The Elbow Grease Legacy

Beverly A. Li

ALL THINGS
THAT MATTER
PRESS

ISBN: 979-8-9862885-9-8
Library of Congress Control Number: 2022946292

"Everyone knows that drunkards and lovers have a protecting deity."

~Dumas, *The Three Musketeers,* (Chapter 23).

"Fear is the path to the dark side ... fear leads to anger ... anger leads to hate ... hate leads to suffering."

~Yoda, *The Phantom Menace.*

PART I
DETROIT, THEREABOUTS

CHAPTER ONE

On a nothing-special, and everything-special, evening, a clunky Windsor bus transported ordinary people from places they left behind to where they chose to go. The inebriated male in the back would disagree, his distorted demons of obligation and whiskey mingling to assure him the world had failed to serve his deserved desserts until he had no choice except to lose all sense of direction—or most of it at least. He might get off at the right stop, if his heavenly escorts were not too disgusted with him, but first he continued his favorite pastime, glaring and muttering at the "goddamn dirty Japs" seated in the middle of the bus as if they had a right to be there. They were an elderly Korean couple maintaining a forward gaze, the wife occasionally catching her husband's chin to reroute his backward glances. "We not Japanese," he kept whispering to his wife. "Our son U.S. soldier!" No one else on the bus offered as much as a sympathetic glance, as if they could sense the swarm of the boozer's irrational aura and they feared contamination, especially the university girl sitting in front of them, her eyes busily absorbing the words of logic presented on the pages of a philosophy textbook, her other books resting in a pile on the seat beside her.

Across the aisle, a man wearing a fedora and clean business suit wrapped one consoling arm around the shoulders of his wife, careful not to wrinkle the puffy fabric or dislodge her stylish hat, hoping the ride would be over before any of his associates happened to see them. By the window, their small daughter held onto her doll, both being well-dressed things with plentiful blonde curls. The girl allowed the woman sitting behind them to have a peek at the doll now and then, pressing it against the back of her seat, sliding it up just enough to let its painted face be admired before snatching it back into her arms and scolding it for being naughty.

The woman sitting behind them dutifully recognized the quartet's fashionable elegance. Feeling diminished in her simple sweater covering a white blouse, she also smirked her small slice of defense, betting to herself they had never had to work a day in their lives. So what if the old skirt she wore once belonged to her mother; it was still good enough. She looked down and brushed it with her hand as an alternative to forcing another smile for the prissy child with the hoity-toity parents, although those blonde curls kept hammering her thoughts, making her self-conscious of her dark hair never curling enough. Idalia turned her head away to look across the aisle at the studying student.

The philosophy textbook looked familiar, reminiscent of her two years of university completed on a full merit scholarship. A year had passed since then, and no money had been saved for her continuation of a stroll through the prestigious halls of higher education. Idalia's days of academic accolades had ended; one more thing taken away from her. No funding could come from her parents, who struggled and juggled to make ends meet; the Great Depression had left its impact, and the harsh war following demanded more sacrifice, only recently declared to end, relaxing its restrictions, leaving scars in the minds and hearts of every working-class citizen. Seeing privilege and money, she couldn't help thinking of the shiny, beautiful red bicycle she had won in a contest when she was fifteen and ready to feel the wind in her hair. It had a basket for books. They took it away from her, without asking, and sold it.

Her kudos for academic achievement had become replaced with orders for table seven, table three. Bring me this, bring me that. I'll have …. Six days a week, she stood and served behind a busy restaurant counter, diligently working up a sweat, proud of at least doing a good job, rewarding herself by occasionally slipping in the back to finish off any piece of pie left untouched by customers, cringing to see other good food go to waste. Clearly, some customers had money. Idalia's money knew no destination other than her mother's hands, the dreary bottomless pit of bills and groceries managed by the old woman since the old man had been placed in a casket. Lately, her mother's commands had become harsher: "Don't dress like a hussy; you're still too smart for that. Get a better job. Buckle up! Keep your seams straight. Don't be late! Stop wasting money at picture shows; you're too good for that low-class trash." Heard most frequently, her mother's mantra had established a permanent shackle on introspective ruminations: "Stop feeling sorry for yourself," delegitimized injured feelings. Deprived of mourning for any loss, Idalia allowed her disappointments to solidify into resentment, stashed deep as a possession they could not take.

Often standing in the shadow of a building to apply her red lipstick, Idalia shrugged off those tiresome restrictions, longing to paint her nails to match, but not enough to go to the trouble of removing the evidence before getting back home. The old woman didn't need to know about the tips Idalia hid in her shoes and other places. Movie theaters served as her alternative realm for encountering new realities in small spaces, big screens painting other worlds, feeding her imagination with glamour and vicarious adventure. Tonight she hoped to meet a girlfriend downtown at Capitol Theatre to see *National Velvet*. Like any caged animal, she had devised her own strategies for making do.

"Bringing in the sheaves, bringing in the sheaves,

"We shall come rejoicing, bringing in the sheaves."

The bus stopped, and she looked outside to see a cluster of Salvation Army women in their drab uniform dresses and serious hats. After the couple with the little girl breathed relief and exited, a handsome fellow wearing a white business suit stepped aboard, scanning the seats for his perfect spot. Idalia immediately imagined him to be a Miami entrepreneur, someone from far away, a pretty place with crystal beaches and warm sunshine. After bumping into the student's pile of books and knocking only a few to the floor, he chose to sit beside Idalia, "The best-looking dame on board," he murmured. *Heavens,* she thought with a tingle. Her visions of palm trees and white sand mingled with his smooth flattery to obliterate her defenses. After thirty minutes of conversation and jostling motion, during which she paid minimal attention to the passing streets and the people progressing around them, his charming blue eyes and soft lips had flattered her enough for her to join him in an early departure into a commercial neighborhood near the dark and wide Detroit River. He spoke of his day playing the ponies, which she knew meant betting on horse races. She knew she'd be late getting home, but she could always tell her mother the movie was longer than expected, and her girlfriend downtown would understand and probably envy her luck.

It felt good to be appreciated. A corrected first guess failed to deter Idalia from becoming engulfed with excitement; the sailor on leave sealed their connection by sharing an intimate problem before the evening ended. Claiming to be distrustful of his own wild *exciting* impulses, this dreamboat anchor-clanker with blond waves gave her two hundred dollars of his winnings to keep for him until the next time they met, ironically an impulse in itself, and she would be oh, so careful with it—and she wouldn't have to give it to her mother.

Lucky dog Jacob Sheridan reported back to his skipper one last time. The euphoria of World War II's end continued to permeate the sea and land and air, banishing precaution wherever possible, hats still flying into the air, folks making the most of every moment, daring to breathe hope again, as everyday life gradually disengaged from the distant vortex that had been sucking away their lives and resources for years, killing more civilians than military personnel in the process. Two weeks later, the bus riders walked out of a courthouse as man and wife, ready to begin their passionate marriage in the rooms above her mother's country grocery store.

Time passed. Responsibilities mounted. Four kids and one more on the way found Idalia and her dreamboat settled in a suburb of Detroit, typical parental responsibilities draining their passion for one another, his blond waves thinning For her, memories of young years in Canada loomed alluringly from across the river, especially of the beautiful horses kept in a nearby stable. She'd steal away from home to watch them run when she could. For him, boyhood days of Georgia danced up from way down south—or perhaps haunted him. Regardless, Detroit bulged with jobs, and the sailor mistaken for a Miami fantasy had flaunted his charm and persuasive verbiage to join workers at a large auto plant, gladly progressing from sweaty line work to delivering messages and small parts from one end of the enormous plant to another, savoring the motion of a bicycle to do so, until that bored him, too.

Multiplying the number of wheels beneath him, he jumped at the chance to spend most of his day driving a car. Following the lure of the green, Jacob began selling water supply parts to Michigan's growing cities and townships, shaking hands with the official "big guns," stepping eagerly into their power bubbles with his ostensibly humble approach to authority, "Yessir, if you have a moment. I know you're mighty busy. I would be honored for just a minute or so, to show you how our new thingamajig will make your day a lot easier. This here is what you need. Yessir, it's a dandy."

He reserved special language for the secretaries guarding the gates: "Hello there, Honey. My, oh, my, you are a good-looking woman. Your old man is one lucky cuss." When eye-to-eye contact had yet to be made, his strategic steps up the schmooze ladder oozed over the telephone. "You sure have a sweet voice, Honey. I'll bet you're a natural blonde." Idalia frowned as she washed dirty diapers nearby, still waiting for his fervent ideas to result in happy victory days.

They'd been treading water forever. All around them, unacknowledged, tenacious memories of military hierarchy had failed to dissipate, permeating social roles and propagating authoritarian conformity, the same authoritarian control they both disliked, yet both accepted as a necessary evil, allowing it to wash over them in waves. If it worked for the military, why not spread it over every facet of society, especially family dynamics? Somebody's got to be the boss and everybody else, just do what you're told; a simple system of obeisance allowing no damn questions. Similar to many others, the two found themselves increasingly frustrated, with romantic notions and clever thoughts failing to provide the monetary foothold expected. Planting metaphorical olive trees round about thy table helped to build the image of virility in an age of post-war productivity, but the quest for immediate success did nothing to quiet the cries of a newborn child. Even worse, the babies began to become miniature people untrained in the ways things were in the world, the ways things had to be.

Their third child, Tallulah, age four, displayed symptoms of said untrained, especially in the busy mornings, when damn questions were least welcome. "Gregory and Humphrey wear pants. Why do I have to wear a dress?" Tallulah asked sister Myrna, who twirled around in her own dress.

"'Cause you're a girl, dummy. Just put it on. Mom said to," Myrna automatically answered. "Besides, nobody likes a little nincompoop," she warned, sticking out her tongue for emphasis before flouncing out of their bedroom.

Tallulah's gaze fell upon the basket of clean laundry left on the bed, and she rummaged through it to find a pair of pants. Humphrey's were too small, but she found a pair belonging to Gregory, and she wiggled into them, rolling up the long legs into doughnuts above her feet. Satisfied, she let her arms help by squishing the waist before she walked into the kitchen, ready for the day. Her resourcefulness met "Hoohaa" laughter and pointed fingers from Myrna and Gregory, who nearly choked on their cereal when they looked up at her. Even Tallulah knew not to laugh when eating.

"Hey, those are my pants," Gregory sputtered. "Get 'em off her. Mom!"

Idalia turned from the sink, her hands dripping with dishwater. "Myrna?"

"I know. Fix the weirdo," Myrna muttered, leading Tallulah back into the bedroom. "Stop with the dumb tears. Nobody likes a troublemaker. Take off the pants and put on the dress," the second child commanded before leaving to finish her breakfast.

Untrained Tallulah harbored no desire to cause trouble, and sadly did as she was told, all the while thinking about that word: trouble. She knew trouble might be what came in the form of loud voices, especially between Jacob and Mom, who raised their voices most of the time. It made her want to be quiet and keep out of their way. She could tell she hadn't caused any trouble yet because Mom still continued her conversation with Jacob, who stood leaning against the kitchen counter, smoking his cigarette, arms folded, not sharing his children's amusement, only glancing at them, his eyes alone warning them to keep quiet.

"Don't you remember the Depression we grew up in?" Tallulah re-entered the kitchen to hear Mom remind Jacob, who paid no attention to his youngest daughter as she climbed on a chair and poured her own dry cereal and milk made from powder. Gregory and Myrna had left, but Tallulah read the box as they had done—most of the letters, anyway. Humphrey remained in his highchair, smearing soggy Cheerios on his pudgy face. "It wasn't long ago. It could happen again. We need to save some money," Mom pointed out. They'd talked about the money things before. A lot. Tallulah continued munching, half-listening to a world not her own.

Jacob's response sounded the same as always. "Save? Those days are over. Everybody else is buying. We have to look sharp to be somebody in this world." Wanting to look like a knife sounded kind of dumb to the daughter at the table. *Maybe that's what nincompoops do,* she concluded. The cereal box had good pictures on it.

Idalia's mirage from the bus had not continued to hand over his money; apparently, he liked the way it felt in his hands. He grinned at the green, he grinned when he donned crisp white shirts ironed by his wife, and when he covered them with a good suit jacket retrieved from the dry cleaners. These adornments made him look like the other men. No rummage sales for him, nope. He left those long walks for Idalia and the kids, reluctantly handing over no more than the minimum to let her buy everyone else's clothes second-hand, and pay the bills, not minding as much as she did if a payment became overdue. Beyond thrifty, the housewife taught her children to brush their teeth with baking soda until they learned their friends all used toothpaste. In reluctant compliance, she taught them to split open any finished tube of toothpaste and dab their brushes into the residue, utilizing every speck, even pulling a tube out of the bathroom trash can in the event some unintelligent human had made an error in judgement.

Their suburban home mirrored the other small boxes uniformly positioned along both sides of the street, illuminated in the evenings by high streetlamps where summer moths circled, caught in the bright light. On a typical evening, inside each residence, an even smaller box emitted noise and images, offering vicarious entry into an alluring realm, one with "Dear" and "Darling" as television models moved around in their own affluent, harmonious homes, presenting incongruent parallels apparent to even young minds. Tallulah gravitated toward the simplicity presented in a polarized world where employment and decision-making belonged to the calm father with the quiet voice. He arrived home every evening, kissed his pretty wife, "Hello, darling," and sat down in his stuffed chair to read the daily newspaper. "Dinner's almost ready, dear," she soon assured him, happy in her subservient role.

With nine-year-old Gregory stretching his bones on the couch,

Tallulah assumed a cross-legged position on the living room floor most evenings, admiring the mother's wavy helmet of coiffured hair, stationed flawlessly above the perfect pearl necklace and spotless, fluffy dress. The preschooler sat mesmerized watching the pretty mother look up and smile at her happy teenage daughter, who came to help with dinner in a typical scene: "There you are."

"Oh, Mother, the most exciting thing happened at school today."

"Well, dear, let's feed our gentlemen first and we'll talk about it later, okay?'

"Oh, of course, Mother dear."

The teen son bounded down the stairs. "Hi, Pops!"

The father glanced at the boy's feet, only slightly jarred out of his newspaper reverie, reclaiming his control. "Hello, son. How about that shoelace?"

"Shoelace? Sure, Pops. Gosh, I don't know what got into me." The boy immediately kneeled to tie his shoe.

"Well, son, we'll let it pass this time," the father said, returning to his newspaper.

"Yes, sir."

One evening, back in the real world, the slam of a screen door announced Idalia and Myrna returning from the backyard with two full baskets of clean, dry clothes. "Whew. We got them in before dark. Lulah, can you clear the table?" Idalia asked, heaving her overflowing wicker basket onto a chair, pushing back renegade strands of dark hair fallen from her signature victory rolls, and wiping her hands on the limp apron hanging on the side of her bulging belly.

"Of course, Mother dear."

"Copycat," Gregory muttered.

Turning away from the television, Tallulah began filling the kitchen sink with the dirty plates and glasses from the dining table, her ears still tuned to the fantasy realm, until another performance commenced to capture her attention.

The corner window of the Sheridan dining room offered a view of the driveway, and a brown station wagon pulled in. Tallulah sounded the alert: "Jacob's home!" Toddler Humphrey immediately dropped his toys and stood up, "Dacub's home! Dacub's home!" he repeated, grinning in innocence. Idalia had thought it cute when toddler Gregory first mimicked her name for her husband, and she never bothered to redirect him or her other children to use any conventional label for male parentage, quietly savoring such minute trophies of noncompliance requiring no action on her part as she took advantage of Jacob's indifference. Being older and wiser at seven years of age, Myrna tensed, as did Gregory, ceasing his sovereignty of the living room couch. "Have homework, will travel. Time to split." The two scooted down the hall, into the farther reaches of the house. Idalia sighed, smoothing her dark, stringy hair, and peeking out the kitchen window. "Can he walk straight?" she said half to herself.

After two weeks on the road, the man of the house entered through a side door, fumbling his way through an enclosed breezeway into the kitchen. Once in, he set down his Samsonite hard brown suitcase and removed his dark fedora. Humphrey's small limbs stumbled over one another to be the first greeted by the tall, thin legs within loose pants. As usual, Jacob carried the pungent odor of stale tobacco smoke. "Well, hee-lo there," he spoke, swaying slightly, aiming one or two tentative hand pats down to the young boy's head. Tallulah recognized a gummy twang in his voice and remained on the far side of the dining table. Jacob slowly focused his eyes on the back of his wife as she gently put distance between the small boy and the unpredictable man. "Did ya forget to comb your hair again, Idy?" he said, reaching out unsuccessfully to her head. Dropping his arm, he instead looked around the kitchen. "Oh, Lordy. Well, a mess. Another mess, as ushual. Can ya get those dishes washed, girlie?" he asked, raising his voice, eyes beginning to focus and glare across the table. As if he felt the commands of expectation upon him, he assumed the ghostly authoritative posture and tone of his old military officers—or maybe it came from his father. "Where's my goddamn dinner? Clean this place up, by God! Filty! Filty! Filty! Pigsty!" he slurred his words out. "Dat's what this place is, a goddamn pigsty!"

The man punished toys for jumping under his feet by kicking them across the room. "Turn off the goddamn TV!" Humphrey scrambled out of the living room, tears on the way. The daughter in the kitchen watched as her father turned to the one person he could not intimidate easily. "Good God, woman, look at you. Baggy britches, a rag for a blouse. Look at dis. You got a hole in the back here." His voice became a sneer as he stuck his finger in the insignificant tear and enlarged it, snickering, not caring if he exposed part of her brassiere. "Mommy got a hole in da back of her blousey blousey, kidz. Looka here. Mommy got a hole. And holes in your goddamn shoes down there! Dirty feet, too. Don't you ever take a bath, woman? What does you do all day, sit around on your Canadian butt? You sure don't kill yourself working. Your old lady didn't teach you nothing!"

Idalia Sheridan had kept quiet when her husband chased out most of the kids, endured the condescending inspection, trying to maintain some threads of peace, trying not to "rock the boat," as she would say, although Tallulah never saw the boat. Idalia accepted the guilt her husband flung at her for the untidiness of their home, she endured his demeaning tear of her blouse, even while her daughter witnessed the twist of pain in her face, but she drew a line. "You shut up about my mother. She worked harder in a week than you do in a year. And I've been on my hands and knees, scrubbing floors all day, I'll have you know! Cleaning your dirty ashtrays and washing your dirty underwear! What do you want me to wear, a mink coat? Why should you care anyway? You're too busy boozing in a bar and flirting with your damn girlfriends to come home on time!"

"Girlfriends? What girlfriends? You're crazy, woman! You dunno what you're talking 'bout. I work hard to make a decent living for diz fabily, and I come home to diz, diz sheet pile!"

"Shit pile? Oh, yeah? Who's the big shit maker?" From the big pot on the stove, she dished his tuna and noodles onto a plate. "I found the latest phone number in your pocket, just like the last time. I found it all right. Liar, liar, liar. That ain't no business number, mister. I'm not as dumb as you think," she continued, ignoring the noodles that missed his plate. "Who is she this time, the dyed-blonde floozy receptionist again, or somebody's stupid wife?" She shoved the plate of food onto the table. "Here. Sit down, you damn fool. Eat your damn dinner, *if* you can."

"Crazy woman. Dunno what you're yappin' 'bout. Nuts! Loony! I married a crazy Canuckian." His flow of half-mumbled words continued as he leaned on a chair and managed to bend his legs until he landed more or less on the seat. "You call this food? Lulah, where did your mamma get this? Looks like somethin' the damn dog spit up, all mixed up. Did she bring it in from the back yard again when nobody was a-lookin'? Did she? I ain't eating this slop. Shit. Fix me some eggs, Lulah girl, and sausage. And grits. I want grits."

Cautiously, Tallulah edged her way around the table, opened a low cupboard, her small hands finding a frying pan, as if she knew how to fix eggs and sausage, while Idalia insisted, "There's nothing wrong with that food. It's good enough for the rest of us, Mister High and Mighty. Better than grits, for God's sake. I'm not wasting money on that southern crap. What's the matter, won't your hussy girlfriend cook for you? Or is she sick of you already."

"Mom, what are grits?" Tallulah whispered, raising the pan.

"Oh, go do your homework," Idalia commanded.

Thinking Mom must be making a joke, Tallulah giggled. "I don't even go to school yet, Mom. How can I have any homework?"

"Go do it anyway."

Jacob ignored his wife's distress, passing out on the couch before she finished sizzling sausage and eggs, the aroma tantalizing the children, making them feel hungry again, but she saved it for him, leaving it on the stove, covered by a lid. As the man slept, his wife's frustration lingered for hours, making her impatient with the kids as they prepared for bed. In turn, they had absorbed enough of the tension to find it easy to bicker, tease, and blame among themselves. Before long, their mother's version of a bedtime song rang through the house as she borrowed the tune to "It Came Upon A Midnight Clear," customizing the words. "Your faaather ii-is a great big jerk," she belted out from the kitchen, loud enough for every young ear in the house, and the verses went on, "the biggest jerk ii-in the world," until she ran out of what gaseous survival sarcasm she could sponge from the air. Other evenings, "Some daaay my prince will come ..." would serve her romantic inclinations, afloat on the waters of disappointment. To anchor something along the lines of hopes and dreams, she had named each child after a movie star, umbilical lifelines tossed out from shifting sandy beaches of dreamy glamour.

As they grew in age and awareness, each child lost the purity of white sand baby trust. Early innocence trickled down the drain as they learned to dread the man and the bizarre disturbance he unfailingly brought into their house, contaminating their young lives with his struggle, leaving each to nurture his or her own lifeline. They found unity in being disgusted by the feet suddenly incapable of serious contact with a flat floor, the legs too wobbly to hold a body up very long, the man's verbal and physical impatience, his constant irritability, his preoccupation with things outside the family, his complete lack of interest in the developing lives of his offspring, and his pathetic days spent in bed following a drinking spree followed, so many times, with a resigned Idalia making her standard morning phone call. "Jacob won't be in today. He has the flu. Yes, again, I'm afraid so. Okay, yes, g'bye."

"They know," she'd say to no one in particular, after hanging up. "They know he's drunk. They know I'm lying. It's the second time in three weeks. Lie for your husband. Hang on to your man. He's better than nothing. Make the most of it. It's good enough. Stop feeling sorry for yourself. She-it."

On such days, Jacob's whining emanated from the bedroom. "Iiiidy. Iiiidy. C'mere pleeease, Iiidy baaaby." Idalia knew he'd soon stick his finger down his throat and gag with full sound effects if she didn't go. The vomit would be his manly gift to her.

The other end of their marriage spectrum boasted of the times the man came home happy, not the kind of happy synonymous with content, but a giddy form of exhilaration, an ecstatic happy, like the thrill of being at the top of a gigantic roller coaster. If he happened to make a good sale, he seemed to be absolutely certain beyond any doubt in the world nothing but glorious radiance could ever flow in his direction again. By the time the older children knew better, Idalia knew better, too. With each of her children standing behind her, they leaned against anything near, anything halfway solid, skeptically watching him beam with his confident, foolish, "Hotdog! I made it this time!"

"Well, we'll see. Give me enough to get the bills paid first," his wife would urge him.

"Nope. I got to get a new car, first thing. Can't be seen driving that heap of trash anymore." He typically owned a used clunker for no more than two years, never performed any maintenance unless something broke, and then hauled it to the cheapest mechanic he could find, some sad old bar buddy. Within a few days, he would have replaced it with another used station wagon, suffocating his regret of the minimal trade-in he'd accepted for the old one. After all, he couldn't let the buyer/seller think he needed the money.

CHAPTER TWO

Idalia directed her mutterings at the floor she scrubbed, or the wall she washed, or at any young ears in the vicinity, those human receptacles occasionally catching her insightful tidbits of information, contributing to their fledgling perceptions of life being a jigsaw puzzle lacking pieces. A week before her scheduled entry into the hallowed halls of kindergarten, Tallulah complained of a sore throat, providing Jacob with material to chat with over the backyard fence, providing him with an opportunity to stride directly into a mainstream medical fad, disregarding his wife's words of opposition. "Kids get sore throats all the time. Makes no sense. Even our good doctor said it wasn't necessary, but he found some fool doctor. He's gotta please the goofy neighbors, above all else. Daresn't think for himself." Tallulah noticed a new floor layer coming into view among the suds her mother's hands induced.

The girl found herself presented to the fool doctor to have her throat examined. Gathering from the linguistic particles floating in the air around her, Tallulah envisioned the existence of strange things inside her neck, things needing to be cut out. A knife slicing into her neck? Vivid memories of creepy television scenes popped up. Monsters laughed.

The next day, the great white cot rolled into her focus as an altar of doomed sacrifice, sucking her into the Twilight Zone, or worse. Dancing natives and an impatient volcano undoubtedly waited in the next room. The young girl's eyes pleaded with her father: *Please tell me I'm not going to die.* Tender hopes of protection disintegrated, however, falling to the underground until the object of her gaze hardened into the heartless tall man who had lured her into this windowless torture chamber. Focused on more important matters, Jacob stood off to one side, fedora tilted on his balding head, jingling the loose change in his baggy trouser pockets, his blue eyes scorching the woman in white who guided Tallulah's road to certain demise, offering his only warm words to the nurse. "You sure do handle yourself well, real graceful like. With your looks, I bet you could have been a dancer, or even a movie star, with your pretty face, your nice figure, and your teeth nice 'n' straight. See now, Lulah? That's how teeth are supposed to look."

Tallulah trembled as she climbed up, hopelessly unfolding her legs on the cold altar, lying back and glancing at the display of pearly whites hovering over her face. The glamorous executioner slipped a framed cloth mask over the girl's nose and mouth. Two long rows of model teeth remained exposed up there, outlined in blood red, as an evil brown glass bottle appeared beside them and began its downward tilt, bringing dark liquid with an abominable stench into the mask. A suspicious motive flashed through Tallulah's thoughts: *A brown bottle. These two cannot wait to get the dumb kid out of the way. Then he'll pour stuff from his own brown bottle into little glasses and grin happy, like he always does. That's why he brought me here. Phew! This stuff stinks!* Her ears caught someone's long scream rising from deep depths, growing distant as she felt the cot being propelled forward.

Idalia tended to Tallulah during the child's next two weeks of unusual, almost pleasant attention at home in bed, bringing her Jell-O and other soft food, freeing her from having to squeeze in at the crowded dinner table. Wisps of pleasantness flitted away with Tinkerbell whenever Idalia entered the room, her words picking up where she had left off on her usual stream of grumbles: "He can't think for himself. He has no willpower. That's the only thing he needs, willpower. That's what I believe in! He doesn't need people as much as he thinks he does. That neighbor Mrs. Shirley is a floozy fluttering her eyelashes, and he's dumb enough to worship the ground she walks on. Weak, that's what he is. She's no medical doctor."

Early one chilly morning, the gray grumbles and colorful Jell-o ceased. Tallulah found herself out of bed, dressed up, and securely wedged between Gregory and Myrna, who had been directed to serve as parental substitutes, trudging down the sidewalk, crossing a street, and maneuvering through a weedy field to a large building. Along the way, Tallulah tried to absorb their flood of information; it filled her with enough apprehension to fill a gymnasium, whatever that was.

"And the bathrooms are separate; one for the boys and one for the girls, but they don't have any bathtubs inside, only toilets, so don't go in the boys' one," Gregory warned, his wavy brown curls recently mowed.

"But how will I know which one to use?"

"They stick a picture of a girl on the door of the girls' and a picture of a boy on the boys', or something. The teacher will tell you. And you get to paint pictures, and don't worry about pencils. They have lots of pencils, the big fat kind, you know, and you can use them, and you get to sit at a desk," he continued.

"Uh-um, no. Tables. We had tables when I was in kindergarten," Myrna corrected, her experience being more recent.

"Tables, okay. Don't worry, the teacher will show you. It's neat, you know, and you get a recess," Gregory said.

"What's a recess?"

"It's not a thing, dumb head. It's a time for. It's when you go play outside," Myrna said, adding, "Oh, they have a bunch of jungle bars to climb on, and this really big slide in kindergarten."

"Jungle bars? Really big slide? How big?"

"And don't worry about your coat. You can shove it in your locker," Gregory assured her.

"What's a locker?"

"Gosh, you don't know anything. They're these box things by the wall and they put your name on it and you stick your jacket in there, not on your desk, and in the winter your boots go there, too," Gregory said.

"I thought you said I had a table."

"No, they don't; your boots go on the floor. But your hat goes in there, if Mom makes you wear one," Myrna said, confident in her female seniority, wearing new rummage sale clothes destined to be inherited by Tallulah. "And there's a bunch of lockers. Everybody gets one. They are like closets, but don't worry, we'll show you which one is yours."

"Everybody gets a closet? When do I get to go home?"

"When it's over, dumbbell. We'll come and get you when the bell rings. First, we'll show you where your locker is," Gregory said.

"You promise?"

"Yeah, don't act stupid or nothing, don't be a weirdo, and don't tell nobody I'm your brother, okay? They already found out I have one sister, and it ain't cool to have another. But we'll help you find your locker."

"Yeah," Myrna confirmed.

Bombarded as the trio became with the noise and tumult of many children entering the monster of a building, the beast of the moment easily devoured their flimsy promise. Tallulah's guardians delivered their bewildered sister inside the door of a bright and busy room full of strange and noisy kids and left.

Realization took only a few minutes to soak in. When it did, Tallulah bolted out of the kindergarten chaos and raced for the front doors of the school, screaming, "Waiiiit! Gregooooryyy! Myrrrrnaaaa! You forgot to show me where my locker is! You forgot to show me! You forgot! You forgahhhhht!"

Alas. One of the more seasoned inmates guarding the door and wearing a bright orange shoulder belt swept up the tearful escapee and returned her to her cell. Without a doubt, she knew Gregory and Myrna had gone home, forever abandoning her.

On top of this tragedy, the teacher had the gall to make Tallulah stand in front of everybody, putting those teacher hands on her shoulders, keeping her from running. "Now, class, class we have a new student. Her name is Tallulah Sheridan." *New?* wondered Tallulah.

What do you mean, 'new'? I've lived here as long as any of these other kids. I just had to get my tonsils taken out, that's all. It wasn't my fault. It was his fault; he made me. Why is this teacher lying about me?

CHAPTER THREE

Two years later, after paying most of the bills, Idalia had managed to squirrel away money for Christmas, and in the wee hours of the holy morning, she and Myrna covered much of the living room floor with inexpensive toys, socks, and underwear from dime stores and rummage sales, equally distributed among her five children. Snowy white tissue paper bundles tied with thin ribbons spread outward from beneath the thin green tree. In addition, Idalia had finally taken steps of vicarious compensation for her own loss: five shiny bicycles filled any remaining walking space in the room.

When daylight made an appearance, Tallulah peeked around the corner, rubbed her eyes, and gasped, "Wow!" She ran back to their bedroom to awaken Myrna. "Hey, Myrnie, guess what? We got bikes! And a lot of presents! And bikes! Real ones! With wheels! Get up! Come see!"

"I know, I know. Go away. Lemme sleep," Myrnie mumbled, burying her head deeper in her pillow.

"What? How could you know already? Did you peek? No way. I got up first." Receiving no more intelligence from her slumbering sister, Tallulah abandoned the puzzling mound of blankets, and zoomed back to the miraculous living room. *It's a reward,* thought Tallulah, *must be, for addressing all those Christmas cards, exactly the way Mom wanted, even without an answer to my question.* She remembered wanting to know why "Mr." gets to go in front of "Mrs." if people really want "ladies first," like they always say. Idalia had merely shrugged.

Almost the last to wander in, sleepyhead Gregory meandered around and looked over the bikes. "Sheesh, Mom, Cary can barely walk, let alone ride a bike."

"Well, he'll grow into it," Idalia replied, wrapped in a tattered bathrobe.

"Ju-dy, Ju-dy, Ju-dy," Gregory mused, shaking his head, lifting his own bike out of the rustling tissue paper ground cover. Glad of the fact Jacob still slept, Gregory headed toward the garage. Before he got away, Tallulah glanced up from the mysteries of something called a paint-by-number set already opened, "Who's Judy? Her name is Mom." Gregory and Myrna knew everything, but occasionally they needed correcting.

Gregory scoffed, "Sure, kid."

He and Myrna made good use of their new wheels in no time, scooting away with their friends. Tallulah's bike sat looking pretty, while Gregory put training wheels on the bicycle for Humphrey.

On a warm Saturday in early spring, Jacob asked Tallulah, "Well, did you ride your new bike yet?"

"No."

"Why not?"

"I don't know how, and it's really big."

"Pshaw, get it out of the garage."

"Gregory said it's too big for training wheels," she ventured.

"You don't need no training wheels."

In the middle of the grassy, lumpy backyard, she climbed up on the seat while Jacob held the bike. He walked for a few steps before proceeding to almost trotting. Tallulah thought she would not mind having a pair of those unneeded training wheels; surely they came in a large size. She bounced as the pedals insisted on playing tag with her toes. "Don't let go. Don't let go," she begged him. He not only let go of the bicycle, he deemed it necessary to give it a shove. "Turn," he shouted at her back, as if she could do anything more than grip the handlebars for dear life. The vehicle possessed an evil mind of its own, bumping straight toward large lilac bushes, whose conspiratorial role became obvious as clustered purple flowers attempted to conceal the sudden sprouting of grasping claws, provoking the handlebars to seek the nearest soft belly as the vehicle collided with demonic glee into the back of the house.

Jacob stood frozen, staring for a moment at the entanglement of moaning child, bike, and broken branches, before walking away without a word. He never offered to repeat the lesson, never mentioned the bicycle again. Scratched and bruised, Tallulah whimpered a painful retreat towards the inside of the house. The aluminum storm door confirmed her unworthiness, resisting her pathetic pull. She would delay conquering her two-wheeler for a year or so, until her legs lengthened and her toes could touch the ground when she planted her bottom on the seat.

With her demonic bike safely confined to the garage once again, Tallulah walked home from school one day to find Myrna and Idalia looking worried, sitting at the dining table. Sharing some kind of mysterious concern, they murmured over the newspaper spread on the table in front of them. Tallulah could see it upset them and sought entry into the sacred team of femaleness by sidling into a chair. A young girl had been raped and left in a nearby field, she read. "So, what does 'raped' mean?"

"Oh, you're too young."

"I am not. I just turned eight. Come on, tell me."

Despite the reluctance of these gatekeepers, their lips pursed like iron filters, she finally extracted a definition.

"Well, it's when a man puts this thing into a girl."

"Thing? What thing?" Tallulah wanted to know.

Myrna had to look at Idalia several times before replying, "A stick thing."

"Where does he put it?"

Again, Myrna struggled for words while Idalia remained silent. "In her bottom."

"Yuck."

Tallulah left them to their secret world, thinking how very strange and uncomfortable it must be to have a large stick shoved into one's butt, and wondering why anyone would do such a stupid thing.

Occasionally, Tallulah got lucky enough to be teamed briefly with the great Myrna. One Sunday, they looked for Gregory, and found him sitting on the backyard fence. Two boys close to Gregory's age lived behind the Sheridans, on the other side of a chain link barrier topped with horizontal wood boards, which offered an ideal perch for human birds. Sometimes Gregory perched. "Whatcha doin'?" Myrna asked.

"Nothin."

"Waiting to see if they'll come out?"

"Maybe."

"They hardly ever do. Who planted such a puny thing?" she asked, her eyes following Gregory's fingers to a young tree of his height entwined in the fence.

"Nobody. It just came up. Look at this."

Myrna scrambled up to join Gregory. "What?"

"The bark is real thin. You can pull it off," he informed her.

"Neat. Let me try," Myrna replied. Tallulah stood by, hoping they would make room for her. They did not.

A few minutes later, holding Cary's hand, Idalia walked towards them.

"Hi, Mom."

Frowning, Idalia threw eye darts at the neighbor's house. "*She* called. Wants you off the fence."

"Why? We're not hurting anything. Look at this neat tree bark."

"Well, you better get down."

"Okay, Mom. Sheesh."

Later in the kitchen, peeling potatoes for dinner, Idalia told Jacob about the neighbor's phone call. "Both of 'em on the fence again? Doing what?" he asked. "Myrna?"

"Nothin'," she replied, coming in from the living room. "Just waiting, pulling a little bark off a skinny weed tree. Nobody planted it. That nosy old lady must have been staring out her window."

"Shit. Hand me a beer, little girl." He pointed at Tallulah searching in the refrigerator for the plastic bag of small apples sometimes available.

"You already had three," replied Idalia's mother, who was visiting for the day. Jacob looked at the old woman sitting in the dining chair at the head of his table while he completely consumed the fourth beer without a pause before bringing it down with his arm to thud upon the table. "Ahh. Where's Gregory?"

"Probably upstairs, doing his homework," Idalia replied.

"Reading those comic books, more likely. Boys his age need discipline to keep them in line or they won't respect their elders. That one already slouches," the mother-in-law stated, triggering Jacob's memories of his military leaders, bringing his mission into focus.

"He's a good boy," Idalia softly countered.

"He won't be a good boy if you let him get away with being a hooligan. He'll turn out rotten to the core. You have to nip that insubordination in the bud. Shape up or ship out," her mother commanded.

"Tallulah, go get him," Jacob said, rolling his eyes in her direction. Tallulah followed his directive. When the boy appeared, "To the basement," Jacob growled without getting up.

"For what? I didn't do anything."

"Now, Goddamn it!"

"But I didn't do anything," Gregory insisted as Jacob grabbed him by the shirt, shoving him toward the basement stairs.

Myrna and Tallulah looked at the floor, retreating to cower in their bedroom for a hollow portion of eternity, feeling the endless whacks and yelps coming from below, trembling, fearing the monster would come after them next, knowing it had been a group amusement to harmlessly pull off a few of those soft, tiny strips from a sapling no one had planted. "How come he never whips you or me for doing the same stuff?" Tallulah whispered to Myrna.

"Shut up," Myrna replied, wiping away her tears.

Idalia kept busy in the kitchen, her movements becoming jerky as her mother stared, reminding her, "We never let you smart-alecky kids run over us. And you had it coming to you too, more than once, missy." The old woman continued to grumble before finally getting up to yell down the stairs, "All right, Jacob, that's enough!" However, Jacob must have decided to make sure everyone knew who was boss, responding by making the whacks harder and louder. When wisps of personal satisfaction finally drifted into his senseless haze, assuring him he had made his point clear to everyone, or he forgot what he was doing and why, or the physical exertion brought weariness to his royal bones, he allowed a boy wounded in mind and body to hobble into a basement corner and cry. The girls received no punishment beyond frowns of disapproval from their mother and grandmother.

The weather warmed into summer. One day, Idalia's older brother invited the family for a swim at his spacious home in the countryside, with no grumpy grandmother around. Gregory and Myrna made their excuses, and Idalia had enough to keep her busy at home, leaving only Tallulah to join Jacob for the drive. Out on the rolling green lawn, with no fence in sight, sat a large above-ground swimming pool. Jacob climbed in to lean against the side. Tallulah compared the pool to their smaller one at home, and didn't see much difference, although she wasn't wearing her glasses at the time. At home, she prided herself in being able to shoot the whole way across by pushing off with her legs underwater, Aquawoman unlimited. The confident torpedo climbed in, filling her lungs before immersion, positioning the bottoms of her feet against the wall, aiming, blasting forward with her perfected burst of power, arms straight as arrows, legs paddling fiercely until the moment arrived to surface and claim her victorious gasp of air.

Somehow, she came up in the middle of a very large and deep pool, not at all according to plan. Her toes begged for the bottom as her arms thrashed, but the bottom had melted away, and her eyes darted to her father for help. Their eyes locked. He did not move a muscle, and the floundering fish had one clear thought: *He is going to let me drown.*

Jacob continued his nonchalant pose standing inside the pool, his thin arms stretched out like bony wings along the side, chatting with his teenage niece, who plunged toward her cousin. Tallulah gushed with gratitude for the rescue. Even as her wonderful, speedy heroine helped the soggy fish girl out of the pool, the unconcerned man-creature remained a few feet away, moving only his mouth, continuing his indifferent conversation, offering his daughter nothing except a seeping token of unpleasant reality. For the remainder of the visit, she sat wrapped in a towel, sitting in the sun, mostly shivering. Having come and gone as a visitor before, a cloud of unpleasant reality attached itself to her as a new companion, following her like a speech balloon in a cartoon.

Tallulah and her new companion mingled their assessments. She could not be certain if things improved when Jacob defied inertia to take action, or if his actions actually made life worse. He appeared to occupy the role of leader like the heroes on television, and Tallulah assumed she needed him, trying to believe Idalia's excuses for his errant behavior: — "Oh, he can't help it" or "Oh, he didn't mean it" — when she wasn't arguing with him, otherwise offering scant explanation beyond her usual shrug, signifying something unseen to be accepted now and put into place later, as if the time would come for a mysterious coming-of-age ritual Tallulah knew nothing about. It, or something like it, would have to endow her with a level of understanding currently looming as nothing more than a wavering mirage glued to a distant horizon.

Jacob's brother in Georgia talked him into a Kentucky rendezvous the next summer. Gregory offered no objection to staying behind with friends and being excluded from the hectic days of Idalia's preparation for the unknown world of family vacationing. "What should we bring?" Myrna and Tallulah asked her, receiving "I don't know" and "whatever you want" enough times to make their own clumsy choices before climbing into Jacob's station wagon, now encumbered with a pop-up camper trailing behind. Uncle Ethan's plans consisted of claiming space in a state park, familiar ground to him, but apparently nothing more than a target to Jacob.

Being a dedicated devotee of destination, Jacob smoked cigarettes and drove for hours and hours without stopping, whizzing along without regard for the backseat moans of "Gotta pee!"

"Can't stop," bellowed the driver, even as the liquid contents of a potty-chair spilled on the floor in front of Idalia.

"I'm too big for that thing! Mom, please make him stop."

"Oh, just hold it."

"I can't. I'm gonna do it in my pants!"

"Goddamn kids. Remind me of your mother, Idy. Got no bladders."

"Mom, I'm gonna throw up."

"Well, use a towel from that blue bag back there."

"Oh, crapola! Mom, he did it all over my shoes. Yuck!"

"Goddamn kids! Not in the car! There's a field ahead. Give 'em the damn roll of toilet paper, Ida. Shit."

At the end of the fun-filled car journey, the woozy family spilled into a designated campground spot, with Jacob and Tallulah eventually joining Uncle Ethan and Cousin Lisa to meander along a woodsy trail to the park's main attraction. A world unlike anything ever seen opened its doors to Tallulah.

Rushing water dashed upon and swirled around huge boulders smooth from years of compliance. Racing to a point below massive green branches, the fluid line abruptly dropped through the air, becoming a wide sheet of animated silk. Joyous sunlight danced in a sparkle of diamonds as bordering moisture sprayed itself into a fine white lace of suspended mist. Crashing a return to land, the water churned wildly in a dark pool. Swirling forces gathered while unseen ushers directed the incessant, winding journey back into the caress of tall, calm, emerald attendants. Fresh mountain air bellowed in strong voice, proud of the sweet music of elemental power and harmony.

Below the roar of the waterfall, spontaneous human laughter and yelps of delight exceeded the distance limits of secondary sound as children of every age clambered upon the sculpturesque rock complicating the water's path. Under the command of imaginative minds, hard nature transformed itself into elegant ladders and lounges and small mountains obligingly conquered.

Along the edge of the high trail, the awkward newcomers paused to view the glory of the falls. Cousin Lisa bent her tanned legs and silently lowered herself into a sitting position, her father remaining standing behind her. Tallulah knelt to join her. Jacob stood behind Tallulah, but instead of allowing his daughter to join the moment of tranquility, he grabbed her arm and jerked her back up to a standing position beside him.

Glancing up at the man for some crumb of explanation, Tallulah met the too-familiar picture of a silent, austere forward stare from a semi-bald head, vibrating with tiny, nervous shakes emanating fear. Logic told her she was old enough to keep herself from tumbling down the slope, bouncing between the tree trunks and being swallowed by monstrous raging water. She and Lisa both held claims to a decade of life. There was nothing wrong with his brother's daughter, no contagious disease or homicidal inclinations Tallulah could attribute to her cousin. Consequently, Tallulah concluded: *There must be something wrong with me, something everyone else knows about.*

She and Lisa made another walk to the falls the next day, without the adults. They wandered through the leafy haven and talked, following the trail. On the way back, they stopped at a point where the trail split in two directions. "I think this is the way back," Tallulah said, pointing to the right.

"No, it's the left trail. I remember it," Lisa assured her.

"Can't be," insisted Tallulah, a remnant of Aquawoman rising. After more of the same discussion, Lisa walked left and Tallulah strode right, feeling brave and correct. However, her choice soon failed to support her determination, disappearing in the underbrush. She held back the stupid tears threatening to spill and kept going, eventually seeing people and a building on the woodsy land rising in front of her. She climbed to level ground, encountering Jacob coming out of a restroom. He glanced at her and continued walking. She silently followed him back to their campsite.

Mistakes and unexplained occurrences continued to baffle Tallulah, unlike Myrna, who seemed to grow wiser and happier every year, flitting about and escaping out of the house into her world of telephone calls and friends, glorious friends who never came home with her, except the giggly one who lived across the street. Earning money from babysitting, with advice from her girlfriends, Myrna learned to buy her own clothes, insisting they match according to current standards, how to tease her hair up into a puffy ball, how to iron it straight, and which creams to dab on zits. She even bought shampoo, taking it in and out of the bathroom with her, disregarding the soap everyone else used.

"What's so great about shampoo?" Tallulah asked.

"Oh, it's just better."

Tallulah stared at a mysterious bottle of something else called "conditioner," reading the label and trying to determine its purpose.

She relied upon Myrna to supply the answers for the adolescent questions Idalia would shrug away, appearing to be too preoccupied to be bothered, or offering answers too vague to make any sense. Neither elder female obliged Tallulah willingly as she became aware of changes in her own body. When she first felt a round lump under one of her nipples, she thought, *Wow. Does this mean I'll really have a woman-body someday? Me?*

"What is this?" she ventured to ask Myrna one night. "Is this the beginning of a, you know, uh, titty thing?"

Myrna brushed her off with, "It's normal, it's normal, it's normal."

Tallulah gave the words a moment to reach her realm of logic, but they zinged around aimlessly. She tried again. "What exactly does 'normal' mean? I just want to know what's happening to my body." But Myrna had already turned away to sleep, leaving Tallulah to imagine her body and mind growing in every direction except normal. The adult planet seemed defined by this nebulous "normal."

CHAPTER FOUR

Limited perceptions continued to be plagued with inevitable experiences for the girl with more questions than answers. Overused adult excuses and empty explanations produced no enticing lure for her into the adult world. For one more summer, Tallulah safely frolicked in the backyard, still pretending to swim in the lesser than large aboveground pool, preferring the company of Humphrey and Cary, along with young neighbor friends, serving a useful role as a babysitter of sorts.

Having advanced beyond the underwater adventures, she sought to impress the young ones by perfecting the big splash. In lieu of a diving board, she had been ingenious enough to place an old wooden stepstool against the outside of the pool. Cool enough. The top of the stepstool lined up level with the top flat metal trim of the pool's perimeter, allowing for many wondrous leaps and splashes before Tallulah climbed up for one more. Unknown to the diver, the stepstool had grown suddenly weary, and began to sink sideways in the mud during the last moment her toes held her up. Perceiving the imminent danger of falling, Tallulah knew in a flash the decision between land or water belonged to her. *Pick one, now!* The water seemed a less painful choice. The girl aimed for it, flailing her arms like guiding propellers, but one of her legs failed to comply. She straddled twenty-eight inches of pool wall as she went down. Managing to remove the cooperative leg from the water and the pool, Tallulah hopped around the backyard screaming and clutching her crotch, the blood running down her legs, and the children stared.

Idalia led her to stand in the bathtub, turned on the water, and told her to sit, before leaving to go to the phone and call Jacob. Tallulah watched the water around her become alive with red snakes. Eventually finding herself on a doctor's office examination table before being driven to a hospital room with identical furniture, every endless probe with cotton wads hurt. At one point, two male Japanese doctors held a technical discussion in their native tongue over her as she lay with her legs spread apart and uncovered. Nothing and no one materialized to warm the human icicle enough to release the battery of questions ricocheting in her brain: *Have I done permanent damage to "that part" of my body? Will I still get a period when I get older?* The great mystery of menstruation had consisted so far of being sent inside drug stores by Myrna to buy those puffy things, and consequently longing to melt into the floor if a boy served as the unavoidable sentry guarding the cash register. *He'll know, he'll laugh,* she always could be sure.

Stitches in her female area kept her in the hospital for several days. Jacob brought Idalia to visit the next day. Tallulah glanced up to see her mom looking unusually pretty, like the Dear and Darling women on television. The second day's visit presented an Idalia who looked less like Dear and Darling, but still showed a trace of pleasant hope and happiness. On the third day, Idalia looked pale and tired. For whatever reason, her preparation time or interest had crumbled. Tallulah detected the reduction of hope and happiness, leaving the daughter to feel remorse for interrupting the woman's busy day. Jacob looked the same every day.

Myrna arrived with Jacob on the fourth day, to take home Tallulah, who appreciated the respectful cloud of silence floating with them into the car, until the man suddenly chuckled, and asked the windshield with a cutting grin, "Well, ain't you gonna show us your stitches?" Tallulah begged the doors of the underworld to open for her, shrinking and hiding her face in embarrassment. She screamed silently: *Let me melt, deep down into the cracks of the seat. Oblivion, please, I need you.* With quieter agony, she realized: *He's put me in the same category as the creepy ink pen he keeps in his desk, the pen undressing the captive woman inside when he turns it upside down, and his ugly necktie with the naked woman posing on the lining. Die, die, die. Please let me die.*

CHAPTER FIVE

With the angel of death offering no rescue from the deepest throes of humiliation, bodies continued to mature, skills became acquired, perceptions persisted in the common struggle for sensible clarity beyond the gullibility of youth. Gregory fixed broken toasters, perfected bicycle chains, washed restaurant dishes, and finally progressed to perform minor repairs on the old clunker of a car he had saved money for and purchased. Occasionally, Jacob claimed the role of supervisor, strutting out to the garage, leaning well away from the grease and oil, advising, lecturing, and otherwise taking advantage of a captive audience.

One evening, curious Tallulah lingered in the doorway, catching particles of the mysterious male verbiage as it fluttered in the air. She heard Jacob suggest to Gregory that he might need to apply a dab of elbow grease. Imagining a slippery, yet tangible element useful to tasks contingent upon the efforts of human hands, Tallulah attempted to verify her mental image by asking, "What is elbow grease?"

Jacob hesitated a moment, then suggested, "Why don't you go see if you can find a can of it in the house, Lulah? Look around real good now."

Eager to please, she heard the suppressed cough Gregory made, hoped he wasn't getting sick, and turned around to enter the house. She began her investigative search with the cupboard under the kitchen sink. "What are you looking for?" asked her mother. "Elbow grease. Jacob said Greg needs it."

"Oh," said Idalia, continuing to dry dishes, one corner of her mouth unable to resist rising. The daughter glanced up at her mother to see semi-compassionate eyes above a conflicted smirk, but maintained her diligent search below, digging through the clutter of accumulated bottles and boxes and cans, hoping her prey had retained its label. The determined detective ignored the feather of doubt drifting down from her mother above.

"I'll find it," Tallulah said, confident of her useful mission; nothing could be wrong with finding something Gregory needed. She progressed from the kitchen to the bathroom, and into the basement, diligently searching, gathering nothing but dust and a few more smirks before realizing Jacob had somehow made a stinking fool out of her, and gave up. *He probably knows we're out of elbow grease,* she concluded.

At sixteen, Gregory also earned steady money by mowing lawns for neighbors, one being an elderly woman living alone. Mrs. Watson apparently appreciated him and his work, inquiring if he had a genetically similar sibling willing to pull weeds in her backyard garden. Not especially inclined to splash in the backyard pool anymore, Tallulah volunteered. "Missus Watson will talk your ear off," Gregory warned.

Ear loss loomed as a minimal risk worth taking for a bit of her own moola. She figured she could hide money from Jacob-the-borrower as successfully as Gregory and Myrna managed to with their nooks and crannies. As she knelt on the edge of the woman's pretty garden, she didn't expect to be bestowed with stashable metaphors to prove their value later in life. "Be sure you pull out the roots, honey. Otherwise, they'll grow right back. Pull easy now, easy but firm. I watered before you came. The dirt should be soft enough to get the whole thing out. Breaking off the top doesn't do much good. It might look gone for the moment, but it isn't. The stronger part is still growing down in the dirt and it will just come up again."

And when Tallulah finished: "You can slip off your shoes and put them right beside mine. These are my garden shoes, and I like the way I can take my foot right out. They're called espadrilles," the old woman declared, standing inside her back doorway. "We don't need any garden soil on my clean carpet, honey. I had the steaming company come last Wednesday and they did the whole house, every room—well, every room with carpet. See how nice it looks, even over there by the front door. That's where most of the dirt was, but they did a pretty good job, don't you think?"

Mrs. Watson opened her refrigerator and allowed Tallulah to choose a can of soda from the small army on one shelf, then directed her to take a few steps out of the kitchen to the closest chair inside the carpeted front living room. A metal TV tray table unfolded over the girl's knees. "Now you just take your time drinking that. I know you won't spill it, although I stayed away from the red sodas when I was choosing flavors. Don't gulp it down." Mrs. Watson settled in her bigger chair close by and continued talking, shifting to family matters. Tallulah drank slowly, wondering how a refrigerator could keep so many cans of soda, how a house could have no more than one inhabitant, how a floor could be free of debris, and if carpet could be slept on. She politely endured the stream of words about people she did not know, grown children who did this and that, said this and that, verbiage merging into a river of other lives flowing past, unhindered by the silence of the audience. Several visits made it clear this would be the routine: listen, work, go inside, listen more, sit, drink, listen. Try not to snatch the two dollars out of the old outstretched hand before the words ended, no matter how loud and large loomed the allure of escape.

At the end of one of those weed removal days, when Mrs. Watson seemed to remember to whom she was talking, she asked about Tallulah's family. "I met your mother the other day. You kids keep her pretty busy. How is she? I stopped in to say hello. Sounds like your father has a drinking problem."

"He's not my father." The chatter crashed into silence. Tallulah shrugged and finished her soda. The words had popped out, something she had heard Gregory mutter in a moment of anger. Mrs. Watson stared with surprise in her bleary eyes, finally getting back on her verbal track. "You mean you disown him."

Disown? What does it mean? What a weird word. "I guess." The girl shrugged, nodding as she imagined "owning" her father: the whining man cringed on his pathetic knees as she flicked a long whip. She smiled.

CHAPTER SIX

Months later, the family's final winter in Michigan blew in. Late one Friday night, hard January snow lay accumulated in deep drifts. Need having finally led her to take action, Idalia worked the night shift at a nearby factory. Gregory washed dishes in a restaurant, and Myrna snoozed on the living room floor. Her giggly friend, Sandra from across the street, occupied the couch. The boob tube hummed with a snowy image, the station's replacement for being on the air. Humor and chatter having ceased, a sleepless Sandra rolled over to reach down and poke Myrna. "Hey, Myrna, wake up. Something smells weird, like smoke."

"No, Mom, I don't smoke. Honest," Myrna mumbled.

"Goofball, wake up," Sandra insisted, shoving the shoulder of her friend.

"Huh? What? Are you smoking? I told you, not in the house. My parents will freak out," Myrna replied.

"I'm not smoking, dodo, but something else is."

"Oh, crap."

They looked down the hallway and saw the wisps of gray cloud coiling out from under the closed door of Jacob and Idalia's bedroom. They heard coughing.

Springing into action, as they would tell the story later, the fifteen-year-old girls looked at each other, rushed down the hall, flung open the door, and gasped at the flames crawling up the drapery. An unconscious father sprawled across the bed, still dressed in his street clothes, one arm aimed at the overflowing ashtray dumped on the floor near the window, his other arm stretched out across the rumpled bedding, fingers glued to a whiskey bottle. Myrna climbed on the bed, trying to shake him awake, grabbing one arm to drag him away from the flames, screaming, "Jacob, Jacob, wake up," but eliciting no response beyond incoherent mumbling. With Sandra grabbing a leg, they managed to slide him off the bed, catching his head to keep it from bouncing to the floor.

"He won't wake up. Whaddowedo?" Sandra exclaimed, trying to keep her cool.

"Hell if I know. Just drag him out. Hurry!" Each grabbed a foot to drag him down the hall and into the living room.

"Oh, shit. The little guys," Myrna remembered. "Get 'em out! You get Tallulah out of there, and I'll go upstairs for the boys!"

"Fire! Fire! Tallulah! Get out of the house," Sandra began shouting, reaching for the other bedroom door as the flames crawled across the ceiling in the first bedroom,

Tallulah woke up, stared at her sister's friend waving her arms for some weird reason, and thought of the snow. She crawled out of bed, aiming for the closet floor thinking: *shoes. Which shoes?* Sandra grabbed a blanket from the bed and threw it over Tallulah's shoulders, saying, "Here. Take this. You have to get out," then pulling her up and steering the younger girl to the hall into and through the smoke. Myrna guided Humphrey and Cary down the stairs.

"Go, go! Just go," both girls commanded, ignoring the proliferation of groggy huhs and whats.

Gregory arrived home in time to perceive the situation, "What the fuck?"

He tried to help Jacob stand, enduring the blubbery, "Ah's a man. Ah kin stand up, goddamn it. Git yer mits off me, boy." Gregory steered him, along with the whimpering children, out to the front porch, where Jacob grabbed a pillar for support, his pants falling to his knees; he had removed his notorious belt, now doomed to burn. Sandra rushed home to wake her parents and call the fire department.

From the front door and windows of Sandra's house, the evacuated children watched in shock as bold flashing lights from fire trucks and police cars battered neighboring houses, shattering the dark, cold night with commotion. Smoke poured from the front door of their home as firefighters charged in with long hoses. Medical personnel slid Jacob into an ambulance as Idalia arrived on the scene. Once determining him to be physically unburned, she joined her children in the neighbor's house to find out what had happened.

Sandra's mother apparently thought a lesson in hygiene to be in order for any small people who would go to bed with their clothes on. She put Gregory and Cary in the bathtub before allowing anyone the luxury of sleeping on her floor. After the bath, the woman insisted Tallulah be given a thorough lesson in removing bathtub ring, and she directed Sandra to instruct Myrna's little sister as to the appropriate method of shaking cleansing powder into a bathtub, soon leaving Tallulah alone, on her knees, scrubbing and stretching to remove the grime of her family.

The day following the fire, Idalia and her five children waded through the mess together. Someone had already covered one of the broken windows with a few boards. Walls and furniture and floors bore the remnants of dirty, wet slop. Ruined pictures and soggy, trampled toys littered the way. Scattered clothing and drenched bed coverings defied former ownership, deepening everyone's sense of personal loss. Muddy water still dripped from the fire's route through the ceiling above the bed where Jacob had sought oblivion, representing his thwarted gateway to heaven. The gaping hole led to the attic containing the drenched beds of the three boys. Everything not burned or soaked stank with the penetrating residue of smoke. While Idalia dazedly wrung her hands and wept, repeatedly referring to her dearly beloved as "that damn fool," Gregory and Myrna hovered near her, setting aside their own weariness and despair to prevent the young boys from climbing the stairs, and supporting Idalia with vague encouraging words collected from neighbors during the night. "It'll be okay, Mom. Let the insurance company handle it."

Newspapers and television reporters fashioned the family into the current charity case, recognizing the heroics of Myrna and Sandra, and decently minimizing the shameful cause of the flames. Over the next few weeks, boxes of donations arrived. Idalia used old clothes to dry the walls and floor of the basement, creating sleeping space before men with clipboards and crews began to clean, repair, and repaint the floors above. School days resumed for the children, who endured innocent and not-so-innocent comments of "Eww, I smell smoke."

One Saturday morning, Tallulah accompanied her mother upstairs. In the bedroom she had shared with Myrna, a man with a broom stood over a small mountain of clothes and toys he had swept into the middle of the floor. He glanced in her direction. Tallulah longed to shrink to the size of a mouse and crawl away in shame, suddenly realizing a stranger could come in and find out they lived in a mess. Her cartoon speech balloon companion of unpleasant reality had filled with lead.

Rather than proving to be a sanctuary, living in the basement brought the family one step closer to hell. At first, the presence of a real mouse threatened to push Idalia over the brink, with her clutching her chest in terror and begging Gregory to put down his Superman comic books and catch the diabolical rodent. The pursuer and pursued almost provided scenes of live entertainment in the process, but no one laughed much. No one could even think of laughing when the real Lex Luther rodent returned.

The following Friday evening, Jacob showed up, defying Idalia's directive to stay away. Doctors had checked him for tuberculosis and lung cancer, confirmed emphysema, settled with removing part of his right lung with a thoracotomy, and prescribed drugs. On the day they released him, he found a hotel and a liquor store, likely in reverse order. Clutching his hotel pillow, he arrived about ten p.m. to find his wife and three children upstairs in front of the donated television. They attempted to ignore him, glancing at each other as he staggered in, feebly reclaiming his authority by shouting, "Go da bed! All a you! In bed! Shoulda been assleep hours ago! What kind a family iss dis? By God! Git to bed! Git to bed!"

"There's no school tomorrow. They don't have to get up early. Leave them alone," a weary but sensible Idalia explained, resenting the intrusion she knew to be inevitable, feeling her harbored hope of his sober return flee from the volatile air.

"Ah said git to bed! You, too, woman!"

"Now, wait a doggone minute. Who do you think you are? Some kind of king? You can't just march in here and start giving orders. I go to bed when I'm good and ready, mister," she retorted.

And the show began.

The children watched their father stumble around the vacant room as if he could not determine the location of steady flooring. They watched their exasperated mother yell in defiance at his irrational demands. Their young ears cringed. The two performers usually managed to keep physical contact to a minimum, fortunately, but this night they veered from the script. Jacob knocked a bottle of beer from Idalia's hand.

Responding to the sound of breaking glass, Myrna removed herself from the bathtub, donned a mighty bathrobe, wrapped her hair in a towel, bid farewell to the sanctity of the bathroom, and proceeded to step between mother and father. "You go away now, Jacob, back off!"

The younger children turned off the television and backed away, watching in a heretofore unexperienced level of fear as Myrna's towel fell to the floor and she found herself being dragged by her long hair downstairs to the basement, her head bouncing against the steps as she struggled.

Idalia scurried to the phone on the kitchen wall, frantically appealing to herself, "He said to call. He said to call. What did he say his number was?"

Tallulah peeked briefly down the stairs, alarmed to see Myrna cringing on an old mattress, Jacob slapping her face from side to side until Sandra's father charged in from across the street, pushing past Tallulah like a big bear. She had never seen Mr. Kowalski in their home before. He went straight to the basement and pulled Jacob away, pinning him against the nearest wall.

His deep voice could be heard upstairs. "Enough of that! Leave her alone, ya damn drunk!"

Two police officers filed in moments later. "Don't hit him, sir. Don't hit him. We'll take care of him. Break it up. Let him go."

They brought Jacob upstairs and across the lawn to their patrol car, where they stood talking to him while Mr. Kowalski stood in the kitchen, patting Idalia on the shoulder, telling her, "You did what you had to do. You're a good woman. He's gone now. You'll be okay."

One officer came back in to tell them Jacob agreed to return to his hotel. Idalia shook her head. "He'll come back. I know he'll come back." As a token precautionary measure, the officers sat outside in their patrol car for another ten minutes, until Gregory arrived home and they informed him of the situation. Myrna remained in the basement for the rest of the night.

Following the officers' advice, Gregory wedged a kitchen chair under the knob of the back door that gave access to a small landing. The landing opened to the kitchen on one side, as well as the basement stairs a few feet further ahead. Sure enough, the villain of the evening soon returned for more action, not daring to use the more visible front door. The kitchen chair remained lodged in place despite Jacob's loud, heavy, pounding demand for re-entry. Gregory bounded up the stairs to wait and watch in the kitchen.

The others remained in the basement, hoping the lunatic on the other side of the door would either come to his senses or vaporize into oblivion. He did neither. Instead, he removed his conventional white handkerchief from a pocket and wrapped his right hand with it. He then shoved his fist through a glass pane in the door, reached in, unlocked it and, shoving away the chair, entered the kitchen.

"No! Get out," shouted Gregory, who had already telephoned the police. "Go away! You're *not* a father! You are a lying, cheating son-of-a-bitch scumbag! You mother fucker! You nearly burned down the fucking house! You are *not* a father! Get the hell out of here, ya stupid bastard!" Gregory's red face ballooned with years of pent-up rage as he raised his fists in a boxer's defensive pose, ready to punch. Tallulah had followed him upstairs and stood by him, mesmerized by the unprecedented explosion, her childish, wavering maturity mirage once glued to a distant horizon now slamming forward as a rock-solid portal into an oscillating netherworld. Jacob's face reddened and began to vibrate with utterances and grumbles, his eyes averted from Gregory's flashing outlets of X-ray vision eager to burn him to a crisp. Lex Luthor struggled to feign indifference, unable to prevent his trembling arms from creeping up in defense, defying his pretense of control. Both faces quivered under blankets of shiny sweat. Punches and blood loomed inevitable when two police officers separated Superman from his foe, breaking into the torrent of hatred, but not before Tallulah felt it, absorbed it, and embraced the existential need to "disown" a monster who would deliberately dump boulders of pain upon those people she knew she loved: Gregory, Myrna, and Mom.

Jacob had given no warning before smashing the window, and a piece of flying glass had flown down the stairs, landing upon his bewildered wife's head. Seeing the blood on Idalia's face, the officers attempted to arrest Jacob for being drunk and disorderly, but Jacob insisted on making his own telephone call. They let him fumble for a number in his pocket and make a call. After a moment of conversation, Jacob handed the receiver to the officers, who soon nodded their heads in compliance. "Yes, sir, yes sir, yes sir," they nodded to the evil one's connection on the other end of the line. Tallulah stood frozen until someone behind her touched her shoulders and led her away.

Thoughts of jail shoved aside, the obedient officers left with the mild recommendation Jacob again return to his motel. For them and their master, Jacob continued his facade of decency by patronizing the fine men in uniform who had been necessarily set straight. He had, after all, won the battle, and a good sport like he could forgive their ignorant error in judgement. Ostentatious grace and pretentious honor flowing, Jacob made a performance of obliging and drove away to his clean motel room.

Although the evening ended without bloody bodies being scattered from wall to wall, the threat of violence proved sufficient for Idalia to file for divorce. Months of hostile phone calls and tears and petty papers from lawyers followed as Jacob pursued various legal attempts to freeze his wife's access to money, including her inheritance of fourteen thousand dollars, destroy her credit, and take the house. Grace and honor made no appearance. Idalia came home from work in the early mornings to fight the legal fight as best she could after getting the kids off to school. Sometimes she could do nothing more than sit at the kitchen table and weep over a cup of tea, trying not to feel sorry for herself . On sick leave and cooped up in a room with a bed and a phone, Jacob made full use of his time and energy to call lawyers.

Fortunately, the house title held Idalia's name, placed as a bankruptcy precaution when Jacob had once flirted with the dream of having his own business. With a show of strength, Idalia refused to sign the house over to him. The attack-and-retaliate game continued as Jacob threatened a dirty and senseless court fight for custody of children who had no desire to live with him. A weary Idalia lost her primary advisor when Gregory decided he had had enough and left for the Army on the day he graduated from high school.

When his employer caught wind of how Jacob was spending his recovery time, he fired him, and having stretched his various buddy-connections to the maximum, Jacob chose to withdraw to his brother's home in Savannah. From there, he watched the evening news on television report on a larger, yet similar manifestation of the seeds and deeds of conflict and inequality.

CHAPTER SEVEN

During the infamous summer of 1967, the city of Detroit ignited from decades of discrimination. Expectations of habitually tolerant, subservient conformity encountered a rude awakening. Late one hot July night, white police officers raided a drinking establishment belonging to another Georgia-born man, this one not so devious. Over eighty African-American adults, having gathered to celebrate the safe return of two local soldiers from the war in Vietnam, never expected to be handcuffed and jailed for the proprietor's lack of a liquor license. Dismayed onlookers became saddened then defiant against the uncalled-for intrusion on a jubilant, patriotic evening, disgustedly flipping a few beer bottles into the air, fed up with a system ready to reward national allegiance and military service with prison, fed up, too, with passive acceptance of years of blatantly unjust deeds confining good people to poverty. In the following hours, more glass fragments flew as fists unclenched only long enough to grab anything of weight to smash store and restaurant windows, feet flying in and out as frenzied bodies captured the merchandise, compensation of a sort for deprivation. Human muscle overturned automobiles on the street, torching the symbols of prosperity belonging to the hated privileged. For five chaotic days and nights, television reporters covered citizens venting their pent-up rage against the segregated city.

During those violent days, talk emerged in the cozy white suburbs. Cars filled with angry men sometimes drove along the major streets yelling insults. Smaller incidents drew nearer to the realms of white comfort. Tallulah heard a neighbor claim his window screens showed knife cuts made during the night. She had no idea why the people with dark skin were angry. She knew they lived a few blocks away, near the factory where Idalia worked, but none had ever come to her school and very few to her neighborhood.

Television reporters hinted at the city's history as home to Ford, Chevrolet, Impala, and other massive automotive manufacturing plants responsible for years of enticing African-American workers from their homes in the South, where daily reminders of Jim Crow laws openly labeled them inferior. Labor agents arriving from the north promised a better, safer life for those of dark skin trapped in a white world they had never chosen, a land rank with habitual degradation and injustice unchecked, frequently allowed to surge into sadistic murder. The northern industrial men needed cheap labor, and often provided the enticing train tickets promising to put hundreds of miles between hardworking people and their misery.

In reality, Detroit built cheap housing, even maneuvering highways to separate the crowded Black neighborhoods from prettier white neighborhoods, where police officers offered Black people no protection from any hostility they might encounter if they tried to move in. Although jobs could be found, promises of northern prosperity and protection proved to be nearly as empty as the crop fields back home. Decades of systematic urban segregation and deception had created its victims. Black disappointment evolved into resentment, a smoldering not unlike the reluctant awakenings of any deceived child relying upon security from those with power and position to provide it. The days of reckoning demonstrated at an intersection about two miles from Tallulah's home caught the national television cameras one day.

"Lawd, Jacob, looka there! Ain't that near ya'll's house? They said *Dee*troit. Mah word. Ah never seen such. You better get Idalia and those children outta there!" Feigning softness in the hands of his southern relatives, playing the role of unfortunate baby brother deserving pity and compassion, and cash "if ya can spare any for a poor lad like me," Jacob calmed down during his weeks in Georgia. Convinced of his sincere decency, Jacob's brother and sister-in-law encouraged him to make peace with Idalia and bring the family down south, away from all that northern nastiness. "Ya'll just need to make a fresh start. Go to church and all," they told him.

Jacob called off the lawyers he couldn't pay anyway and put Ethan on the phone to persuade Idalia into giving her boozer another chance. Idalia remembered Ethan as the boozer who had come to visit early in her marriage. She had once cooked breakfast for him, but his level of inebriation commanded the fried egg to keep slipping off his fork, repeatedly avoiding capture by his gaping mouth, and she couldn't help laughing at the memory.

Jacob drove back to Michigan, blamed everything on the booze, and persuaded his exhausted wife into allowing him to take her and the children away from the neighbors who knew too dang much and kept interfering. He would not live alone. She had never lived alone, he reminded her, kindling her doubts about single parenting. Her old philosophy arose, that having something is better than having nothing, and losing something you had is the worst. And Gregory was gone. She imagined every negative scenario and mustered no threads of courage for the positives, not even when she held the upper hand.

He took her hand. Against the advice of her legal counselors and her supportive neighbors, Idalia agreed to give her blue-eyed, maybe not-so-royal-but-still-charming prince another chance. Among the shards of reason, she selected a slim favorite: at least she could keep an eye on him.

Myrna went to live across the street with the Kowalskis, who assured Idalia they would keep an eye on the house. Tallulah and the young boys were told it was a vacation, and they would return in time for school.

PART II
SAVANNAH, THEREABOUTS

CHAPTER EIGHT

"Why are there so many Black people down here?" Tallulah asked as her father drove through scattered clusters of humdrum buildings. Unhurried people strolled or languished on street corners, perhaps using them as daily meeting spots. "I thought they had a lot of trouble down here." After over eight hundred cramped miles in the station wagon, with minimal stops, no one answered.

Jacob landed what was left of his family in a municipal campground on the edge of Savannah, where he'd promised to find a job, although why he'd look for a job while vacationing seemed a bit odd to Tallulah. Setting the thought aside as one more adult mystery unsolved, she accepted an invitation to become a guest in Cousin Lisa's nearby home. The contrast between this home and her Michigan one soon sparked a realization: not every family lives the same. Some differences surprised the "yamn dankee," this being the label Uncle Ethan waved around to tease his brother's kids. Other words were new. The first time Lisa's mom yelled "Heyyy" to a neighbor from a car window as they drove past, the yamn dankee in the car jumped, the words sounding to her like a chop on the block. Tallulah looked around for the emergency, then settled back, realizing, *oh, they actually like each other.*

For one thing, the house exhibited open spaces, uncluttered corners, reminding her of Mrs. Watson's tidy domicile. No toys lay forgotten on the floor; no clothing sat in neglected piles; no stinky ashtrays overflowed. Some people might have considered the home dull with its typical middle class furnishings, an unimaginative tribute to Sears, Roebuck and Co., but to Tallulah it brought relief. She discovered a fondness for clean sheets and comfortable pajamas. For another thing, Lisa's mother had time to be kind. Aunt Lizzie actually asked Tallulah what she liked to eat, and made sure the girls had ice cream, real ice cream, not occasionally-provided ice milk, available every night for a bedtime snack.

Uncle Ethan shared his brother's addiction to alcohol, and the family had endured their subsequent years of hell, but this uncle had learned years ago to stay away from the booze, and he survived quite peacefully without it. *If his brother could put down the bottle, why can't Jacob?* Tallulah wondered. *Same family, same background.* Tallulah envisioned Idalia's usual bucketful of excuses for Jacob and dumped them out onto the ground. He could indeed "help it." The whiskey bottle held no magic power over him or anyone else. It was nothing more than an ordinary glass container; it required a human hand to pick it up. She began to perceive Jacob's behavior as deliberate choices, repulsive choices so damaging no one with half a brain would keep repeating them over and over. His choices made no sense. He made no sense.

She thought how lucky Lisa was to have a father who came home from a steady job every evening for dinner, a man who spoke calmly to his daughter and to his wife. He relaxed in front of the television at night, with nothing more potent in his hand than a newspaper and a candy bar. This man even cared about his house, fixing whatever needed repair, busying himself on weekends with the lawn, organizing and caring for hand tools he did not hesitate to use.

Lisa and her parents made Tallulah feel welcome and wanted. Uncle Ethan even talked to her sometimes, as if she might be more than a dumb-punk, in-the-way burden. Apparently, she held genuine opinions, tucked down deep, in a safe place, and she allowed a few to peek out. People listened. *How different,* she thought. They may have disagreed with her, but their disagreements floated light and humorous, never the hostile, hammering, insulting torrent pouring out of the man-beast contaminating every interaction in the house Tallulah knew too well.

Taking a break from daily swims at the community pool, one day Tallulah and Lisa rode a city bus to go shopping, rumbling along old streets lined by historic buildings, bordered by looming woody perennials, their long branches laden with chains of Spanish moss. The cousins seated themselves behind a young Black girl about their age, travelling alone. Lisa began to sing a ditty, barely loud enough to reach the ears of the girl, "I see your hiney, so black and shiny, if you don't hide it, I'm gonna bite it."

"Shhhh. Stop it," Tallulah whispered, jabbing her cousin in the ribs.

"It don't hurt nothing," she snickered. "It's what we always do."

"It sounds mean."

"No, it ain't. They're used to it."

"How can anyone get used to being hurt? She's a girl, just like you and me."

"They ain't the same."

Baffled, Tallulah tried to keep the subject open, bringing it up off and on during the day, but Lisa brushed it away, passing it along to her father in the evening, leaving the two in the living room. "Daddy, you need to explain things to this girl."

Tallulah had not considered approaching her uncle, but she plunged ahead. "Uh, okay. Why are Black people treated differently from white people?"

"Because they *are* different, that's why," Uncle Ethan replied, easing into his armchair for an evening of television.

"So what if their skin is darker? Two arms, two legs, one head. People are people."

"They ain't the same."

"But white people are no better than Black people."

"They don't look like us, they don't talk like us, and now they're stomping around all over the country acting crazy."

"They have a right to be angry. Good people can get angry, really angry, when someone around them acts like he's brain-dead and does mean … stuff."

"They can be angry all they want, as long as they stay put." Uncle Ethan had his feet up on a footstool by this time.

"So if a Black family moved next door, would you welcome them?"

"Pshaw. Never gonna happen."

"What if Lisa wanted to date a Black guy? You'd have to let him in your house."

"I do not have to let one walk through that door, into my house," Uncle Ethan replied, his voice rising, his arm rising in anger but then relaxing to wave her away like a pesky mosquito. "Heck. Go on now girl, git. Shoo. I ain't giving you no history lesson."

Tallulah shooed, not angry, feeling instead a sparkly, new iota of self-worth, vaguely grateful to be considered worthy of verbally sparring with an adult, even briefly, like being allowed to place her toe upon a threshold without anything exploding. And she knew she was making sense.

More potential shuffling into the mature cosmos of reasoning adults brewed as Tallulah savored high hopes of returning to school after summer; the grand and wonderful halls of junior high, including swimming lessons, awaited her and her Michigan classmates, friends since the days of kindergarten. They felt thrilled with the prospect of becoming bona fide teenagers and having legitimate entry into the sacred land of developing bodies and developing ideas, love and dreamy romance, freedom to make their own choices, to follow or to lead, ready for the gauntlet of pre-adult passage. They would face it together.

However, the supposed two-week vacation in Georgia dragged on for three weeks. On one of her campground visits, Tallulah caught up with Idalia returning from the laundry room, "Hi, Mom. When are we going home?"

"He wants to stay here," she replied, moving forward with her full basket.

"What? Stay here? In the campground?"

"No, find a house."

"A house? He's looking for a house? We already have a house. He doesn't even have a job here. What about our stuff? What about our friends? I didn't say good-bye to anyone. What if he starts drinking again?

"Well, maybe he deserves a second chance."

"That's what you always say. Why? Do you want to stay here?"

"No, but what can I do? If I get on a bus and take you guys, he'll just find a way to drag us all back here."

"You're giving in? Gosh. Crapola, I wish Gregory were here, and Myrna. I'm staying with Lisa."

Within a few days, Jacob and Idalia extracted Tallulah from her relative sanctuary and brought her to the dismal dwelling they'd rented outside Savannah. They moved in with no furniture, and washed clothes in the bathtub. Lisa and Aunt Lizzy came during the day to cook and help out while Idalia flew to Michigan, staying a week to sell or give away everything in the real house, put the empty shell on the market, and bring back Myrna, who wouldn't speak to Jacob for months. Toys and mementos sacred only to their young owners, furniture and books, bicycles and clothing, remained behind, scattered among strangers, entombed forever in the now hallowed Michigan of origin and identity.

Tallulah found every savored anticipation of returning to school with her friends tossed into the southern heat to fry and evaporate. Conquest of the grand and glorious halls of junior high with people she knew became nothing but a dream ripped away from her, leaving no need to feel any thrill with the prospect of becoming a bona fide teenager. The majestic door she had anticipated passing through disintegrated, leaving her to crawl into a stupid world of stupid odd people close to her only in age. The memory of her mortifying, new-kid, first day of kindergarten came back to her, merging with the explanation she'd have to provide to her Michigan friends someday for not returning: *It was his fault; he made me.* She wanted to puke. Hadn't he done enough damage already? Unsatisfied dancing natives and an impatient volcano had returned.

In the strange land of their father's reclaimed childhood, Myrna, Tallulah, Humphrey, and Cary began to ride school buses for the first time: noisy, crowded vehicles whose stupid passengers seemed to be well acquainted, and laughed loud together, and whispered about "those new kids" as if they bore green skin and antennae. Local youth did not hesitate to bestow the stigma, "Ya'll talk funny," repeatedly, loudly. Alien Tallulah kept quiet, regarding them as the ones who talked funny, letting words slip slide out of their ole mouths like they was a-coated with the awl the food is fried in, and nothing in their whole, wide, itty-bitty world was worth a-hurrying up for. "'Ya'll' is not even a word," she muttered to herself, resenting the subtle hostilities supplanting her initial exposure to Southern ways; the fun days with kind relatives in Savannah had been tons better.

On this sticky, warm planet, adults wore the crowns of Ma'ams and Sirs without needing to earn the respect of such formal titles. *Why do they still bow and scrape?* Tallulah asked only herself, feeling shoved into a cage every time grown-ups reminded the quiet Yankee girl to use the titles—and she would not use them unless poked. *Am I a wild thing needing to be controlled?* she wondered, remembering her one sixth-grade Michigan lesson about the South of today, wishing her teacher had elaborated more on this sicko place mired in its self-induced misery of the past.

Slavery might have been forced to end a century before, but a volatile avalanche of resentment and ignorance had taken its place. White inhabitants made no attempt to disguise the obliteration of genuine human decency. Tales handed down to "my daddy" from "his daddy" bragged of violent days, when the breath of old rage blew out from under mossy tree branches, across the hot, neglected fields, and into the vengeful minds of pale men struggling to retain romanticized interpretations of the inglorious past. Deceitful memories elevated whites into god-like positions of ease and dominance, preferable to the confusing challenges of their current life requiring "some Yankee thing called edy-cashun," and learning new ways which took too damn long to figure out. Tallulah could not believe her mother accepted this warped land of obvious cruelty and falsehood. It felt as if someone had taken the ugliness of Detroit and ripped off its camouflaging blanket of prosperity.

When alone, Tallulah refused to forget the Michigan friends stolen from her. She possessed no phone numbers, no addresses, only her last class group photo rescued from an envelope in Idalia's luggage. She wrote down everyone's name so she would never forget anyone, knowing they must be wondering what had happened to her, wishing she could tell them: *No one told me we were moving. He lied. I hate this pukey place.*

Idalia mentioned an upcoming interview arranged by Uncle Ethan at the big paper plant where he worked as a supervisor. Tallulah could not help imagining if Jacob took the job then maybe she could embrace a modicum of the stability Lisa enjoyed. Such a naive hope lasted about as long as one of the big cockroaches dumb enough to crawl across the kitchen floor during mealtime, signaling two pairs of young stompers into immediate action. "I got it!" "No, I got it!" Humphrey and Cary often battled for this victory, leaving a smear of guts and carcass for someone else to clean up. The roaches failed to diminish in the winter, or during the months which normally would have been winter. When a sprinkle of snow fell one day in December, the schools closed.

"Today is a snow day? You've got to be kidding." Myrna laughed.

For some strange reason, Jacob did not take the steady job, or any other job. His self-sabotaged body and history of job-hopping in the far-away north failed to make the greatest résumé. Idalia said he didn't want to be confined in one building. Tallulah thought what she probably meant was he couldn't go for two hours without a stinky cigarette in his mouth. Months before the school year ended, Jacob and his promises of stability took a new direction: he found a way to use Idalia's savings, while she attempted to reclaim a meager fragment of her own childhood, when days were easier.

With a faraway look in her eyes, she spoke of being a youngster in Canada, underfoot in her mother's country grocery store with its upstairs living quarters, while her father meandered the roads selling kitchen supplies door-to-door. She seemed to have erased the troubles. Jacob's frequent excuses for meandering the highways had unearthed an empty country store with attached living quarters.

Not far north of the southern city heralded for its historical street squares stretches the Talmadge Memorial Bridge, a massive metal arm reaching across the Savannah River into South Carolina. Marshland preceded the woods, where undergrowth and dense pine trees discouraged disturbance. "You know, you could just keep driving north, back to Michigan. We're headed in the right direction," Tallulah ventured aloud to the back of her father's head, its forward focus unchanging, cigarette going in and out of the mouth, offering no response. She slumped back among the bags and boxes and rattling dishes, not surprised to be ignored again, glaring ahead. *I hate you I hate you I hate you.* Myrna stared out her side window while the boys fought for space in the back.

Change crawls even more slowly into the quiet, scattered communities of the low country. Most of the tiny clusters of wooden homes along the two-lane highways boasted a church or two, and typically one country store to supply groceries, gas, and chewing tobacco. The stores bestowed monetary credit upon their local customers, some of whom would pay, and some of whom didn't worry much about owing a wee bit of money to a familiar face behind the counter. All of this the family soon discovered.

Fifty miles from Savannah and Lisa, Jacob and Idalia appeared to be in agreement on this one store as the true solution to their problems. Tallulah felt them succumbing, breathing in the stagnant atmosphere of the land around them, becoming two more adults seeking refuge in the past when the future appears bleak, pulling together their ragged memories of times gone by, weaving the selected scraps into a destination of nostalgia, or sewing the scraps into an easier, cozy quilt to wrap around their sagging shoulders. It did not matter to her if the man sunk to new lows, but the woman mattered, and she clung to him. The human mind can savor slivers of justification, and Idalia appeared to be resigned to slivers, excuses. Perhaps this store decision stood as some kind of inner tribute to Idalia's mother, or Idalia felt her life to be an inevitable rerun of her mother's, or maybe she followed her mother's path in a way still longing for approval not offered in younger years. Tallulah could only wonder, while her insides churned. "Cheap family groceries" stood as the only verbal reason her mother offered for giving the children a longer bus ride to rural schools even more lost in time than Savannah.

Two outdated gas pumps in front served to distinguish the building as a business to passers-by who otherwise would glimpse no commercial activity in the area. Living quarters existed behind and above the empty store, complete with a large yard in the back, so said the parents, as if their children cared. A dry, slight, aged man had agreed to rent this empty store, the hub of a humid, sparsely-populated community rumored to have been tramped through by General Sherman's troops. *At least someone from the north has been here before,* thought Tallulah. The elderly man and his wife remained living in the back and above, while Idalia dusted and scrubbed the wooden, U-shaped countertop and wood floor before the merchandise arrived. She included every one of the old wood shelves lining the walls behind the long counter, shelves designed to hold most products, requiring every can of beans and every bag of flour to be handed to the customer.

Not quite matching the convenience lodged in Idalia's idealized memories, down the highway a mile or so, a rural mailbox marked a single-lane dirt driveway disappearing among tall pine trees. It led into a clearing dominated by a large, neglected, two-story remnant of the slavery era, clearly diminutive in comparison to "the big house" reigning somewhere else on the old plantation. Jacob introduced his northern family to high and wide steps once elaborate enough to compliment the swishes of long southern gowns. Young hands of the present era soon discovered how easily flat pieces of a crumbling concrete surface yielded to reveal a foundation of very old, red bricks.

Enough strength remained in the structure to lead leery souls of modern times six feet up to a wide, wooden porch streaked with souvenirs of gray paint, stretching across the front and along two sides of the house once painted white. Double front doors with cracked glass panes opened reluctantly to reveal a dusty entry hall leading straight back to a plain door at the rear of the house, a design accommodating breezes before the days of air conditioning, which had not been added. To the right of the hall, a large room boasted a crumbly fireplace, peeling paint, and carved woodwork both on the mantle and along the tops of its high walls. The similar room to the left of the hall, boasting another fireplace, became a bedroom for Jacob and Idalia.

The central hall also contained a once-sturdy staircase leading up to two more rooms, both large enough for several beds. The house boasted of added electricity, with quality control being something only fancy-pants city folk required; some of the lights worked. Gas heaters defiant of safety standards sat in the old fireplaces. Cockroaches thrived in numerous cracks provided by old boards subjected to years of long, humid summers, the critters massing especially well in the tiny kitchen at the back where the hearty old boards presented a generous slant to the floor at one end, depriving a newfangled washing machine on spin of its usual resistance to travel, Idalia soon discovered, as she accepted everything with acquiescence, increasing her consumption of cheap beer.

Tucked under the two fairly spacious stories with their high ceilings and wide walls lay genuine slave quarters for those in servitude to the supposedly higher life above them. Low beams promised to bump the heads of fools daring to stand erect, and a single fireplace apparently had served as kitchen and heater for the unfortunate inhabitants of times past. Crude concrete walls and sandy, gray cobblestone floors would have hosted untold mildew had they not been accompanied by one door and three large, square windows substituting glass with hinged wooden covers ready to swing open, barn-door style, like loose lids on a box.

Even so, barely any sunlight could find its way into the dark, dank interior still moaning with misery and human suffering for anyone with ears of sensitivity, more than a hundred years after the end of the shameful practice. No light or breeze could erase the spooky misery of old despair and dust. At the far edge of the grassy yard behind the house, where the woods began, stood a distinctly large old tree, its massive branches providing a thick, wide canopy. Standing under it one day, expecting to share its cool peace, Tallulah instead felt the painful human history man had poisoned it with; undoubtedly a site of punishment, unseen agony emanated from the ground, the grass, the branches, the leaves. She never visited it again.

The entire house, guaranteed by a local spiritualist to be haunted, had plenty of noises and darting shadows for anyone who wanted to hear and see them. Humphrey and Cary encountered the most obvious. "Hey! Did you see that? A thing, some *thing* just flew behind the bathtub. It looked like an owl."

"An owl?"

"Yeah, a black owl."

"Where did it go then? There are no holes back there."

"Come over here and take a look back there for me."

"Not me."

"You big chicken. I will. I don't see anything now. Well, I swear I saw it."

"Yeah, I did, too. It just flew right back there, with no noise. No noise. It was weird. I saw it. It's gone now, whatever it was. Sheesh. Who wants to take a bath? Not tonight. I think I'll wait. When are we going back to Michigan?"

The two goats Jacob purchased to nibble down the tall weeds surrounding the house consistently pooped out pellet droppings around it. Not content with soil contact, Nanny and bearded Billy did not hesitate to scamper up the porch steps and christen it with their calling cards whenever they could. A sudden clomp-clompity-clomp on the wooden porch in the middle of the night might be the goats and might be something else. Idalia often heard footsteps. Jacob never heard anything. He still managed to be away most of the time, driving around God knows where, leaving most of the store time and tasks to his wife, leaving the kids on their own in a strange house, letting them all, except him, walk through the snake land, high grass bordering the lonely highway to and from the store.

When he happened to remember having made himself as well an occupant of the old dump, Jacob stomped about demanding superfluous nonsense, ordering "all hands on deck," with no deck in sight. Instead, only his two youngest, landlocked sad excuses for sailors complied with his commands to clear underbrush along the sides of the long driveway, fumbling confusedly while their father stood watching, smoking, yelling, slapping them if they ventured too near him. Petty frustrations, cuts and scratches on the bodies of young boys meant nothing, remaining part of an annoying background buzz as his allegiance to appearances remained the priority, and the long, hot walk to the store served as a frequent escape for Myrna and Tallulah.

"What about snakes?" they asked him.

"Hell, no. I never got bit by no snake, and I used to go all over the fields 'round our house down in Georgia. Saw a few once or twice, and there was one time—heck, git on out there and git to work, boy! G'wan now. They ain't gonna bother you." During the following weeks, he also compelled the two young innocents to whitewash the lower portions of tree trunks along the driveway, for some unexplained reason. "Probably to keep himself from driving into them some night coming home late and loaded," Myrna whispered to Tallulah.

Idalia's eldest daughter was smart, but her college goals nurtured by years of good grades in Michigan meant nothing in a school system too minimal and too disinterested to offer more than the lowest compliance with state mandates, and her mother had chosen to remain married to the man who rewarded his daughter's saving of his life and others' by dragging her down a flight of stairs into hell. Her high grades of the past met with irrelevance from officials in the nearby town. Consequently, Myrna's academic goals spiraled down to the local good-enough philosophy of "Just do what you are told and don't ask questions." More kindhearted than ambitious, she eased into compliance. "Linear equations? I don't even need to ask questions. I can't believe they're just now teaching what we did in Michigan two years ago. Baby stuff." With high school classes devoid of challenge, Idalia's eldest daughter waded into the playful mainstream, carelessly making friends more easily than Tallulah could, accepting the fun of it more than Tallulah could, ignoring injustice more than Tallulah could, such as the failure of schools to teach the price Black people had paid for the white man's prosperity.

Many Black people lived in the area, all with their faces sad and their eyes lowered, in contrast to the angry mobs of Detroit. Across an acre of neglected corn near the house sat an unpainted, wooden shack. The Black neighbors who lived in it kept to themselves, curious young faces offering only an occasional peek through the dry stalks, the kids riding a different bus to a different school. Heavy Black women with shiny faces came into the store and bought kerosene to splash on their skin to keep the bugs away while they worked in the fields.

Tallulah sat alone at the store counter one day, setting aside the copy of *Newsweek* she was reading, to wait on a customer who had strolled in, a scruffy local man in work clothes, complete with the confederate flag emblazoned on his sweat-stained baseball cap. She hoped to someday figure out why the flag of a war finished over a hundred years earlier, confined to textbooks in Michigan, still flew on southern hats and window stickers and car bumpers. He asked for flour and sugar and bacca. She turned around to get the first two items and brought them to the counter to see him stabbing his middle finger on a *Newsweek* picture of twenty beautiful children gathered for the sake of their diversity. He grumbled, "That's what's wrong with this here country."

"Children?" she asked innocently.

"Puttin' 'em all together like that there ain't right," he declared, his grungy finger still tapping on the photograph."

Tallulah paused, remembering her conversation along these lines with Uncle Ethan. Sensing the offer of bait designed to feed racist ranting from a man who smelled like Jacob on his worst days, she chose to remain focused on the groceries. "I'm sorry. Bacca?" she asked, tilting her head gently, trying to look politely unsure when she genuinely held no idea of which third item he wanted.

"Bacca," he repeated, flicking a dingy hand toward the cigarettes.

"Oh, okay. Salem?"

"No, no, no. Bacca, I said," he replied, becoming suddenly gymnastic in his long reach across the counter to the shelves behind her. She managed to capture one of the petite packages before he did.

"Oh, chewing tobacco. Now I get it. Here you go." She smiled.

He dropped a crumpled bill on the counter and she politely gave him his change before he sauntered out the front door with his purchases, muttering, "Damn Yankees."

Jacob grew suddenly proud of his roots in this bizarre land, the same roots he had never raised above a drunken murmur in Michigan. When a passing townsman issued the obligatory verbal invitation to bring his whole bunch to Sunday worship services, the man who aimed to please strangers made a point of rounding up his wife and young-uns, a sharp point.

Suddenly they had to go to church, every damned one of them. Without explanation, without the handy benefits of the common comprehension constantly eluding Tallulah, into the house of God the children stumbled with their parents, for the first time in their lives. "We're gonna fill a pew, a whole damn pew. Fill a pew," the man insisted.

What the heck is a pew? Tallulah wondered, thinking it sounded like a bad smell. Sunday mornings became hell. As before any departure, the man would stomp around impatiently, periodically shouting, "Lezgo,lezgo,lezgo!" chain-smoking like a maniac in order to survive the hour of service without a cigarette. His nervous impatience obliterated any chance of mental pleasantness, creeping into the neurons of every vulnerable soul, and the combination of cigarette smoke, closed windows, and his whisky-risky driving continued to upset young stomachs. Tallulah thanked heaven for short distances.

Church meant sitting still on hard, wooden benches for an hour while some fellow wearing a long black dress stood at the front and told everyone how crummy they were. With strange "thee" and "thy" words, suffering this and suffering that, he spoke passionately of people who lived a long time ago and who liked to fight, apparently. Tallulah had witnessed enough battles, held no desire to suffer, and she didn't appreciate the way this man tried to drill his ideas into their heads. Even stranger, no matter how loud this fellow shouted or how fiercely he swung his arms, the audience stared blankly at him, standing when he told them to stand, sitting when he told them to sit, singing boring, tedious songs when his vocal cords required rest.

The fellow with the dress wanted payment for all this, payment for the discomfort and harassment he manufactured, making folks pass around a big shiny brass bowl with a circle of felt glued in the bottom of it. To Tallulah, neither he nor the building looked like they needed any money.

When he finally released them, people exercised their voices with the happy relief following a fulfilled obligation. They stood around outside admiring each other's good grooming, flirting with those they were not married to, inquiring about those who had not shown up, and gabbing about the weather. When insignificant chatter had filled the proper number of minutes, the people disappeared into their automobiles as if on cue, returning to their indifferent, normal lives once again. Tallulah saw nothing sincere, nothing worth joining. Weeks later, when Jacob's enthusiasm for pew-filling wilted as suddenly as it had sprouted, no one objected. After the family's few token appearances, sleeping late on Sunday mornings once again became the welcome norm.

Each of Jacob's remaining offspring endured the uncomfortable choice between slipping in beside local mediocrity, thus dulling their northern aspirations, or struggling to retain those distant threads of identity, and consequently be guaranteed loneliness. Being only human and thus uninclined to savor isolation, Tallulah eventually made a few friends, and attempted to absorb their sage gossip and some of their local habits. Occasionally, her social education warranted a demonstration, like the time a soft-spoken blonde girl she was walking with through a residential neighborhood unexpectedly stepped inside the exterior foyer of an African-American church, promptly squatted in a corner, and defecated, never ceasing her gentle stream of words, never picking up her substantial feces, left like an unsigned souvenir of routine contempt. Tallulah stood in disbelief, finding within herself a complete absence of any capacity for joining the duplicitous world this girl represented. Loneliness gained in its appeal, isolation a safe sanctuary at times not to be discounted.

At home, Idalia began to identify more openly with her roots as well, the remote distance associated with Canada conveniently enabling her to look down in detached judgment upon the racist chatter frequently prevailing among white customers lingering in her store. Their complaints against "Blacks taking over," and "them darkies getting uppity," failed to seduce her into their cauldron of camaraderie, generating smug frowns of disdain instead; she repressed her verbal disagreements for later. When customers and Jacob were not around, she coached her children with lofty platitudes, like throwing seeds out to the wind. "Think for yourself! Use your imagination! Don't follow the crowd! Be different!"

The consequences of being different became painfully apparent for Tallulah as she waded through the halls of another junior high, always a hellish zone of pubescent vulnerability. In any geographic realm, the age of authenticity demands mainstream acceptance, the bloodline of adolescent survival. Some gauntlets extract a heavy toll. Every zombie in her school viewed and rated each other through the narrow lens of popularity. Unpopularity felt ridden with inescapable drawbacks in a pathetic system designed to destroy individuality. Clothing and hair fell prey to the scrutiny of a few self-appointed judges seeking to deflect attention from their own imperfections. Tallulah couldn't even begin to compete. Intelligence suffered as a disease to be avoided, with good grades labeling girls as eggheads no boys would ever date, as if the male gender held every key to the symbiotic dance of existential happiness. As a result, Tallulah welcomed the end of every school day, getting on a big yellow clunky bus and getting away from the school and the town, even if it meant fewer chances for friendship. Helping Idalia in the store after school proved to be a convenient refuge, while it lasted.

CHAPTER NINE

Jacob's smooth persuasion skills failed to deter the old store owner from booting out the Yankee family after less than one year. Either the old guy's wife wanted to run the store again or he'd forgotten it could make a profit, according to Idalia. Then again, Jacob might have been too inclined to negotiate instead of actually paying rent. Regardless, no Sheridan objected to leaving the loose boards and dark shadows of the drafty slave house. In the town the school bus called home, Jacob embraced what had already repulsed his junior high daughter. He located another empty dream store, a larger structure meeting Idalia's preferred layout of attached living quarters. Tongues wagged about the previous tenant who had quenched the community's thirst for sexual promiscuity by adding a couple of bedrooms and an additional bathroom along the back. Jacob could ignore the history of any establishment as long as it put space between him and his crazy teenagers and kept his wife busy. She scrubbed counters and mopped floors again before filling the place with groceries. At least in this store, customers could pick up their own items.

However, the town of Aaron already boasted more than one grocery store, along with a few motels and restaurants, enough to require two blinks instead of one to miss it from travelers passing through. Having grown more restless than usual living in the rural world, Jacob aimed for the bright lights of the city sky, although Aaron lit its evenings with nothing more than a dozen hazy streetlights. Silly specifics aside, he muttered his visionary plans for a grandiose grocery store, as if his heroic revitalization of an ugly, vacant cathouse would undoubtedly bring him the stellar recognition he so rightfully deserved. "Yesiree, I'll be in the Rotary Club in no time. To heck with Ethan and his highfalutin' Masons," he tooted.

Regardless of the building's position on the edge of town, regardless of its being set back from the highway enough to be largely unnoticed by passing cars, regardless of the busy and well-established Piggly Wiggly stationed closer to houses where people lived, Jacob advertised on the radio station and paid for a billboard announcing Sheridan Groceries 'n' Gas. It's Sher-a-dandy place to stop! In addition to the same basic groceries offered in the first store, Tallulah found herself arranging tourist souvenirs, trying to hide the beach towels emblazoned with the ubiquitous confederate flag, but Jacob noticed, demanding she "Get one of those damn things up on the wall where the old boys can see it."

With more town life infiltrating her days, Tallulah couldn't help noticing the conservative polyester and unencumbered shirt collars prevailing among the male residents of Aaron, while the youth of the rest of the country flaunted flowers, beads, long hair, and blue jeans. Only the miniskirt had infiltrated the local ranks; sexual invitations readily received. In this blip of urban existence, she thought it odd how frequently young people seemed to refrain from questioning authority; not favoring consequential beatings, she supposed, choosing instead to remain as safely dull and traditional as their parents to the point of not seeming young at all, more like by stale duplicates of the older people. The label "damn hippies" zinged out of mouths like a bullet, aimed at any males with hair below their ear lobes, and the few females who dared to be associated with them. Friendly travelers venturing in from the highway encountered more ridicule and rudeness than even mild "southern hospitality" from other customers, passing through what must have seemed like a time warp, an embarrassing situation to some of Jacob's offspring. A rare and scrawny species, southern hippies required none of the political principles and anti-war demonstrations of their fellows in the north and on the west coast; they acquired the label by avoiding the barbershop.

Gregory returned to his family with long hair, jeans, and the occasional loud nightmare about Vietnam. His soothing guitar and the strong anti-establishment philosophy passing along the highway of contemporary life had morphed a protective soldier into an independent soul with ideas of his own. Within him lurked kindness patiently waiting for fairness, intelligence longing for encouragement, and a thread of hope dangling for his acceptance. Tallulah could identify with each of these qualities, because Gregory remained the only male in her world with whom she could hold a conversation, who would talk to her, and who had enough patience to answer the endless questions popping up as freely as the pimples on her face.

One Saturday evening, she slouched in the doorway of Gregory's bedroom as he sat on his bed tuning his guitar. "What is wrong with these people? Did you see the men in the parade dressed in white bed sheets with wizard hats covering their faces? What dummies. You can still tell who they are by their eyes and their shoes."

"Yeah, it's the way they were brought up. Small worlds make small minds."

"I think I should run away. How do you do hitchhiking?"

"No," he warned. "People get really messed up doing that, especially girls. Besides, Mom needs you here."

"She needs a new brain."

"Yeah, ask the heart transplant guy in Africa."

"You're not going to tell me to go look for a can of elbow grease, are you?" she asked.

Gregory chuckled and shook his head.

Tallulah said, "Mom said she took Jacob back to keep an eye on him, so he can't sneak in one night and shoot everybody."

"Sheesh."

"I don't understand why he doesn't just put down the damn bottle. Stop the stupid drinking. Put down the bottle. How hard can it be? Uncle Ethan did it," Tallulah informed him.

"He's an alcoholic, too?"

"Yes, but he stopped drinking a long time ago, when Lisa was little."

"Must run in the family. Hand me that pick on the floor, will you?"

Not only had Jacob pushed Uncle Ethan and Lisa out of her reach, now he did his best to keep Tallulah's primary hero from becoming too comfortable at home. Wise enough to avoid direct confrontation with a veteran, and lacking his old safety net of city officials, Jacob used a finger as his shield, keeping it pointed at Gregory, complaining to anyone who would listen, "Why in hell can't he be like everyone else around here? He don't need long hair, for God's sake."

Idalia and Jacob ceased to agree on anything.

"Oh, leave the boy alone, Jacob. He's not hurting you."

"The hell he ain't! I'm trying to establish a business here. Trying to get off on the right foot. I got to fit it with these people in town. They don't like this long hair stuff. It makes me look bad. Crazy hippie shit."

"There's nothing crazy about it. The rest of the country tolerates it. A sign of the times, that's all. Men have had long hair before. Look at the history books."

"I ain't living in no history book, Idy. I'm talking about here and now. This is the South. Today! Goddamn it."

"He is your son. You ought to be glad he's here and safe."

"Bullshit, woman. He's here all right. But is he working? Is he gonna get a job? Or is he gonna be a freeloader. No sir. I ain't having that kind of crap in this house. People won't like it."

"You're not perfect yourself, mister. The whole town is full of crap. Gregory just needs some time. He's a good boy. You were young, too. Be patient for once in your screwy life and stop picking on him. You don't have to listen so much to other people. Think for yourself."

"Shoot. You're a crazy woman. Gregory. Useless Gregory. Your baby."

"Maybe you could try to be a decent father."

"Don't start your crap again. He ain't my problem. Hell, he probably ain't even my son. Shit with that."

Jacob never told Gregory he wanted him to leave; instead, he repeatedly poked him verbally in a self-righteous, petty stream, spouting underhanded remarks about pretty hippies, dirty hippies, lazy hippies, long hairs, insinuating he himself ruled as a truly decent man, the innocent victim of a wild young thing his wife had failed to raise properly. Within a few weeks, Jacob used the presence of one of those mind-altering hippie-creatures transcending local norms in his house as an excuse to get drunk, a condition quite preferable to holding himself accountable in any way, shape, or form for fatherhood, or for the minimal number of townspeople and tourists who trickled in through the doors of his magnificent establishment; the stampede he'd imagined had failed to materialize. It was dang tough for a man to have to keep waiting for some kind of red carpet to be rolled out. He deserved a drink for everything he had to put up with. And another one.

Gregory tolerated the stares and mutterings of grocery shoppers when he helped at the register or stocked shelves. He chuckled at their grumbles, ignoring the louder peeps of ridicule from rednecks in pickup trucks when they came in to buy beer and stand around chomping pre-packaged sandwiches, hot from the microwave.

"Boy there needs a haircut, don't he?"

"We'll be glad to give him one. Take 'im out back in the woods and trim 'im up real good like."

After a few months, not surprisingly, Gregory moved out to stay with cerebral acquaintances in Savannah. Tallulah inherited his bedroom, which she had helped him paint a far-out solid black. Making it her own, she used fluorescent poster paint to emblazon the top of one wall with the funky bright letters copied from a box of Screaming Yellow Zonkers. A growing collection of psychedelic posters and ubiquitous peace symbols, highlighted by a black light, united to create an oasis of self-expression where she pondered the unfair treatment of the kind individual who had formerly occupied the room, and the mean drunk who had pushed him away from the family again, out of her life, away from Idalia, who longed for him to stay. Gregory's departure brought obvious sadness to his mother, but she failed to cease serving her platter of excuses for Jacob's behavior, again offering passive platitudes to throw a blanket over the deep wounds her husband continued to inflict. "He didn't mean it. Just let it go. That was the booze talking. Don't rock the boat."

What boat? To Tallulah, this brother represented her last connection with intelligent conversation and with Michigan, the familiar world where she had fit in, where she was not weird or different or unpopular—well, not quite as unpopular. Gregory sought nothing more than essential freedom, identity, respect, and love, with Jacob depriving him of everything. Tallulah sat left behind in her hero's former prison cell, feeling doubly abandoned in the land where nothing made sense.

With no comforting cloak of logic to be found, a pitter-pattering dance of survival began between the neurons and neurotransmitters in her brain. She chose to carry on her own crusade of memorial tribute to Gregory by immediately leaving any room her warden-dictator creep of a man-father entered, by refusing to speak to him, by refusing to ride in the car with him, and by slamming the hell out of her bedroom door every day or so with a few hearty, profane expletives thrown up into the air for good measure. Watching television shows took second place to showing the bastard she detested him. Not a word left her lips when she abruptly exited any room he entered. Jacob said nothing when she did this, only glancing in her direction, shrugging, and brushing her off as another crazy dumb teenager.

Being the target of adolescent anger was nothing new to Jacob, eternally preoccupied with his own brain battles. Pretending to work in a store every day predictably made him stir-crazy. Plus, he could never stand the sight of anyone at ease, and kept his wife and kids busy constantly loading coolers, stocking shelves, cleaning floors, raking yards, and bowing to customers, especially the ones who did more than browse the merchandise.

Whenever restless, which was often, his life mission compelled him to stand around and bark orders. He didn't care if his commands put tears in a daughter's eyes. "But I have homework!" He didn't care if a customer saw him grab and shove a young son—or maybe he did care, performing for an audience. One could never tell. The inferior peasants of his plastic kingdom slouched and complied if they had failed to see him coming in time to dart away, enduring the crowning status of dirt if any idea other than their holy master's dared enter a child's tinny head. They all waited for the moment he would conclude, "To hell with this," and stomp out the door. Then they could breathe again.

Lacking Myrna's convenient excuse of a boyfriend to be away as much as possible, Tallulah continued to help her mother in the store. Humphrey did duty at the gas pumps, with Jacob taking full advantage of the boy's infantile stage of adolescence; this one could still be bossed around. To Tallulah, Jacob and his facade of omnipotent authority prompted a visualization of every stage of oral food ejection. The hypocrite who came into the store for ten minutes a day and took public credit for family labor—the stocked shelves, clean windows, and ding of the cash register—began to make a habit of escaping to the freedom of the road. His first step of the daily exit led him to the register, where he stuffed his pockets with the cash Idalia needed to pay the wholesaler often expected to arrive at any moment.

The king of nothing eventually found employment again as a traveling salesman, accepting the throne in a van of hand tools. He proved capable of selling an adequate number of those small heavy things other men knew how to use, while he indulged his insatiable thirst for warm cash, fresh booze, and the personal freedom road travel bestows upon the driver; a hand-size, brown paper bag with a flat bottle in it lived under his seat. Consequently, his social life improved as local members of Alcoholics Anonymous made room for one more. It was, after all, an effective method of societal assimilation. When one of Jacob's drinking sprees would peak, another man carried him through the inevitable crash, sitting in the bedroom for hours with the begging and puking and whining thing stretched out on the bed. When the thing fell asleep, its weary sponsor would speak quietly to a weary Idalia and depart.

Jacob began having too much fun to put down the bottle.

Whenever his paltry commission from sales allowed, and even when it did not, Jacob demonstrated a preference for the extended attention bestowed upon him at a halfway house. He relied upon it, beginning a second career of making the rounds, jumping from one halfway house to another in neighboring towns, basking in the professional patience and compassion served to pathetic dancers on the staircase to hell. At home, Idalia frequently hid the booze from him. Her hiding places had a way of becoming cute surprises for the rest of the family.

After school one day, while Idalia worked in the store, Tallulah decided to bake a cake for the evening's dessert. After turning on the electric oven for preheating, she began to follow a favorite recipe. Before long, she filled the pans with smooth batter and carried them to the hot oven in true baker anticipation. Opening the oven door produced something quite unexpected, however. Whoosh! Flames jumped out, right at her. Nearly dropping the pans of batter, she caught a glimpse of the culprit. Stationed directly in the middle of the middle rack, carefully placed on its side, lay a pint of Seagrams, its flaming contents pouring down in a steady stream through a melted plastic cap. The stuff was puddling in a pond of flames on the oven floor. Furious, she set aside the pans and grabbed a box of baking soda. "Goddamn it! Who the hell put that thing in there? Goddamn it! Goddamn it! Why didn't she tell me? Goddamn it! Goddamn it! Why didn't she tell me? Goddamn it! Goddamn it! God*damn* it!"

But how could she blame Idalia? Left with store duties from dawn to dusk and beyond, with no hope of plugging the bottomless pit devouring profit, Idalia lost her enthusiasm for her mother's lifestyle, but somewhat weirdly, it seemed to Tallulah, retained her belief in not letting go of her man or her failing business. Idalia dragged herself out to the front every morning and somehow made it through the long days. Her appearance began to reflect her *what's the use of trying to make money when a damn fool spends it all?* despair. She no longer dressed for the public, usually appearing bedraggled, as if she intended to spend the day mopping floors at home.

Tallulah continued to help for a few hours after school, learning to leave the kitchen to her mother, finding it safer to sit by the register or run out to pump gas, even when those moments outside the family deepened her confusion. One afternoon as she pumped gas into a car, a man slouching in the back seat asked, "Hey, hon, can ya bring me a chaser? Ya got any chasers in there? I need a chaser."

"Sure," she replied, and brought out a few samples of fireworks bearing the same name. The man stared with a vacant, glazed look before Tallulah caught a whiff of an odor too familiar to her, and she guessed he probably had another type of chaser in mind, a liquid one. He confirmed her conclusion with his slow googly eyes and his wordless, weak grin of amusement, turning his head, back into oblivion, away from the stupid girl.

During the merry month of May, the family drunk managed to produce the down payment for a sporty new Oldsmobile for Myrna's graduation present, she having become the lone teenager who tolerated him. Determined to not rock the boat, the one who would stay afloat regardless of monsters lurking in the deep, Myrna wanted to do what she could to help people, even when they had hurt her. She could straighten the living room in a snap, arranging the furniture beautifully, as if everyone would be nice to each other if the couch sat in exactly the right spot and nobody's shoes occupied the middle of the floor. Anything ugly was thrown into the nearest closet and the door pushed closed. In addition, she easily obtained employment in her favorite store, a retail clothing shop selling lots of pretty stuff. In the owner she discovered a happy woman who did more than yield to misery; this odd businesswoman laughed a lot and made a profit.

Tallulah would wander into the clothing store and find her sister laughing along with the owner. They were both odd to her, and she wondered why she lacked any desire to act nice and dress nice and be friendly like Myrna. The ingredients, the incentives, the desire, whatever it was fueling Myrna's connections with people had never been handed out to Tallulah; perhaps she had been absent that day in heaven. She watched her smiling, laughing sister, and continued a familiar conclusion: *something must be wrong with me.*

Then again, Tallulah almost wondered if Myrna put too much trust in people. Leaving the tool truck home, Jacob began to borrow Myrna's new car for what he referred to as weekend business trips, and his motive for assisting with the purchase came into question. One Sunday evening, he staggered in, passing the living room and through the kitchen to land on the swing on the back porch, unable to get up. It wasn't daughter number two who put her arm around him and pulled him halfway up before she noticed the growing wetness on his pants' crotch. "Oh, shit. Nope, can't do this. I cannot do this." Myrna left him on the swing and went out to her car. The ashtray overflowed with lipstick-smudged cigarette butts. The next day, she began looking for an apartment of her own.

A week later, Idalia sat late at the kitchen table, teacup and a stack of yellow invoices in front of her. She looked like she'd been crying when Tallulah walked in to get a box of Zonkers. "What's wrong now, Mom? Money problems again?" Tallulah asked.

"Oh, worse than that," Idalia mumbled, elbows on the table, one hand slowly massaging the flesh of her teary face, her other hand flicking in the direction of the invoices. Tallulah picked one up.

"What does I.L.Y. mean?" she said, unable to not notice it scrawled boldly in the top margin. "Some kind of delivery instructions? Isn't this the company Jacob works for?"

"I love you," mumbled Idalia.

"What? That's really nice. Gee, thanks, Mom. I guess I love you, too." Tallulah patted her mother's shoulder. Idalia began weeping again. Tallulah walked slowly to Myrna's room, where things were being pulled from dresser drawers.

"What's wrong with Mom? She said 'I love you' and started crying."

Myrna stopped folding her clothes and stared. "The invoices, nitwit. Did she show them to you?"

"No, I picked one up."

"He's cheating again. Another girlfriend, dummy. She wrote it."

"Wrote what?"

"I. L. Y. I loooove you."

"Oh, to who? Not to Jacob. You've got to be kidding. Creepy shit. She had to know Mom would see it. Bummer."

"I don't care. I don't care anymore. I tried to help and they are both crazy. I'm getting myself out of here." Myrna continued her packing.

Of course, the next day, Jacob denied everything. Idalia waved the papers at him, and he used the moment to deflect the attention to her "pinned britches," uncombed hair, dirty blouse, and so on. Week after week, every disagreement led to loud accusations, heavy with obvious guilt. The remaining offspring took refuge in their bedrooms or sat outside the house and bit their fingernails. The school year approached as a welcome escape.

In 1970, while things rotted at home, long-overdue compliance with federal integration laws brought its own demonstrations of escape to the public school system in the South. Most of the white students fled to quickly organized church schools in a desperate effort to avoid rubbing shoulders with Black students reassigned to what had been the whites-only high school. The few whites who remained found themselves evolving into role models for the many new students. Tallulah and her few quiet friends made a sudden rise to the top of the popularity ladder and had fun becoming heavily involved in school activities, as if they knew what they were doing. The administrators allowed them to observe the first Earth Day, releasing all students from classes for an hour of campus clean-up. Providing trash bags and directing classes to specific areas of the campus proved to be a positive experience. Near the end of the school year, a counselor summoned Tallulah to her office.

"We are planning an interracial committee of student advisors next year and would like you to be on it, since you seem to get along well with everyone. It would be a discussion panel to voice and resolve conflict. Are you interested?"

"Yes," she responded sincerely. The Black students were much friendlier than the whites had ever been, and she loved the thought of being part of a mechanism striving to dispel the omnipresent ignorance, fear, and hatred.

"Good, we'll be counting on you. We'll organize in the fall. See you then."

A feeling not felt in a long time tingled Tallulah's spine: hope. *I have something to look forward to. Somebody wants me. Super groovy cool wow.*

Before fall school days could come close to arriving, however, Jacob succeeded in draining every drop of financial resources, as well as every hope of his community assimilation, and Idalia closed the store. The adult members of the tight, well-dressed group of citizens whose numerous relatives controlled the social, political, and law enforcement entities of the town had rarely stepped into the Sheridan store, adhering to the fundamental rule disdaining any substantial association with a newcomer fellow contaminated with northern iniquities whose kids depended on the school's free lunch program, regardless of how frequently the fellow had managed to pull up a chair with a "How do, ya'll?" and join them for coffee at the proper restaurant. His visions of community support had crumbled, leaving young male hell-raisers to dominate the scene on Friday and Saturday nights. They had made a game of flushing whole rolls of toilet paper into the public toilets, flooding the restroom floors, with weary Idalia being the lone custodian endowed with the task of feces and urine removal. Jacob's typically polarized perceptions swung the esteemed community from the top plateau of his accolades down into his intolerable bin of trash. It was hard to say who rejected whom.

Once again, the rollercoaster uprooted his dependents, aiming away from town life and its busybody inhabitants he had no use for. Way down the highway, back into a rural world again, away from the town's schools, he moved them, disintegrating Tallulah's long-awaited chance to participate with a few sane, positive people trying to accomplish something important. Before they left Aaron, the girl stared at the family telephone, badly wanting to call the school counselor and confirm: *I am not intentionally running out on you.*

CHAPTER TEN

Set back in the tall trees, off a minor highway, a hapless, ranch-style house received fewer cool breezes than one would expect. In fact, Jacob had given it a rather hot beginning. In the weeks between finding the house and actually moving in, he had decided he needed to go and sleep there, "to keep an eye on the place," he told Idalia. To Myrna, he confided, "I'll be having a friend with me at the house this weekend, and I'd like for you to come and meet her." Myrna trembled at her father's audacity, but drew the line, saying, "Na, I don't think so. No, no, I can't do that." Undeterred, to Idalia, he suggested, "Why don't you go on up to Canada for a weekend before we move," although the packing had already begun. "Go on and go. You're always talking about going back. I'll pay for the flights. Go on and go for a short little visit."

As much as she longed to visit her homeland and relatives, Idalia knew her husband well enough to suspect a reason for suddenly trying to get rid of her, and "a short little visit" could mean many things. Myrna found a private moment to whisper to Idalia, "Don't go to Canada. I can't tell you why, but don't go, Mom. Don't go."

Idalia took another look at the tool company's invoices, found the names she needed, and used a time when Jacob was not home to call the long distance operator and get the boss's home address in Florida. She sat down and wrote two letters. Revitalizing a technique she had used in Michigan for achieving her peculiar goals, Idalia informed the boss, in detail, of how one of his employees was attempting to break up a family.

Apparently incapable of not looking a gift horse in the mouth, she mailed a second letter to the hot new number. "…You're not the first and you won't be the last … He has five children conceived in lust inspired by others … There is more to love than scribbling on invoices … If you had a husband, you would follow him to the ends of the Earth … You know nothing about love."

After moving into the new old house, Tallulah noticed letters scratched in the bathroom woodwork and showed them to Idalia, who assured her they had no meaning, leaving her to dismiss them as someone's initials. When Myrna came for a visit, she quietly assured Tallulah, "Those are not initials. Mom knows damn well B.T.T. means 'best tail in town.' Jacob had his girlfriend here and wanted to introduce her to us. He tried to get Mom to go back to Canada for good." Myrna did not even spend the night, smart enough to avoid the consequential and inevitable domestic battle producing another torrent of anger, threats, and tears. Predictably using the same old nonsense, Jacob criticized the old clothes Idalia wore, the clothes she wore to save him money.

This time Tallulah stepped in. "Mom works hard. Leave her alone. Why don't you go away? You're not a father! You stupid cheater! I hate you!" Red-faced Jacob slapped her. She turned away, picking up her eyeglasses from the floor. *Surely,* she thought, *now Mom will kick him out.* Later the same day, Tallulah walked past the bedroom of her parents. With the door open about a foot, she glanced in to see both of them dressed and lying on the bed, her mother's eyes directed outward, seeing another world as she curled with her head nested below the chin of Jacob, who lay on his back, reading the newspaper. She clung to him. Tallulah nearly gasped, trying to ignore the crack threatening to penetrate the beloved image she held of her stalwart, victimized mother.

With Myrna gone, and no store for anyone to worry about, Tallulah obligingly assumed a new role, becoming useful as Idalia's confidant. Deducing from his new habit of carrying a large amount of change in his pockets, Idalia suspected her unemployed husband continued to call his lover from a truck stop down the road. Having lost a business, with the kids back in school, and a husband not worth keeping, Idalia sat alone most of the day. She allayed her worries by reading her teacup leaves or dropping black ink into a glass of water as a makeshift crystal ball, trying to foresee the future enough to claim she had seen it coming, "it" most likely to be trouble. Out in the expansive front yard, a highway patrol car sat parked daily under a massive, old tree, presumably waiting for speed violators along the lonesome highway, but Idalia speculated about its real purpose, wondering if Jacob had made connections to keep her from leaving, or maybe to help her leave if she started out the door. She mumbled periodically about someone having had to give them permission to sit on private property.

Months later, in a behavior pattern Idalia congratulated herself for predicting, Jacob confessed and told his wife the letters she had written compelled the woman with a job to pause and reflect. The company boss told the secretary to choose her job or her lover. She chose to keep her job, while Jacob lost his. The slightest wisp of victory passed through Idalia when she relayed this to Tallulah, who heard her proud mother whisper, "Word power. You may say 'em but I can write 'em." Tallulah listened, thought about it when alone, and shook her head.

With the new schools thirty miles away, Tallulah, Humphrey, and Cary spent much of their time riding big yellow buses again, their ears bombarded with the boisterous chatter of young people whose families had lived in the area for generations, who held no interest in newcomers. Not having the greatest respect for the male gender, Tallulah made no attempt to be friendly to boys on the bus or in the classrooms. Therefore, when one demonstrated an interest in her, his sincerity required a certain amount of proof, and therefore could be perhaps subjected to a test.

A few nowhere dates had been arranged for her back in Aaron, but for the first time, a guy in one of her classes went out of his way to talk to her, while other people watched. One day, when her history teacher gave the class a study day, Gentle Clyde Murphy casually invited her to walk to the library with him. Since she had no idea how to find the library, and Clyde seemed fairly harmless, she said okay, nonchalantly setting her stack of books on top of a desk to get a hall pass from the teacher. Crash! Books toppled to the floor as the desk tipped forward. Complete betrayal by books and desk. How could they not appreciate her cool, although thoughtless balancing attempt? They had to have plotted against her, she felt sure. Even more jarring, Clyde stood still, not blasting her error in judgement the way she knew Jacob would. The absence of attack upon her failure impressed Tallulah; a void to be appreciated. Neither did Clyde run for the hills in embarrassment. Instead, he ran his fingers through his curly locks, and kindly helped her pick up the mess, while she fought against her own desperate urge to dash out the door in humiliation. After a few more conversations with this oddly persistent male, Tallulah dared to hope, and dream of the possibilities of a friendly bond, a true acceptance of her real self. A week later Jacob announced they were moving again, smashing her foolish glimmer of hope. Clyde calmly accepted the fact they were leaving, deepening Tallulah's sense of loss.

CHAPTER ELEVEN

Once more the cardboard boxes came out, and the books and the clothes and the dishes went in. Conveniently, some boxes remained unpacked from the last move. Once more the reluctant nomads followed a mirage to say good-bye to a house they had not yet become acclimated to as any kind of home. The concept of home had been claimed by the nest of rattlesnakes Humphrey discovered under the house. The vipers coiled near the top of everyone's list of no-regrets-to-be-leaving-behind.

Obvious to the powers that be and wonder why-o-why, a zigzag pattern began to emerge in Jacob's restless relocations: urban to rural and back to urban, landing the diminished family this time in a somewhat larger urban entity way down in southern Georgia, close to Florida, which worried Idalia. Jacob had replaced his tool van with a potato chip van, spuds for a stud, and claimed the town to be in the middle of his new route. He chose one of the numerous, fossilized late nineteenth-century houses, now split into awkward duplexes, leaving each tenant to assume the other enjoyed the original kitchen. The roots of old sentries lining the streets cracked and buckled the sidewalk, making it necessary for Idalia to watch her step when she walked the six blocks to the retail district in search of employment, an area with sunshine and commerce, blinding in its contrast to the high ceilings and small heaters reminiscent of their plantation house, minus the slave quarters. Subjugation became apparent in other forms.

For one, the local churches stood as old, dominant lords of the land. The sight of children carrying boxes into a house prompted a vigorous watchdog of a soul-winner to approach Jacob, encouraging him to revive his church attendance. This time Jacob succeeded in dragging only Humphrey and Cary into a pew, but that did not stop him from signing up his entire family as members, although most held no intention of ever stepping inside any place he selected. Only the young yielded.

For two, the unexpectedly modern high school building appeared inviting, physically. On her first day, Tallulah discovered its precise level of friendliness. A male student directly behind her in the crowded hall between classes welcomed her with a quick squeeze of her butt. Turning around, she encountered a foolish grin planted on a dark face, gleeful eyes carefully focused forward on the empty air above her head. Faces of wiser, embarrassed companions followed him. In such a corridor of obvious racial tension, one thought came to her mind as she continued forward: *Do you not know how much trouble this could create if I reported you?*

On her second day, a student in her art class told her wearing blue jeans violated the school dress code. Tallulah had worn blue jeans for both days, never noticing no one else wore them. It was 1971; what else was there to wear? Blue jeans stood as the national symbol of youth and freedom, not to mention practical comfort. She really couldn't believe so many people could be so Neanderthal.

Idalia the empowered letter-writer claimed to be appalled as well. "That's not fair," she insisted. "People have the right to wear the clothes they want to. Blue jeans do not interfere with the educational process. This is a public school system, not Nazi Germany. You should write a petition." And her eyes brightened with the intrigue of another exercise in combative composition. "That's what I would do."

In perfect agreement, Tallulah stayed up alone until two in the morning writing and perfecting her magnum opus. At every opportunity during the following school day, she took a brave step and approached students unknown to her in name or reputation, the guiding beacon of high school life. Many of them signed, but muttered warnings of the futility of "another petition." At the beginning of her last class of the day, her pretty history teacher quietly informed Tallulah that the vice principal, who happened to be the teacher's husband, "would like to see you in his office immediately." Tallulah carefully balanced her books on her desk and left, expecting perhaps administrative praise for practicing her constitutional rights, hoping to regain the hint of value bestowed upon her by the Aaron counselor, or at least academic recognition of good composition skills. Her work was well written.

After a friendly greeting, and the careful closing of his office door, the lean, relatively young self-proclaimed buddy-of-all-students metamorphosed into a hostile, raging tyrant, rapidly pacing the floor and spitting out furious words without inviting his shocked victim to have a say. "You're a new kid here! You don't know anything about the way we do things!" Bang! His fist hit the desk. "Do you know how many of those petition things we've already had to deal with?" Bang! Fist hit desk again. "I could take that damn paper now and throw it in the trash can!" Bang! Tallulah managed a thought: *So now I know what happened to the other petitions.* "I could send you home today for the pants you're wearing now!" *Green and white tie-dyed jeans are not blue.* Bang! "You are totally out of line with this garbage!" And so on and so on.

His fierce opponent sat in a chair staring at the floor, trying unsuccessfully to keep the tears from rolling down her cheeks, attempting to quell the seismic response of her torso to every bang of his fist on the desk. Weary, silent, she thought of the time and effort put into the paper, and the hypocrisy of this so-called leader of education's refusal to read it or discuss anything with her. Apparently, only power mattered to him. *Another stupid jackass like Jacob, with no interest in fair communication,* she concluded.

When the jackass finished dumping the tirade of his frustrations, he directed Tallulah to leave. She sought refuge in the closest restroom, crying in the corner before heading back to her classroom. When she arrived, the other students had completed their class and gone home for the day. Tallulah picked up her books as the history teacher moved around busily straightening the empty desks, suddenly announcing to the air, without stopping, without looking up, "Ah just think young ladies should dress like young ladies," as if those images of dainty delicacies justified verbal abuse and subjugation. *Now I know who makes the school rules,* Tallulah thought, walking out.

Arriving home, Tallulah described the school's reaction to the petition. Idalia shrugged, said nothing, and continued to mop the kitchen floor. *No offer of support, of defense for your idea? Your idea?* Tallulah wondered, wounded for the second time in the same day, but unwilling to bring any kind of grief to her mother. The girl walked to her bedroom and fell across the bed, confused and tired.

However, the school had not finished injecting her with its required dose of local education, making sure she received her share of its abundant angst. She had noticed the Black students seemed angrier in this pretty building with its phony administrators. On the previous Christmas, Myrna had given Tallulah a warm fringed jacket, and it became the object of attention one day in a crowded restroom. As Tallulah washed her hands at the sink, she heard, "Look at her jacket, huh. Hey, white girl, what do you think you are, some kind of honky hippie?

"Look more like cowboy to me."

"Woo-ee!"

The group laughed at their own humor and started touching the fringe, getting somewhat too close for comfort. Baffled Tallulah remained silent. From out of the corner, fortunately, one voice spoke up. "Hey, she's all right. She's in my French class." And the others allowed her to walk out unmangled. Later she supposed she had violated some unwritten law of student-directed segregation by going into that particular restroom in the first place, because there were no other whites to be seen. In the French class, she sat as the only white person, and did not mind being the oddity; in fact, it felt typical, her normal, her destiny. She liked the teacher and wanted to learn, and thought that to be sufficient. When she paid attention to the social dynamics, she gradually perceived most of the classes, like the restrooms, appeared to consist entirely of either white or Black students. Integration occurred only in the halls.

Another day, she provided the entertainment for a large cluster of chatty white boys sitting and standing outside before the morning bell rang. Tallulah didn't mind being labeled as the only teenager weird enough to ride a bicycle to high school; it was better than the bus. Having finally conquered two-wheelers, she usually rode her own bike, but it happened to have a flat tire. On this day, she'd borrowed Humphrey's, rescuing it from sitting unused by one who chose to conform to the idiotic, local taboos. On arrival at school, dismounting, she forgot to swing her leg behind her. Instead, she swung her leg forward as she usually did with her own bike, and her foot hit the stupid bar distinguishing a boy's bike from a girl's. Bike and rider fell to the ground, much to the uproarious delight of mindless malodorous masculinity.

In her dreams at night, Tallulah flew past and above the dark green sentinels of foliage permeating the neighborhood, looking down at the empty sidewalks, watching the insects buzz around the streetlights, feeling their soft wings brush her cheeks. Some nights she flitted all the way back to the streetlights of Michigan, to the neighborhood they had lived in, where summer moths still circled, entrapped in the bright light. She often landed and followed the sidewalk to her old elementary school, walking the grounds, remembering the teachers and friends she had never had a chance to say goodbye to. Eventually she approached the house they had lived in. She made many visits before she found the courage to knock on the front door and talk to the woman who lived there. The woman politely let Tallulah in, and Tallulah drank the moment, detecting minor changes, but, more importantly, her memories revived the good times of belonging, brothers and sisters filling the rooms with noise and play.

Tallulah welcomed Jacob's next move, despite being a few weeks into twelfth grade. Less than a year after arriving in We-hate-blue-jeans Town, but longer than forever, the potato chip job lost its appeal, and Jacob announced his plans to retreat toward Savannah. Idalia suspected he had failed to win back his Florida girlfriend. Regardless, Tallulah's best moment took place on her very last day in Polyester High, when she experienced her second verbal exchange with the mister-cool-buddy-to-all-students vice principal, this time a chance encounter in the hall. "Hey, there, Tallulah baby. How's it going?" he asked.

She lightly replied, "Oh, it's going goood." Chuckling to herself, she continued walking, away from him, muttering under her breath, "Yep, real goood to be getting away from this crappy place and away from crappy you."

CHAPTER TWELVE

Jacob claimed to have found the next house, rural again, smothered in pine trees, on one of those potato chip routes. Nothing steered him away from unemployment before they moved in; he depended upon Idalia's renewed desire for a miniscule, empty grocery store. The store and the house sat within easy walking distance of each other, the only other structure in view being a dinky white church standing between the two, providing some social connections for Humphrey and Cary. They became friends with the preacher who avoided any consumption of alcohol by not eating cake or cookies containing vanilla.

More sky than land surrounded Idalia's tiny store sitting at the intersection of a quiet highway leading to nowhere of much interest and a dirt road or two. Neither parent seemed fond of steady employment, or of stepping away from holey business ideas prone to failure. Once more, Idalia scrubbed and stocked what served mainly as an honor zone for customers to occupy while she pumped their gas outside. After expressing a token interest, actually standing behind the counter a few times, Jacob left it to his wife while he hit the road again in a quest of that ephemeral thing referred to as a job, supposedly to conquer its nasty habit of slipping away from him, dang it. Idalia's retail mirage supplied him with endless cigarettes and gasoline, while he scooted about in a gas-guzzler presumably seeking the quintessential boss man, one capable of appreciating the astronomical values of Jacob's stellar qualities.

Cloudy at best described the latest local high school's system of control during those early years of segregation. This time, boys and girls responded to separate bells, safely conveying the fragile females before any nasty young males could venture forth into the same hall. *Not much chance of getting a butt squeeze here*, thought Tallulah, but at least she could wear blue jeans again. In her English class, four large tables seated students: two for boys and two for girls. Within each gender category, the separation process continued, placing those of higher social standing safely away from those of lower economic status. Tallulah chose the poor girl's table; it seemed less frozen.

Her first day at this dreary school had almost come to an end when one of her new teachers, one who strode the halls with the rigid stature of a miniature dictator, being shorter than most of the students, swooped down upon her. "Ah didn't know you were Jacob's daughter," she exclaimed, thrusting her wrinkled face into Tallulah's, every crease of sternness obliterated, waiting for a response as if Jacob's daughter ought to be elated by this woman's remarkable discovery. Tallulah halted long enough to stretch her lips and force the corners of her mouth to rise, suffering through a pat on the back and a reluctant release. *What crap,* she thought, *An old school mate. I can't even get away from him at school now.* Those ancient eyes twinkled with rekindled memories, prompting Tallulah to wonder what delights her mother had missed. Before the exit door became hers, a second teacher smiled at Tallulah with more Jacob Sheridan memories, mentioning something about a pleasant old swimming hole.

After school, the three youngest Sheridans climbed aboard another unpleasant, old, clunky school bus, this one driven by a fat, tobacco-chomping farmer with thick, pale hands, slits for eyes, and an endless supply of blue-and-white-striped overalls — or maybe he wore the same pair every day.

Other old farmers in overalls emerged from the land, stopping in to sit around munching peanuts and sipping Coca-Cola in and outside the store, providing the newcomers with tidbits of the slim local history, more real to them than any current events. Tallulah tended the store after school, and every afternoon her most interesting customers were the cute Black kids who lived in one of the unpainted wooden houses scattered down the highway. They would sass and scold each other, immersed in their own roles of domination and submission, occasionally pocketing a few more pieces of candy than their sparse coins could cover. Tallulah enjoyed the show.

The farmers agreed among themselves that a girl of seventeen ought to be married, and when their verbal efforts to match up Tallulah with a younger version of themselves kindled no flames of interest from either side, one of the old guys summoned up his courage. Mr. Stone took the liberty of using the counter beside the cash register for his chair one day when no other customers occupied the store. He hopped up, crossed his thin legs, and started swinging one foot like he was revving up an engine. *Oh, God,* Tallulah thought, *here it comes.* The old flirt looked down at her toenails painted purple, as if they substantiated an invitation, and said, "Well, if nothing's gonna happen 'tween you and Willie's boy, how's 'bout you and me going out and having some fun one of these nights?"

"Naw, don't think so," Tallulah replied, trying not to be too quick, polite but clear, saving the urge to vomit for later.

"Got yersef some purple toenails there. I got my own trailer back down the road aways. I could show it to you sometime."

"Naw, don't think so." The persistent buzzard gradually got the message after she repeated it several more times, and lowered himself back to the decency of the floor. From then on, Tallulah made a point of keeping a distance between her and this hot-to-trot old bachelor.

One afternoon after Tallulah relieved her from store duty, Idalia walked back to the house to find a note from Jacob. With his anticipation of worthy employment plummeting as low as it had been high, now unappreciated and depressed, he had packed his suitcase and left, saying in the note he thought they would be better off without him. He left his intentions to the imagination of a woman he knew would worry, and she did, wringing her hands until a few hours later, when an acquaintance drove up and informed Idalia that Jacob had checked himself into a nearby halfway house for alcoholics. Not even boozing yet, he had sold himself to the staff, convincing them to admit him sober, because, as he told them, he knew he'd get drunk if they didn't. His persuasive words laced with charming scenarios resulted in the assimilation he endlessly coveted.

Idalia did not sing anymore, but her Michigan melodies remained mired in Tallulah's collection of northern fantasies. One day after school, a young man driving a bright red Volkswagen Beetle stopped for gas, emerging from his chariot to rescue Tallulah from horny farmers and a nowhere father. The someday prince had come, brandishing a crown of glorious hair long enough to actually touch his collar, making Tallulah wonder how he managed to escape the local razor. Apparently, the Sheridan store sat at a turn he made on his way home from classes at a nearby college. With his subsequent stops, he and Tallulah came to view each other as welcome exceptions to the omnipresent vortex of the past and its graveyard snooze.

Roger lived with his parents, who had also made a recent decision to return to the land of the father's roots, but only after a successful career in business. At college, this prince studied music, practiced his deep, rich singing voice, and played the acoustic guitar, reminding Tallulah of Gregory and other young men of the day struggling to retain their innate freedom to be themselves. She admired his achievement of vocalizing "ya'll" minus the image of feet being dragged through syrupy mud.

Lisa had driven from Savannah to sleep over one Friday night, and waited at the house when Roger happened to invite Tallulah out to a movie in his college town. After closing the store, Tallulah went home to change clothes, providing entertainment for Lisa, who watched her deprived cousin go gaga over "some guy." "He asked me out! Oh, I can't believe it. He asked me out. Somebody actually likes me!"

The silliness continued when Roger objected not to having Lisa come along. In order to make her feel less like number three, Tallulah lured Humphrey and Cary to join Lisa in the back seat of the VW bug until no one could do much wiggling. After a movie and popcorn inside a theater, Roger impressed them by pulling up to the fanciest restaurant in the small college town, hauling them inside, making the waiters shove a few heavy tables together, and ordering pizza. *Flexible with a flair. Pretty cool,* thought Tallulah.

Weeks later, when Jacob finally returned and noticed the steady dating, he felt compelled to issue a warning on a subject he knew too well. Arriving home late one night, Tallulah found him standing between her and the back door to the house, and he began a long ramble pertaining to Gregory and where he lived, to Myrna and where she lived, to family responsibilities. Putting one foot up on the front bumper of his car, lighting a cigarette, and staring at the graveled ground, he floundered around "society" and "obligation," and "people talk," which Tallulah interpreted as his fear of gossip. Eventually, he meandered to the subject of male and female physical relationships. Tallulah sat on the doorsteps, head in her hands, enduring the hazy air as it filled with hazy words, gradually concluding she was being told to back off "when things get hot," as he said. The gist of his message came into focus: the hypocrite of the ages didn't want her to embarrass him by getting pregnant, being worried more about himself than any consequent pregnancy of hers and the changes it would bring to her body and her life. When he felt he had given the subject adequate coverage, the man ended his irrelevantly-woven basket of a monologue with, "Welp, it's gettin' late. I gotta get up in the morning," and she moved aside, allowing this phony father-thing to enter the house. At no moment had the completely one-sided conversation invited feedback from Tallulah, consequently she said nothing, leaving him to his own bizarre illusions of his personal protection duly fulfilled. She noted clearly how his manufactured shield radiated around himself, not her, pushing her to go elsewhere for any hint of her own significance.

Tallulah loved having Roger like her; it was a new feeling. Having Roger love her made a lot of unhappiness slip away, encouraging hope and inviting sparkling dreams. He often visited in the evenings, after store hours, and they sat together in the living room, talking. Like his restaurant choice on a first date, his words could lean amusingly into the dramatic. "My mother made the most atrocious monstrosities for dinner today. She called them drop biscuits. I mean, what is that? Everybody knows biscuits are round and flat on top, not these horrendous lumpy mounds."

"Uh-oh," uttered Cary from his spot on the floor in front of them, distracted only momentarily from the television. Without turning around, he waved his arm at Tallulah. "She makes them all the time."

"Yeah, we like them. They're easy." Tallulah smiled, guilty as charged. Roger seemed confused. Sensing the need for a diversion, she asked, "So what else did she cook?"

Roger attended a weekly prayer group at his college, and she didn't even hold it against him. After a few months, she almost dared to speak of a future together, despite opposing biscuit preferences, until he returned from a weekend in Atlanta with his Christian friends and dropped a bomb on her.

CHAPTER THIRTEEN

Jacob need not have worried. Roger and his quite decent friends sought the will of the Lord for their lives and chose to worship God sincerely yet informally. On the floor in a student's apartment, young adults uncomfortable with the formality of traditional churches sat and sang passionate, cheerful songs of praise to their shepherd. Two or three spontaneously shared their interpretation of specific subjects in the Bible. Others asked questions or talked about school or home situations for which they needed support. Respect and freedom erased the need for a formal program of worship, and they prayed in a special way, usually in a quiet, although powerful, glossolalia given to them by God, acquired for the asking, a token of the baptism of the spirit. Most conventional churches rejected this direct channel to Jesus, but the more charismatic followers of the day believed the gift of speaking in tongues to be manifested by the presence of the Holy Spirit, in accordance with the Bible's description of the day of Pentecost.

The founders of Roger's college prayer group had graduated a few years earlier and returned home to Atlanta, where the parents of one held the same type of weekly charismatic meeting on a larger scale in their home. Several times a year, Roger's friends who could left their studies behind for a weekend and traveled together to join Atlanta's larger group, from whom they could receive the benefits of mature experience and guidance. Guidance must have been on the mind of the Atlanta brother who directed Roger to II Corinthians 6:14, discouraging his unequal yoking with an unbeliever.

Tallulah knew Roger attended a variation of church, one place she had no desire to follow him to, even when he played guitar at the dinky white building next door. He never pressured her to believe in Jesus, and she genuinely appreciated the respect he gave her doubts: *No way can there be a kind and loving God in a world where hope gets continually clobbered by disappointment, and nascent dreams are trampled by the whims of a self-centered, hypocrite father who torments those who depend upon him, telling them to take what you get and be glad you get anything at all and shut up about it. No way.*

Long before their lives intersected, Tallulah had selected the label of agnostic for herself and Roger had found his way into Christianity. Now she was being told God did not approve of their relationship; they were unequally yoked because he was a Christian and she was not. Suddenly-pious, religiously-obedient Roger remained late outside her house on a Sunday night, having dropped by on his way home from the big city.

He declined her offer of coming inside. Instead. they stood and spoke outside his car. He let her down gently and promised to pray for her as he climbed back into his snazzy red VW, waving farewell. She frowned at his sheepish grin, wondering if she had underestimated the power of biscuits.

The object of religious rejection stepped inside the house, quietly retreated to the back bathroom, locked the door, sat on the floor, lodged herself in a corner, and caved in. A waterfall of tears and self-pity and agony receded after a few wet hours of generous tribute to the facial tissue industry. Sidling into the gully cut by the cascade, a crust of anger began to form, morphing into pronounceable clusters of letters, but the indignation made no target of Roger, who had only done what he had to do, of course. Sobby, soggy Tallulah located the real culprit, pounded the floor, and screamed out her soul in the fiercest whisper privacy allowed in a house full of people.

"You stupid God! Who do you think you are? Who are you to disapprove of our relationship? We were not bothering anyone! How can you claim to be a kind, loving God and snatch from me the only love I have, the only person I belong with, the only connection which makes sense to me, the only person who makes me feel halfway human? How in the hell can you do this to me? Do you get some kind of perverted kick out of giving someone something precious and then taking it away? I hate you! Do you hear me? I hate you! What's wrong with you? I love him! He loves me! Ain't that good enough for you? What the hell do you want? Are you having fun destroying me? Goddamn it! It ain't fair! Ain't fair! Ain't fair! Tell me why! Why? What can be the sense in tearing apart something good? I haven't hurt you. I simply want to be with him. He's mine. Go snatch somebody else. Nastier people than I exist. Go pick on them. How could you do this to me? Why? Why? Why?"

Like storm clouds clearing and sunshine falling, it finally dawned on her: what she ranted, the irony slowly gurgling up into her cognitive caverns, splashing its whopping heavy sloshes upon her dumb brain. Whop! *Wait a minute.* Whop! *To whom am I talking?* Whop! Whop! *A god I don't believe exists?* Whop! *How can I be talking to him unless I believe he exists?* Whop! Whop! *How can I possibly believe in God without having any brain-awareness of believing in God?*

"What a jerk I am. What a real jerk. Shit. Shitshitshit. Caught red handed. What a mess. I have gotten myself in too deep, way too deep. What an agnostic failure I am. My fantastic logic and reasoning down the drain. Crapola."

The worst of the worst possible scenarios fluttered down to besiege her: *Egad! Does this mean I have to go to church? Does this mean I have to become one of those smiling zombies reeking of phony, fake proclamations, out to save the world by pretending to be happy-o, plastic polite, and squeaky-clean? Fake fake fake?* She held her tormented head in her hands as more dastardly thoughts stabbed and swirled. *I could pretend nothing happened. Deny the touch this thing my soul has already somewhat warmed to. No, it hasn't. Yes, it has. Sweep under the rug a glistening moment of honesty, my most vulnerable spot exposed. I hate sweeping things under a rug, but the alternative is dreadful exposure. For God's sake, ignore it, moron. There I go again; for who's sake? Shit shit shit.*

Honesty of the bare bones, naked variety prevailed, grounding her with the realization she lacked any momentum to run away from the moment, the stabbing glimmer of real stuff, feeling truer than anything else around her ever had. Undoubtedly, many questions lay ahead — *Shut up, Brain* — but she chose to allow the closeness of a warm and loving spirit to remain, opponent or partner status yet to be determined.

"All right, all right, all right. So you exist. I acknowledge you exist. I acknowledge I believe you exist, anyway. If I'm nuts it's your problem, not mine. You got me into this. You pack quite a wallop, you know. Nobody else could hit me this hard, right where it hurts. Nobody else would bother. Roger is — was — my only foothold on the path to sanity, and you snatched him away. As for you, you're not much of a goody-goody yourself. Pretty darn sneaky, if you ask me.

"I may be making a commitment here, but I swear to God — yeah, you — I swear to God I ain't going to wear one of those dime-a-dozen smiles I see on the faces of people who claim to belong to you or claim to represent you. And I ain't going to parade around looking so damn polished every damn minute of the day. I don't like the slick and slimy look. You either take me the way I am or forget it. I hate their phoniness, the same way I hate my father's phoniness, and I refuse to become a part of it. You're getting a weird one here, you know. I don't fit in anywhere, but if you think you can handle it, I'm in. Maybe I'd better let you think it over. I'm going to bed. G'night."

Tallulah's bed was lodged next to a large picture window in a room intended for use as a family den. That night she half expected a lightning bolt to smash through the big window and zap her brains. However, the night remained quiet.

She spent most of the next Saturday sitting under a pine tree in a far corner behind the house, the bathroom being occupied. Leaning against the trunk of her chosen conifer, she laid everything on the line to her new God. Her life seemed like nothing but a hollow compost pile to her, but He could have it if He wanted it. She didn't consider herself bad or unworthy, merely rather void, useless, without purpose, without hope, without dreams, something dragged along in the mud for a long time.

Only the vague possibility of following Gregory through the gates of college provided any dim reveal as to what lay ahead. She carried no confidence in herself, and no confidence in life. Living had no point; dying had no point.

Tallulah told God about the genuine contempt she harbored for her father. "The man's lust for booze is an abominable disgrace to common humanity, and he tops the list of destructive, spineless weaklings not willing to put down the damn bottle. I justifiably hate him for the misery he chooses to shower upon a woman of common sense and tenderness. My mother's pain permeates every child the two of them brought into the world, and, like her, we learn to suffer, seeking refuge in skepticism, self-defense, and sarcasm. We teeter on the edge of lunacy because of Jacob."

Tallulah sought reasonable explanations to justify her agony from breaking up with Roger and found none. Apparently, some pain reaches beyond logic, to twist and torture the searching mind. This inner gap between logic and misery is where the intangible God fell in, a glue pulling together pieces of herself which otherwise hung loose and lost. The more she talked to the new holy man in her life, the more she began to feel an affinity with her surroundings: the clarity of the clear blue sky, the warmth and light of the bright sun, the tall, flexible strength of the towering pines, and the solid foundation of the rich, fragrant, fertile ground beneath her. The delicate beauty of the pine needles, neighboring green leaves, and various grasses rested like a complimentary veil over all, kisses of delight upon the land. In the natural richness, she felt the blessing of God upon humanity. Lessons in harmony stood near and ready for any human willing to pause and perceive. A more glorious congregation could not be hoped for. Wherever she went from there, she knew she would carry faith in God's love for humanity and for her, with proof visible available from almost any window. Life was worth living, perhaps.

In order to be on the safe side, she laced her backyard résumé with church words. Pieces of the Lord's Prayer popped in here and there, as did other tidbits picked up during the weeks of mandatory pewing. She knew she was supposed to ask forgiveness for sins, although she didn't feel guilty, so the heck with that; fire and brimstone made no appearance. Instead, a surreal door opened within her consciousness. For as long as she chose to hold the strange door open, a soft, peaceful breeze came through, and this breeze carried threads of self-awareness.

"I want to understand myself," she said, "to comprehend why I am the way I am. Then maybe I can understand other people more than I do now. If there is any rationality in this nutsy universe, I'd like to find it. You must have it. You must know. You put it together. You see what's going on. It's your world. Don't you think you could open those massive doors for me, every now and then, just a crack or two? In return, I'll give you what I can. I'll do my best for you, but I have no idea of how good that will be. Maybe I don't have much to offer. Lord Jesus, please take me in. Please forgive my sins and let me learn what the heck a sin is. And forgive my trespasses, too, whatever those thingamajigs are. See what a jerk I am? I don't have a clue about this stuff. If you've got room for me, you're doing pretty good, I'd say. I guess I need to talk to somebody human."

Receiving no rolls of thunder in response to asking for permission, Tallulah called Roger. He sounded delighted with the conquest, as any good soul winner should have been. During the following days, she allowed him to introduce her to his religious friends, and the two of them resumed their relationship, with a new twist to it. Tallulah never regretted establishing a private line of communication to God, and the people who would or would not influence her from that point on could never equal the warmth, insight, and catharsis of the first private moments spent sitting on a bathroom floor and deepened on the good earth with her back against a pine tree.

CHAPTER FOURTEEN

Tallulah revealed to no family members her commitment to God. They would only laugh and prod, she knew. Soon enough, her behavior did the speaking as she allowed kindness to emerge where hostility had been the usual behavior. Among themselves, the boys remarked that "the bitch" was becoming less of one. She ceased slamming doors and cursing the slowpoke of the hour who monopolized the bathroom. Resisting the old urge to pound down the door, she unearthed a miniscule amount of what appeared to be the thing called "tolerance" within herself. As for Jacob, she even allowed herself to remain in the same room with him, with effort.

Tallulah's graduation rolled around, but not before she happened to pick up a certain book in the high school library one day. A casual glance at the card in the back of Thomas Hardy's *The Return of the Native* told her who had been the last person to check out the book. Only slightly less shaky, her father's handwriting had not changed much in forty years. Uncanny. She could not determine if God had sent her a topic for father-bonding, evidence of community illiteracy because no one else had checked out the book since, or a holy see-what-I can-do initiation prank. Absolutely weird, ironic, kooky miracle-thing. *I guess you have a sense of humor*, she spoke without speaking. *I should steal this card; no one will ever believe me without the evidence. Nah, maybe not. You win.*

A new connection to God did not make up for years of alienation at school. Cap and gown measurement proved easy to avoid, since Tallulah sat stuffed away in a sophomore business class when the loudspeaker summoned seniors to the gym. A week later, she was called into the counselor's office to watch as a female relic of days gone by claimed she, for some odd reason, couldn't find Tallulah's measurements. With no offer of guidance, without caring enough to ask why, the counselor never came near to counseling. "We've never had anyone do this before," appeared to be the only words she could mutter, keeping the focus on her victimized self instead of the distressed student standing in front of her. Tallulah felt no sympathy, and walked away.

Jacob and Idalia never inquired about the when, where, and how of their daughter's graduation ceremony, or Tallulah's lack of attendance, even with his old acquaintances running the show. No one expressed any interest in why she chose not to participate in the town's educational event of the year, except a mild inquiry from Roger, who now kept their relationship appropriately platonic.

Without any college or paying employer within bicycle range, transportation became a problem. For some strange reason, Idalia had never learned to drive, leaving Tallulah no alternative to accepting Jacob's presence in his car if she wanted to acquire a legal learner's permit. Consequently, at age eighteen, eons later than any normal teenager, and with God's help, she finally commanded herself to sit in the car with that nervous wreck of a man long enough to comply with the state procedures required to obtain a driver's license. Jacob sat on the passenger side, chain-smoking, braking the empty floor with his right foot, and mentally writing his Will as she struggled to block out his damnably contagious anxiety long enough to stay on the road during the drive back from the test.

Always ready to help someone spend money, Jacob presented her with a clunky old reddish Ford for her to purchase with her savings, the fruit of sporadic employment taken whenever Idalia could get by without her, or between her mother's grocery store gambles, the latest of which had already come to the usual profitless demise. With the store closed, groceries needed to be purchased from retailers, and Tallulah assumed the family role of kid with a car, playing chauffeur for the brief excursions Idalia and the boys desired, trivialities Jacob regarded as unworthy of his time.

Local employment opportunities remained thin for young adults choosing the "real world" instead of college. Most being accustomed to having aspirations shot down, they had grown incapable of strategizing for a fulfilling future beyond the sensible needs of here and now. Every threadbare town in the area seemed to extol its lone garment factory, which employed mostly middle-aged Black and white women for pennies above minimum wage. The majority sat at noisy sewing machines for eight hours a day. Others stood and wrestled with hot, steamy irons, removing the wrinkles from life. Tallulah soon found herself standing at a large table with three other inspectors, occupying their designated spots on a concrete floor. Each armed with a strangely short pair of scissors, the inspectors busily snip, snip, snipped long threads from bundles of newly-sewn girl dresses, which journeyed next to the pressers, each standing in their station with individual ironing boards. From the pattern cutters to the final stage, the various workers collected their designated tag from each bundle they completed, enhancing by pennies the amount of money they could take home for the day. The women stayed focused, speaking sparingly, with tidbits of conversation usually focused on their children or the work waiting for them at home.

One day the four snippers caught sight of unusual seam holes left by the sewing machine operators, who routinely sewed to hide these guides left for them by the pattern cutters. The snippers mentioned this to their supervisor, a long-time fixture who shook her head and said to let it go, and thus they did. Later the same day, she marched the four snippers into the main office to be reprimanded by the factory owner, a loud man who did not know or use their names. "We can't have this happen! Every single one of these dresses has to be redone! I should take it out of your pay! How could you not see these holes? I pay you good money! Don't let it happen again!" Tallulah thought maybe an explanation would help get the blame off the backs of her co-workers, good women who did good work, and were losing money with this encounter. Before speaking out, however, she glanced at her supervisor's eyes only to get hit with lasers of caution, warning her, begging her to keep the blame where it stood, and thus she withheld her breath and her voice.

A few months of stale "real world" inequity and swollen legs prompted Tallulah to consider attending college before she suffocated completely, and she began to make plans. She held no idea of how to choose a college but knew she would require the thing they called financial aid, so she applied to the one Roger attended, fifteen miles away, down a country highway. *At least I'll know someone there. Knowing someone is even better when that someone actually likes me.*

One evening during the regular Tuesday campus prayer meetings she'd been driving to, Roger asked her to step outside for a moment. Without warning, he dropped the bomb again, saying he didn't think they loved each other "enough" to continue seeing each other. This time, however, she let him go. This time, Tallulah had someone to catch her, and she remained outside alone in the dark while Roger went back in to join the happy group. She had her new faith, and she used it. Apparently, the only male she could depend on appeared to be the one who dwelt inside of her. While the others disappointed her in one way or another, she felt her Jesus holding her tight, cushioning the blow. She had his love, and it felt warmer and more lasting than anything else.

"I have no idea of what is ahead for me," she whispered into the darkness, "or if I will ever have anyone human to share my future with, or if there will even be a tomorrow, Lord, but I have you. I don't have to let go of you. I don't have to lose you. I know you are with me, and I know you love me. Your love makes me strong, and I can go on. I know you are with me. Thank you, Lord Jesus. Thank you for your love."

After a few minutes, Tallulah quietly rejoined the group inside. Roger grinned a little too much and spouted, "Praise the Lord" at her return. He knew she had been free to hop in her car and drive home. Roger had introduced her to the group months earlier, and the members consistently welcomed her with friendly arms, so now she stayed, making her own claim on a territory that had proven to be beneficial. The neophyte did more listening and watching than participating, but no one minded her silence, and someone always helped her find the verses in the Bible. She knew she had much to learn, technically and spiritually.

That night, she remained later than usual. After Roger departed, with another dumb grin on his face, she wanted to tell the few who remained about their breakup and ask for a prayer of support. The power of prayer in this group could make a person glow. However, someone's sister was having problems with her marriage, and Tallulah's pint-sized personal devastation did not seem worth mentioning.

As the weeks passed, she began to wonder if Roger's college was going to be the best place for her; she worried, like any good converted soul. *Maybe God wants me to go somewhere else* kept running through her head when the financial aid letter arrived, but no official letter of acceptance found its way to the Sheridan mailbox sitting out on the edge of a highway. *Is this a sign from God? Does he want me to go to a different college? Maybe I'm not supposed to be around Roger and his friends anymore. I won't know how to act. What does God want for me? Something else? How am I to know? Where is my acceptance letter? Why hasn't it come?*

Finding no answer in her impatient worry-prayer, Tallulah took an afternoon off from work and drove over to the college registrar's office. Yes, they told her, she was accepted, and, yes, the letter had been mailed. But where was it? Still confused, she wanted to talk to someone who held a more mature relationship with the Lord than she did, and she wanted to talk immediately. *Someone from the prayer group should be able to help me, but I have no idea of their class schedules.* She drove to the parking lot of a shopping mall, sat in her car, and prayed.

Way down not-so-deep, Tallulah had one particular brother in mind, an outdoor type who carried a calm, strong aura of fresh mountain air, but they had never shared more than casual greetings. Having no idea where he might be, she concentrated her thoughts on him anyway, and within minutes she knew where he was. Tallulah arrived at the town's Christian bookstore barely in time to see Tod swinging one of his handsome legs smoothly over the back of his ten-speed bicycle, alone and ready to depart. *Oooh, another little miracle of my own. I think I like this God business.*

At the hamburger restaurant next door, Tallulah ordered a soda, while Tod drank milk. Fighting back nervous shivers at an outside table on a cool spring day, she dumped out her college dilemma, only to discover some of the brethren could be pretty adamant about their personal convictions. After she explained it all, he nodded at his milk carton, and stared into the tall trees beyond her.

"Do you remember the girl, Marty, who came to the meetings a couple of times?" he asked.

"The one with the long brown hair? Yes, I remember."

"Well, the Lord's going to reach down his hand upon a group of brothers and sisters up around Atlanta and do a work among them," he said.

"Really? What's going on?"

"Yeah, the Lord's really going to step in and touch those folks. Just imagine the power of the Lord among them. I wish I could be there just to see it."

"What's going on?" she asked again.

"Well, the Lord told me Marty is my helpmate. We belong together, and you just can't go against the word of the Lord," he said. "She's planning to get married to this other guy, today."

"Today?"

"Yeah."

"And you think she's supposed to be with you?"

"I know she is. It's the Lord's will. I would appreciate your prayers for her and those brothers and sisters there. When the hand of God strikes them, He's going to wipe out their plans. Man, it'll be a big zap all right, and time is running out for them. They need our love, because God's really going to do a work on them." His mouth smiled his easy smile of hope and faith, but his eyes remained private territory. Finally, he said he didn't see any reason for Tallulah to change her original plans, declined her offer of a ride back to campus, and they parted.

CHAPTER FIFTEEN

Shattered heart aside, Tallulah loved being where the brains were. The campus presented its own large pond, complete with spacious, encircling lawn, shade trees, stone benches, tables, and ducks. *A student can actually sit alone here,* she thought, *unlike high school, where a moment without companionship screams social abnormality, and petty mouths constantly spurt petty labels. Here, nobody cares. What a relief.* People sat alone in many places at college, and she joined them, gladly.

Not each and every adjustment floated into place, however. Tallulah suffered from a typical disorder of enthusiasm common among green freshman, spurting her own smiley "Hi!" to nearly every passing face. The consistent flow of blank stares often glaring in return had the effect of curing her of this malady, eventually.

Using a dormitory toilet with other people in the room proved to be the most challenging obstacle. Even out of view, every stall wall loomed as a massive microphone, broadcasting her tinkles to all ears within a mile or two, Tallulah's bladder insisted, freezing vehemently. For a long time, her bathroom trips had to be lonely trips, taken during less popular times of day, until she finally learned to clamp down on her own ears to appease her lower body's fierce resistance.

The subject she decided to major in more than compensated for awkward obstacles. Out of habit, her thoughts had floated toward Gregory, who studied psychology as his field of potential expertise. *To follow or not to follow. That is the question,* she mused. Equally influential ran a gap produced by the numerous cruddy high schools in the numerous cruddy towns of her past, meager environments plotting against her to not offer art when her schedule had room for it. In one of the first schools, however, Myrna had emerged as a memorable celebrity; her drawings consistently claiming the distinction of Drawing of the Week among the student work taped to the wall outside a certain classroom Tallulah could only make excuses to meander past.

In college studio classes with other longhaired nonconformists, extracting a smidgen of peace from the constricted educational system began to emerge as a possibility at last. Learning to see by drawing, discovering the rational essence of two-dimensional, then three-dimensional design, these journeys began to offer a remarkable naissance of fundamental simplicity and control. Harmony, balance, and unity made sense. They could be created and held in the hand. *Far out.*

An early lesson in drawing her first human model rewarded

Tallulah's concentration. As she stared at an arm, the wrinkles in the model's sleeve began to distinguish themselves as hills and valleys rich in various levels of light and dark, evolving her eyeballs into magnetic conduits for details. Without speaking, she attempted to relay the nuances from vision receptors to paper. The elderly professor strolled by, perceived the results, and praised her, dismissing the rest of her drawing as irrelevant, but this was enough. Tallulah felt she had touched a treasure; art classes in general began to give her hope and confidence, petite seeds of perception pinging at dingy old walls.

Not completely transformed, her mind playing reruns of Idalia's frequent praise of Gregory the great, Tallulah deliberately paid familial dues by selecting the intangible rewards of psychology as a minor subject, acknowledging its potential to serve as a tool, human perception in general being contaminated as it was with the convoluted paths of influence, as well as being receptive to new concepts. Using visible or invisible tools, she hoped to understand human behavior someday, especially the irrational aspects of it. She had already confirmed the existence of a sublime transcendence which had knocked the socks off her, and art seemed to be some kind of bridge between worlds seen and unseen. Psychology might help build bridges, especially when moving forward carried with it a sense of leaving behind other good folks. The former chauffeur hoped one day to extend rescue routes for her mother and younger brothers.

With surprise being a common feature of unknown territory, her classes produced more light than she expected, shining upon her own ignorance and naivety. Survival compelled her to set aside those gallant hopes of extending lifelines strong enough to undo the turmoil of her father's dysfunctional influence, pulling the others to sanity and safety, away from Jacob the monster. Despite her intentions, however, Tallulah's big balloon began to drift without the rest of her family, the basket taking her away from them, preventing her from doing more than struggle with the heavy, muddy boots encumbering her own progress.

Occasional weekends at home served to remind her that old laces encased in mud could not easily be undone. Jacob never had more than one question for her: "Gonna make the Dean's List this semester?" He never asked if she liked the teachers, if classes were interesting, if she needed money, or if she had goals for her future. He wanted to see his family name reported in the runt of a local newspaper. Bragging rights would be something to slap down on the table in front of the cronies he met for breakfast in a local restaurant, and nothing more.

Tallulah lacked local cronies of her own with which to compare opportunities and accomplishments. She barely knew the kids from her high school senior classes, having given up any hopes of success in the realm beyond oddball. Her years of being "the new kid" had effectively destroyed those futile adolescent hopes, yet simultaneously prepared her well to receive the new seeds of freedom breaking dry ground to reach the warm rays of sunshine. Unhindered by peer pressure, she felt free to explore the world of academic opportunity in any direction she wished, savoring positive mental health avenues gently meandering through the verdant gardens of academia, nevertheless taking a practical turn now and then.

Leftover financial aid prompted her to make her first trip ever to a dentist's office, breaking one of the family cycles of negligence. She ventured further from the shackles by replacing her thick eyeglasses with contact lenses, not to expose her glorious eyeballs, but to broaden her view of the big picture. To her, these common steps glowed as uncommonly delightful achievements.

Tallulah's social activity remained thin, with the same weekly Christian prayer meetings more appealing than unending beer busts and wet T-shirt contests held nightly at the local watering hole. Roger remained polite, but she missed his old passion. Pretty Tod's eyes remained focused on another girl, in another time, another place. Fraternity boys seemed to regard Tallulah as a challenge to be imposed upon each other, for reasons failing to emerge after a polite offer of a car ride across campus, or a few, obviously pre-packaged, interview questions of "What's your name? What's your major?" at the cafeteria dining table. *What was that shit?* she wondered afterward, assuming she must have made it onto some kind of checklist; be it the checklist of "freaky" or whatever, she cared not. Encounters of a more genuine nature emerged along other paths, like on the warm day she walked with another male friend from the meetings, sharing ice cream he had bought. The fun lasted until she kept spooning up the melted goo to prevent it from being wasted, her giggles failing to slow the frown deepening on his clean-cut face. *No Depression-era habits passed on from his parents,* she guessed. Then came Tony.

An unimposing, well-contained individual, Tony fluttered his elegant ivory hands in the air to accompany the verbal expression of his endless feelings. While most guys stuffed their emotions into their hairy chests, Tony spoke openly of his subjective responses to everything from the latest fads to roommates to the gentle commands of Jesus, offering a refreshing, authentic sincerity with unrehearsed prayers during the meetings, where spontaneity mirrored consent politely given. Tallulah appreciated the empathy and compassion he held in his heart, unlike Jacob or any other males she had encountered. Also unlike Jacob, this Y chromosome carrier also knew how to listen, and applauded everyone's diverse, yet harmless, opinions and views.

Tallulah listened as well, enjoying his companionship. After a while, she could not help wondering if their friendship would ever go beyond the easy flow of words. Months of dormitory visits and meals together and long evening conversations passed with no attempt at hand holding, no kiss, no warm embrace beyond a friendly hug with no squeeze. Finally, Tallulah took the risk of embarrassing him and said, "You know, I really wouldn't mind if you held my hand sometime or touched me. We're friends, aren't we?"

The poor guy nearly fainted before he could speak, "Sure, we're friends. You're a great friend, but I don't have those kinds of feelings for you. I don't know why I don't, and I'm so sorry."

"But it's important to me to be touched," she explained. "There's nothing wrong with it. I like it. It expresses the way people feel, that's all."

"I get it. I can understand it being important to you. But it's something I can't give you. Oh, gosh. This makes me feel like a real crud. I don't want to hurt you, Lulah. You're so important to me. You understand the way I feel about so many things, about how important being real and being honest is to me, about how much I hate phony people, and I can talk to you about almost everything. And I can't even give you this in return. I'm too selfish. I'm sorry. Here. Put your hand in mine. Come on, let's walk outside."

After a few tense yards of striding and staring at the grass, she told Tony to forget it, the effort obviously equaling torture for him. Tallulah forbade herself from forcing anyone to love her. The last thing she sought was a fake relationship. Whatever it was they had at the moment remained more valuable to her than nothing, thus she settled for conversation and companionship, nurturing the slim hope his passions would ignite, and thinking, *Oh, well, something must be still wrong with me. Maybe I need more deodorant.*

The final critique in her first painting class produced a deeper personal clarity. Like everyone else's, her four paintings sat mounted on easels for the other students to analyze. While most comments pertained to the use of color, brushstroke, and aesthetic elements, Tallulah could not ignore an unexpected commonality between her subjects, despite their random selection: a doorknob, a long woodsy path, a dormitory exit sign, and a view looking out of a second-story window with its big trash dumpster planted below, this last view failing to capture the pleasant motion of a primordial metal beast with its kind limbs as it reached out to grab and lift everyone's garbage, devouring it, taking it away forever. Tallulah wished the garbage of life could be removed as easily, but the four paintings could not be silenced, each having something to say to her, each presenting a perspective of getting out of something. Together they presented one of those bridges between two worlds, leaving her to wonder about the unseen. *I did not deliberately choose these subjects as an associated group,* she reminded herself. *Each was created separately. Is there something I want to get out of? Maybe so. My relationship with Tony?*

Hearing about how well some other chick's jeans fit indeed had proved to be wearisome, along with Mr. Friendly Fun's growing penchant for unbridled flirting with every female. She came across an extra spiral notebook and began using it as a journal, not heeding the limitations of a lined page. Her unfiltered words sprawled large and expressively angry, frustrated: *Fuck it fuck it fuck it! Shit shit shit!* After the initial spew, her thoughts settled into a calmer route, rationalizing: *But how can I give up Tony? Someone cute, kind, gentle, fun to be with, and grateful for something as simple as my ear? A male open with his feelings and honest about his reactions, one who actually likes to spend time with me. It isn't as uncomfortable as going to the dentist or eye doctor, both of which he encouraged, so what's the big deal? Why do I want out? He's good enough for me. At least he isn't dumping me. The physical stuff will probably come later; I need to be patient.*

She ignored the warning, said nothing to Tony, and plowed ahead with classes. In her sculpture professor, Tallulah found an older, bearded man with the patient sensitivity of Tony, but much less chatter. The first assignment he gave was to shape a hand sculpture from clay, destined to serve as the model for a sandstone carving. The students were told to make it appealing to the human hand, "something you would want to pick up and turn over and over." Tallulah thought of the pinecones littering her parents' lawn, and made hers bumpy and lumpy.

On the due date, the students anonymously placed their assignments together on a table for inspection. The professor stroked his beard and browsed the results, sadly shaking his head; not a single one had met his aesthetic criteria. Picking up the worst one, shuddering with disgust to get his point across, "This," he said, "is repulsive." As the guilty party, Tallulah froze, dreading having to face the blazing light of exposure. Without asking whose work was whose, fortunately for her, he gave everyone twenty-four hours to, "Do it again." And Tallulah breathed.

The next day the students, each daring to hope, placed their renewed attempts anonymously on the same table for scrutiny. The sage artist strode around again, gazing down, finally picking up only one. In his hand, it sat smooth and sensuous, turn-able, like two merged, round doorknobs. "This one is right," he said, nodding in approval. Again

Tallulah froze, silently thrilled her transformed pinecone had somehow risen from worst to best, confidence pricking her nitwit head like the wake-up flick of a finger, the hint of a Jesus wink in the background.

Weeks later, Tony demonstrated progress of his own. A confession sat in store. "I have something not very pretty, actually almost rotten, to tell you about me. I plan to tell all the brothers and sisters at the next prayer meeting, but I want your reaction first. You won't like it. I just hope you won't hate me after I tell you." The trodden victim of a southern Baptist fire-and-brimstone church upbringing always expected the planet to crack open and swallow him alive. He and Tallulah sat at one of the picnic tables near the pond on a spring afternoon.

Slowly, finally, he stared at his folded ivory hands and let the long-hidden truth escape in a quiet voice of doom. "I ... am ... a," he said, then paused for an even longer moment, " homosexual."

"Oh. Okay. You're gay? Is that all? I thought you were going to tell me you raped your mother or something," Tallulah responded. *So much for hand-holding.*

Slightly swooning, he said, "No, no, God no." Breathing a deep sigh of relief, chuckling, he asked, "Still friends?"

"Still friends. Why not?" Tallulah replied. "It's no big deal, really. If that's the way the Lord made you, who am I to question it? I'm glad you can be yourself now, your God-made, honest, true self. Maybe some people won't care too much for the news, but their response doesn't matter. This is truth. This is between you and the Lord, and I don't believe he hates you for it, so why should I? You're not hurting anyone." *Except me and my stupid hopes,* her brain chirped.

When no one in the prayer group condemned him, Tony gradually felt he had enough freedom and honesty in Jesus to seek the discreet fulfillment of his desires, filling Tallulah in later on the whos and whens, having enough mercy to omit the details. He seemed to rely on her more than ever, and she almost wished she had heeded the warning from her paintings. Even worse, his opened mind continued to wander to females, he continued to flirt outrageously, and most objects of his attention, male and female, adored his easy, playful manner. He exhibited no predatory practices, and both genders welcomed his conversational agility, a precious and rare commodity in the traditionally tight-lipped male world. Shoving aside the hellfire hammerings imposed upon him during his youth left space for many new experiences, like his question of what it felt like to be drunk. "Well, if you turn your head to the side, you have to wait for your eyeballs to catch up," Tallulah supplied.

Tallulah could down a few beers from time to time, but steered clear of ever becoming dependent on the hard stuff in brown bottles, and she held no interest in smoking anything, strongly preferring to maintain a lucid grip on her God-given free will as opposed to yielding to the snake of addiction ready to permeate families as a shared trait, as the psychology books informed her.

At home, Jacob continued to flop in and out of Alcoholics Anonymous meetings and halfway houses. Having eventually learned of Tallulah's commitment to Christianity, he took advantage of the cessation of slammed doors and swearing and exits executed on his behalf. She tried to ignore his sudden pride in having a college daughter, looking at her like he had never seen her before, a creepy interest not to be trusted, mutating her into a potentially useful thing to show off and brag about. Unfortunately, she failed to come up with a good excuse when he asked her to present him with a chip at his next AA meeting. As much as she dreaded it and hated herself for being stupid enough to step in the mud again, the night arrived. On the way there, she walked beside him along a street in town, only to have him suddenly stop, grab her shoulders, and push her against the brick building beside the sidewalk. "Ow," she said, bewildered.

"Man walks by the street," he muttered, some kind of primeval decree of tribalism shooting up from inner earth. She rubbed her arm and continued allowing her feet to move forward, soon finding herself planted in a long meeting hall stagnant with thick cigarette smoke. A chattering, nervous crowd, clones of her stupid father, eventually seated themselves at long rows of cafeteria tables.

Tallulah had never attended one of these meetings before. Beyond Idalia's reluctant accompaniment once or twice, Jacob went by himself, no one in the family being willing to tolerate his display of unboxed solicitude blatantly absent at home. At one end of the room stood a lonely lectern, Tallulah noticed, and the presentation of poker chips for specific periods of sobriety began. After listening to several tales of how much trouble and pain and anger had led to this night, it dawned on Tallulah that she, too, was expected to accompany the presentation with a personal testimony of trials, faith, and tribute to the receiver. *Shit*, she thought. He had not prepared her for this, as he had not prepared her for anything, once more leaving her to drown.

When her turn arrived, Tallulah deliberately broke the chain of winding stories by hastening her steps, quickly uttering her just-memorized sentence, hating the moment, but making it honest enough. "I'd like to thank the Lord, AA, and Jacob himself." She then unceremoniously handed chip and podium to her father and returned to her seat, leaving him to stand in her place and feign surprise at the brevity of his child's introduction. He stood, shrugging, savoring the public moment of being once again a helpless and innocent poor-me victim no one could possibly expect to do more than stammer, "Gosh darn ... well, I reckon ... what the heck ... just gotta make the most of it."

Tallulah yearned to get out of the building and away, away from these people with their power to evoke mud memories, themselves being creatures ejecting endlessly as if from an office copy machine, their sameness rattling the bars she put up between her and them. *Besides,* she reasoned, *he deserves no more. As for the father thing, he remains grossly inadequate.* Before she could somewhat politely make it to the door, however, Tallulah received a reassuring pat on the shoulder from a prune of a woman who forgave the obvious incompetence, "You did real fine up there, hon." Outside finally, away from hollow words and horrid memories, fresh evening air never felt more fresh. She rubbed her sore shoulder.

While social reinforcement fed into Jacob's sobriety dance, and he skillfully alleviated any threat of boring steps by getting drunk again, Tallulah continued to move in what she hoped to be a logical, healthier direction. Unlike the trampling rush permeating her mental past, she found no opposition within to a slower pace. Allowing herself frequent immersion in the throes of contemplation, she simultaneously examined telling details of life past and life present, applying explanations from the textbooks of human behavior, weaving them into the emotive visuals of fine art. She attempted to piece together the reasons for a multitude of people's lives becoming miserable and stagnant, hoping to learn enough to avoid most of the numerous camouflaged pitfalls.

Perhaps life-future required the element common to many artistic creations: a model. Something to start with, something to build upon, not necessarily to copy. Her case sought an operational role model. Like any daughter, Tallulah looked first in the direction of her mother. She thought if she overlooked the parenting shortcomings, the shrugs of indifference presented in lieu of support, maybe she could objectively focus on the person named Idalia Sheridan. She longed to find positivity and courage leading to success of some sort, accomplishments beyond scrubbing floors and doing laundry and repeated failures in the self-employment realm. "Did you take business classes back in college? Who taught you to keep the books?"

"Nope. No one. I figured it out on my own." As an afterthought, "Maybe with a suggestion or two from the wholesaler's rep."

The woman had brains, but apparently something obstructed her path, repeatedly. Tallulah used her art classroom skills to ponder perspectives of her mother's puzzling life from every angle, without being confrontational; she observed and remembered, figuring it out on her own. The lack of any evidence for a happy life well lived confirmed how much the years of worry and grief had worn down an intelligent woman, crushing her into passive dependence and despondency undeserved. Asking "why" led to finding something or someone to blame, something or someone had ripped to shreds a gessoed canvas of potential. Only one creature deserved the blame for blocking this woman's rightful journey to self-fulfillment.

Men like Jacob held no right to their destructive selfishness, Tallulah concluded. Weaklings presented as strong heroes, gender-appointed, omnipotent authorities on everything they knew nothing about, made life second-class for the women who supported and loved them. Tallulah may not have constructed a vision of goals for herself, but from her parents she formed a solid scenario of what she did not want, what not to do. When one of the pages of her psychology textbook revealed the scenario of most girls being attracted to, and marrying, boys similar to the girls' own fathers, usually not intentionally, a red dart of warning! warning! shot through her entire being. The thought of being chained to a cold-hearted, womanizing alcoholic made her want to vomit. She vowed to *never ever* become someone else's aproned asshole, living in a man's shadow until she could no longer find her way out, suffering like a doomed insect trapped within a spider's web. If she found anyone to share her life with, he would clearly have to be very different from Jacob.

She could recognize truth in the textbook scenario. Young women around her appeared to play thoughtless games only to have their lives taken away from them. Roommates fawned upon the male species: "Oh, he's so cute, so dreamy." Tallulah held no desire to manipulate a man with the flutter of heavy eyelashes or the puckered pout of painted lips. The myths of feminine helplessness and male superiority resulted in much pain for too many people. These were games she banned from her embryonic identity. She revered truth, natural honesty devoid of pretense and deception, regardless of how weird it might make her appear.

One day, she happily consented to give the wife of her painting teacher a ride home. The woman worked at the college in one of the administrative offices. Some of Tallulah's art pieces sat in a display case outside the office. As they passed by it, the woman commented on the pieces, "Those things are so ugly."

Tallulah laughed spontaneously, saying, "Those are my pieces."

"Oh! I didn't know. I am so sorry, very sorry."

Tallulah repeatedly assured the kind creature it was okay, really okay, amused at the embarrassment, delighted to experience a success in upsetting someone's expectations of conformity. The pieces were never meant to be pretty; they represented the crude, primordial honesty of earth elements with a bit of human rage woven into the natural fibers, the baked clay, and the unpolished cast metal.

Love of truth continued to be the one thing Tallulah and Tony shared. Being unlike Jacob made Tony valuable. He did not pretend to be the dominating decision-maker or to have the answers to everything, and she remained free to be her unadorned, natural self. They did not try to change each other, but continued to grow spiritually, and mentally, with a genuine acceptance of self, each building a solid foundation without conformity, neither one knowing the direction their future lives would take, but both clinging to one important perspective: the authenticity of bringing a blurry world into focus.

So she thought.

Building upon the good earth of theoretical idealism, rising above common fallacies of genders' societal roles, adhering to the clarity of high vision sometimes became a blur. Tallulah allowed freedom to flow in a weaving class sampler, leaving some strands unconventionally long and loose, showing them to Tony and expecting his usual cheerleader support. Instead, he offered a silent response, with only his face offering any signs of motion, his upper lip rising in disdain before being squashed into politer indifference. Once again, Tallulah failed to heed the warning whispered by her art. She found herself cutting the long strands down into something closer to the expected standard, thinking, *He's right. This is too wild. It won't hurt me to make it more like everyone else's.*

Another day's stroll in town took the two into a fabric store, where they compared patterns and colors, each expressing personal preferences. Tallulah chose a delightful Monet style of freely blended colors leaving shape definitions to the imagination. He groaned at her choice, choosing miniature, consistently pale blue cookie-cutter flowers evenly spaced, the antithesis of art. Tallulah stood silent, soused with a bucket of conformity, suddenly wishing she had not clipped those long, lovely tendrils of free-flowing yarn.

The summer before her last year of college, Jacob surprised her by asking her to accompany him and Idalia on their first visit back to the Wolverine state and to relatives in Canada. A year of sobriety had made him almost human, and Michigan lingered as a stolen fragment of Tallulah's identity. She did want to see it again, but felt no honor bestowed upon her by his invitation, only a forewarning of doom pertinent to being cooped up with the battling duo in a moving car. She wondered how Idalia had finally persuaded him to make the trip.

On the road, the trio frequently fed oil to Jacob's latest thirsty, neglected brown station wagon, devoid of air conditioning. The equally questionable driver sweated his way through traffic all the way to gloomy Detroit, a city clearly drained by a greedy automobile industry and corrupt politicians. Jacob's first stop consisted of a visit to an old associate living in one of Detroit's lush, green suburbs, the big house standing tall, looming as the status symbol of profit from selling the company Jacob claimed to have helped build. He sauntered into the man's home with an arrogant shrug, as if to say, "Was it my fault I moved on to bigger and better things after having bestowed my golden seed upon the less gifted?" Jacob donned his thin robe of entitlement, hoping for a share of the fortune produced after he left the company. At their kitchen table, the host and his wife treated their Georgia visitors to a minimal lunch of cold cuts while Jacob presented his case, man to man, with the three women beside them. At one point in the polite chit-chat on the sidelines, the wife asked Tallulah her age. "Twenty-one," she replied, quietly.

"How old?" the husband bellowed, bursting out of his conversation with Jacob, nearly knocking everyone to the ceiling. Being fairly sure of her own age, Tallulah repeated the answer, only to be showered with bizarre mutterings of disbelief in the authenticity of Jacob's college daughter. "Can't be! She looks no older than high school," they insisted. *Why would you care?* Tallulah wondered, an ugly jab of realization poking her, whispering, *you're a trophy.* Her counter thoughts immediately responded, *I am not, most certainly am not!*

Jacob manufactured his own line of mutterings as the rejected trio drove towards the Detroit River, nearing the idolized realm of Canadian relatives. Once across, and in someone's home, Jacob played the role of rehabilitated husband while his wife flaunted painted fingernails and donned her own robe of sudden nobility, a proud queen among her admiring relatives. More than once, Jacob and his pseudo-trophy daughter sat forgotten in the background as nephews and nieces cuddled at the sides and feet of their revered American aunt, who smiled and spun chatty reminiscences of a past rich with details Tallulah had never heard before. Adding to the surrealism, Idalia appeared not only flattered, but dignified and happy. *Who is this strange woman?* Tallulah wondered.

The return trip included a brief stop in the neighborhood Tallulah had flown to in her high school dreams. From the car windows, they viewed the suburban house bulging in their memories with years of drama, disappointment, and tears. For the entire time of her nine years since forced extraction, Tallulah had loyally stowed the image of a unique giant of a structure among her mementos; something loved and cherished because it had been ripped away from her. Now it sat, looking ordinary, dull, and diminished. "It's only a two-bedroom house. How in the hell did you think you could raise five kids in a two-bedroom house?" Tallulah asked.

Idalia glanced at the salesman beside her in the front seat, shrugged, and offered her typical crumbs of make-do defense. "Well, we used the attic." Jacob stared straight ahead, gripping the steering wheel, lost somewhere in his menagerie of private recollections, obviously unshared, depriving of any reward the trophy-college-child who had failed to be as useful as he had planned; her presence had not helped get him the money he knew he dang well deserved, dang it. Unaware she had been expected to shine, Tallulah could not determine whether to admire the tenacity of these two people who were her parents, or to forgive them for their mental deficiencies.

With unadorned reality imposed upon thoughts of an irretrievable past, and befuddled by the behaviors of Jacob and his latent Canadian queen, Tallulah returned to college even more confused by her journey through the Twilight Zone. Awareness of her own ignorance sat undeniably renewed, shoving aside nearly everything previously dragged into focus, leaving her with diddly-squat. Some kind of enigmatic lump waited to be brought into the light, like the clay she mixed and prodded and slammed onto the table. Slamming she enjoyed most, ensuring no air bubbles remained to burst later and destroy her piece of exquisite beauty, perhaps functional, to come. She wished she could remove her brain bubbles as easily.

Why am I always using my right hand more than my left? she wondered. *I'd do better using both hands.* Days later, a direct question to Idalia confirmed what Tallulah suspected; family policy had included restraining, holding down every young babe's left hand when it reached for a toy or spent time in the highchair picking up food and other manual endeavors. "But why?" Tallulah asked.

"Well, I don't know. I guess we didn't want a leftie." Idalia shrugged, her eyes on the bushes outside the window.

Why is it people don't believe, don't live, their own words? First Tony with his flamboyant praise for art and freedom, shunning the undefined stroke of color in useful fabric. Now my own mother, who admonishes us to be ourselves, don't conform, yet don't be left-handed? It's the same as telling a child to color always within the lines, with your right hand. Good doggie. A pat on the head for squelching your true self.

Heart-wrenching hypocrisy aside, Tallulah chose to retain the tenet of personal freedom as her own, letting others do as they chose, hoping she would be able to maintain her grip, avoid falling into the cesspool of conformity, into a world which did not want her, a world she felt would eviscerate her. She treasured the few fibers of identity thus far gathered: honesty and truth about what she felt, what she thought, the validity of herself, what God had made her to be. She supposed He knew what He was doing. Maybe that murky thing they call "faith" could come into play during times like these, perhaps.

She continued to incorporate personal honesty into her art and her life, watching as her art pieces became organic on their own. One she had thought hopelessly resembled a fish as it underwent construction on the floor instantly became the iconic union of male and female forms when placed upright. Without any intention of creating sexual forms, bosomy bulges and penetrated circles began to prevail in her work. Once again, her art revealed more than she intended. The rising sexual awareness becoming obviously evident to those who could interpret abstract art began to embarrass her.

Mostly men, her art instructors shrugged off the sexual display as nothing new. However, Tallulah savored this unearthed facet of her identity, stowing it away for future reference. A consequential radar emerged and pinged her attention upon the printmaking instructor. A transplant from Massachusetts, this tall, boyish newcomer to the Art Department had not impressed her until he made a point of asking her opinion during class critiques. Repeatedly, he singled her out, although her prints were not the best. He never explained his attentions, and never took them beyond the classroom, but the poofs of respect fell as fairy dust upon Tallulah. He made her feel especially valuable, actually in possession of credible perspectives during a time of personal uncertainty. *Am I so lacking in personal confidence I lap at crumbs?* "Oooh," her classmate whispered. "He has his eye on youooo." Tallulah held onto her doubts, but she tucked away this slice of unexplained extra attention, preserving it for later deliberation, perhaps something to return to.

Life had grown less encouraging for the prayer group's base in Atlanta. The house meetings disintegrated when the steadfast, prosperous married couple playing host suddenly announced their plans for divorce. The kind, soft-spoken salesman of a husband had become involved with a younger woman—several, in fact. His devoted, flawless, Jesus-loving wife who never looked Tallulah in the eye transformed into a berserk basket case, reportedly screaming "Harlot" at the young woman, an attractive divorcee she had been acquainted with for years. Violations of trust and commitment came as no surprise to Tallulah, especially from another traveling salesman. She realized her friends had idolized this man and woman more than they should have. She could not share their multitude of tears. Pleas for explanation from heaven above poured forth from members of the group, especially from Tony.

On a return trip from Atlanta, he asked her how she could take it so calmly. Having been injected with similar doses of reality, she shrugged and replied, "People get divorced every day. Why should we expect these two to be any different? The guy is only human after all, another cheat-on-the-wife salesman." Tony said he found her words harsh, but the mountain of despair spilling forth from naively misplaced faith in people dulled her interest in the prayer meetings. While she appreciated having learned the meaning of the ubiquitous suffering among the thees and thys, the last thing she needed was to focus on a husband's infidelity.

Her wandering, yet solid, steps through the utopian, but trustworthy, garden of academia teetered as she neared the end of the trail. With graduation, Tallulah removed her hallowed cap and gown only to find herself standing on the edge of a cliff. The great and nasty unplanned, unnamed abyss of the future ballooned in front of her, its dangerous depths imminent. Assessing potential directions brought to mind faraway Gregory's sanctuary of graduate school, Myrna's settling for office employment, Idalia's total avoidance of planning a tomorrow, and Jacob's constant battles with it. Tallulah sighed. She suspected her skills of slamming clay and getting good grades were unlikely to be appreciated going forward.

Without a doubt, the monster thing commonly referred to as the "real world" and its superficial glorification of tangible possessions began to snicker at her opposing view of "real world" and its sincere reverence for intangible treasures accumulated within and unseen. Feeling enriched in one way but dreadfully ill-equipped in another, how could she expect to step into a daunting galaxy where many people wallowed in torment? Reading the Bible twice had revealed the root of all evil to be the love of money. Jacob epitomized this soul-sucking, ruthless quest for the greenbacks. *How can I expect to do any better?*

Tallulah allowed her vision of a canyon to mist into an ocean. She saw herself floating in deep waters, wearing a life vest. To head for shore and landing would require removing her life vest, where it was not needed, starting over again, accepting new standards again, encountering strange people and strange value systems again, leaving behind four stable years of enrichment. The only trail to be seen on any shore revealed Jacob's haphazard stumblings in the sand, headed in many different directions, a glaring testimony of his repeated grasps for support, his dire clutches at standing trees, the young native plants in his path ripped up and burned. His repeated attempts to blaze his insane trails of ambition led nowhere. *Do I really have to stumble along as he has stumbled along, into his crappy money world of crappy chaos?*

Work-study and summer jobs had been fun, but now something about full-time-forever employment gave her the heebie-jeebies. Most of her art friends, including her hopelessly hopeful Tony, planned to move to big cities. While she had basked in college as a rejuvenating end in itself, others wisely viewed it as a stepping-stone, preparing themselves for the same geyser of employment, money management, and bills she saw hissing and bubbling in the canyon, laughing and swinging from branches in the trees on beach shores. She shed her friends as nothing more than the passing waters every friend had been to her. Alone again, what choice remained for her but to jump and be devoured, swim to shore and starve, cease to exist, no matter the analogy. *Shit.*

She vaguely contemplated opening an art supply store, becoming a practical asset to the numerous art students in need of the tools necessary to carry them into the precious self-enlightenment guaranteed to rise in opposition to the rat race when they graduated. She could use the customer service skills acquired by years of working for her mother, combining her new life with her old, but she doubted self-enlightenment would mix well with habitual failure, and she had never taken a college business class.

She considered graduate school, but lacked any professional goal to serve as the carrot at the end of a stick; classroom confinement had its limits. Several art professors casually encouraged her to go for a Master's degree in Fine Art, but true artists had a habit of chopping off ears and screaming, and the partying pot scene resembled alcoholism, and she feared it. A lonely art therapy brochure tacked to a bulletin board in the Art Department held some potential, possibly, until realizing she would most likely become her own patient. Scary. And the graduate school was in another state, meaning another move, another uprooting after four cherished years.

She considered stopping at a local construction site, imagining herself acquiring the steadfast skills of a bricklayer, building some functional and concise structure of longevity, able to withstand the perpetual onslaught of devastating change. Almost immediately, up from the roots of hammered memory sprouted the ingrained, omnipresent disdain from macho Jacob males, laughing at her lack of know-how, ridiculing her inevitable struggles, teasing her for girlie weakness in general. A patriarchal world reeking of misogyny guaranteed to drown her. She had no courage.

CHAPTER SIXTEEN

Tallulah landed on Myrna's couch. With her office job and apartment in Hotlanta, Myrna allowed her aimless younger sister to lodge in her pretty living room while the tadpole of self-supporting employment squirmed through its metamorphic transformation into a warty amphibian of general acceptance. It took its time. Vague newspaper ads and daunting transportation within a crowded, noisy city where huge bus tires threw their heat into one's face felt rather hellish to Tallulah. Crossing such a threshold required strategic planning, the application of logic, and the courage to have hope; her weak spots.

Struggling with her own divorce entanglements, Myrna offered simple advice. "Just get a job," she said. "Don't make such a big deal out of everything."

"Yeah, but, I dunno. It feels like a huge step, a giant commitment, and I don't know what I'm good at."

"Good God, you've had jobs before, moron."

"This is different. College taught me to think, how to create. I can't throw away four good years. I can't just become a mindless stooge employee again, doing what other people tell me to do."

"Gee, thanks a lot."

"The walls of my blessed sanctuary have collapsed, and I stand naked in the cold wind."

"I'm glad I didn't go to college," Myrna scoffed.

Between the two sisters, they arrived at "maybe an art museum," before Myrna walked away, shaking her head. And Tallulah considered it. *But why would a monolithic art museum hire less than the best of the best? And taking care of someone else's good art isn't the same as making it.*

As she wallowed in excuses, she was introduced to a neighbor of Myrna's. Big sister seemed to have found her own chatty male friend, attractively promising no sexual entanglement for those of the female gender, slightly older. "She can make something for me," Bernard told them, swinging back his long blond hair with a sleek hand adorned with lengthy red fingernails. "I'd like to have something exotic, an oriental man, made of fabric, to hang up on my wall." Tallulah set to work, looking for a typical Asian man's face in Myrna's encyclopedia, and finding a noble one wearing a cap. For two weeks, she cut fabric and sewed it by hand, putting puffy stuff behind segments of silky fabric, taking up the living floor until completing a dignified, serene three-foot high face. "Uh, okaaay," Bernard said when he took it. He had promised to pay one hundred dollars.

"I'll give you the money," Myrna assured her, and she did, later, saying it came from Bernard. He laughed when the three of them sat in a restaurant, saying he and his roommate referred to Tallulah's creation as "the head." On a napkin, Bernard cheerfully sketched for her what he had really wanted: a grinning, toothy person on a tricycle, his one long, braided pigtail flying in the wind.

Suspecting she had been bamboozled, Tallulah felt her precious self-actualization slipping away, something to be ridiculed, like the grinning fool on three wheels. Her naive baby step in the direction of money had proven to be the antithesis she feared, leaving her with a sense of no gain, no hope of any good grade appearing out of sparkling fantasy land to ignite encouragement. *Crapola. I am getting nowhere fast.*

Part of her knew she must become her own hero, she must stop clutching at trees on the beach, become her own best Mighty Mouse, boldly go where no available role model had gone before. However, since flight remained absent from her skill set, she determined to hang on to what modicum of identity solidified from the molten and muddy experiences of her past, even as her precious college days threatened to mingle deeper with the tumultuous family years, both anchored in the past according to any timeline, yet both remaining quite alive in her head. She knew this, but remained stubbornly reluctant to become part of anything commercial. Since the Atlanta hugeness guaranteed to swallow her into anonymity, she opened her old jar of fairy dust, something Tinkerbell had left behind. *Just to be sure,* she reasoned.

A greenhouse environment nurtures young plants, yet who is to say those young plants don't scream in protest when they are plucked out of their sanctuary and thrust into the harshness of direct sunlight and ravaging storms. With art professors having functioned so well as Tallulah's gentle horticulturists, consistently encouraging and supportive, her separation from them conjured ghosts of being ripped away from all the other classroom worlds where she had begun to grow roots of identity. The ivory tower beckoned, in a way.

She latched her anchor upon the idea of the young printmaker, relishing anew the tidbits of attention this handsome, smiley, single, not-gay guy had doled out in her direction, invoking handy fantasies of romantic substitutes for self-sufficiency. Justification emerged from a compliment he once gave on her Canada T-shirt. *Maybe I wasn't responsive enough. How stupid of me.* Even after sculpting these certainly-valid tidbits together into a pleasing, conclusive form, she lacked the courage to pick up the phone and call. However, the winds of opportunity brought a breeze other than the blast of hot bus tires in an asphalt jungle.

A telephone call from a former roommate informed her of a public school art teacher job opening ten miles from the town her parents had moved to after she began college. Nothing had cured their rootless zigzag of mobility. Fifteen miles from her old college, the school registered enough in her mind as sitting in familiar-enough territory. She called the Board of Education.

When she drove down for the interview a few days later, she took time to stroll around her alma mater, and happened to encounter the object of her current passions in the art building's elevator, alone, the two of them. Following the standard greetings, Tallulah threw caution to the wind, deciding to find out if her romantic fantasies embodied any jewels of truth. While the doors closed, and with time at a minimum, as the building consisted of only four floors, she looked him straight in the eyes, turning on her deepest smile, radiating the warmest glow she could muster, full sexy power, exactly as former roommates had rehearsed, waiting for him to melt accordingly and release his suppressed love, or at least ask her for a date. Poor soul. He squirmed, begging eye contact with every corner of the elevator. The doors opened and he flew. Tallulah remained. *Ah, well, at least now I know.*

With her wispy hope of rescue disintegrated, employment offered itself in no other easy path except the teaching job, the thought of which gave her bad dreams, student and teacher relationship cuckoo dreams. Nevertheless, she left Hotlanta to Myrna and moved back to her college town, finding her own apartment, fearing the noisy, nasty, miniature people would scorn her, and the art she loved would receive none of her devotion.

She placed her favorite sculpture piece on top of the old bedroom bureau borrowed from Idalia. Second only to the reborn hand carving, bulges simultaneously inviting and repulsive, resembling a compressed cousin of Thing from the Fantastic Four, her cast aluminum manifestation of human rage unpolished, chunky, and screaming, prompted a smile of growing appreciation. "Hi, buddy. Still with me, aren't you." Serving as a reminder of the unresolved, as well as skill worthy of development, it whispered the consideration of graduate school, but the idea of any classroom situation conjured images of restriction, confinement, and strangulation, when she craved freedom. *Better to be at the front of the room than to be a disciple locked in a desk, perhaps, maybe,* she hoped.

Wishing for a miracle and finding nothing but freedom within a fence, she held her breath, mumbled. "What the hell," and jumped off the cliff. Tallulah landed in a tangled world, but at least it wasn't about making money; she told herself she had avoided the vortex of Jacob's perdition. A jumble of five hundred hormonal and not-yet-hormonal junior high school creatures became her art education responsibility. Her goal could be nothing less than to give every single one of them his or her own version of the insightful personal growth the art world had given to her. Building a one-to-five-hundred bridge couldn't be too difficult. She watched as herded young bodies entered classroom after classroom as if condemned to prison cells. Every class groaned and moaned. They really needed art.

It surprised her to see the old serpent of racial segregation still entwined around the legs of the students, confining them into grade levels of A, B, C, D, and E groups allegedly according to achievement, as if they could possibly have the same aptitude for every subject. The system reeked of adult subjectivity. Teachers did not pretend to hide the stigmatic labeling from the students, whose behaviors reflected accordingly: The A group consisted of a bored white majority; racially-mixed B group knew they were second-best and demonstrated resentment; mostly-Black C group exhibited downright anger; D lacked enthusiasm; and E students wallowed in hopelessness. Art class offered less peer grade pressure, but the students knew they would get only a P for Passed or an F for Failed on their report cards, and only a few displayed interest. Regardless of their skill levels, Tallulah loved the kids for their honesty and rowdy candor, from the cute fifth graders to the tall, muscular eighth graders.

With a broom closet for her office, she pushed a film projector cart from classroom to classroom, a situation allowing for hardly more than drawing exercises. Memories of spacious studios remained fresh in her mind, and she had no idea of how to expose the young people to every rich facet of art while they each sat at a writing desk with no storage space for any project requiring more than the few minutes allowed. She only knew her role had been trivialized, with art being trivialized, begging for counteraction.

She finally convinced the principal to let her use a bona fide classroom, which otherwise sat empty. The classroom offered no sink and no storage cupboards. The only tables allowed were constructed by janitors mounting full size sheets of plywood on sawhorses, while sturdy cafeteria tables sat in storage after having been replaced by new ones. No money in the school system had been allocated for art supplies; nothing more than a few jars of paint, crayons, scissors, and a week's worth of construction paper sat in the supply room for each and every teacher to consume at will.

"You could ask the kids to each bring two dollars for supplies," the principal suggested, but Tallulah lacked the heart to ask kids for money, not when so many appeared to come from low-income families. Instead, she asked them to bring articles from home, like coat hangers, which they turned into squares and began weaving with yarn she purchased. The school had no objection to her spending her own money for supplies.

Regardless of her intentions, the miniature wizards taught her there is more to teaching than teaching. The students seemed to have been trained to talk and play until screamed at, or until frightened into stopping by a showy display of primitive adult anger. Tallulah held no desire to yell at them, or stomp around shoving children, as other teachers did, and possessed no background in educational training to supply effective alternatives. Consequently, she faced the predicament of obtaining their attention in a peaceful manner before any teaching could enter the realm of possibility. Something about commanding their attention repulsed her.

Observing most of the other teachers presented no solution. She was bothered by their displays of control. Somehow, their actions never failed to trigger vivid, negative flashbacks centered on Jacob, who had no business invading her world. Tallulah tasted disgust, finding herself at an impasse, unable to see any alternative to either joining the ranks of the abusive adult bosses tied to dastardly Jacob, or kissing the soles of five hundred not-so-small feet that did not hesitate to run over any new teacher if she lacked a clear and monstrous vehicle of control over them. *God knows I do not want to be like Jacob. I will not become what I hate,* she promised herself, wondering how the hell her father managed to infiltrate so much of her identity quest. Every day she fought the internal dilemma of how to control without controlling, while giving the freedom she knew to be essential to self-discovery and positive development. It did not go well; things got messy. Too embarrassed to leave everything to the janitors, she picked up and cleaned up every day.

If the regular teacher remained with the group when they arrived for their art class, the constant threat of chaos settled down to a murmur, with the one or two exceptions being inexperienced teachers whose presence made the situation worse. To her surprise, another novice actually demonstrated less control than Tallulah, quitting before the year was over, while an old-timer decided her students could not handle the freedom Tallulah wanted to give them, and this teacher directed a child to face Tallulah one day to prove her point. Nervous, fearful little Bobby obediently repeated his dismal analysis of the new art teacher's effectiveness: "You are too nice to us."

"There," the regular teacher said, without a glance in the direction of her dismayed colleague. "Let's go, Bobby." The duo marched out of the art room, the class never to return. Tallulah could only wonder what nasty hindrance to Bobby's development had taken root. Her own psychological development dropped a few notches.

Weekly faculty meetings turned Tallulah to stone. As the confirmed adults discussed policies, plans, frustrations, and changes, she scoured her psyche in vain for any evidence to justify her presence among bona fide educators. She could not open her mouth. She still felt very much like a caged, dumb kid, with no more right to be in those meetings than the students who had already escaped for the day. Unfortunately, no one offered the guidance she knew not how to ask for.

Between her weekend shopping trips for supplies, a telephone call to Gregory, who was married, had a baby on the way, and teaching psychology at a junior college, assured her every faculty conglomerate contained its fair share of jerks. Being the new kid on the block, or the new teacher in the classroom, could be counted on to be an adventure, with inevitable ups and downs. *Crazy ones,* she thought. He mentioned his own classroom approach. "I'm throwing Plato at them. It's pretty cool."

"Play Doh? You're throwing Play Doh at your college students? Why would you do that? Do they get to pick a color?"

"Sheesh. I said Play-*toe.* The philosophy guy. You know."

"Ahh. Well. Play Doh sounded like a better solution. I might use it."

"Good luck with the authority figure shit. My students come into class and sit down. "

"Is that what it's called, authority figure shit? It feels more like jackass master, cruel browbeating sewage."

"Yeah. It is that, too."

Jacob held more pride in her teaching position than she did. When Tallulah occasionally stopped by her parents' latest abode, his glances in her direction acquired a spooky, reminiscent smile, as he saw not a daughter, but a deceased sister. His mother had given birth to six boys and one girl, who had grown up to teach school, and passed away early. Tallulah began to think she understood why.

Idalia demonstrated her support by donating an old stack of magazines to her daughter's art classroom. Tallulah appreciated the support until her students discovered pornography among the politics of the day. "Ms. Sheridan, you ought not to give us those kinds of pictures," they told her. She collected the magazines and threw them into the trash dumpster outside. Before long, "Ms. Sheridan, those big boys are crawling all into that dumpster."

Away from embarrassing situations and the frustration of trying to reach kids who needed more than she could give them, she kept an apartment to return to every day, a cat, and a few distant friends. Occasionally, Tony still called or dropped by to spill his affairs with other males past and present. When she couldn't avoid it, Tallulah continued to serve as the neutral, open ear for the muddled guilt contaminating his good heart. The more she encouraged Tony to be himself, the more he illustrated his tales of sexual escapades and bawdy humor. Oh, it was great fun, great fun, but comparable to watching a show; after turning off the television set, the dismalness of her own life stared her in the face. Inertia preserved fragments of her self-awareness, but not much more. Even quiet Leo, another buddy from the prayer meetings, and who people often thought to be her brother because they resembled each other in appearance, didn't offer much of a roar when she gave him the chance.

Having found employment as an accountant with a large company in the area, Leo invited Tallulah on a winter weekend hiking trip up to and along the Appalachian Trail. They lay side by side on a dark Friday night, in cozy sleeping bags inside his tiny, secluded tent, after a four-hour drive. Outside, the still night air held no intention of letting the snow melt. Tomorrow it would crunch under their boots as they reveled in brilliant sunshine and crisp mountain magic. But tonight ... "You know," Leo remarked, looking at the roof, "being out in the woods like this makes me get kind of wild."

"Oh, yeah?" Tallulah grinned, waiting for the wild part of this tame fellow to take over. The next thing she knew, however, sunshine dominated the land and they joined it, casual and friendly, sharing a love for nature and plastic bags of granola. The second night with Leo meowed as well.

Back in the bustle of weekly work, traffic lights prompted Tallulah to admit something had gone seriously haywire. Those hanging colors became fun to zip through as she drove through town, especially right after the red light came on. The perpetual sentinels seemed to challenge her, continuously dangling above, daring her to go past. Several polite police officers lectured her, and she paid one fine before staring in the bathroom mirror, trying to determine what was wrong with her life that would compel her to take such a stupid risk. *Do I want to die?*

"Well, dipstick. Sort it out. Critique it, art class style," she directed herself, sitting alone, staring at the empty walls in her living room one evening. "I don't know how to get any better at my job. I don't know how to keep down the roar in my classroom. I have gained a new respect for teachers who accomplish teaching without going nuts, but I obviously have more to learn, and should probably go to graduate school, somewhere, somehow. As for here and now, living alone endows me with prolific freedom, so it isn't that. I can arrange the furniture in my apartment any old way I desire, without having to share with a roommate, or worry about a sister changing everything, or a brother dumping his belongings in the middle. Everything gets done my way, for once, from meals to television scheduling to picture hanging, and it is good to look around and get acquainted with my preferences."

She stood and walked to the bathroom. The strange creature of solitude staring back at her from the mirror lacked something, even when examined from different perspectives, right tilt, left tilt, a poke in the cheek, and a prod to the nose. "Yuck. I have no sparkle, no spice. Well, I can try fattening up my social life, I guess." Mild-mannered males made safe friends, but the relationships would never bring fireworks to her soul. *All the patience in the world doesn't seem to change my passive pals*, she concluded. *My female friends seem to have no trouble finding someone to screw. They speak glowingly of their sexual adventures. I am running out of reasons not to join them.*

Tallulah turned to her hero of the spirit. "Well, Lord, here we are in another bathroom. You've been with me for a long time now. You're always around when I need you. You have taught me many things, shown me I'm not so smart, sheltered me from harm, comforted me when I needed comforting, directed me when I lost my way, and I love you. I'll always love you, deeply. You will always be a precious part of me, a truth I can never deny. Sometimes your spot is the only warm spot within me. I don't think I could get rid of you if I wanted to. Most of the people I used to share you with have grouped together in a private utopia. Tony still keeps me informed about what everyone is doing, and I care about each one. I also care about my college friends, but college was enough utopia for me. I don't want isolation, religious or intellectual. I've hidden from the real world too much, Lord. What I want is to see your love work in everyday happenings, in common and uncommon folks, where it is most needed. I have felt the power of your love, of your ways, of your work. Real love does not selfishly sit and nourish itself. It reaches out. It creates bonds. It communicates. Your love needs to spread over the Earth; let everyone feel it as I have felt it. I cannot hide any longer. I want reality, Lord. I want to die having faced the real world. Eventually die, that is, not right now.

"I may not succeed. I may never become a competent, functioning asset to society. I feel extremely ineffective, as proven daily by my lovely job. My life may never have meaning. It may never be remembered, but I want to try. I'm tired of living under a rock. I want to be normal. I need to be normal, although there is no normal. I want to have your love become effective with me. I want to follow your will out there in the nasty jungles of the real world, where roads are not paved with goody-goody well-wishes. Please help me, Lord. Please strengthen me. Please be with me.

"There is one more thing, Lord. I love you deeply, but you dwell inside of me. Forgive me, but I want someone of flesh and blood to share my life. I want someone I can touch."

CHAPTER SEVENTEEN

To the creature in the mirror, normal reality at the time meant following the mainstream trend of living with fewer moral restrictions than commonly found in platonic Christian circles, after active participation in these circles had ceased or the façades had fallen. Moral principles remained among individuals who chose to retain them. Tallulah detected no harm in putting aside those restrictions and engaging in a bit of her own exploration. Part of her longed to walk the earth before she flew to the heavens. She wanted to take off her boots and feel the clay and earth squish again between her toes. *To feel in touch with the whole terra firma planet. To feel alive. To feel human. To feel, to feel* .... Mustering her meager threads of courage to face the walls of her apartment, she announced, "Okay, I'm ready. I'm loose. Come and get me, men!"

While she waited for the stampede, weeks later, her youngest brother, Cary, stopped by. He had enrolled in her old college the same time she began teaching. No one had expected this family clown with the low grades to make it to college. When he somehow managed to get accepted and make the housing and financial arrangements, Tallulah felt pleased, although she still did not take him seriously. Unlike her, Cary immediately had acquired a cluster of new friends. He sat down to eat one day in the cafeteria across from someone who resembled his Korean high school pal, and soon found camaraderie within the International Club. According to him, the foreign students and their American friends frequently gathered on weekends to travel to a big city night club for fun, or remained in town and scraped up enough dough for beer and pizza.

As more weeks went by with no rush of hooves, Cary continued to stop by Tallulah's apartment to describe the lively Brazilian guitar player, the sexy French student, and the Hong Kong friend he nicknamed "Grandfather" because of the "deep thoughts" they shared. "They call me Elephant," Cary proudly proclaimed.

"Why on Earth?"

"Because I can eat thirty-two pieces of pizza on buffet night. Thirty-two. I hold the record," he gloated.

On a March evening: "Hey, guess what. They asked me to get my sisters to go with us to the Holiday Inn.

"The Holiday Inn? For what?"

"Dancing. They have live bands. It's fun. So I'm asking. Wanna go?"

"With friends of yours? Gotta think about that one."

Tallulah reluctantly accepted, expecting to have unserious fun with unserious people, at best. Her stampede of risqué invitations had failed to materialize, and, at least for one evening, she hoped to forget about obstreperous classes guaranteed to disintegrate into pandemonium with the slightest slack in traditionally crude reins of domination, and the plethora of art never taught by a neophyte babysitter/goddamn janitor. She smiled and danced often during the carefree evening; she needed to.

A few days later, Cary telephoned her. They spoke of how much fun the night had been until he abruptly changed the tone of the conversation. "Grandfather has been sort of sick since that night," he said.

"Oh? What's wrong with him?" Tallulah asked, alarmed.

"He says he has a fever."

"A fever? That doesn't sound good. Has he been over to the health clinic yet?"

"Nope. It's not that kind of fever."

"Not that kind of fever? What kind is it?".

"Grandfather calls it Tallulah fever," Cary said.

"Tallulah fever? What are you talking about?"

"The uh, well, the fever of uh, love, he says. And he wants to know if he can call you."

"What? Is this one of your corny jokes, Cary? I'm gonna kill you if it is."

"No, no, I'm serious. He's serious. He likes you, I swear."

"Oh, come on. This isn't funny. A bit early for April Fools." Cary could come up with the dumbest pranks.

"I'm not joking, honest. He wants to know if he can call you. He told me to ask. You think I'd make up something like this?"

"Yes."

"All right, just humor me then. Come on, can he call you or not?"

"Sure he can call me. Anybody can. I'm here. Let me pull out my little black book and check my appointment list."

"Okay, I'm serious now. I'm going to tell him you said he can call, and he will. You'll see. Bye."

"You're nuts."

Tallulah had danced with Grandfather more times than anyone else during the evening, and when she had tried to sit, he had pulled her back up for more. The fellow smiled a lot, but didn't say much. She remembered thinking he looked like a choir boy when they were introduced. Anyone who could put up with sloppy Cary and his callous humor couldn't be too bad, and this buddy must be older, with some brains, if he was studying for a Master's degree, as Cary had mentioned.

She decided to be a good sport and give Grandfather a chance. *What the heck.*

Grandfather's name turned out to be Jay. On their first date, they spent two hours watching Richard Dreyfuss and Marsha Mason fight like tigers before *The Good-bye Girl* managed to settle into domestic harmony. After the movie, Jay bought a chocolate bar to share as they walked across campus. When part of it fell to the grass, Tallulah quickly picked it up and brushed it off, noticing the lack of a disapproving frown from Jay.

Over the next few weeks, Jay made his moves quicker than any true grandfather could. He soon said he loved her and spoke of forever. Tallulah said thank you and she had no plans for forever. Actually, she needed time to catch up. She thought about it. *Somebody likes me. Somebody really likes me. I don't believe it. Somebody loves me? I must be dreaming. Oh, my gosh. Astonishing! Frightening! Why am I being such a nitwit about this?*

During the following weeks, a great door manifested itself in front of Tallulah. She knew not where it would lead, but it did stand mighty beautiful, she had to admit. A glorious portal, trimmed with fresh, colorful flowers, bright with warm promise, scented with an elegant aroma, soft to the touch. This was her door. Could she trust it? Of course not. Jacob's rug-pulling shenanigans had obliterated her innate trust. She needed to reach higher, finding the one proven plateau providing solid ground, allowing her to take one safe step at a time. Thoughts flowed: *This is my gift from a graceful God, who has stayed closer to me than I ever expected him to. This is my door, and I have the honor of going through it, if I choose to do so.*

With the exception of her free will, nothing became more important to her than her relationship to this new person. The value of each day became directly proportionate to the amount of time spent with Jay. Quite often, she wanted to grab this person and shove him deep into her pocket, not trusting the alluring hints of romance and fantasy floating around their heads. *Too time-consuming. They never lead to anything but disappointment, anyway.* The diamond sparkle of sunshine upon his wavy ebony hair would have to wait to be glorified another day. *"What else do I see?"* she asked herself, seeking the scrap of logic she should probably look for.

Using her art-trained eye, she gradually perceived in Jay tidbits of everyone she had ever loved: hair reminiscent of Roger's, patience evocative of Tony, the bright eyes and mature quietness of her art professors, but Jay's steps came toward her instead of heading for the hills from an elevator. Simultaneously, he held a distinct identity uniquely his own, making other relationships seem trivial; they dropped to the wayside. She found she could talk and be herself around him, and he didn't even run away. *How different.*

In the summer, Jay presented a bottle of champagne to celebrate her birthday, and a most wonderful discovery fluttered down from heaven above. After consuming not even one half-glass of the sparkly stuff, his satiny face began to acquire the strangest red glow. His arms and neck began metamorphosing into a mottle of red spots. Tallulah's eyes widened in alarm. "Allergic," he explained.

"Allergic? Allergic to what?" she asked, looking around the room for the likely cause. Dust? She wasn't the greatest housekeeper. Feathers?

"Alcohol."

"Alcohol? What? You are allergic to alcohol? Really? I've never heard of anyone being allergic to alcohol. Will it get worse? Do we need to go to the hospital?"

"No. It goes away in a few minutes."

"By itself?"

"By itself."

And it did, pulling Tallulah into a new realm of realizations. A door within a door? More like a gift being chunked down in front of her. He had shared a drink with her, well aware of his inevitable, unpleasant, physical reaction. She felt touched by the sacrifice, really she did, but, more significantly, she could not help being delighted with the news. A frisson of excitement tingled her spine. "Wow, this is great. You are really allergic to booze? You can't drink it? How cool. This means you can never become an alcoholic. Fantastic! I can't believe it. Yippee!" Heaven and its angels had showered Tallulah with a custom-made insurance policy beyond her imagination, a guarantee this man would never become a drunken nightmare disaster like her father. It crushed her dread of the psychology textbook's prophecy. *What a relief. Way to go, God.*

Of course, there existed no guarantees as to what he would become, but she held no dreams to come true or fall short, because she had no dreams, and no goals. Tallulah held fast to her determination to not repeat the mistakes her parents had made. She did not want her life to turn out like theirs. She could wade through rough times if she had to, because she knew she carried blessings from above. Whatever direction her road took, it looked like she had found someone willing to walk beside her into the forever fog. A month later they spoke of forever.

"Are you sure?" he asked.

"I'm not sure of anything," she replied, smiling, "but let's give it a go."

Not everyone shared their courage. On the Fourth of July, the couple joined the masses to be awed by the town's evening fireworks. Among the crowd, Jay recognized one of his sponsoring teachers for international students. Dr. Vaughn lounged on the grass with his family, and Jay strolled over to share his happy news of engagement with them. In a few moments, Tallulah strolled over to join them, listening. Instead of offering congratulations, Mrs. Vaughn was asking Jay when his visa expired. "Next June," he dutifully replied.

"Oh, well, you don't really have to get married until then do you," she concluded, with the emphasis on "have to." Her insinuation did not sink in until later, when the smiling couple discussed it. A disappointed Jay realized Mrs. Vaughn fell short of being a friend.

A week later, they invited a student friend of Jay's to dinner at Tallulah's apartment. He brought his wife, and they spoke of their missionary work in South America. When the subject of Jay and Tallulah's engagement came into focus, the guests spoke about how very long they had been acquainted before they had married. "When you find out you really can't live without each other, that's the time to think about getting married," the friend told them, without a smile, still eating Tallualh's pasta. Neither he nor his wife came any closer to offering words of congratulations.

Tallulah tried her friends, telephoning an old roommate, whose first question was, "Well, have you slept with him yet?"

Taken aback, Tallulah laughed. "Is that a requirement?" The old friend seemed to think so, but Tallulah had no intention of yielding to interrogation. "That's the easy part," she replied, shortening the conversation, and her list of phone calls to make. Tony stopped by, responding to the news with, "Yeah, that's cool. Let me tell you about my lover." She shook her head after he left moments later.

Subtle snubs from new acquaintances helped the couple adjust their expectations. At a party, Jay and Tallulah met a recently married couple who seemed friendly. After a good chat, they parted with a casual invitation from the man, "Ya'll come see us sometime."

Jay and Tallulah both said, "Sure, we'd love to."

"Okay, be seeing ya." He waved as he and his wife turned to walk down the road to their car.

"Did they tell you where they live?" Tallulah asked Jay.

"Nope."

"They didn't tell me, either."

Jay wrote to his family back in Hong Kong, only to receive a long, angry letter from his father, who insisted: This kind of interracial marriage will never work. Disappointed, Tallulah and Jay did not see the differences between them as being as problematic as they seemed to appear to other people. The couple noticed only similarities, such as the love of things natural and real as opposed to the superficial and phony. Shrugging off the scarcity of support, they went ahead and discussed wedding plans with the priest in a local Catholic church Jay occasionally attended. The simplest ceremony would cost six hundred dollars, the old priest informed them. He also said in the meantime they would be inviting him over to Tallulah's apartment for dinner; he needed to test her cooking skills. At this point, the couple readily perceived the bullshit, thanked the priest, and dropped the church route as an option. Between them, they didn't have the money for it anyway. After buying art supplies for her students, Tallulah had splurged on presents for her family, and Jay's only income trickled in from a graduate assistantship.

Placing aside hopes for endorsement, choosing instead to expand their universe, positive Jay suggested they use their free time to hit the road. Simple enough, so she thought. Tallulah considered the idea with high hopes, and good vibes, but, once again, Jacob's abominations flared up from hell, uninvited, as soon as she sat in the passenger seat. Tension engulfed her body. Perhaps the adultness of the situation froze her into the conditioned combatant, ready for battle; something did. Getting in a car, hearing the ignition, eyes forward, triggered a predetermined, blind thrust of a mission to capture the destination. Neither hell nor high water nor any child who needed to pee would justify a stop along the way. Why Jay even wanted to do this, she suddenly could not fathom, but she soldiered up. However, before bladders even had a chance to fill, she found herself saying, "Why are you stopping? We're not there yet. Is something wrong with the car?"

"I want to read this historical marker."

"Historical marker?" Tallulah groaned. *Why did I let him drive? This is not the way to travel.* He kept doing it. Bit by bit, with Jay stopping at tiny historical sites, scenic parks, and local museums, Tallulah began discarding the now-useless cannonballs of angst she carried, often wrenching her familiar old ingots from their rusty barrels, slowly. She even ventured forth from the car, sometimes. "Stopping again?" she asked, her voice angry, then relaxing, "Oh, okay, good. Stopping again." For the next few weeks, Grandfather began to introduce her to her own country, starting with a visit to the hometown of the President of the United States.

Plains, Georgia, presented minimal variation from the other small towns she had already endured too many times, but, seeing it with Jay, it acquired something of a tolerable personality. A low-budget drive to an overpriced amusement park in Florida followed. The free monuments and museums of Washington, D.C. presented a more appealing significance. Brimming as they did with knowledge and inspiration, these rich giants succeeded in re-defining the dismal turn her employment road had taken, reminding her of the insignificance of her conundrums, as well as her fortunate history among the verdant gardens of academia as a plethora of resources readily available, not to be cast aside, instead to be utilized as a key to many doors, requiring more initiative from her than showing up for class and following instructions. Appreciation made an additional appearance in the form of Jay's insensitivity to her sensitivity, allowing her traditionally frigid cell of automobile travel to become comfortably warmer.

Near the end of the summer, a delayed decision became easier to address. Looking back, she had begun to trot along a potential career path only to be yanked by a leash she hadn't known she wore. Nauseated by the thought of a mental connection to her putrid father apparently bridling her behavior, contaminating her free will, Tallulah disqualified herself. She had no right to ferment chaos in the lives of children. Not even creativity justified the absence of qualified preparation. She had failed to pass on to her students how the glory of a waterfall could be hiding in the wrinkled sleeve of an elbow, failed to uncover the rich sublime sparkle possessed by every human being, failed to present perception as a key to comprehending their very own world, and failed to convince them of how different perspectives from different angles increased the humanity of the entire planet. Vehemently opposed to wallowing in any mired mental muck related to the repulsive Jacob, she chose to ignore the authority figure shit, leaving the job to a qualified art teacher. When the final paycheck showed up in her mailbox, Tallulah looked around town for simpler means of employment, while Jay continued with his classes.

A printing company hired her to work in the paste-up room for minimum wage. She arrived on time every morning to arrange images and text on brochures and flyers. After a few months, the busy season passed, but Tallulah's younger, high-school-graduate supervisor made it known she carried an unrelenting prejudice against "college girls," despite Tallulah's lack of experience and quiet, unthreatening manner. One morning, this supervisor moved beyond muttering to convince the shop's manager to hand Tallulah a final paycheck. Speaking privately to the targeted college girl, the manager fumbled with a flimsy explanation and apologized for things somehow not working out. Tallulah pitied him, realizing it was only personal politics which had not worked out. She had never meant to be a threat to anyone, floating through her time spent there, her mind focused more on Jay than an insecure supervisor having her own insurmountable insecurity obstacle of God knows what. Getting fired still hurt.

CHAPTER EIGHTEEN

Back in the parental world, Jacob encountered his own employment problems. He had been selling flat, magnetic signs designed to be slapped onto the doors of automobiles. For months, family members had been listening to him crow about his smart, generous, fair, good buddy of a boss. When the roller coaster reached its summit, predictably, it headed down. Overnight, the boss man morphed into a worthless, cheating, lying, no-good son-of-a-bitch. As Idalia maintained, it was usually an attractive, virtuous woman who transformed into untouchable trash if she refused Jacob's sexual advances, but, not to be left out, bosses, too, could slide down the ladder stupendously fast if they did not give Magnificent Man whatever he wanted, usually more money. Predictably, Jacob quit his job. This time he decided to create a competitive facsimile.

The impatient beast couldn't set up a three-foot sign press in his garage to start modest and logical. Nope. His emotional majesty hankered for the limelight, and before Idalia had time to think, she had thrown to the wind her steady retail job to become his receptionist, bookkeeper, and manager of a downtown space soon filled with everything needed except customers, those incidentals yet to be persuaded into existence. A table-size magnetic sign press glorified the back room of the former dry cleaners, with several lime-lighted portable signs bearing changeable letters set up in the reception area for good measure.

After being fired from the printing company, Tallulah's confidence in herself as a valuable employee took the typical downward dip, especially after several local interviews proved fruitless. Even K-Mart turned her down for a simple sales position because "teachers usually go back to teaching." She assured them one year had been enough, but did their ears connect to their brains?

"No, no, you're a teacher."

"I'm not a teacher."

"Yes, you are."

"I'm not a teacher; I don't have an education degree."

"You're a teacher. We don't want to hire you."

Jacob held no objection to hiring someone plastered with the label of teacher. Eager to brag about having his college-teacher-daughter working for him, he offered to pay Tallulah a smidgen over minimum wage to operate the sign press in his new shop, and she succumbed, soon finding herself acquiring inky fingers and playing audience to bickering parents. The two argued daily, with Jacob spending money before he collected it, insisting they "think big and fly high!" while Idalia mumbled about maintaining contact with the earth beneath their feet.

"Can't you wait until you have a deposit from the customer before you order the material?" Idalia asked, repeatedly.

"Hell, no! Call in that order to the manufacturer right now, damn it. We got to get moving on this. It means big money for us," Jacob insisted.

"But what if the customer changes his mind? You still have to pay for the material. Those big panels are expensive. We haven't paid for the last order yet."

"God, woman. How can you be so lame-brained? That old boy ain't gonna change his mind. Just do as I say. I'm the boss now. Quit trying to work against me."

But that old boy customer did change his mind, as did many, once released from the clutches of a salesman's persuasive aura. Jacob would curse everything in sight when reality derailed his aspirations, but he never learned not to trust the initial thrill of excitement conjoined to the possibility of a sale. The magical scent of money erased all caution.

Sometimes Tallulah wondered if the man had air pockets in his brain. Near the reception area at the front of his sign shop, he maintained a private office area for himself. Plywood walls stood at a height of eight feet, leaving four feet of empty space above them, resulting in much of the shop noise making its way into his sanctuary, or maybe too many of his frequent telephone conversations traveling out to unintended ears. One day, Tallulah noticed the addition of two foam indented rectangles of used packing material for something about the size of a boom box. These white chunks had been attached to one of the walls inside his office, occupying space most people reserve for a scenic picture or two. She asked him why those foam things were stuck up there. "That stuff absorbs sound. Fella told me that's what they use to line telephone booths." She tried to imagine sound waves zeroing in on those white masses, but somehow the image eluded every realm of possibility.

As much as she wished to subdue her raging soul with tolerance, it bothered her greatly to still feel susceptible to the tentacles of his nervous energy, and the power they held to permeate any opposition to stress in proportion to his proximity, like an indefatigable osmosis she could not shake off. His regular attendance at Alcoholics Anonymous meetings kept him mostly sober, but he continued to smoke cigarettes like a maniac, cared about nothing but money, and was incapable of sitting for more than ten minutes unless chained in place by the telephone. The cloud of discernable tension enveloping him evaporated from the shop every time he went out the front door, leaving Tallulah and Idalia to breathe and share a moment of peace.

The income paid her bills, and driving home to be with a loving, calm person proved to be an essential daily relief. Jay came to accept his friends' and family's disapproval as something he could live with by setting it aside. The woman from Canada and the man from Georgia offered no objections to Jay, and Tallulah did not seek their approval. For the time being, she could tolerate the workday tension as something separate from the peaceful life she chose for herself. She had no need to bring home the garbage; it no longer polluted vulnerable young lives. Her two worlds remained safely isolated from each other, her naive brain deduced.

Tallulah and Jay used the end of his semester to make a trip to the courthouse, where they encountered an unexpectedly kind, old judge who presented them with his unique approach to discouraging slap-happy hitches. He persuaded particular couples of his choosing to delay their immediate wishes by returning the following evening and allowing him to perform the court ceremony at his private house. Apparently, Tallulah and Jay met his criteria, and obliged. With his wife serving as the witness, smiling as she played something romantic on the piano, the judge spoke his words, provided them with a license, a printed list of marriage dos and don'ts, took a photo, and wished them good luck. They appreciated the gracious beginning.

Nonetheless, doubt had its way of creeping in. The musty hats of traditional marriage slowly dropped with clunks upon their individual heads. For the first few weeks, everything seemed hunky-dory in their new apartment, including daily tasks. Tallulah cooked and cleaned as usual, not minding the extra laundry, not minding the additional dishes left in the sink, trying to maintain the obliging attitude she had adopted before donning the official headdress of marriage. The thing was, that same headdress landed on each of their heads. Love acquiescing to expectations might be sweet for a time, but it melts like sugar, quickly, easily. She noticed an increase in her chores, but said nothing about the lack of an equivalent increase in his. Jay came and went as usual, studying, attending classes, acquiring odd jobs, doing minimal housework.

In late winter, she dreamed of being showered with flowers. Light and lovely, they floated down to land in the palm of her hand, each one consisting of the same pale blue color, each one perfectly symmetrical, each one forming a tidy, conventional quadrate of petals, oddly familiar. She looked up to see a darkening cloud as their source. The pretty things continued to rain in a steady pattern, each equally distant from its neighbors. As she watched, their softness began to harden, and they steered away from her outstretched hand. They began flicking her head, top and sides. "Ouch. Stop that. Go away. Just a dumb dream," she mumbled as she awoke, appreciating the warm body beside her.

While washing dishes in the evenings, she began hearing a strange whisper in her ears, a creaking noise, hardly noticeable. At first, she ignored it, until she looked down once or twice to see the hazy image of a strange old box sitting on the floor. "Where'd you come from?" she asked, never expecting a reply. She watched the lid lift as slim, snickering snakes emerged, sliding along until one of them began wrapping itself around her immobile ankles, giving a squeeze, triggering red-flag memories of her mother washing dishes, always Mom washing the dishes, never Jacob washing the dishes. Succeeding snake squeezes flashed similar memories, endless scenes of laundry, taking out trash, every type of cleaning, always performed by Idalia, never by Jacob. Never.

Her brain could not avoid making the connections; it began working like a machine to gather empirical evidence. *If Jay does not wash the dishes, it can only mean he expects me to do them. He expects this! He expects me to wash all the dishes. He expects me to perform every menial chore of housework, like laundry and cooking and making the goddamn beds and dusting the stupid furniture, and I will get stuck in the monotony, swallowed alive by snakes! I will become stupid, and boring, an aproned asshole, his shadow, and, oh, God, it happened to my mother and tons of other women, just by being sweet and "nice." Didn't I avoid dropping into hell by marrying a man who could never become an alcoholic? What is this garbage?*

In addition to the busy brain gears, a weird sense of belonging winked at her from the sidelines, welcoming her. Not only could she find acceptance within a group of good women who understood her woes, another facet of the sly invitation spoke in her head: *Join us. Jump in. This is what all wives do. Later on, perhaps you can free Idalia and all the other women, be their hero. Sure, honey. They will love and adore you forever and ever.* She could hear the snickering. *Oh, sure,* she retorted. *Just like I rescued Idalia and my young brothers by drifting away in a balloon basket. Just like I rescued all of my art students from the suffocation of a pigeon-hole system. Do I have some kind of Moses complex?*

An image of herself with flailing arms, reaching skyward but unable to fly, stumbling feet scrambling atop the snake-covered paddles of a giant waterwheel, endlessly churning boiling molecules, each composed of twice as many hydrogen as oxygen atoms, floated before her eyes. Hot tears fell.

Jay asked, "What's wrong?" In swooped Mighty Mouse, ready to save the day, poised high in the air. Tallulah wiped her face, vaguely wishing he could make it easy for her, fly down, grab her and proclaim,

"Oh, my precious darling! Your pain is my pain. Allow me to share it, I beg of you!"

"Nothing," his young wife lied, and the male mere human walked away, believing her.

As the weeks progressed, the snakes deposited Tallulah into a coffin, her mother's coffin, long nails hammered through the walls. Tortured tradition wreaked havoc upon her wobbly, undefined contemporary concepts, like a newborn calf facing an old bull. Bible verses depicting her role as a clinging vine did not help. Hell on earth radiated from the stupid wife hat glued to her head.

At the same time, her safe, separating bridge between employment and home began to creak and sway. Daily witnessing of verbal battles between the married people whose sperm and ovaries and hormones had conspired to land her on this planet began to irritate the heck out of her. Tallulah inadvertently brought home the battles, tentacles infiltrating her own, unguarded arena. She began arming herself with defensive weapons against her own married man, leaking out her old anger, the hate, the rage, fueled by her new fears of suffocation.

She confronted Jay, slim threads of academically-acquired identity keeping her from dropping completely into the boiling pit, but not from reflecting its rising heat. "Why don't *you* take out the garbage? Why don't *you* wash the dishes!? Why don't *you* mop the floor?"

However, Jay harbored his own demons. They danced in a world other than alcoholism, and they awoke. Until then, he had appeared to step easily into the role of husband, the traditional role of authority, too easily. And why not? However, Tallulah's revolt triggered a link to his past. He argued back without thinking, without magically discerning her underlying cry for help and rescue, instead insisting, "You can't tell me what to do! I am busy doing other things! Marriage isn't supposed to be like this. My mother never told my father to help with cleaning around the house."

And on it went, until her words sounded too much like her mother's and Jay sounded like Jacob, or, more likely, another man made of the same cloth, and Tallulah realized she had met his father. Jay's parents lived on the other side of the globe, but something had transported them into the kitchen of a couple of newlyweds in the U.S.A., and they manifested themselves as the same dominant man-monster and submissive woman-zombie as Jacob and Idalia. Tallulah looked at Jay's face during their arguments, and she perceived a deeply entrenched pain readily kindled by selfish emotional outbursts, a far cry from any avenue of logical resolution. The battles accomplished nothing.

So she spit out her frustrations in the old spiral notebook: *What do you want from me, you MAN you? You lead and I follow? You talk and I listen? You think and I agree? You say and I obey? No way! No way! No way! No way! I cannot die in order for you to live. I don't believe I have to. I have learned from my God, real strength lies in truth. The truth is, I have feelings. You have feelings. I have thoughts. You have thoughts. I have ideas. You have ideas. I am alive. You are alive. I have value. You have value. I need to respect myself as much as you need to respect yourself. If I can top off my life with your respect, that's even better. I see you at times suddenly becoming another person, saying things you do not mean, with an anger I do not deserve, reacting without the love which bonds us, and I suppose I have met your old man, although oceans separate me from him.*

Why do we have so much garbage within us? I wanted our marriage to be fresh and clean and beautiful. Instead, I fly at you with a self-defense system shutting out everything else. Words and expressions come to my mind and leak out of lips not entirely mine, all too familiar to me, and I see my mother defending herself from my chauvinistic pig of a father. Dear and Darling, where art thou? Don't I even get a pearl necklace? Lies lies lies! Marriage is shit. It reeks of crappy double standards. Tradition slithers and torments me. This is not the direction I want to go in. I have a brain! To lose the ground I gained will be to lose my life, and I will fall backward, into Idalia's pit of despair and frustration no one can climb out of. Here I teeter.

Entangled in a bizarre conundrum, Tallulah stepped back to critique herself, like a painting in her old art class. Somehow, *some crazy goddamn fucking somehow,* something in her pathetic brain presumed Jay would be a rerun of Jacob after all, her father's influence permeating her expectations by equating one husband's behavior with another, old traumas popping up, barging in uninvited. But at the same time, part of her expected him to be Mighty Mouse coming to her rescue. She wouldn't have minded. *What is wrong with me? Why am I so fucked up?* she demanded, quietly, of herself. *One thing I will not do is to sweep this shit under a rug and pretend it doesn't exist. No, leave it in the open. Face it. Ugly is okay.*

Vaguely recalling something called "free will," she decided to do house chores only when and if she chose to, not because she "had to," or was "supposed to," grasping the despicable feeling of obligation by the throat, throttling it, flinging it to a distant dungeon, slamming the door, turning the key. Her free will she placed upon a golden throne, complete with doves fluttering above, and a goddamn tight seatbelt.

Her friend, the spiral journal, recorded her spirals. *Our marriage would be easy if we were both realistic, mature, sensitive people. But we still carry years of youth, and the crappy impressions absorbed during those vulnerable years. Perhaps we would not need each other as much if we had conquered perfection. I suppose we must grow up together, and allow each other the space to do it in, somehow.*

One evening, after the tears and anger, with the wisdom befitting a young sage of the old Orient, Jay shared a thought, "Marriage is like two rough stones, tossed against each other until the sharp edges wear down, and each stone becomes smooth and beautiful. Let's keep trying."

"Ouch," she replied.

Tallulah had her doubts, but with obligation incarcerated and free will consecrated, she stood her ground as psychological warden, not trusting herself, and not trusting any behavior or words resembling noxious Jacob. In her journal, she told Jay: *Marriage is a minefield, where any careless step can bring disaster. You're ready to float through it; I have to know exactly where I'm stepping and why, and you are not going to rescue me, probably not even understand my predicament, but I still wish you would. Can we remember to talk to each other? Can we remember to listen to each other? Can we set aside those vile expectations collected subconsciously throughout our young years? Can we concentrate on the present, on each other, on what's actually before us? Can we build a loving life together?*

For the first time, Tallulah felt the imminent need to define her expectations, first stomping the old inherited ones, then somehow begin the process of molding new ones into existence, taking deliberate steps to equip herself for the journey ahead, accruing her tools to sculpt a realistic marriage onto the armature of her future. In one hand, she held the totally fake image of Dear and Darling Harmony and the too-quiet wives. In the other hand, she held the screaming disaster of Idalia shackled to the unsound Jacob. She remembered Idalia's motto: *Having something is better than having nothing.* And responded to it: *Well, Mom, I'm not so sure.*

She sought no bridge between the two extremes; she wanted to fling them both into a distant galaxy, but possessed no substitute. Consequently, she did as Idalia had claimed to do with Jacob long ago: she kept both handfuls with her, as identified monstrosities locked into cells, to keep an eye on, to live with and guard against, so they couldn't sneak in one night and shoot everybody.

Do healthy alternatives float somewhere between a fake heaven and an undeniable hell? She scribbled. *Both scenarios twist and distort communication. I confess to be ignorant and inexperienced in any healthy equivalent, but I can be honest. Can I be me again, and you be you? Can we wait for a reaction instead of anticipating it? Don't tell me my thoughts. Don't tell me my feelings. You don't know them. Don't tell me who or what I'm "supposed to" be. Damn the "supposed tos."*

I love you. You love me. Let's clear the clutter from our love before it is choked by crappy old weeds. Don't wrap me with those weeds, and I won't wrap you. I don't want our marriage to be a rerun of someone else's marriage. I don't want my life to be a rerun of someone else's. I have struggled for years to find myself, and I'll be damned if I'm going to get lost now.

She could stomp and curse and rebel against the old ways she knew too well, but when the moment came to replace garbage with a positive form, she possessed nada, as blank as an actor forgetting her lines. The horizon before them lay broad and empty, with no markers to guide them, no role models to follow, piles of mistakes behind them, and only their hearts to lead them. Tallulah shook her head with the realization: *The oldest trail in the world must be re-blazed. God help us.* She preferred a road map.

CHAPTER NINETEEN

Carefully, very gradually, Tallulah pulled herself up and out of the coffin, realizing she needed to teach herself to call upon the honesty and truth rooted in her God, to flick herself in the head from time to time, to remember the genuine love she felt for Jay, instead of playing stupid performance roles rotted with time, devoid of anything good. She owned tools; cognitive resources had been acquired. Most sat in the pages of dusty textbooks waiting to be picked up. Others required the raising of eyelids, allowing light to pass through the pupils, hit the lenses, and make its way to the receptive retinas. Awareness could bring pleasant surprises, as in seeing a bona fide change in the images transmitted from the box containing her old Dear and Darling.

The *All in the Family* television show grabbed her attention with its honest portrayal of a dysfunctional family dominated by an angry bigot. "Wow, that actually looks familiar," said she, applauding the realism, deeply encouraged by it. Finally, she who had always followed others, now pushed herself onto center stage, appearing clothed in rags, naked in experience, holding no script." Somehow, I will try to act from the heart, and try to do what I do out of genuine love, because I have free will, because I choose to do so. My actions shall not be plagued with 'supposed to,' or 'that's just the way we do things,' or, God forbid, 'that's how my parents did it,'" she promised herself. Such pledges arrived none too soon.

Jay wanted to have a baby. Tallulah thought about it. She harbored no wishful imaginings of finding personal fulfillment in motherhood. Neither could she claim dynamic career plans bound to be ruined by a dependent tyke in diapers. As a result, the possibility of having a baby stood as no big deal to her. "We can give it a try. After all, conception may take months, or years, or may not even be possible for us. Who can tell?"

They found out. Before she had time to contemplate the deeper pros and cons of parenthood, within weeks a home pregnancy test showed positive results. Without asking for her permission, Tallulah's digestive system began rabble-rousing, as if responding to a stage director in the gridiron above, who, having caught her standing idle, and deciding to call for action, tossed down a rolled parchment for the slow brain. Hey, you. Lazybones! Yeah you, Socrates. Here's your script, stupid. It's called "life." Live it!

The stage director must have flipped a switch as well. A most primordial, elemental form of gestation began to set the scene. Time of day as well as meal content commanded her obedience. Forget sleeping late; any attempt at breakfast after nine a.m. met literal rejection. Onions, spices, and chocolate became banished from the realm of acceptable edibles, as demanded by the decrees of her rebellious stomach, "Throw them out! Throw them out! Throw them out, out, out of my kingdom!"

As milk, cheese, vegetables, and vitamins invaded their refrigerator and entered her oral portcullis, shoving their way past off-guard, silenced taste buds, and Tallulah's autonomous belly swelled into dictatorship, booties and bassinets joined the mutiny. If she happened to find herself in a department store with her eyelids open, pupils, lenses and retinas conspired to zoom in the direction of those itty-bitty ruffled pink and blue garments clustered in their own retail universe. Her complicit feet followed. She looked, she touched, and she wondered how such a small human creature could incite such a comprehensive digestive riot in an adult human.

Hormones and emotions pranced in what would be a nine-month heyday of freedom for them, paying minor heed to any puny cognitive guidance. With the slightest invitation, tears fell in joy or sadness, whichever lay at hand. Serious conversation with other people, and even with herself, took second place to caring for the promise of life growing inside her body. Protective instincts arose, warning of the danger in continuing to tolerate the two people who paid her salary, even if they were related to her.

With Jacob and Idalia bickering in her ear throughout the day, shaping a marriage on uncontaminated principles while simultaneously building a nest of peace and safety proved to be about as easy as building a sandcastle on the beach in the rain. The principle of honoring thy father and mother, coupled with lingering dreams of extending lifelines of something or other to combat the turmoil of their dysfunctional influences, pulling everyone to safe shores, conflicted with an itch to get away, get away, get away from them.

The letter helped her decide. She received a response from Gregory, to whom she had written weeks earlier, seeking his coping-strategy advice. Unceasingly, this first son sought to analyze the two people who had brought him into this world, but only from a distance. He could make jokes when he spoke, but when he took pen in hand, it was as if the house fire still smoldered within, its embers destined to never be extinguished. He wrote:

My days in the Army gave me confidence enough to face an opponent, taught me the value of having supportive buddies, people I could rely upon and who relied upon me, how a team can work well to resolve conflict, especially if guided by someone who knows what he's doing, and appreciates the value of every human being on this beautiful planet, instead of being so fucking insecure he has to step on people.

When I got out, I embraced the peace and love shared by many good people. I tried to put the inevitable trauma of combat behind me. Going back to Jacob and Idalia was like a passage through hell: no love, no peace. Nothing but constant battles. They are stuck in a cycle of self-destruction, one being a fucking egomaniacal jackass and the other a dependant mouse. I have tried to talk some sense into them, but they don't listen, and they don't want to change, either not seeing the shit they spread, or seeing it and embracing it.

I had to get the fuck away from those two. My advice to you would be to stop wasting your energy on them. You can't change people who don't want to change, and you can't rescue mice who don't want to be rescued. I'm glad you found some space for expression in my old bedroom. More importantly, congratulations on the promise of new life within. Protect it. We try to keep our bambino away from contaminants, especially the human ones, and it's therapeutic to watch him grow in peace and love.

Good luck,
Gregory

His acrimonious perspective prompted an examination of her parents in a harsher light than usual. She could not deny the truth in his depiction of them as wandering in circles, moving in a cycle of perpetual animosity. Neither would ever change. For some unfathomable reason, both embraced adversity, rollicking in the fight, rolling over their children like dough under the pin.

While the man and woman rattled in disagreement over an order a few days later, Tallulah walked out of their sign shop for lunch, never to return as an employee. Tears rolled down her face as she and her belly drove back to Jay and sanity, but big brother's description of Jackass and Mouse helped to steer her away from two people she genuinely feared duplicating. Jackass and Mouse. The verdict tore into her heart, but her eyes brought into focus the abyss, the nothingness between Jacob's chronically monstrous schemes catapulting into the pecuniary sky, and Idalia's grasping foot-paws mired in the earth, repeatedly revealing levels of steadfast sadness. Bearing the bruises from her last metaphorical canyon, and yielding to the precious dynamics of new life left Tallulah in no condition to wander into that chasm, with no fiber for weaving her heart and soul into a sacrificial bridge across it.

Jacob telephoned when she failed to return. He refrained from using the rage and fury he would usually dump upon an insubordinate child. Tallulah stood as a college graduate, another man's wife, an employee, and soon-to-be mother. He chose his words carefully. "You're not sick, are you?"

"Nope."

"We thought you'd gone down to the house for a bite to eat. And you didn't come back, and your mother here got a little worried."

"I'm not coming back."

"How about tomorrow?"

"Nope."

"Well, I'm sorry to hear that. We hate to lose you. You're better at that sign press than anyone else. Is there something that made you think you couldn't work here anymore?"

"The fighting." She exhaled, not allowing any more tears, detesting the traitorous trembles her body wept with.

"The fighting? Oh, you mean me and your mother? Aw, heck, we thought you were used to that by now."

"Used to it? No, I'll never be used to it."

"Well, it's nothing. So you think you won't be coming back then?"

"I won't."

"Guess I'll have to find a new press man, then. You and Jay don't forget where we live, now. You'll still drop by, won't you?"

"We'll still visit."

"Okey-dokey then. We'll be seeing you."

Having stood her wobbly ground, she hung up. Apparently, the fighting was nothing to Jacob, a mere eerie, unbelievable sinkhole of dysfunctional normalcy sucking the breath out of everyone else in his vicinity.

Even more determined to keep away from her father's insanity, Tallulah pursued new employment. After several job interviews, she learned not to mention she was pregnant, and wore loose clothing. Finally, the manager of a pint-size clothing store hired her for a full-time, permanent position. Two months later, when he worked near enough to catch the sound of her vomiting in the back restroom, a confession emerged. He said, "I thought so," with no hint of empathy, no forgiving grin. She knew she had deceived him, indirectly, and he could fire her if he chose to, but she did not mention the subject again, and neither did he, replacing his usual smile with a frown of resentment every time he allowed his eyes to travel in her direction. *So what.* Having been perched forever on the outskirts of conventional popularity, Tallulah impenitently accepted one more person's regard of the clumsiness of her journey into adulthood, a place permeated with sinkholes. Focusing instead on a horizon of glorious possibilities, she moved forward as best she could, needing the money.

Actually, her enlarging belly made conversation easy with customers. Many other people were pregnant, or knew someone who was, and they loved to chat about it. Grins came easily, except from her offended manager. He and those in the field of professional health services appeared to be the only ones who did not approve of her condition.

In addition to hoping for a glimmer of empathy from her employer, Tallulah made the mistake of expecting sympathy from people who had chosen medicine for their careers. Between Jay's part-time jobs and her minimum-wage fling with clothing sales, they qualified for the government's Women-Infants-Children program, which greatly discounted medical care during pregnancy, and provided coupons for appropriate food, but also carried a stigma. Tallulah held no qualms about receiving help from the federal government; the government had helped feed Idalia's children during the numerous times Jacob's dreams flipped and crashed. College funding had stemmed totally from the government. But this was different.

In the months of examination and testing, Tallulah never adjusted to the iciness of people who chose not to display the compassion which surely must have once steered the course of their professional lives. Procedures eroded into apparent monotony for them vibrated as brand new experiences to her, her mind threatening to burst with questions and fears too tangled to verbalize. Without any display of sympathy, they in the white coats chattered freely among themselves, fumbled between her pried-open legs, and discarded her humanness like the rubber gloves they repeatedly peeled off their hands and tossed into the nearest trash can.

"Only the stupid get pregnant," their attitudes announced, maintaining a sterile hauteur, sprinkling disdain upon the ignorant, indigent objects. A chasm of perspective surged between those engrossed in tedious routine versus Tallulah and countless other women experiencing a strange, uncomfortable, and even holy bodily transformation. Incredibly, the self-appointed saints of indifference never appeared to perceive the profound hunger for a morsel of conversant compassion, or else recognized the need but did not care. A kind word or two could have eased loads of anxiety, but mere employment must have smothered the myth of dedication long ago, or the caretakers chose to focus on their own horizons. The human victims could only gasp as they became objectified: "That one has a lousy diet but her blood's okay. This one's got a pretty good diet. But her blood is the pits."

From the very beginning, the supposed professionals tossed conversation back and forth among themselves in front of the pregnant women, behind them, over them, and around them, as if these women were dead specimens under a microscope. Many times Tallulah felt like shouting at them, "Hey! I'm going to have a baby. You know, one of those fragile, teeny-weeny creatures of new life. It's my first time. Can't you help me relax, since you possess the educational training I lack? Don't you understand how frightened I am? Do you even see me? I have a mind too, not just a belly. Talk to me!" What these government-assisted patients did not pay for with money, they paid for with their dignity.

Near the end of Tallulah's seventh month of pregnancy, Jay completed his college graduate work. A long and solitary drive to visit a friend in boomtown Houston landed him a job, and he paid for an apartment before returning to Georgia. Within a week, the two used cars Jacob had sold to Tallulah became stuffed with books, clothing, and dishes. Jay drove the tiny, old Toyota, while Tallulah and her belly squeezed under the peeling vinyl roof and behind the wheel of what had once been a luxury model Oldsmobile. With boxes and baggage bulging from every space, they completed the classic image of hillbillies on the move by tying an old rocking chair to the top of the wheeled remnant of glory days gone by.

PART III
HOUSTON

CHAPTER TWENTY

For eighteen mostly straight miles, Louisiana's concrete Atchafalaya Basin Bridge shoots level across vast swamp and wetlands. It is a double bridge, with one direction built separate from the other, as if to ensure the flow of traffic during inevitable hazards. Tallulah and Jay passed the Whiskey Bay exit before they pulled over to let the big Oldsmobile's engine cool. Cars whizzed by a very pregnant Tallulah as she stood in the breeze, admiring the massive, enduring bald cypress and water tupelo trees, their lower trunks swollen by dark water, slow to circulate, much like her unhappy ankles. Hours later, the travelers made one last rest area stop before turning their wheels forward to the massive metropolis, looming in the distance like Oz, crowned at the moment with a heavenly rainbow of reassurance.

In Houston, the yellow brick road turned into a definitive armature of highways surging from the ground to overlap in multiple layers reaching neck-stretching heights, teeming with amniotic automobiles. The humid air pocketed odd puffs of chemical pollution. Hotlanta's huge bus tires purred in comparison. More like a descendant of Detroit, petroleum's booming land of plentiful jobs and apartments soon enveloped the newcomers. Tallulah smiled as she noticed the plethora of Michigan license plates. *It seems Michigan has come to me, instead of me going to it.* She smiled too to think she had finally replaced the muck of small town mentality with the big city, where thrives intelligence, diversity, and so many people no one cares to monitor every neighbor. However, despite yellow brick smiles and rainbow assumptions, the newcomers soon discovered they retained the mantle of low-income peasantry.

Within days, Tallulah and Jay registered at Jefferson Davis Hospital, a huge, crowded, county facility serving a conglomerate of indigents who spoke little or no English. Several visits shuffled the couple from one clerk to another, all asking the same questions: Are you employed? What's your income? Are you allergic to any medication? Have you ever been admitted to a hospital before?

Eventually cleared for physical examinations, Tallulah found herself elevated to the basement for the next visit, where she proceeded along a long hall with thickly-painted pipes and heavy wires a foot above her head, to join others in the maternity clinic. This clinic required all patients to sign in before eight in the morning. A room full of ninety heavy women spent the rest of the day waiting for their five minutes of examination by a nameless intern. For any one of them, leaving the waiting room to eat or make contact for a moment with the outside world meant taking the risk of missing her turn, as Tallulah discovered on her first visit, when she ventured out to call Jay. Upon her return, asking at the counter if her name had been called stirred impatience from the unconcerned clerk who sat five feet behind it and didn't care to lift her broad bottom from a cushioned chair in order to check the list.

At times, that five minutes of examination might be extended to fifteen, as happened for Tallulah on her second visit. "Oh, that's cold," she told the intern as he inserted a metal speculum into her vagina.

"No, it isn't," he corrected her. "I put it in that bowl of warm water first."

"Right," she replied, thinking, *And then you left the room for ten minutes. I guess I just don't know what cold is. Silly me.*

Once a week for a month, Tallulah endured long, lonely days sitting on uncushioned small chairs, with release and daylight never arriving before four p.m. During one of those days, a plump, small Hispanic woman with few teeth sat beside her. The woman spoke of her husband and asked about Tallulah's. "Do he beat you, your husband? Mine, he knock my teeth out," she said, gesturing toward her ventilated grin. A few moments later, when Tallulah stood in response to the sound of her name being called, the same woman said hopefully, "Maybe I see you again, in there." She nodded at the door Tallulah would enter, her dark eyes trying desperately to share a portion of the sad despair that emanated not only from her life, but from the chilly walls of that creepy building as well.

Pregnancy progressed as a woman's publicly private enterprise. So much unknown, so much unseen, so much sensation, all contrived to produce much uncertainty at a time when she preferred to be certain, to be ready, to be prepared. Most people spoke kindly to her, but they could not share her coming role, a unique experience, mostly hidden, yet very recognizable. No one could tap into her growing solicitude.

Tallulah longed to minimize the agitation brewing in her body and permeating her mind. Her body the master continued to compel her to yield to the didactic rumbles and grumbles from within. Her body the master demanded a royal level of obedience, her head remaining subjugated on top, serving as useful radar but not much more. As the final day approached, this deference of control became more compulsory, crowding out uncertainty until it could only dance on the sidelines. She continued to comply, taking the big vitamins, exercising, eating healthy, giving all priority to her woefully distended belly, continuing to believe someone would guide her, would tell her what to do when the time came, carry her safely through a very natural climactic moment.

Some credit could be given for having taken a pregnancy class in Georgia. Tallulah had felt a dire need after speaking to Idalia one day. "Well, Mom, what's your advice for making it through this pregnancy?"

Idalia shrugged before replying, "Beer."

In the Lamaze world, the good student's old habits of classroom objectivity popped up readily, actually hindering application of the subject matter to a personal level; she could only grin as Jay squeezed her arm to simulate labor. Overall, Tallulah received the impression she could expect hours of gentle labor, giving her plenty of time to pack her bag of nightgown and toothbrush and sip warm tea before she needed to go to any hospital. Maybe read a book. After all, they said, twenty-four hours of labor was not uncommon with a woman's first pregnancy.

CHAPTER TWENTY-ONE

Tallulah woke at four o'clock on the morning of her due date to discover that her belly boss had chosen to begin the coronation of the new prince or princess. Standing in the bathroom, trembling with trepidation, she timed the gripping sensations that must be contractions. Two minutes apart seemed mighty closer than what she had been told to expect. She waited an hour before waking Jay.

Jay felt the sudden reality of imminent fatherhood too fearfully to wrap her in any blanket of calm reassurance. "Where are my pants? Where are the keys? The car keys! Got to find the car keys! What else do we need?" They tossed Tallulah's toothbrush in a paper bag and fluttered awkwardly out the door.

Traffic clogged, heavy as usual for that time of morning. As solitary joggers braved the early fumes, the warm glow of an orange sunrise offered competition to fading headlights and misty streetlamps. Camouflaged potholes and the lumps from past repairs threatened bouncing interruption of the rhythmic breathing which had become necessary. The Lamaze instructions seemed remote and difficult to remember. Bracing her feet against the floor, Tallulah lifted her thirty-pound belly protectively out of reach of the Oldsmobile's worn and wiry seat. Muscles in her middle continued to tighten, then ease, as if to gather momentum for the next wave.

This strangely independent activity of her body surged, more frightening than painful. Unanticipated mental anxiety increased the physical tension until she found herself a long way from the relative calm and tedious pace of the incubation months. Six a.m. arrived before they caught sight of that massive concrete structure, rising to both of them as a promise of reassuring, gentle hands ready to tenderly guide a precious new life into the world, gentle hands and gentle words anticipating and melting all the natural anxieties of the latest duo of potential parents, who tried to ignore the indifference of fluorescent lights glaring in rude contrast to the warm morning dawn.

"Can I help you?"

Tallulah let Jay answer the question, avoiding the direct look of doubt cast in her direction.

"Third floor and to the right."

On previous visits, she had viewed women in agony being rolled down this hall, their wheelchairs and stretchers pushed by pale and rushing ambulance personnel. Tallulah was glad she could walk it, slowly, in spite of the skeptical glances and comments that began to fall like rain.

"She don't look like she's in labor."

"Probably going back home, that one."

"Hmmph."

Jay's arm, light and unsure, slipped around her, and they exchanged nervous smiles of excited anticipation. The two expected to share every moment of the intimate experience ahead. The elevator opened to a replica of the first floor. A turn to the right revealed a colorless corridor ending with two massive, ominous metal doors. Despite her past requests on examination days, Tallulah had never been permitted even guided access to this mysterious, heaving heart of the hospital. The unfriendly, unfamiliar surroundings added to the apprehension and tension that didn't want to let go of her. A uniformed guard stood outside one of the numerous doors along the way.

"You'll have to wait in here, sir."

Jay was suddenly gone, to sit and be pacified by television in a room of silent male comrades. Fully desiring the best of care during this miraculous event, fully expecting the education, dedication, and experience of trained professionals to provide a safe, snug environment, they cooperated. They trusted. Even in the face of this unexpected separation, they demanded nothing.

Tallulah continued alone. She pushed open the heavy, stiff doors, and a high counter confronted her. "Can I help you?" spoke the dull face behind it, displaying all the concern of a bored store clerk. "Are you sure you're in labor? You don't look like you're in labor. They'll probably send you back home, but go ahead if you want to," and the store clerk of birth pointed to another door, without receiving the apology she seemed to expect to draw from Tallulah. A stronger contraction caused the unconvincing annoyance to slow her steps, providing evidence more in line with the local expectations. Age emanated from the thick paint and worn tile of this finally-confronted sacred ground. An odor of disinfectant prompted the mental image of a scrubbed toilet bowl.

Once through the door, another mask of apathy inquired, "Can I help you?" The hard wooden chair alongside her desk offered no comfort. Noticing the absence of any nearby wall for support, Tallulah balanced fat and wobbly upon it. More paperwork and the same questions provided an opportunity to look around. Cluttered desks greeted her, clumsy metal filing cabinets, dingy walls, and, out of the way, she saw them: the horse stalls, each boasting a rather nauseating pink-and-orange-striped curtain. These continuous compartments outlined with metal poles formed a two-sided perimeter of the condensed room.

"Okay, c'mon."

Tallulah accepted the brown paper bag handed to her for her clothes, and the metal curtain rings scraped along their metal rod, leaving her alone with the taunting height of a flat and skinny cot. After removal of the final remnants of the outside world, the climb aboard proved to be a discouraging reminder of her non-athletic condition. Finally sitting atop her conquest, she shivered. The gown was thin, ugly. With envy she noticed all staff were fully clothed. When she lay back, her eyes had nothing to focus upon except two aluminum shelves above her feet. Sound consisted of sprinkled conversation trailing shuffling footsteps, with the occasional eruption of a moan from somewhere. One of the stall mates seemed to be muffling sobs. *With what*, she wondered. *A pillow would be nice.*

A silent custodian entered and completed light duties, careful to avoid eye contact, as if giving birth were contagious. Tallulah's belly continued to work gently, steadily. She wondered what Jay was doing, and wished he was with her. She had mentioned their Lamaze class to everyone she spoke to since entering the building and expected to see his reassuring smile appear any moment. In the meantime, still ominously far from the relaxed accompaniment she intended to offer her body, she tried to ignore the dismal surroundings and focus inward. Each trembling muscle proclaimed an unwelcome tension. Thoughts covered all the months of effort and patience preceding this grand and final day. "God, I sure do wish I could relax."

A body with a clipboard and pen entered her stall and barked the worst possible question, "When did the pains start?" Tallulah could not answer immediately; her mind being slammed into a wall. *Pains? What pains? Am I in pain? "Pain" is exactly what I have spent months of education trying to avoid. Pain is what I lie here now trying to prevent by relaxing tight muscles.*

Pain was what she did not want, did not want, did not want. The suggestion of it fell hard and heavy upon her. Trusted modern medicine had given her a shove into the Dark Ages. *Oh, shit.* She sighed and complied, yearning to correct this nurse or attendant or whatever she was. Tallulah longed to inform the misguided creature she was having contractions, not pains.

Instead, the cooperative patient set aside her own needs, telling herself the good woman had made an ignorant choice of words and shouldn't be blamed for it. So Tallulah responded calmly to the questions, like a good dog. Moments after the clipboard left, a male entered and examined her. Assuming him to be a doctor, she asked if he would inform Jay of her progress. "Well, you're doing so well, you can go tell him yourself," he replied, and walked away.

Go tell him myself? Now? Like this? Well, if a doctor says I can then I suppose I must be able to. Reluctant to acknowledge the red flag of sarcasm in this young man's voice, and fleetingly wondering why she deserved it, Tallulah told herself he was just being friendly. She would be a good sport and try. With her belly feeling much closer to her knees than before, she slid down the side of the cot and slowly made her way out of the room and down the hall to the high counter. She stood there panting while they called Jay. When he arrived, a strong contraction prevented her from speaking. Treating her like a naughty child, a nurse helped Tallulah walk back to her cot, leaving Jay to stare at the puddle of his wife's blood on the floor.

Behind the striped curtain again, every referral to contractions as pains now made her a bit angry. Between the people interruptions, Tallulah tried to think of what would soon be in her arms. A baby. She couldn't remember ever having held one, much less caring for one of the odd little creatures. They always seemed to be either frantically helpless or screaming for mercy at the top of their lungs. *Why am I always so far away from history's image of the unquestioning, submissive woman, slipping naturally into her assumed role of child-bearing, blessed with practical body knowledge and the contentment of self-sacrifice? Maybe I missed something by not taking home economics in high school.*

A familiar sensation began to develop in her stomach, and she saw the trash can as the only available receptacle. Tallulah asked an attendant to please hand it to her, but watched as the attendant disappeared through the curtain without speaking a word, leaving Tallulah to imagine what a very sloppy mess she was about to make of myself. Barely in time, the attendant returned with a small curved bowl and handed it to Tallulah, still without a word. A slop of last night's dinner presented itself.

"You have to lay back. Spread your legs apart. Bend the knees up." A queer disturbance between her thighs led Tallulah to assume that the head in view belonged to a pair of hands, which seemed to be shaving her pubic hair. So much for having a choice. *Do they also intend to surprise me with an enema? I hope not. These people either hate their jobs, or hate me, or perhaps utilize mental telepathy above my level of perception.* No one bothered to speak any more than necessary.

Tallulah began to realize she had a choice to make: *I can dedicate my energy to bombarding these reluctant medical matrons with polite questions, perhaps receiving a genuine answer or two, or I can continue my breathing pattern, greedily seeking as much physical relaxation for my body as possible.* As it had for the last nine months, her belly and body won the day while her brain whined with neglect. Keenly, she felt the absence of her trained coach of a husband, who would have bridged the communication gap.

"She's about five."

Abruptly and without warning, her conquered cot and she exited their cozy stall. They found themselves suddenly mobile in an open room. A door frame rushed out to greet them, and Tallulah quickly gathered fingers and elbows. Long ceiling lights of a fluorescent corridor flashed and passed rapidly. A brief halt squeezed them through another doorway, followed by the expanse of another room. Tallulah obediently rolled adieu to her preliminary cot. Apparently, she had been promoted to an almost-bed.

Before she could congratulate herself, however, Tallulah's ears cringed. From the other side of a heavier curtain, a frantic female voice assaulted the air with painful, intermittent cries of "Have mercy, dear Jesus!" Beside Tallulah squatted an imposing cluster of cryptic machinery, dutifully awaiting employment. The air hung tense with the expectation of trouble. From across the narrow aisle at her feet shot a spasm of profanity, bombarding any open senses foolishly seeking to maintain calm. Tallulah longed for the power to transcend mental captivity.

"When did the pains start?" Although the room differed, the choice of words remained repugnant. Other questions danced across the stage as dull duplicates of the ones she had answered an hour earlier. Her expectations of basic communication skills between medical professionals evaporated along with any hope of simple courtesy.

She longed again for Coach Jay's presence, her sentry of freedom from this annoying human interference expressing irritation when she paused in her answers, allowing herself to breathe deeply and steadily through a contraction. Her body demanded the return of lost attention, while her jealous senses gobbled every exterior irritant. She felt lost between two worlds, in harmony with neither.

"Give her the I.V."

"I want a natural childbirth. I took a Lamaze class," she managed to tell them for the hundredth time, still expecting some form of positive support. Instead, narrowed eyes stared at her as if she had been naughty again.

"You could bleed to death without it."

How dare she try to undermine the authority of experience, the eyes glared. Tallulah suddenly felt ashamed at the thought of sacrificing safety for stubborn independence, and allowed the needled restraint of one hand. The enemy was winning.

"You have terrible veins," spoke an encouraging intern, moving his probing search to the other hand. Tallulah's contractions deepened. *I must relax, every muscle,* she told herself, trying to ignore the probing. She realized now the real battle was not with the forces inside her body.

She wished she had taken seriously the childbirth books favoring home birth. They had seemed too radical during the calm before the storm. Now she knew they did not exaggerate. She had neglected to install defense mechanisms in her brain, and it was too late.

Mind and body threatened to part, as body demonstrated its clear intention to continue, regardless of mental accompaniment. Surprised at the autonomy of this awakened warrior inside of her, and awed with respect for its power, Tallulah struggled to prevent what she knew would be a dangerous separation. More than ever before, she wanted to be in tune with her body, to harmonize, to gracefully perform the inherent role which belonged to her alone.

"Are you scared? You looked scared to death."

New faces emerged, each with a more stupid comment than the one before. She grasped for block-out of this endless, asinine, fear-breeding expectation of her failure. In vain she searched for reassurance among the staring white coats, while her muscles refused to ignore the noises, the distractions, and the negative insinuations she absorbed so fully.

"How far along is she?"

"Where's all the blood coming from?"

"I dunno."

"How far along is she?"

"When did the pains start?"

"When did the pains start?"

"Hey, it must be a full moon, the way they're dropping in here today!"

"Where's all the blood coming from?"

"I dunno."

Every thoughtless comment pushed her farther from her goal as it receded to a far horizon. She considered giving up and giving them the hysteria they stood waiting for; at least then they would stop gawking. She wished just one of them would tell her to relax; she needed to hear the word, more than anything in the world, she needed to hear the cue. Only five letters: R-E-L-A-X.

"We're going to break your water. Don't move."

Now why are they going to do that? It will speed the labor process. I have only been in the hospital for two hours. Maybe they need the space I'm in. Within minutes, the contractions became much closer and stronger.

"Where's her chart?"

"How long's she been bleeding like this?"

"She should have a file downstairs in the clinic."

But nobody bothered to go get it. *The dumbheads don't even have my records, after all this time.* She turned her head to the side, in disgust, only to catch sight of another approaching pen and clipboard.

"Have you ever been admitted to a hospital before? When? For what?"

Again, an impatient face spouted rotted old questions. No longer in the mood for cooperation, she let the incompetent idiots wait for their answers. *My body comes first, damn it.* All the faith she had ever held in the experience of trained professionals gurgled its way down the toilet, never to return. The only sane choice left was to get through this nightmare with as little friction as possible. She had become the unfortunate victim of an insincere, inefficient, pretentious excuse for people-employment. *They can all go to hell.*

"Lift up."

Two wide belts went around her middle, but they hung loose on one side, making hardly any contact, and she didn't care to try to inform the idiotic white coats. Modesty was gone, and her crotch public property. The coats continued to stand around, each concerned only with their turn at donning rubber gloves and spouting another opinion of her condition. All chose to ignore the head attached to the specimen.

"How's she doing?"

"Wow! Looks like M*A*S*H in here."

Rows of bloody, mutilated, agonizing soldiers flashed before Tallulah's eyes.

"Are you allergic to anything? Any drugs? Penicillin?"

Sensing the use of the machinery, she would have liked to see the mechanical interpretation of how she was doing, but she did not possess eyes on the top of her head. *Inadequate again I am.*

"She said she doesn't want anything." *The owners of those skeptical glances just don't know what to do if they can't shove another needle into me.*

"Something's wrong."

"Who checked her in there?"

"Where's all this blood coming from?"

"That doesn't match with what I have over here."

"Good God, look at the blood."

"Heartbeat's too slow."

"She's ready to go."

"Are you having another pain?"

"She's ready."

"We can give her a spinal."

Tallulah's lower back felt ready to explode with pressure, right along with her patience. The only real pain she felt was the tearing of her hopes, the crumbling of her trust, the lonely mile between her body and her intentions. Nature's ultimate stamina test held her enslaved, and stupid mankind stomped on her as its doormat.

"She's ready."

Ready for what, she did not know. From somewhere out of the blue behind her head, one new voice uttered a sentence that actually made sense. "Tallulah, you should be doing your shallow breathing."

Yes! Yes! Shallow breathing! I remember! Where have you been? Who are you? Oh, where have you been? Tallulah wanted to twist around for a glimpse of this saving angel's face, but she had to be content to let her ears snatch one precious crumb out of the cluttered cluster of verbal nonsense. *Had humanity arrived? No, humanity had passed by.* The white coats continued their irritating chaos.

"Where's all the blood coming from?"

"I dunno."

"We're going to give you a spinal. Is that okay?"

Too busy to argue, or even ask why, she nodded in agreement. *Just get it over with, you morons.* They probably needed a demonstration for medical students. A new intensity in the contractions told Tallulah, "Push!"

"Don't push now."

"Let's go."

Not again. Around her, a doorframe materialized and just as quickly disappeared. The rush to get out halted ten feet out from the door, and she found herself abandoned. She recalled hearing a yell as they had begun their movement; she wondered if it was hers, a trip back to tonsil days. Two desk workers in the distance offered brief, patronizing smiles. She felt more like slugging them than offering a lip-stretcher in return, as she waited for the mysterious voyage to resume.

In the meantime, she tried to remember what a "spinal" was, but her body's next command to push arrived simultaneously with the resumption of travel. Doorway number four plunged her into an icy interior. Caught off guard, all fragments of body relaxation vanished. Tension reigned in victory. Perspiration chilled. *I cannot believe it's so cold in here. An icy reception for a newborn!*

"Okay, let's move her."

"Hey, hang on to that cot! Anytime you're moving a patient ...."

Yes, they almost dropped her. The most tremendous experience of her female life served as nothing more than an exercise for clumsy students. Her body a shivering mass of clenched flesh, she waited for someone else to take control, to finish.

"All right, roll on your side, on your side."

Very small, very reluctant relief told her she needed merely to cooperate now. Mind and body had separated, one no longer heeding the wishes of the other. With deliberate effort, she obeyed, muttering her frustration, "So cold in here. Don't you know that only makes it worse?"

CHAPTER TWENTY-TWO

In the recovery room, as she lay on her back with legs gone to jelly from the spinal shot, a young intern approached. He had been present in rooms two and three. A rare moment of honesty from him confirmed her despair. "It probably would have been all right without it," he confessed, referring to the spinal. "But, just to be safe ...."

"Yeah," she echoed. "Just to be safe." *Safe for whom? Shit.*

Tallulah told every white coat checking her during the next hour that she wanted to have the baby with her in her room. "Sure," they typically replied, if at all. Despite those verbal reassurances, she found herself wheeled into a room and dumped into a bed on the only maternity floor of the hospital not allowing babies in the rooms. "Has anyone ever been able to keep her baby in the room with her here?" she asked.

"Only one, and that was because she raised such a fuss," a floor nurse admitted, tossing Tallulah a glance of apprehension that said, "I hope you aren't going to be a troublemaker." Being stretched flat on her empty belly for twenty-four hours to prevent side effects from the spinal didn't put a patient in the best position for raising "such a fuss."

"Spinal? Who in here just had a spinal?" a voice in the adjoining room bellowed. "Where is she?" Tallulah had lost all interest in cooperating. She didn't bellow a reply, instead she thought, *Lady, if you don't even know my name, I'm not about to break my neck answering you. You can get lost for all I care, and take that stupid ham hock posing as meat on my lunch plate with you.*

When they allowed her to get up the next day, Tallulah walked to the nursery. Three women attendants watched as she opened the tiny diaper, viewing strange black goo inside. "Honey," one spoke, while the others grinned in mild amusement, "you might want to get a copy of Dr. Spock's book."

The new parents carried their bundle home to an apartment nearly void of furniture beyond the portable vinyl bassinet they'd purchased at a Goodwill store in Georgia. Cake and popcorn and welcome home posters made by a proud father greeted mother and son. The star of the show had arrived, and everyone else took a back seat, including Tallulah and her rage.

From the wrinkled little lovely bundle of arms and legs they named Zachary, the new mother strove to separate her sad jumble of hostility and disappointment. She began reading Dr. Spock's book, attempting to ascertain how to care physically for a fragile cherub, what he needed, what to watch for. Common sense told her she could not blame the bundle for the faults of his porters, but she felt the stage had been set for her to lapse into a mental depression. She saw the laughing faces peeking out from behind their heavy theater curtains, waiting for her to crumble, expecting her to slide into dark corners for their entertainment. *Screw you! I've been laughed at before. I have endured, and I could have endured more.* She had expected to work through the labor, to feel the agony, to survive it, all of it, to claim it as her body's union with the substantial forces of genuine life. The need to experience the climax, the culmination of her body's intensely focused activity, its transformative journey, this incredible physical force her subservient brain had bowed to, seemed to go unacknowledged. No one could say Tallulah had not earned her moment. Part of her felt robbed, useless. *They gave birth. I gave bother.*

It had nothing to do with caring for a baby; the baby was not a consolation prize. Labor had been her distinct, separate experience. Only some kind of superwoman could have maintained the role of calm assistant to the fierce intentions of her body in that dismal environment of swinging doors, swimming lights, hollow voices, and cold eyes. Of course she had been afraid. Her imperfect system of defense had submitted a convenient surrender to those who had no right to expect it, to those who betrayed her trust. She insisted on figuring out why it had been taken away from her. *Why? Step back. You know how. Change the perspective. Look at it from another angle or two.*

Human birth is the strangest thing in the world, an oddity in our obsessively material lives. It begins as the door to glory floats down on a nine-month cloud, opening slowly almost as if to welcome someone to its interior, preparing the mother-to-be not only in body, but in spirit, as its chosen initiate. Daily, she feels herself special as a selected participant in a realm of warm possibilities, miraculous developments, becoming included in something heavenly, familiar, but also unpredictable, even harsh at times. As it continues, if it continues, she carries the tender hope of life to an anticipated culmination of completion. A woman's body bleeds in readiness for this natural moment. *Nope, they couldn't teach that in Lamaze class.*

One day, instinctively responding to signals of completion, woman nears the threshold to heaven only to be reminded, "No, you can't come in yet. You are here to receive. But you must remember your closeness to this door, you must perceive its power, the radiant force, so you embrace the sanctity of life as no man can." With that salute to her soul, her feet remain glued to the threshold, ready to receive. Her bones vibrate with the power of the universe as her child begins its passage out of the glory realm, aiming for her trusted arms. Together, they work through the holy energy field, until.

Until it stops. The door is slammed shut in her face. "Wake up, silly. We took over." Woman's months of preparation, mental and physical engagement, fall to the side, discarded, devoid of acknowledgement, devoid of completion, devoid of climax.

Damn them! It was my body! It was my role! What right did they have to take it away? Once more the fool, she had misplaced her trust in an authority system, expecting protection, guidance, finding instead another hierarchy slicing off compassion in deference to the delegation of quantitative duties; achieving targeted end goals by unencumbered means. Her anger at herself would linger for weeks, pulsating through her bloodstream. She had only wanted to give birth. She had only wanted to feel birth, to feel a new human being emerge from her body in a personal, well-earned, sacred moment.

Somehow, the so-called professionals brought to mind Jacob, although he had expressed no interest in her pregnancy. The lack of emotional support, of compassion, of empathy, people aimlessly standing there, she looking up to them as they looked down on her. Their indifference to her plight brought tears to her eyes, just as he had so many times before.

It was as if they had removed art from life and made everything paint-by-numbers, making her into one of the numbers, a dehumanized object on the assembly line of procreation, a pulpy mass of skin, bone, and muscle stripped of personal humanity within an institution controlled by robots in disguise, trashing her feelings, discarding them as irrelevant to the situation they dominated. The robots had no intention of supporting her humanity; such was not their job. *How could they offer no moral support with the gates of heaven open? Most likely, they were afraid,* she guessed. *Their own souls worked in close proximity to the gates of glory. Their eyes needed to look away to avoid being blinded. So they mechanized the process, like taking a free flowing river from the land and freezing it into ice cubes they could place anywhere they chose at any time of their choosing. They enslaved nature.*

That was the problem. Men tried to assist a natural process. They approached it with a businesslike, apathetic indifference, hiding behind the mechanical instruments providing quantitative justification. They pushed aside their own humanity. Not even knowing when to bow, their male bodies lacked the uterine blood and pangs bonding one to a natural veneration of life, and the lengthy, central preparation for its arrival, not to mention the female body's responsive sustenance sacks so well positioned to partner with a cradling arm. *What would it be like if a man gave birth? Would the hospital staff yessir him and follow his orders? Or would he too bow to the gates of glory, savoring the sacred holiness of life, but falling prey to pseudo assistance? If someone had pretended to care enough to hold my hand ....*

Molecular maelstrom aside, the new parents had no way of realizing how deeply Number Three would alter their lives. Being kind folk, they tried not to mind the multitude of delicate needs beginning to blast adult routines. Tremendous responsibility replaced relaxation, which began to seep out of their lives. A constant alertness for signs of baby trouble took precedence over everything else. Even when the helpless noisemaker slept, Tallulah and Jay would check on him frequently, interrupting their own conversation, just to reassure themselves he continued to breathe. Tallulah's bathroom showers became brief, the sound of running water masquerading as a dangerous muffler for the possibility of distress signals. Her ears attuned themselves to every small sound. Night after night, she would still be dripping wet all the way to the infant's bed as she made sure those had not been baby whimpers she thought she'd heard. Soft and peaceful, he would lie sleeping. The whining and gurgling had been the water running through the pipes, again.

As the weeks progressed, night no longer served as peaceful compensation for the turmoil of the day; her time transformed into a series of two-hour rests, with snatches of feeding and cleaning serving as dividing lines. Darkness and daylight did no more than take turns making appearances.

She deliberately intended to give Zachary the attention she had not received in a dysfunctional family of seven, and she could not trust anyone else to care for him so carefully, so lovingly. Buying furniture could wait. New clothes could wait. Even her entangled sanity could be put on hold. This baby could not be, would not be, put on hold. She knew her years with him were limited, and the earliest years, the foundation years, stood out as the most important years, so she read. He grew older every day. Her heavy sense of responsibility also grew old, naturally, expedited by gravity's forces upon the vulnerable human body.

Okay, you little dictator, you. I'm coming. Always I am coming. I am tired, but you don't care. I want to sleep. God, to stay in bed. But you don't care. I want to think about something other than the milk that so quickly goes in one end of you and out the other, and those stinky diapers, one after the other. Ugh! You don't care. How could you?

How could you come along and complicate my life like this? You are revealing my lack of genuine patience. I'm beginning to feel like a train wreck. And the little bundle seemed to say: *Shut up, you stupid adult. Yeah, you. At least you're supposed to be an adult now. Whether you like it or not, I am here, and you will care for me. Cease your whining. You will reach deep, deep inside of yourself into the well of necessity, back into the depths from which I came, and draw out more patience whenever I require it. You will reach deep, deep, inside of yourself into the well of necessity and find empathy. One of these days, dingobrain, you will reach deep, deep inside of yourself and find true joy.*

And Tallulah felt, not really reaching syntax: *Reach deep inside of me? Huh! I am beginning to turn inside out from all this darn reaching. I don't want to change, you little varmint. I was just beginning to like myself the way I was before you came along. I don't want to become a mere caretaker. A caretaker has no independence, no will of her own. I don't want to lose my freedom or my will. I don't want to lose anything. I don't want to lose myself. Me! Me! Me!*

And the bundle spoke without speaking: *Don't you know anything? You are not losing yourself, but adding another dimension to your being. It's called growing, maturing, learning the stage limelight need not always shine on you. I said find joy, remember? It is there. Inside of you. And it is greater than any substitute you might stumble upon without me.*

And a weary Tallulah wallowed. *It's too hard, this motherhood stuff. It's too hard. I can't. I can't change. What am I? Some kind of lump of clay? Ground beef? That's what I feel like: ground beef. I don't want to fail you, little one. God help me. But I like being free to express my real emotions, and you, little thing, demand that I filter them, filter them. Winds and wants stir me to agitation, but I must be calm. When I feel like screaming, I must be calm. When I feel like stomping the floor, I must be calm, calm, calm! Where is the automatic mellow that mothers are famous for? I certainly haven't found it. I guess it doesn't come bundled with the daggone diapers. I love you, little thing, but, God, you make me feel like exploding. Never have I had to stifle myself, so often, so much.*

I feed you and I clean you and I hold you and I walk with you and sometimes wrack my brains trying to figure out why you won't stop crying. This is not the way I want to be. Suffocating. I can't stand the pressure. I have to change. Somehow. I must become both driver and vehicle, and I will make myself shift gears, shift those deep emotional gears that scream for release. Their intensity frightens me, but the alternative looms as unthinkable. A lot of downshifting lies ahead for me, I expect.

Manual transmission downshifting, transmission, transmission, transmission. *Okay, okay, okay.* A clutching, shifting transmutation of behavior and attitude surfaced as the price Tallulah paid for stubbornly insisting upon playing a positive major role in her baby's life. She knew she held in her arms a genuine, realistic opportunity to create, to sculpt, to weave, to watch, to understand the young and tender compositional elements of a human being as near to herself as she would ever come. Sacred raw material.

She could and would contribute healthful fertilizer, though it be created from her old shit, her personal junkyard. *I get to contribute to the foundation of another person's life, and God has blessed me with this honor and opportunity, I think.* As she rolled out of bed on one of those segmented nights, the light in her wristwatch failed, as it had been doing for several nights. Instinctively, she spoke to her Holy Spirit. "I bet you can make it come on." Without so much as a pause in her steps to reach her child, she chuckled at the suddenly illuminated watch face.

While time passed and the nights gradually became nights again, from that small sponge sprouted a duplicate of any mood, attitude, expression, or gesture left lying around by careless Mommy and Daddy. They began to witness the development of a personality, and as man and woman they both learned to shift gears to make their constant contributions as unpolluted and positive as possible, struggling to dance the good dance of parenthood. Old habits and expectations and bitterness continued to pop up in Tallulah like evil weeds, distracting her, causing her to stumble, but she chose to be content with snatching off the tops for now. Root removal postponed, as in the practice of a wise gardener who avoids rooting out big weeds during the months of lawn dormancy when nothing is available to fill the barren patches they would leave behind.

Downshifting brushed aside enough dirt to reveal the door to joy alluded to, occasionally glimpsed in the years before, but never opened. Apparently, it required the hand of an innocent babe to reach up, turn the knob, and lead the way, slowly. Her little one, like any child, became the greatest of teachers. If Tallulah allowed him to, he actually expanded her narrow character by teaching her to laugh, not the old cocky sarcasm poking fun at others, but an innocent appreciation of simple things, like his soft, stubby baby fingers and baby toes, primordial appendages reaching and curling, his surprising splashes of bath water, bright rays of sunlight dancing across the floor capturing his attention, his gestures and gurgles and darting eyes expanding her connection to the realm of wristwatch lights appearing when summoned.

His needs were so immense, yet so simple when accepted and met, although far from predictable. They became fluid, beyond the endless ins and outs of his bodily functions; his needs kept changing, evolving. Once she adapted to his diet of liquids, it became time for solids. Once she adapted to his immobility, he became mobile. Crawling led to new perspectives, like how much she needed to vacuum the floor.

She ventured into his realm by becoming aware of the manifestations of the world as he targeted them through his uncontaminated eyes and grasping fingers, and he rewarded her with bits of joy. As the months went by, his reaches and babbles taught her to recognize the wonders of the universe in the many directions male urine can shoot, in the hairs upon her busy arms, in ordinary parking lot pebbles and their conduciveness to stroller wheels. She caught herself singing "Old McDonald Had A Farm" when alone. She chose to join him, tentatively, in his world, rather than go bananas expecting him to fall into place in hers, like some kind of miniature adult.

Others stepped in and out of this baby world with more ease. In stores, strangers smiled and spoke freely to her son, as though he were an old Army pal of theirs or something. "Hi, there, little buddy. How ya doing, fella?" His weary young mother rarely received a glance. *Sheesh and double sheesh, what's wrong with me now? Has my whole body become invisible?*

Beyond the insensitive shoppers, joining the social ranks of motherhood included taking Zachary to the playground and maneuvering him into a baby swing, while noticing how frequently women denied creative freedom to their child rather than accompany the great explorer a few yards or be bothered with soiled clothing. In an area designated for fun, adult impatience popped up easily, crowding efforts of mature respect for a child's innocent approach to the environment, and she saw her mommy frustrations to be far from unique. One morning, a three-time mother sitting beside Tallulah expressed the typical exasperation over a young adventure with the good earth, impatiently brushing it from her child's pants. When the woman exclaimed, sincerely, "Thank goodness for Tide," Tallulah looked around for the television cameras.

Television seemed to exploit the immense influence it held over women remaining home day after day, their vulnerable world impaired by the flimsy motivation of monotonous and menial chores. At least other adults existed in that cubicle container, speaking adults with more adventurous moments confronting them than a melted popsicle on the carpet, or oatmeal on the ceiling, or dust under a table. Apprehensive enough to maintain the self-willed, yet thin, wires encompassing her own mental wellness, Tallulad steered clear of the soap opera trap, leery of anything akin to addiction. She kept the television off during the day, but evenings still presented a plaguing, dim-witted image of the homemaker: She wears plaid shirts and ponytails, and a clogged kitchen sink boggles her poor little brain. Dirt and grime threaten her very existence, attacking in cute but nasty teams cementing themselves in an oh-so-telltale ring around the inside of her family's bathtub, not to mention around the collars of her precious husband's precious shirts. Oh, my! She cannot function without using those numerous handy cans of pretty magic to make her appear clever, when we all know her to be just a normal ninny, the butt of every home. Let us praise the heavens for this divine, useful creature, whose greatest joy in life lies in maintaining a good relationship with her toilet bowl. Now put her back in the closet.

American society of the eighties seemed to hold no respect for a woman who chose to stay home and care for her child. She had to be stupid to get pregnant in the first place, and she had to be stupid to ignore the popular trend of daycare facilities.

As a necessary contribution to the child's sense of security, routine reigned at home, but as with all things, perspectives of it differed. The same years of living that enabled a somewhat mature adult to establish those routines beneficial to new members of the human race also doused that adult with a slosh of personal regret. For these taller, larger creatures, the undeniable passage of time regarded monotony as a draining force upon their personal hourglass, a waste devoid of immediate reward, a dimming of the telltale sparkle keeping eyes bright, thus providing most women enough excuse to flee to the world of employment and its cognitive activity. Most women celebrated contemporary liberation by jumping into business jobs, thinning the old-fashioned motherhood role to a minimum, and Tallulah could not blame them. *To each her own.*

Indeed, her stubbornly chosen alternative of mental atrophy lurked as not the brightest of horizons. Every weekday morning, after the front door closed behind Jay, a big, hazy beast Tallulah named Boredom loomed up, snickering in her ear, threatening to envelope an idle mind. Two feet behind Boredom stood fat Bitching, hungry to devour another female recruit: *You are left behind. You are an insignificant housewife, the shadow of a man with no worth of your own. Your brain will turn to mush, and nobody will like you. It takes two people to bring a child into this world, but now he's out having all the fun.*

Weekends were easier. Day trips to the museums and parks of Houston relaxed everyone. At the zoo, Jay held up his wiggly infant to see the monkeys, the giraffes, and the native predators of the Gulf of Mexico swimming behind glass. Tallulah couldn't help feeling somewhat alien around this playful father who bought kiddie train rides for the three of them. He not only endured the pointless clackety-clack ride around the park, but enjoyed it. Miller Outdoor Theater offered an expansive grassy hill to sit on and do nothing other than absorb live music. The natural history museum required visitor patience to present its dinosaur bones and the man-made strategies used to access their liquefied remains, or the liquified remains of earlier plants and animals, depending on one's view of the crude.

These days were good not only because Jay helped with Zachary, but Tallulah saw, she heard, she allowed herself to experience the expanse of a diverse world larger than her own vulnerable brain bubble.

She slowed her steps in this expanded environment, and she began to think perhaps she belonged in it as much as any of the goofballs dropping their ice cream in the heat and massing the freeways like maniacs. "That must be the Astrodome," she offered, as they drove home on the southwest zoom route.

"Yep. Hey, Lulah, maybe we can go to Astroworld."

"An amusement park? With rides and roller coasters? Maybe when he gets a little bigger." To deliberately pursue ups and downs while defining stability for her child might be more than she could handle.

Although diverging from the mainstream felt normal to Tallulah, *her* normal, the thing planted above her shoulders insisted she figure out what she was doing and why she was doing it. Her growing appreciation of slowness, of gradual and continual growth, of changes subtle and wondrous, stood in opposition to the outside world racing for money, possessions, and starry recognition. Hunkering in her weekday mommy cave reminded her of the intense concentration required for the creation of a good piece of art, yet such an environment could so easily become dark and unhealthful.

Jay did not deny the importance of her childcare immersion, but Tallulah's commitment compelled him to carry the burden of their financial responsibility alone. She knew she would not forever postpone her responsibility to share that load with him, and after a year had passed, reluctantly agreed to accompany him to a company party, a step beyond his easy company picnics welcoming children. However, the friendly adults and delectable refreshments failed to convince her the time for separation had arrived.

With a nagging feeling, she insisted they leave early to rescue Zachary from a babysitting service in a strip mall, where they had left him. The woman at the counter, where she surveyed the children from a distance, assured them their boy over there had stopped crying after a while and fallen asleep in his crib. He had been crying when they left him, and "after a while" could mean nothing less than eternity to the woman whose womb still throbbed with symbiotic vibes. If re-entering the workforce meant trauma for her child, she would stay poor.

Other times, if she took Zack with them to a party, someone would come up to her and say, "I think it's so cool you brought your kid," as if Tallulah had brazenly defied an etiquette rule, and she realized she probably had, although not so brazenly.

Jay watched the wife he loved struggle to keep her brain alive while other women worked beside him; Tallulah tried not to think of the other women. When she did, old ghosts of a husband and his habitual infidelity rose, swirling around her head, bringing waves of doubt to the reasons Jay gave for working late. Suspicion lay more readily available to her than any facets of trust. *Oh, shit, here more of it comes,* and she clung to the side of her boat in rough waters, watching slimy Suspicion join the taunts of Boredom and Bitching.

Maintaining a distance from the beasts demanded a fortification of identity for Tallulah, and she searched for foundational building blocks. On top of the mindless housewife package, television commercials presented a second image of womanhood waiting for viewer adoption: the socially radiant, successful, non-mommy woman. A Christmas tree of a creature, the adorned woman in the tube, along with posed and poised mannequins in store windows, reminded Tallulah of a principle taught early in her college fine art classes: anything without function is decoration. Decoration is not a form of contemporary art, they had taught, and therefore not to be regarded seriously. Aggressive cosmetic companies presented beauty as a desperate, artificial, yet essential mask for the contemporary woman, produced only by their sleek, seductive, and profitable products: Her eyes must be fully open, with night-black borders for emphasis. Lashes thick, long, fluttery. Eyelids must carry rainbow hues bright enough to allure like magnets. Eyebrows, evidence of the clumsiness of nature, must be redrawn. The nose shall disappear. All visible skin shall mesmerize with the flawless satin of superior dairy cream. While cheekbones glow with enhanced, handsome height, the lips, ah, yes, the lips ooze with wet, red lusciousness. Every physical and mental element dedicates itself to the essential entrapment of some glorious specimen of the male species, tantalizing his hormones until he cannot resist being manipulated by those long, red claws. Only then is a woman a woman.

Tallulah watched and thought, *Good God! Am I supposed to be a person or a Venus fly trap? A human being or a limp dishrag? I have no desire to deceive anyone. I want truth in my life, remember? I have no desire to be an ornament. I want to be able to respect myself. Who respects a decorated, empty shell? There is nothing inadequate about the natural beauty and power of the female body, or the female face. This womanhood stuff is for the birds. Better to leave make-up for the circus clowns.*

Still not fond of breaking new ground, she longed for an image of a positive, productive, honest, natural female she could emulate, one she could follow, one who could bring into focus the daily blur hanging in front of her face. All potential role models seemed negative, unsatisfied, bored, phony, or frantic with impatience. The modern concept of adulthood reeked of shallow traits. Self-fulfillment trampled compassion, integrity, and responsibility. She mused, *I could easily pretend to be a woman encumbered with a child instead of accepting motherhood as a serious role, and no one would object if I chose to pursue a time-consuming career instead of being with my child. I could justify my hours away from home with the money that would give my child a higher standard of living.*

For Tallulah, however, getting away from home to alleviate restlessness and gain hollow prestige in the name of money reminded her too much of the contemptible father who had never been close to his children, who had always been too busy with money pursuits to reach out to them with any sincerity, who would not or could not find the fundamental words of approval, who contributed nothing positive to prepare them in any healthy way for the jungle of the world they must face. The complex sadness his neglect and anxiety instilled in her young heart lingered without mercy.

She had no desire to exist solely in the shadow of her husband or her child, but neither did she wish to trample her child for the sake of her own personal fulfillment. "Parent" stood as a permanent title, not a passing fling. *For the rest of my life I will be a mother. I have to find peace where I am, and with whom I am with, and with what I am, whether anyone else on Earth has ever done so or not.*

Neither escapism nor pretense could be allowed to substitute for truth. Too frequently, psychology textbooks had presented denial as a sure road to duplicating the monster behavior one abhors, and she had already felt the poison creeping in. Finding her truth was no pretty joy ride without consequences. *If I am frustrated with myself, then I am frustrated with you. If I am unhappy with myself, then I am unhappy with you. If I am angry at myself, then I am angry at you. If I don't like myself, then I cannot like you.*

Response to any home situation, from a broken, gloppy jar of peanut butter to a sudden kiss from her child, required as much uncontaminated honesty and truth as she could dig up. Honesty from deep within always brought love, which could mend a moment in a moment, she discovered. Tallulah relied upon parenting books to open the doors that jammed, to help shoo away the damnable self-pity and despair haunting her, to allow light to shine in those dark corners of her mind. Basically, a child needed respect, the same respect due any human being, the books seemed to say. So simple a word, "respect," so why did it take hundreds of pages to explain how to give it to a child?

Feelings dominated the realm of a small one too young to carry the heavy coatings of reason. Tallulah began to remember reactions and feelings accumulated during her own young years. Re-examining them, she perceived that they consisted of not the people, places, or events which had glued themselves into her brain, but the unseen rippling sensations produced by those elements. The tremors associated with her parents' incessant battles and abuse, the angst of strange school days, her negatives playing ping pong with positives, such as conquering the backyard swimming pool before it retaliated, and the happy cohesion among brothers and sisters sharing popcorn as they sat on the floor absorbing evening television, the popcorn always popped by Idalia in a heavy old pan with an odd lid and a broken handle, then coated with the cheapest margarine, and sprinkled with the cheapest salt after being dumped into a speckled oval roaster pan because big bowls cost money. Sometimes chocolate milk made from the cheapest dry milk would be an added treat. All dropped the seeds of feelings.

This arrival of small clarity told her she did not need to supply her child with the latest creations of the manufacturing industry, or with zigzagging lessons and activities, in order to fulfill his growing needs. No, she felt the challenge of cultivating in him a sense of security, confidence, love, and belonging, including a sense of respect for himself and as well as others. She had to give him good feelings.

Her own conclusion frightened her: *I have to give him good feelings? And where are these good feelings supposed to come from? And how will I recognize them even if they do come along? And how, God tell me how, can I pass on something buried so deep? I have but slim holdings.*

As with her role as a parent, Tallulah's role as a partner in marriage hung heavy with mossy chains of what not to do. Her parents and couples like them did battle over the flimsiest excuses they could find, using each other to vent their anxieties while a dumbfounded child with unclosable ears sat swallowing dose after dose of insecurity. Jay came home with his problems, and she tried to help him redefine them as challenges, thinking beyond the old and easy, "Screw them. What a bunch of idiots. Your work is always better than that jerk's!" She stopped short of telling him to quit.

As with any lonely new road, forward movement encountered barriers, stone walls inhibiting her progress. She found herself repeatedly halted, unrescued, seeking to go around the walls, over them, under them, wishing she had a big spray can of rock-melter in her pocket. *My future manufacturing and marketing endeavor, I suspect. It could be an easy sell.*

Like it or not, ingrained behavior patterns duplicating the miserable torment of adult life she detested sprouted within her again and again, reminding her of a certain arcade game whacking popping-up insectivores also of the burrowing mindset. Complaining and finding fault with others was so easy, too easy, but accomplished nothing. She usually stumbled right into her habitual mistakes before recognizing them, losing her temper only to hang her head in shame and apologize, and she struggled to find suitable replacements. Seventeen months after her son's birth, while she corralled enlightening moments of meaningful motherhood, sorted motley marriage strategies, and struggled with an amorphous personal identity, the telephone rang.

CHAPTER TWENTY-THREE

Early brilliance danced upon the concrete, promising an illuminating day. Visions of pink azaleas and blue wildflowers perked in sleepy minds. Bayou City residents smiled on such mornings and tried to leave early for work so they would not need to stay late.

Abundant employment and affordable housing had drawn many transplants from east and north. Change and adaptation graced everyone's lives. Immediate comfort easily lulled them into not worrying about the relatives left behind. Letting go of the past and the frustrating feelings of helplessness it had engendered could be dealt with at will, until the telephone shattered the walls of contemplation, but even long distance phone calls seldom dared to interrupt the glory of an early morn.

Seldom dared. In one of the many apartments, an unsuspecting Tallulah routinely opened the drapes and focused on the smiling man she had married. Across the room, he had his hand on the front doorknob, about to be gone for the day, a day she would routinely spend buzzing in and out of, and around in, their home. At the first ring, her thoughts raced to little Zachary still sleeping upstairs, while her hand immediately halted the abominable noise.

"Hello, Tallulah. This is Humphrey."

Humphrey, she thought. *Good! We've been remembered by somebody back in Georgia. An Atlanta resident dares to violate all those years of anti-long-distance-phone-call training by Jacob. Maybe a move to Texas wasn't a drop off the edge of the planet after all.*

Having acquired a direct and dispassionate approach, Humphrey's voice continued, "I wish this could be under better circumstances."

"Oh? What's wrong, Humphrey?" The roll of sunny delight in Tallulah's mind came to a halt. Rumbling, dark clouds gathered in its place.

"Jacob died last night."

And the blast hit. "Whaaaaat?" She gasped, deeply, inhaling half the air in their apartment, hardly hearing the ensuing explanation. All morning sunshine, glory, and smiles vanished. Poof! Ordinary hand-held polymer pulsated into a vicious, loathsome, slimy, hissing, sickening, snake-thing, metamorphosing with an eruption of fleshy bumps and scales, writhing and wriggling like a gloating demon in her hand. Gasping repeatedly, she shoved the monstrous thing at a bewildered Jay.

Feet usually steady and light stumbled heavily across the room while her limp body fell into a bizarre world without floors or walls or ceilings. Disbelief, shock, and a bit of blinding horror blasted away years of an excellently constructed and, until now, quite effective, barrier of interior defense. A sinister, slick blade of raw pain stabbed her chest. Her body staggered, shuddering, moaning, spinning. Her head churned and heart pounded, heaving with wave after wave of deep, shaking sobs. Uncontrollable sobs. Tallulah hated having no control. Down and around through turbulent air, not unlike the interior of a notorious Texas twister, she fell, into a phantasmagoria of unsummoned, fragmented memories: his home arrivals, her tonsils, bike lesson, tree bark, nearly drowning, stitches, waterfall vacation, the fire, leaving Detroit. They all zipped past her like machine gun fire, slicing the air. Long-ago images of her father's rough and distant face, his silky stabbing voice, his rare and stale closeness, all ballooned and popped around her in rapid succession. Her mind erupted as a volcano of emotion and thick tears gushed from somewhere within, pouring forth like molten lava, melting her face. From the inside out, her body alternately froze with shearing pain and melted with scalding emotion, froze and melted. Shuddering, shaking, on and on. Uncontrollable chaos.

When glimpses of reality finally broke through the devastation, Tallulah found herself on her knees, hugging the bathroom wall, wringing the life out of an innocent hand towel, both hands grabbing and twisting until the rack the poor thing still hung from threatened to come off. Sobbing, sobbing. Logic and sense slowly emerged. *My god,* she thought, when she could reclaim her brain. *What the hell was that all about? I hated the man.*

Soon after the maelstrom subsided, she and Jay gathered a few days' worth of clothing for all three and exited their boomtown. Most of the drive back to Georgia Tallulah spent communicating with her father. Jay drove, and Zachary sat in the back seat playing and making up songs, innocent and unaware of the absurd pain adults endure.

Unseen scenery whizzed by as Tallulah pinpointed the questions in her embattled brain without debating the validity of ESP or other forms of telepathy, and listened to the calm, soothing responses that floated to her, unlike any conversation ever experienced when the nervous, impatient, demanding son-of-a-bitch lived and breathed.

What happened to you, Jacob?

My time came, that's all.

Where are you? What's it like there?

Oh, not bad. Kind of nice, pretty. Get to see all the old folks again. Sorry it had to be so sudden for you.

What happened? I thought you quit the booze years ago.

I did. I did. I don't know. Just started back. Thought I could handle it, I guess.

What made you start back?

Oh, just things.

It really hurts, you know. I never expected this. I feel as if I'm ready to join you.

I know. You'll be okay. Don't worry, baby.

What about Mom? What's going to happen to her?

I don't like leaving her like this, but it couldn't be helped. I want you to help look after her now.

Look after her. Tallulah imagined Idalia would be crying, quietly, deeply, her strong, proud face distorted with the suffering not new to her, but now dragging her to a type of finish line. She would be letting someone else make all the calls. Tallulah wanted to be with her, to hold one of her strong, weak hands.

"Yeah," she told her father. "I know. We'll try."

"She needs you," he continued. "She ain't gonna beg for help, but she needs you, and don't let her tell you otherwise, the old hardhead. I'll do what I can from here. I'll be around for a while. Who knows, maybe I'll be of more use to my family from here than I ever was alive."

"Are you all right, Jacob?"

"I'm all right. I knew my days were numbered. It got a little scary at first, but I'm home now, and I know it. The Big Guy has His ways."

"I can't believe all those years of trouble are over now. I'm real sorry for bitching at you so much. I'm just beginning to understand the pressure and all. I'm sorry, Jacob. I'm really sorry."

"I know you are, baby. I'm sorry, too. We had some rough times. Things just never seemed to work out for me, or maybe they did and I missed it. I don't know. You just go on with your life now. You've got a fine family. They need you, and when it's all over you'll take your place here with the rest of us. You've got a fine spot waiting here for you."

"Is He around?"

"I ain't seen Him, but I can feel Him, kind of close and warm-like. This is a real powerful place, and I've got a lot ahead of me, rehashing my time and cleaning up some things."

"I'll pray for you, Jacob."

"Thanks, baby. It helps."

Her floating conversation fluttering away as easily as it had come, Tallulah and Jay and Zachary were the last family members to arrive. Jacob had checked into a drug and alcohol rehabilitation clinic to sober up for Easter weekend, the others said. He didn't want to embarrass Gregory, who had summoned the courage to bring his wife and kids for a rare visit the following week. Three years on the wagon of sobriety had not prevented Jacob from falling off a few times in recent months.

A fellow member of the local chapter of Alcoholics Anonymous had driven Jacob to the clinic that evening. Jacob wanted to go and had made the arrangements without the consent of his wife, who still urged him to use his willpower instead. Idalia had watched the man of her faded dreams go out in search of help many times before, and she didn't bother to say goodbye anymore to the blue eyes that could not focus. She stood and watched her husband, the father of her children, the supposed rock tradition urged her to cling to, allowed his baggy trousers to drop to his knees as he staggered through the doorway. He had forgotten to put on his underwear again.

Her thin gray hair coaxed into long, girlish curls around a dignified, lined face, Idalia had telephoned the clinic later that night to check on him and give instructions to the staff, " ... and don't take away his inhaler. He has emphysema."

"Sure," they told her. "We're keeping an eye on him, he's fine."

"I thought he'd be enjoying the attention, as usual," a tearful Idalia told her children. "Never has there been a man who cherishes attention from doctors and nurses more than your father. I can't even remember all the times he went to halfway houses. Always thinking he could fool people, hide the drinking, hide the booze, and then go begging for pity when things fell apart. He didn't even have the willpower to stop smoking one damn cigarette after another. I wonder if they took those away from him."

The medical professionals failed to reciprocate the respect one more drunk held for them. That night they had followed routine, letting another patient watch over the new arrivals, who were always given "something to help them rest" by a nurse. In Jacob's case, the dosage proved more than adequate, and fifty-eight years of life came to an end as he dozed off. The staff later claimed to have performed cardiopulmonary resuscitation and a tracheotomy to no avail. A doctor decided to put arteriosclerosis on the death certificate as the cause.

Idalia held no interest in challenging the actions of the staff, because, as she put it, it wouldn't bring her husband back and she didn't have any money for lawyers anyway. She didn't even have enough for a funeral but that was all right because she hated funerals and didn't want to ever go to one, not even for him. She chose cremation for her husband's body, because they had discussed it and he had said it would be all right.

A few aunts and uncles joined the gathering at the house to comfort Idalia, express mild complaints about not being able to view the body, and their general surprise at the suddenness of it all. They all thought Jacob had looked fine the last time they'd seen him. Everyone said it's good to see you and wouldn't Jacob be glad to know he brought everyone together like this. Yeah, he's probably smiling. Smiling. The ashes sat in a sealed box on the mantle above the fireplace.

The price of gasoline in Houston carried some of the conversation, and Idalia stood by quietly wringing her hands and waiting for everyone to leave and dreading the sound of an empty house. No one bothered to wear black.

Idalia had always experienced difficulty with company. Her physical appearance, her home, placed before judge and jury, would never be good enough, she was certain. Any visitor's politeness undoubtedly concealed undivulged disdain ready to spill forth later, once the door closed behind them. As usual, Myrna tried to help by tidying the main rooms, making things pretty. She rearranged some of the cheap pictures covering most of every wall. Idalia did not tell her to stop, but she wanted Myrna to stop, because Jacob had been the last one to arrange those pictures, and he had never shown an interest in wall pictures before. Silently sacrificing threads of value felt normal to Idalia, her normal: having everything taken away from her. It gave her something to be morose about later.

Her sadness laced with fantasy, Idalia thought maybe the death was another one of his lies. "I wouldn't put it past him. Who knows what kind of promises he would make to get out of this life and start a new one somewhere else? That's one way to get out of debt, like in a movie," she conjectured in a private moment with Tallulah.

Imagining Jacob in any state of relaxation required effort. The skinny, shaky, buzzard of a male creature had always been around, even when he wasn't around, irritating his family with his constant restlessness, making demands that accomplished nothing except endowing himself with chimerical power and authority, living beyond reason, battling with his wife, establishing destruction and difficulty as his norm, their norm, warriors forever. Years before, Tallulah had spoken to Humphrey about the inevitable collapse of the thin man's weak, wheezing, blue-veined body. *His death should not have surprised me.*

CHAPTER TWENTY-FOUR

An assortment of bare feet trod past, some thick and heavy with the bodily weight they bore, others small, nimble, and dancing in anticipation of the cool water ahead. All towels dragged, soon to be flopped over the low fence or tossed upon the hot concrete. Splashes and laughter beckoned from around the corner. Tallulah sat in a cheap lawn chair outside the door to their apartment, shaded from the hot sun, watching the passing steps of others, her embers glowing like smoldering coal beneath the surface.

She spoke without speaking. *Why are you still with me? Evaporate and allow me peace. Dissolve. Be gone. Scat. Our rendezvous is over. Your presence cannot be claimed beyond the standard status of temporary. Go away. You are the guest who overstays his welcome. I wish I could reach inside my chest and yank you out, blade thing. I don't want you. I do not understand you. I never asked for you. It has been two years. According to the books, you get one year, no more. Two years is too long.*

The thought of another sudden loss occurring constantly dangled above her, taunting her. She doubted if she could survive a second stab of the knife, since the first once refused to evacuate the premises. *Nothing lasts in this world, so why do you linger?*

What was it about him that haunted her? Her old hate remained valid; the man's actions and their consequences had not died with him. She had no intention of denying the evidence even without its connection to a living source. Hate sat within her as an unseen yet stable element of her identity, something definite and keepable, a channel of energy redirected from being aimed at a bullseye to encircling her like a mantle falling to the shoulders. She had expected it to protect her from the pain. Instead, life had lost its smile.

Whatever happened to my good old days of insensitivity and fortified barriers? I worked hard to build those. They at least kept him away from me, most of the time. Now the damn tears keep popping out any time they please. He invades my privacy. He infiltrates my public life. Why can't I prevent him from jumping in when I least expect it? Why the hell is this pain thing lingering, a perduring metal intruder? I find myself stupidly suffering for people I do not know, or for fictional characters I know damn well have never taken a breath.

The doors swing open, and two perspiring male surgeons emerge, peeling off rubber gloves as they stride forward. The compassionate eyes of the handsome young one meet the gaze of an anxious, stylish brunette, who stands, continuing an obvious, valiant struggle with self-control, her finely manicured nails restless and tapping. Connie has already guessed the results of her husband's operation, yet clutches her noble torch of hope.

"I'm sorry," the surgeon says, dashing those hopes. "We did everything we could."

A handful of loyal friends remain glued to their chrome and leafy waiting area long enough to see if the omnipotent facade of courage and strength will crumble. Expectant glances flash across the faces of a cosmetologist's pride: make-up flawless, hair precise, contemporary, fashionably hot stuff. The rebellious teenage daughter displays only the slightest disfiguring frown before dropping her lined eyelids. Finally, Helen from across the street stands up to supply poor Connie with the appropriate shoulder and puppy dog face.

Tallulah supplied the tears, enough for everyone. *My God, it's only a stupid T.V. show*, she had thought, last night, her face soaked. *My gates possess no will of their own, and the flood crashed through.* She had not been thinking of her father at the time, but old memories slashed uninvited, each screaming at her like some dreadfully lost opportunity. *How absurd.* The barbed sobs had continued until her own embarrassment arose, though she sat alone, and she stumbled to the bathroom refuge. There she had allowed the anxiety to dump itself out. *Dump. Dump. Dump. So many damn tears.*

Weeks before, in a movie theater, she had remained in her seat and weathered another private storm as a country singer attended her father's funeral in the hills of the coal miners. "Amazing Grace" had been Jacob's favorite song, and the dreary old church hymn tore into her heart, pulverizing defenses, making the sobs drench her face, embarrassing her again.

Beyond the passing feet and limp towels, Tallulah's truncated gaze fell upon a garden, not much more than a line of shrubbery edging the next building. Plants grow pretty in Houston, if they can take the heat. Verdant rewards await the diligent gardener. The trick is to get the plants in the ground soon after the heaviest months of heat. In addition, one must be kind to the roots, giving them a soft, nutritious pillow with moisture as needed in a location with only as much illumination as they can bear. They all have roots, tenacious tentacles reaching for sustenance within the soil of the earth.

Somewhere within me, the blade must have a root, despite its lack of chlorophyll and carotenoids. A source, a reason for its existence, a reason for lingering so damn long.

Ever the student, she had been reading books about the impact death leaves behind for the survivors, attempting to build herself into a solid person with a life worth sharing, grasping at bits and pieces of insight occasionally fluttering up from the pages, applying the various stages of grieving to herself, trying them on like hats: *What about something called Acceptance? Well, his life ended; no argument there. Here's a familiar one: anger. Anger? Yes, I am angry this thing still hurts. How about Bargaining? Sell my soul for alleviation? Not likely. Perhaps Denial? Mom covered that. Any Depression? Yes, plenty. Guilt? I already apologized. Pain? Way too much. Shock? Yes, the news arrived suddenly. Suppression? No way, not my forte. Reinforcement? People don't offer much sympathy after two years. I receive no attention for suffering, and I do not pity myself.* Her mental efforts browsed in vain, burdened with bearing the drag of heavy metal. Scarce enlightenment rose from the pages of books attempting to bring a remedial, yet simplistic, order to the usual pain of losing a loved one. In Tallulah's case, an elusive something remained un-typical about her god-forsaken agony over a highly-non-loved one.

So she prayed. "Please God, with thy holiness and strength, Lord God whom I love and cherish, please be a good guy and help me get rid of this heavy, ugly thing. I cannot enjoy the life you have given me with the blade blocking joy, blocking happiness. I know you must have a reason for slamming—I mean planting—this slicing knife in me. I'm ready to learn whatever it is you're trying to teach me, honest I am. Many times before I have learned from what you put before me. I want to grow, but I feel stuck, and for such a long time. Come on now, be a good sport. Yoohoo. Tell me. Show me. I'm listening. Seek and ye shall find? Open closed doors? While dealing with the present? You've got to be kidding.

"How about maybe a little hellfire and brimstone approach: get thee behind me, Satan, and all that? You could do it Texas style, with a self-righteous fury thrown in. Lasso that blade thing and yank it out. Yeeha! What? No go? Then any style would be okay with me. Feel free to step in and do a work, a zing zang zap from heaven, as Tod the beautiful bike rider would say. Nah? Sheesh. Yeah, yeah, I know, but I don't want to know. You are not kind. Back to the doors, the deeply closed doors."

Three years of parenting had opened a few smooth portals for Tallulah. They certainly held more appeal than any old ones rusted shut. *More joy has surfaced with our second child, but I can't help wondering how much of this new child's life I will be allowed to witness. As a parental responsibility, I choose to be the most well-balanced person I can be, by recognizing my weaknesses and overcoming them on a daily basis. I have no right to harbor anxiety. With these two little human sponges around, every modicum of my time holds the potential for establishing a portion of another human being's personality. I'd rather not be anyone's source of contamination. Apparently, I cannot go back to seeing but avoiding obstacles, trotting over and around like any sensible person. My personal commitment to bare naked*

160

honesty is encumbered by something especially heavy from my past. My good feet, usually able to kick aside the scattered garbage, can't move through this clunker. Together we weep in apprehension of the inevitable rot inertia brings. Snickering stagnation stands on the sidelines. Oh, Lord, what a monster blocks my path.

More brain browsing headlights caught a time past when she enjoyed living and learning. One of the field trips included in her college sculpture class consisted of a visit to the local junk yard. Each student followed the instructions to find his or her own path among the heaps and hills of rejected stuff. Strolling and responding to voices chirping about potential enabled each explorer to select a few treasures and transport them back to the classroom, where young sculptors-in-training either cut, sawed, glued, welded their winners together into masterpieces unparalleled, or made plaster molds from them to fill with epoxy resin, thereby creating new and aesthetically dynamite forms. While those goat horns and hubcaps and radiators and tea kettles no longer served their original functions, they gained new distinction by deliberate changes in perspective, imagination, and swabs of elbow grease.

As Tallulah and her classmates manipulated pieces of repurposed junk, they removed loose wires, pounded out dents, sanded, and stripped old finishes which distracted from the basic forms. Had they real lungs, the things would have yelped and whined in pain, the way people do when they resist change, but the students worked with careful respect for their selected objects, creating memorable moments by immersing themselves in the challenge, scrutinizing society's rejects, imagining new possibilities, nurturing hope and rejuvenation scrap by worthy scrap. *Tangible challenges are so much easier to overcome.*

Relinquishing her lawn chair and the foot parade, Tallulah quietly retreated to her life on the other side of the front door. Reaching her bedroom, she slammed her fist into a pillow, pounding and pounding the innocent bag of fluff into the mattress beneath. A single thought permeated her brain, each blow to the pillow coordinated with a single word, collectively building a full sentence: *There. Is. No. Reason. For. The Pain. There. Is. No. Reason. For. The. Pain. And yet there must be one, somewhere, behind some goddamn internal, infernal, rusted old door.*

"Why are you hitting your piwo, Mama?" Tallulah swirled around, and there stood her three-year-old radar system, in the doorway.

Uh oh. "Um, just making it fluffier, Zach. Is Arnie awake, too?"

"Yes. I wet him play wif *my* Cookie Monster, and he made doodoo."

"He doed the doodoo, eh? Let's go clean him up." *Finding the goddamn internal, infernal door will have to wait.*

"I could shmell it. Phewy poo poo," said Zachary, holding his nose as he walked. "Babies are stinky. I'm not."

Arnold's nine months of turning his mother into a subservient duck had culminated much in the same pattern as his brother's, minus the trauma engulfing the climax, and minus a good portion of the uncertainty. The second time around, Tallulah knew better than to lean on the white coats, and she wanted Jay to be taking care of Zach while she made a second go 'round to achieve harmony with her body's adamant pursuance of propulsion.

At a different hospital, where patients encountered respect because they possessed medical insurance, birth came smooth and tremendous, all the way to its fulfilling completion. The final moments emanated wonder, warmth, and a sacred sprinkle of transcendent unity with God's world. The arrival of an exquisite creature from a holy realm evoked reverence and pride. Soft and vulnerable he lay, as threads of euphoria mingled their way up to his mother, defining her as the one he reached for, crowning her with the responsibility to envelop him in the security and comfort every newborn individual is entitled to. This time, she could smile at him and say, "I know where you came from."

Despite the unidentified heaviness lingering in her heart, she could not deny feeling the twinkle of hope a healthy baby brings, glimmers emerging with the glow of a bright dawn from behind another new door sweetly beginning to open, even as the other portal tormenting her the most remained rusted shut. The responsibility felt tremendous, yet she knew somehow she would reap benefits. In order to minimize contaminating him with her personal garbage and that of the societal forces he would grow up in, she accepted the challenge of distilling accepted standards of social behavior into basic, sensible elements, providing the essential building blocks of beginnings, and discarding hindrances and contaminants, somehow. She pledged to contribute her finest to his untarnished, sensitive system, as well as to the ubiquitous receptors of his older brother, and learn to juggle her attention between their individual needs.

The second time around, loss of sleep was nothing. The baby world of diapers and feeding and mushy food had become accepted elements of the prioritized identity Tallulah claimed, despite its job requirement of sometimes enduring wrenching personal adjustments. She adapted, embracing the evolving responsibility, searching to find and follow the uncommon, mostly unwalked paths of natural development, avoiding familiar potholes of authoritarian roadways riddled with misconceptions and nonsense. She gained confidence in her own judgement, setting aside personal dilemmas as needed to enjoy the softness of a baby while balancing it with the needs of an inquisitive toddler.

Her first months as a mother of two continued to exemplify the deliberate gain of knowledge as a superior tool over any supposedly innate female skills of baby care. One day when reddish spots appeared on Zachary's chest and arms, she telephoned Idalia and described the symptoms present in her toddler, only to hear, "Oh, well."

"What do you think it is?" Tallulah wanted to know.

"Kids get things sometimes."

"But what is it?"

"Kids just get things sometimes."

"Things?"

Worn and stained, her copy of Dr. Spock's book remained an invaluable reference. She tentatively identified Zach's skin symptoms as roseola, a condition unfamiliar to her, and a visit to a doctor confirmed her amateur diagnosis. She experienced minimal success in restraining a victory smile over her sick child.

Tallulah's pleasure lay in having taken a deliberate step away from Idalia's complacency, her mother's view of trouble as something acceptable, nothing more than another inevitable storm to be endured by sitting and waiting for it to pass, ignoring resources of definitive information, of alleviation, ignoring the unused umbrella over in the corner, choosing instead to applaud each difficulty endured by adding a token credit to the chain of trouble she wore around her neck. *No. I took action. I found out exactly what it is and now I can deal with it.* Success in unraveling the mysteries of the young required immersion, not passive acceptance, nor denial. She would not be a spectator. She had jumped into the lake of child development; it felt good to keep her head above water. *Now and then I might get it right.*

"Mama, can we go to the wiebawee?"

"Good idea."

The public library's easy-reader picture books ensured shared journeys, offered vicarious adventures, eased tension, and opened beautifully illustrated gates to creative learning. Emperors with no clothes, talking rabbits, and elephants getting their noses stretched into the trunks they carry today made for shared giggles, and often supplied subtle clues for positive nurturing, such as Kipling's exquisite weaving of the spanking do-or-don't controversy in *The Elephant's Child*. The new mother adopted the young pachyderm's painful response to having his nose stretched into a trunk by Crocodile. "This is is too butch for be!" became a favorite response in her mind if not always verbalized in the range of small ears. From within the young, receptive minds of her boys, natural inquisitiveness and curiosity bubbled forth with the slightest encouragement. When Zachary asked what was real, Santa Claus and the Easter Bunny remained wonderful stories spreading love and kindness, nothing more and nothing less. Monsters also found themselves lassoed with Mama's rope of honesty.

Along with a selective choice of words, Tallulah had discovered how tone of voice played a major role in guiding her firstborn's behavior. Adult loudness inevitably instilled fear without understanding, and maintained a position of last resort when better strategies eluded her. A soft voice, reasonable yet firm, kept emotions from igniting on both sides, avoiding a stupid power struggle. While the common dictator approach of Jacob jumped up and down on the sidelines, outraged to be left off the team, she recognized his salesman smoothness as something not unlike the calm voice of gentle persuasion effective in eliciting desired results. However, patronizing a child had its limits. Her three-year-old's radar system detected and blasted insincerity; there were no shortcuts.

"You don't mean it," Zachary would say, stabbing Tallulah's heart with his direct gaze. He wouldn't go for promised mountains of candy any more than she would. Directives needed to be real enough to provide him with the same "why" she demanded from the world.

"Take your dishes to the sink so you can have a clean place to draw pictures."

"Okay."

"Put your shoes in the closet so you can find them when you need them."

"Okay."

"Let Arnold sleep so he will be fun to play with when he wakes up."

"Okay."

Along with help from baby care books, she took cognitive travels back to her college psychology classes redundant with the principle of "all behavior is reinforced." Unaccustomed to receiving or giving praise, Tallulah made a deliberate effort to dig up genuine words of warm kudos, and hugs and kisses for reinforcing moments of positive behavior. In contrast to authoritarian and superficial control, she realized behavior restrictions could be minimal as long as Zachary felt good about himself.

However, her angry words of criticism still popped out when she'd banned toy guns, but he used a banana to shoot the bad guy, and simulated loud battles between his toy elephant and his giraffe, reminding her of boisterous brothers, making it too easy to treat him as a familiar nuisance instead of her own son. *Good Lord, I have to monitor my behavior as much as I monitor his. Mama, how are you doing? Mama, cool it. Discipline without anger means putting aside my abundant emotions even as they race around within me. My brain shall rule over my emotions, somehow, someday.*

A multitude of optional responses presented themselves. In particular, she found herself compelled to stand guard against the readily-available, slap-whack do-it-because-I-said-so approach, even as it, too, bounced up and down on the sidelines, expecting to join the team, antsy to get in the game, hankering to slip in as a slick demon of superiority. Like a red flag, its appearance signaled the urgent need to find a thoughtful alternative and block the bastard. Dousing challenges of disorder and danger with rational, honest encouragement repeatedly proved to be a more effective strategy. Learning and re-learning self-control, ascertaining the guiding logic, provided both parent and child with their boot camp doses of self-respect and kept Tallulah from morphing into a warden, so they picked up toys together until Zachary got the hang of it, and because it made the room easier to walk around in. "Fewer things for you and Arnold to trip on, right?"

"Yeah, Mama, wike when dat wock wan under my shoe and the twees fwipped upside down and said heywo monkey boy. Ha ha."

"Right."

Along with respect for themselves and each other, Tallulah sought to cast a wider net, to instill in her children respect for non-human creatures, if only the rescue of the caterpillar Zachary tried to poke with a stick while his captivated younger brother watched, or the noisy squirrel in the park who begged to have a stone tossed in his direction. Neither appreciation of nature nor the value of property appeared to be innate for long in a child, both areas soon trespassed by the young curiosity and quest for discovery rising intermittently as treasures in themselves not to be extinguished. She found herself balancing the negatives with the positives, becoming nearly level-headed. "No, don't poke it with a stick because it will hurt the caterpillar, and then it won't be able to eat leaves and make its cocoon and come out as a magnificent butterfly."

"Magwificent?"

"Magwificent."

"Okay, Mama. Arnie, wisten to Mama."

At the library, they were stacking their selections on the checkout counter when Tallulah's eyes wandered to the "New Books" display, catching a title about the children of alcoholics. Interested, she added it to their pile. *It might be magwificent food for my brain.*

Food and eating and talking swirled together at dinnertime for the jazzy quartet. "Does bwead gwo on twees?" her little wizard wanted to know, holding up his piece of baked grain, snatching his mother's brain into outlier territory as she wiped up the pool of milk puddling its wet way across the dining table.

"Bread is made by people." Not every reply needed to be

encyclopedic. Patience could be acquired even as urgent urchin voices, promisingly silent a moment earlier, immediately battered adult ears during the mysterious endeavors redirecting adult attention without their young permission, such as telephone conversations daring to interrupt mealtime.

"Can I have my bwead metted?" Zachary continued. Jay held the telephone receiver, stopping mid-sentence to stare at Tallulah.

"Melted. He means toasted."

Arnold managed to bubble out an adoring giggle at nearly every Zachary moment, meanwhile smearing his own face with food before some of it found its way into the orifice above his chin, and much goo became incorporated into the moving masterpiece created daily on his highchair tray. Mama didn't mind wiping the glop from his chubby cheeks and dark, curly hair, but her thoughts traveled to the standard mother objections zinging from wall to wall in her head. The standard and familiar sought a verbal exit she refused to provide: *Oh dear heavens you are a mess mess mess we cannot have this you are making too much work for me don't be embarrassing for me now sit up and eat like a normal person for me be good for me and don't move blah blah blah.*

Shopping trips bombarded her with prosaic negatives at a time when she would have appreciated support for attempting to establish a positive route. Encountering handwritten directives such as Parents! Control your children! taped to a store's front door didn't help; instead, it motivated the continued motion of her feet past the ignorance. *As if parents can set dials and flip switches. How moronic.*

Children are not programmable robots, but they do require attention. *No kidding.* Freedom to explore and discover with the inquisitive mind bore no resemblance to the rampant destruction of an unthinking or neglected child gone awry, as commonly feared. Surely, calm parents could raise calm children. *But where art thou, calm parents?* The nervous and negative ones appeared to hold the prevalent claim on attention, particularly for a novice attempting to avoid pitfalls.

Tallulah's acute awareness pinpointed the negatives as they popped up in public, causing her to shudder at a passing thought of duplicating the speeches made by the mamas who used harsh words to bludgeon their children in pseudo guidance, employing a volume loud enough for the edification of every soul within a fifty-foot radius, as if they needed to prove to strangers they knew what they were doing, or how they deserved pity as victims of the devious plots emanating from the limp and pale creature they dragged by the hand, or arm. "I have told you and told you …." Any inspired pity within Tallulah flew to the child sinking in the mire of adult insecurities and laziness, despite the commonality of stress.

Obviously, tender minds new to a conventional, hackneyed world required bridges. Guidelines pertaining to adult concepts of territory and material possession did not exist in their innocent realm, a situation remedied with a touch of expository introduction: "You cannot pick up things in a store and play with them because they do not belong to you. They belong to the people who work in the store. You wouldn't want those people to come to our house and start playing with your toys, would you?" Tallulah discovered such basic explanations, being adventitious, required being repeated several times before the mind of a three-year-old reluctantly allowed them into his territory of acceptance. Grocery store workers did not help when the completion of a successful journey through the aisles led customers to the check-writing stage only to have the cashier ask, "Do you work?" Tallulah looked at the children with her, and the full cart. *Nope, I just play all day; no cognitive responsibilities whatsoever.*

Dammit. How can any rational society maintain a negative attitude toward its own children? Progress? Civilization? Are these good or bad? Young, innate values stood to be melted beneath the heat of materialism and commercial energy, leaving sparse space for soulful innocence. By functioning as the link between the two worlds, sometimes Tallulah wondered if she served as a key unlocking the gates to Beelzebub land. Nowhere did she see wickedness more evident than in the clever marketing strategies of hamburger restaurants, toy manufacturers, and clothing designers who manipulated children for monetary gain. Otherwise nuisances, the vulnerable little buggers became quite valuable if their dinky desires and demands could be agitated into life and heated to combustion.

Observations heavy with materialism and the greed it engendered corroded the joy of innocent living, but she noticed something lighter as well, momentarily familiar. It dawned on her that many of her old college buddies had landed in the field of commercial advertising. *Hello. I recognize this type of work. It's beautiful, very effective. Too effective for me now, I'm afraid.* Clever slogans, harmonized colors, and powerful imagery strategized without mercy to capture the better judgement of every slightly naïve, trusting consumer, young and old. The deliberate yet subtle manipulation battled to not only sell useful commodities, but to conjure into existence a need that did not previously exist, appealing to human insecurity, making women more womanly and men more manly and children ecstatic with joy joy joy. *How will I teach you, little ones, to fit into this society without being trampled by it? Thrive in it without succumbing to its superficial deceptions? Be happy without being foolish? Somehow, discernment and personal integrity must be slipped in somewhere between learning to tie shoelaces and donning graduation caps, like an essential constant undercurrent, the flow of personal integrity against the odds.*

At certain times of the day, she had help. "Sunny day, sweeping the clouds away. Can you tell me how to get, how to get to Sesame Street?" Tallulah wondered if the theme song had been written for parents or for children. She certainly wished to sweep her clouds away. The show presented a world inhabited by friendly monsters, daily activities interspersed with people of different colors, sizes, shapes, and ages. *Sesame Street* gave her hope for the world her children must learn to navigate, despite the turn her stomach took very time she heard one particular song: "One of these things is not like the others. One of these things just doesn't belong ...."

As the boys napped after lunch one day, Tallulah picked up her library book. She hoped to see where she might belong in someone's attempt to bring order to the chaos ubiquitous in the lives of children produced by booze lovers, who established "crazy" as their contagious normal. She also hoped she might find a key to identifying her weird blade-pain-thing-that-did-not want-to-go-away and banishing it to the great beyond. *Maybe I'll get lucky.*

Alcoholism defined as a disease placed it in a new light, perhaps as something curable, and not the demonic forever-plague of shame and embarrassment that consumed Jacob, wrung the life out of Idalia, and deeply damaged each of their offspring. Familiarity rose from the descriptions of mothers who lied for their husbands, embracing the habitual lack of responsibility for problems avoided, silently ignored, never acknowledged, never resolved. Emotionally ill adults spawning emotionally ill children. Young ones adopting various roles of compensation along the way, heroically or rebelliously trying to save the day, or clownishly laughing it away, or hiding in the nearest corner to avoid becoming the unlucky scapegoat. Actors in uncoveted roles, deception prevalent within all intentions, good or bad. Suppression and repression of feelings until they propagated and tangled into an inseparable mess. Frequent grabbing of any physical labor and sweating through it always being a safer bet than daring to playfully play among the feet of addicts programmed to blast foolish games to smithereens.

Unexpectedly, another ray of light revealed the consistency of behavior among club members as a diminishing factor for the uniqueness of her family's traditional muddle. The more she read, the more the Sheridan shroud branding them as different from other people, and therefore special, therefore proud, slid to the ground. They were no more than cookies cut from the same cutter as other progeny of drunks; they fit in perfectly. Uncovered, not a single individual stood disrobed in shameful exposure, as they had always been assured they would. This second daughter felt the hoarded family treasure of being unique dissipating and draining away down a definitive sewer of shared reality. *Damn. An ordinary dysfunctional family? Where's the fun in that?*

Dead-on personal exposure enveloped Tallulah; the complexity of her parents and siblings dissolving in the simple pages of a simple book. She closed her eyes in disbelief only to encounter a tamer phantasmagoria swirling, pelting and welting Gregory, Myrna, Humphrey, Cary, and herself in endless Superman, Batman, Mighty Mouse, Popeye the Sailor Man, Bozo the Clown battles against Lex Luthor and Bluto, seasoned with sappy Olive Oyl on the sidelines. The Good Humor ice cream truck zoomed in and out as an unattainable treat beyond the worth of Sheridan children, who stood and watched as their pals remedied hot days with cold and delicious. The misfit young Sheridans craved sanity, simple stability permitting them to grow and develop into confident individuals, free to love and explore unencumbered interests, to find themselves, to spend their lives as more than janitor to their father's mess. *Ah, shit. Well, I asked for it. Seek and ye shall find, indeed. Dear God, where's my spinach?*

"Mama, don't cwy. Here, you can hold Poochie Bear for a wittle bit, then I want him back, okay? Can I have some paper? And a pencil with a button, wike yours." Tallulah set aside the book, along with the notebook she had been using for scribbling the finer points and barbs, to accept the stuffed toy. Having discarded the coloring books of conformity that came his way, she handed her sweet son clean blank paper, unlined, free of expectations, free of strangling tentacles, free of murky waters. She also provided him with a click-click ink pen.

In addition to smashing secrets as common stuff, the alcoholism book mentioned a truth she had begun to witness: her own power. How she set the tone for her children and for her husband, regardless of whether she deliberately sought to do so or not. Her tears induced their tears; her happiness, their happiness. These days she couldn't get away with a sullen wallow in self-pity without dragging three other people into it, and then it became pointless. Light years from regarding herself anywhere near being worthy of serving as a role model or leader, she fit more comfortably as a follower of her own children, appreciating their slower, fresher, and uncontaminated approach to everyday happenings.

With a couple of kiddos to open her eyes, she began to perceive two realities, two vaguely distinct worlds, existing simultaneously but not blending well, having some type of oil and water relationship, perhaps reflecting a yin and yang concept of dualism, as Jay would say, or not say. "When are you going to explain this cosmology circle thing to me?" Tallulah asked.

"It's just some old Chinese stuff."

On the one hand, young children exemplified the innocent and unseen primal universe swirling with emotions, wonder, unlimited creativity, and trust. On the other hand, the existential human quest for food, shelter, clothing, and money reigned and ballooned, spreading into an unchecked, greedy flood wherever an avenue presented itself. *Undeniably, bodily needs exist, but why should the attainment of those required things necessitate manipulating and drowning the tender, young essence, burying it as insignificant?* The sovereignty of conformity seemed ruthless in its extermination of any thoughtful wandering off the beaten trail. The protection civilization claimed to provide as justification sat bloated with heaviness.

It wasn't that Tallulah couldn't see or didn't notice what could be perceived as missteps off the ordinary trail, aka errors, in the actions and behavior of her young ones. Early in that college drawing class, the queen of self-consciousness had learned to see details, beginning with those remarkable rolling wrinkles in shirt fabric produced by a bent elbow, but her brain didn't always know what to make of what her eyes landed on. Browsing gallery exhibits with other classes, she had asked why a particular artist deliberately left his teaspoon embedded in his highly textured painting, and why another master allowed the plaster used in casting his metal sculpture to lie sprinkled like snow on its dark base. They were not mistakes, obviously. At the time, she wondered about her own reluctance to accept these divergences from standardized norms of fine art presentation. Professors supplied answers in the form of more questions: "Well, what does it say to you?"

She had gradually accepted these "errors" as signs of a thought-provoking freedom she lacked. *But I thought I was free, open-minded. I don't have shackles. Not me. Fuck it. I do have shackles. Wait a minute. Do I like my shackles? Of course not. No one likes shackles. But I'm used to them. Yeah, that's the problem.*

Being weak in matters requiring personal courage did not prevent her from making somewhat grinding adjustments to her perspective of so-called mistakes, scooting her off the hard bench of judgement. She rubbed her bum, continued to see details, recognized the standard perceptions of error, but became less eager to correct them. The student of yesteryear had yearned for more of the bold freedom expressed in the professional artist world, perceiving it as a luxury beyond her reach. The mama of today looked at her munchkins naturally expressing something adult artists strove to rediscover. Consequently, she rarely demonstrated "the correct" methods for stacking blocks, or empty boxes, or couch cushions, or connecting those incredible Danish building blocks. Tallulah usually managed to relish the everyday adventures, scribbles, and verbal nonsense constantly emanating from her unadulterated creatures of discovery and exploration.

However, from adults, those graduates of childhood, thereby endowed with the responsibilities of guidance and leadership and protection of the young, she demanded more, holding them to higher standards, or perhaps alternate standards. Applying the benchmarks she demanded of herself, she expected big people to navigate the physical world with acquired skill, to have less ambiguous behavior, to be able to regulate their emotions, to possess more empathic thoughts than a child, to wisely accept the largeness of the universe, to boldly go forth. As she dug her own way up to a new plateau of maturity, her hope flickered with the assumption that most older human beings, other than her anomalous parents, must already be there, must have already pursued the path of enlightenment, and resolved problems of their past; she hoped to catch up with them.

Twinkling her Tinker Bell assumptions, she reached into her savored past to again don the silly glow of a college freshman exercising her first steps on campus. Relaxing in public finally felt somewhat permissible. She had gained admission to the campus of grown-ups, who, after all, did not come out of their pretty homes just to judge her. She gave less attention to so-called proper behavior among the remaining delinquent adults continuing to steal the stage from natural responses in children. She expected their insecurity to diminish in their lives as it had diminished in hers, closing her eyes to the evidence speaking otherwise. Although family fun remained as alien to Tallulah as it was new to her youngsters, she allowed herself to trust her surroundings enough to put up her feet on a park bench now and then.

Of course, unaware of their mama's progress, her kiddos wasted no time reminding her of the vigilance required to put lovely theoretical conclusions into practice. Noisy young wiggles in a restaurant continued to attract attention, but progressed as not so embarrassing after all. She continued to see not only how the slow appreciation of life through a child's eyes contrasted with the speedy attainment of adult goals, but how her role as mother held an essential, natural purpose, kind of cool despite the societal view of it as a stupid waste of time, a view she also flicked away with her magic wand.

Waving that wand in a circling motion with a sparkle of fairy dust revealed how the bare ground of any loving partnership required ongoing maintenance, deliberate tending, and protection from the rain of ordinary expectations and perceptions too readily available, too eager to wash away good soil. She allowed Jay to continue to play the role of bread winner, although it traditionally reeked of a power she would never yield to should he ever be so dumb as to wield it over her. Viewed from a certain angle, she felt Jay's long and inconsistent work hours squashing her into the traditional role of motherhood, the mindless housewife. Viewed from a different angle, her newly acquired adult angle, they did not push her into anything, not really. She simply found herself planted in a stereotyped role encumbered with detestable traditions camouflaging an altogether different reality. She chose the altogether different reality, remaining cognizant of her God-given free will, not trusting the myriad of daycare options available, not trusting anyone else to care for her children, not viewing herself as a flawless parent, but aware of many things, one being her inability to trust others, not when she did not have to, not as long as basic needs were being met. Beyond her lack of trust, something deeper, something stubborn connected her to her children; probably a many splendored thing.

As the April rose anchored her to her children, it also climbed away from the thorny traps of traditional marriage. With neither she nor Jay being acquainted with a model marriage to emulate, Tallulah chose to use her power to build their working and loving relationship from scratch. She had decided there was no such thing as a "happy marriage" anyway; only happy people sharing their lives. Nothing could survive on emotion alone. While she chiseled and hammered and welded an adult from the rubble she called herself, romantic Jay did not seem to need answers to every conceivable question the way she did. He just loved her.

But I have to love me, too. I have to be happy with myself, and I have no right to expect Jay to make me happy. He cannot. I am responsible for my own happiness, and for my life, whether married or not. I will always keep learning, stumbling along. Along with self-examination, being joined in marriage requires a change in perspective, how I perceive my partner, adjusting my view to blur the damn old tradition of male authority and see him as a human being, like me, and unlike me, different from Jacob, thank God. If we can get away from the poisons of the past, we can focus on each other's positive qualities. We can build something strong and new to both of us. We can push aside old dirt.

Old dirt seemed to be everywhere. As in any close relationship, living with someone day and night revealed all the loose wires and dents in a person's character, and they each encountered a plethora of expectations popping up like poisonous pimples from God knows where. Money, messiness, and mood could wreak havoc if not addressed, but how to address these infectious agents? *Blind infatuation may keep the bumps in the road negligible for a few years, but that kind of love, if it is love, flickers out as quickly as it flares up, and offers no foundational solidity. I do not trust infatuation. A solid love sees the shortcomings, tries to not trip over them, focusing on the basic form, always treating that partner with respect, with hope. That is what I reach for, elusive as it may be.*

Frustrations of ordinary living required release, and screaming at the nearest person remained easiest, but bursting her highest vocal volume into any convenient pillow proved to be much less harmful. Emotions cluttered the bridge of communication, shoving rational honesty into the river below, if they let it, whenever they let it. So much needed to be learned and practiced, such as pausing to listen, instead of waiting for a chance to blurt out whatever weighed on her mind. Tallulah's expectations of adult behavior as being easily evolved and mature frequently ended up in the toilet. Even so, she knew she could adjust, adapt, acquire, and apply knowledge. She perceived marriage as the bare ground of a garden, where brilliant flowers could bloom if planted, once she figured out how to break the dry dirt. Obnoxious weeds did not hesitate to jump in and flourish in the same bare ground, if given any chance at all. Along with the ruts and ridges of child development, Tallulah strolled progressively among the marital flowers and weeds, getting dirty from kneeling and digging, stumbling occasionally, making mistakes, correcting them, inhaling the smell of manure-rich soil, cultivating at a confident pace, when an odd wind brought in the distant rumble of heavy machinery. "Ever notice how often Houston tears down a gas station to build a gas station?" She asked Jay one day, as they drove through the city.

"Yep. Lots of bulldozers," he replied.

CHAPTER TWENTY-FIVE

It was a quiet evening. Jay sat reading a letter from his parents, who seemed to have forgiven him for marrying a round-eye. After Zachary's birth, they had mailed box after box of clothes from Hong Kong, impressive double-thick cardboard boxes, each stuffed with sometimes-fitting clothing for all three. Shirts, blouses, baby clothes, pants, all precisely folded and arranged to fill every pocket of space to an amazingly generous capacity.

"Tallulah, they are coming," he said, without looking up.

"Who's coming?"

"My parents. They are coming to this country."

"For a visit? You mean I finally get to meet them?"

"No, not for a visit. They want to stay."

"Stay? With whom? Your sister in Dallas?"

"I don't know. They just say they are selling their house and coming, in about six months."

"But they don't speak English. Did you invite them?'

"No."

Are they saying they will soon be moving in with us? Tallulah wondered. *They cannot live alone without learning the language first. Jay's sister in Dallas has ample space in her house for two more people but cannot offer them much attention with a management job that keeps her away from home all day and many evenings. Without children, she lacks the pitter-patter of little feet adored by grandparents of any nationality, surely.* Tallulah looked at the chubby baby on her lap and his brother sprawled on the floor, slowly flipping the pages of a *National Geographic. Perhaps it is time for us to bring our days of apartment living to an end. A house with a yard would be great for the kids, and they would surely benefit from additional elderly attention.* The next day, she told Jay, "I'm okay with it if you are. Go ahead and invite them to stay with us. We'll work something out."

"Are you sure, Lulah?"

"From what you've told me, your mom cooks, she cleans, she used to care for young kids. Sounds about the same as my mom, who can't stand the thought of making another move. I could use the help."

Tallulah had often longed for the helping hands of Idalia, instead of the vague answers floated over the telephone. For whatever reason, five children had not made her mother an authority on childcare. Idalia's standard, "Well, wait and see." did not ease the cries of a baby with bubbles coming out of his butt, nor ease the worries of his young mother.

"I'm sure."

As spring heat and humidity began to make their presence felt, Tallulah began a daily drive around Houston for the right house, wondering about these two old people and what they would prefer. Cruising neighborhood after neighborhood, her thoughts often wandered to Georgia, and Idalia, who carefully avoided getting in anyone's way, a hard-working timid creature who would try to give her daughter the sweater off her back if Tallulah said she liked it. A woman familiar with struggle and full of empathy, careful not to be a burden, careful not to interfere, yet always willing to lend a helping hand if asked.

Movies and history presented Asian women as being similar, humble, submissive darlings, silent, gentle, graceful, quite lovely. She remembered good people in old movies, such as *The World of Suzy Wong* and *South Pacific*, an enticing favorite. Hop Sing, the cook on *Bonanza*, always seemed like a nice guy. *Jay's mother is probably sweet and passive, a lot like my own*, she concluded. Tallulah was sure they would get along.

Jay's father worried her more. Tallulah hoped he shared few, if any, of Jacob's maddening personality traits. One sleaze-ball boozing dictator in anyone's life is too much. *Nevertheless, I admire the courage of these two senior citizens, uprooting themselves so late in their lives. Maybe I'm being selfish, but part of me is very eager to accommodate them; a little compensation for my fumbled relationships with my own parents might be obtained by making life easier for Jay's folks. Who knows, perhaps they can dissipate my blade-thing pain; release would be magwificent.*

Summer brought their first hurricane, a direct hit upon The Bayou City. Jay applied masking tape in an X to their downstairs windows, and they remained inside the apartment with extra canned goods and flashlight batteries, peeking out to witness the ferocious wind stripping trees of their leaves and small branches, hoping the roof would not fly off. Electricity and water stopped working. During the eye of the storm, when the air clogged with heaviness, they picked up a bucket and followed their neighbors to the swimming pool, scooping enough water to flush the toilets. Downtown, unanticipated force popped windows from tall buildings built bold enough to reach high and provide views. Put on hold while the city cleaned broken glass and fallen live oaks from its streets, Tallullah's neighborhood excursions resumed a week later.

In the early eighties, Houston offered the beginnings of a second Chinatown. Away from its old one crunched under a noisy downtown freeway overpass, this new area seemed likely to be the most comfortable environment for his parents, with its one big Asian grocery store propagating smaller offspring shops. Tallulah and Jay chose a three-bedroom handyman special house as near to the large market as their income permitted. Tallulah envisioned her in-laws walking from store to store, making friends, being happy.

When the elderly couple arrived in the autumn, on a Sunday, they were given the large master bedroom, with its separate bathroom and walk-in closet. Playground and library visits had become supplanted by the priority given to preparing these areas. Tallulah had painted all three ceilings, and the walls in the closet, wallpapered the bedroom and bath, scrubbed and bleached the shower and toilet areas, before she steam-cleaned the carpet, setting the stage for the new bed she and Jay bought and assembled, with its matching bureau and desk. New bedding, fluffy towels and elegant soap dishes, the best in the house, completed the sanctuary.

"Fancy," Jay said.

"Do you think they'll like it?"

"Oh, yeah."

In the kitchen, Tallulah had scrubbed the grimy floor, caulked every roachie entry point she could find, painted the ceiling and walls, scrubbed every inch of the scummy cabinets, finally stocking them with whatever Jay pointed out. "C'mon, tell me what to buy," she insisted. Chopsticks, rice bowls, ceramic soup spoons, wooden spatulas, an electric rice cooker, and a big wok, all situated well in the kitchen she intended to be a pleasantly-shared territory.

Given the tour, Grandfather and Grandmother responded with many an appreciative "good." Friendly nods and smiles accompanied by the multitude of small gifts they brought promised happy times. Zachary grinned and furnished delight with cute bowing to his expanded family. Pudgy Arnold endured an abundance of approving squeezes and kisses.

Grandfather dressed well and maintained a calm dignity Tallulah admired. In the days that followed, the cigarettes and booze and womanizing she watched for appeared absent from his vices.

Jay's mother and Tallulah shared joy in finally meeting, with Jay translating for them. The friendly, casual appearance of Grandmother allowed Tallulah to relax a bit. Looking forward to working with another down-to-earth woman, gaining from her experience, sharing female perspectives, fully envisioning the development of a collaborative, equal, fun partnership between them, but also realistically anticipating the likeliness of overlap in their individual intentions and territory, Tallulah intended to patiently acquiesce until their smiles brought them into the harmony she knew would be perfect. Grandmother's repeated promises of learning English, and the energy she exhibited in talking to Jay reassured the assumptions of her daughter-in-law. *This likely diffident creature will feel more welcome if she has freedom to do things her way for a short time, and I can gently steer her into our preferred waters if need be, as she and I sail across the open sea together.*

A hint of discord arose early the first morning, but it was nothing, just a Monday. Something sounding like dancing dishes, and pots clattering and clanging, abruptly docked all seafaring dreams. *A clumsy burglar?* "What on Earth is that noise?" *Can dishes polka?* "Someone's in the galley—I mean kitchen." After peeking around the corner, Tallulah roused a groggy Jay. "Go see what she's doing." Grabbing a robe, he stumbled out of the room. In a moment he returned and collapsed back into bed.

"Cooking breakfast."

"Cooking breakfast?"

"Yeah."

"For whom?"

After a few tolerant days of early rising to soft rice complemented with small meats and chopped vegetables, Jay again explained to his mother that she didn't need to have breakfast ready by seven a.m. every morning. His irregular working hours, sometimes lasting long into the night to complete a project, had always made it quite permissible for him to sleep late the next morning, and Tallulah let the kids sleep as late as their developing bodies needed. Although she nodded and appeared to quietly consent when he spoke to her, the next morning, and every morning after that, Grandmother continued to rise before seven and put hot soft rice and meat on the dining table, clattering and clanging only a smidgen less. Gone was the usually private time of peace Jay and Tallulah shared before he left for the day.

"Why doesn't she stop?" Tallulah inquired.

"I don't know."

"Did you tell her she doesn't have to do this?"

"I told her."

The two new people wasted no time settling in. They apparently did not see any need for altering their regular routine practiced in Hong Kong. After breakfast every day, Grandfather, in his pajamas, retired to their bedroom, appearing to read and write letters all day, not bothering to get dressed, while his wife washed all the dishes herself, gently but firmly shooing Tallulah away if the younger woman attempted to participate.

This woman likes to keep busy. Okay, I can respect that, thought Tallulah. So she began straightening the boys' room instead, or some other spot that needed tidying, keeping her sons in sight as they played. Every time, every day, in a few minutes, Grandmother materialized beside her, taking over, elbowing away her daughter-in-law, regardless of what the younger woman chose to do. It was weird. Even when Tallulah put the boys in the backyard and she began washing windows, Grandmother followed, rag and bucket in hand.

Day after day continued this bewildering pattern. Tallulah was not allowed to help Grandmother with anything, but Grandmother always had to help Tallulah, shoving any daughterly concept of gentle steering into the nearest corner. *So I am useless to Grandmother, but Grandmother is essential to me. Oh, Lord help me.* The baffled young mother shook her head, soon feeling she was expected to sit on the floor and play with toys all day beside the boys. Her towering aspirations of equal womanpower sailing the open sea began to shudder, threatening to disintegrate into watery threads.

Between snatchings of Tallulah's chores, God's gift to grandchildren began to do all the things for the little boys their really-not-so-stupid mother intended for them to learn to do by themselves. Four-year-old Zachary found his bed made every morning without his lifting a finger, his shoelaces tied with no chance of an attempt on his own, and every toy he and his toddling brother dropped swooped up immediately. Arnold lost his highchair tray masterpiece moments, returning to the days of spoon-feeding, and having every dribble wiped from his chin.

Good Lord, do my children now have a personal servant? What is going on here? Why does this woman carry Arnold everywhere he wants to go, and why does the sight of her carrying him so tightly, as if he were her possession, rip at my heart? I don't need any more pain. Arnie has just learned to walk, and he needs to use those little legs.

At the end of his work days, Jay served as a conduit to explain their preferences for Arnold to walk and for the boys to become responsible for their own messes, and Grandmother nodded in agreement, but the next day, she continued her same actions, bulldozing forward, ignoring any expression of dismay from Tallulah. The evening brought a repeat of explanations and preferences, more nods of agreement. The following day, as soon as Jay left, Arnie found himself scooped into his grandmother's arms, landing on his grandfather's lap while Grandmother made up Zach's bed, picked up every stray toy and dropped clothing, tied Zach's shoes, cooking and cleaning more than humanly possible. With the standard definition of help flying out the window, Tallulah recalled the adjustment necessary in her earliest days of parenting and took a deep breath.

Despite the unsteady waters, Tallulah appreciated the humble manners of her in-laws, feeling they likely required more time to adapt. She noticed they removed their shoes every time they entered her house, although everyone else kept theirs on. *They are not Japanese. Maybe their shoes are not comfortable,* Tallulah surmised. One morning, after getting an okay from Jay, she planted Zachary in the front seat of her compact car and strapped Arnold into the child seat tucked between Grandmother and Grandfather in the back. Arriving at a shoe store, she managed to guess at and select a comfortable pair for each of the grandparents. She stood by juggling her boys while the shoes were tried on and approved with affirmative nods, chuckles and a "good" or two. At home again, more chuckles and shrugs accompanied the removal of the shoes upon entering. His parents showed their gifts to Jay when he came home, and never wore them again. Tallulah returned the direct display of smiles aimed at her, ignoring the grumbles tossed underhand in Jay's direction.

Stubbornly hopeful of harmony and the benefit it would shower upon her children, Tallulah strategically attempted to get to the kitchen at mealtime before Grandmother, several times. The young mother desired no slave labor in her house, and she savored the kernel of creativity cooking offered. Before she could get the vegetables cut, however, Grandmother never failed to magically appear, immediately trying to figure out what was being made, and snatching any task she recognized. Both women offered nervous chuckles to cover up the growing urge to punch the other out of the room.

When Jay asked how things were going, Tallulah replied, "Well, she's certainly consistent. She's your mother. I hope we can work together, and I am doing my best. We say 'good' and 'okay' to each other a lot, and sometimes, 'no' and 'thank you' and this is how it goes, all day long. I feel like a traffic cop. I try to express appreciation, and demonstrate as best I can, and she nods, like she gets it, but she turns around and keeps doing things her own way. I'm probably not being clear enough. It will help when she learns more English; then she'll be able to talk to the kids, too. Your father mostly stays in the bedroom. He smiles but doesn't get involved. Maybe we need a little more structure. How about negotiating guidelines into the situation? Maybe a schedule, so we can each know more of what to expect."

With Jay's help, they set up a cooking schedule, alternating days. Grandmother agreed to cook on Mondays, Wednesdays, and Fridays and Tallulah cooked on the other three days, and the seventh night they all ate out. That was the plan.

Theoretically, such a system should work, fair and square, Tallulah thought. She liked the idea of a logical solution, one they could all be happy with. On her first Tuesday, she opened the refrigerator, noticed the abundant leftovers, and sighed. *Well, maybe this will take some time.* She cooked a little macaroni and cheese, warming up some of Grandmother's leftovers so food would not be wasted, adhering as she always did to her training of Idalia's insistence upon frugality, especially with food. Tallulah made a mental note to tell Jay to tell Grandmother not to cook so much, *please.*

On Thursday she discovered even more leftovers, and so the pattern continued. Sometimes she warmed the copious leftovers and sometimes she forced herself to ignore them, depending upon how close she had come to the tipping point that particular day. Needless to say, the refrigerator bulged.

Just as she refused to believe that Jay could work late and sleep late, Grandmother would not put her prepared food on the table until the breadwinner arrived home, usually around eight or nine p.m., but sometimes midnight. The unhidden hunger and frustration of her grandsons did not appear to move her, but it jarred their young mother to her bones. Consequently, her patient tolerance of her husband's parents discovered its limits. It, like the crackers she had been giving to Zachary and Arnold three days a week, could not last forever. *The hell with this.* After about three weeks of deliberate compliance, she quietly dished up plates from the prepared food on the stove and fed the boys and herself, while Jay's parents watched in disbelief, refusing to join the sacrilege. *Sorry, old folks. My children have to eat. I hope you can understand, although what I see on your faces is clearly not approval.*

On Tallulah's evenings to cook, she put the food on the table at six-thirty and called Grandmother and Grandfather to come, hoping they would get the message after a while. Instead, Grandmother never hesitated to raise her arm, point to the front door, and make a dramatic, unsmiling question out of her son's name, "Jay?"

On cue, her daughter-in-law learned to reply, "At work."

"At work," Grandmother echoed in feigned surprise every time, shrugged, and reluctantly joined her husband at the table, two condemned victims obviously wondering what kind of terrible wife is this who eats before her poor husband gets home. Their unyielding perseverance confused Tallulah, repeatedly, shaking her benevolent intentions to the core, wrinkling her road map of collaboration.

The preparation of rice helped drive Tallulah to the boiling point. On the day she first noticed Grandmother rinsing those white grains before cooking, she waited until Jay came home, then asked him to politely, kindly tell her she didn't need to rinse rice before cooking. "It's on the bag. It says to rinse before cooking washes away vitamins. We like vitamins around here." The next day Jay told his mother, and showed her the directions on the bag, and Grandmother nodded her consent, and Tallulah had hope, standing beside her husband, watching her desired potential partner in womanhood stand there with the filled pot in her hands. The moment the young couple turned away, however, they heard the sound of water being poured into the sink. Jay and

Tallulah looked at each other, giving Tallulah a memory to be stirred from the ashes every time Grandmother nodded her consent.

After two months, with the creeping realization that Grandmother had no intention of adapting to her daughter-in-law as an equal, Tallulah's patience began trickling down the sink with the rice water. She started to complain to Jay in the evenings about the way Grandmother "just jumps in and takes over" every time she tried to do something, and the way both grandparents stuffed candy into Zachary's and Arnold's little hands every chance they got, forcing Mommy-the-Monster to uncurl their tiny fists and remove the candy so they would have an appetite for their meals.

"And what is this cluck-cluck of disapproval every time, *every time* ignorant daughter-in-law puts fewer than six layers of clothing on the kids? I'm sorry, Jay. I know she's your mother and I want to work alongside her and I'm honestly trying, but they won't let the kids play in the backyard sand that I bought, and she frowns at decongestants and insists on her muddy, cooked twigs, herbal remedies for a runny nose, and they don't like the dog because it poops on the grass, and your mother always carries Arnie around the backyard, pointing out the leaves and flowers to him instead of letting him explore on his own like we did with Zachary, and feeding him and not letting him play with his food and rocking him to sleep in her arms instead of putting him in his own bed and then putting him in her room on her bed instead of his room and covering him with jackets when he doesn't need them. Her room! She puts *my* baby in *her* room!"

To herself, Tallulah tried to think about what she was doing and why. *I want to be polite and respectful to his mother, because she is his mother, but I have no desire to be thrust down into helpless little girl mode again. Knee socks and lollipops loom on the horizon, no, they are clunking me in the head. Do you and I have to become docile children again? I am trying to grow up!*

"What is going on here? She treats us like incompetent children, Jay. Jay. Jay? Are you listening?"

The pain in his contorted face when he looked at her melted any hopes of a planned offense. She backed away, changed to a lower gear, reduced the heat to simmer, and found herself standing alone on another cliff, the one many women encounter when they realize men are not great protectors of the wives they vowed to have and to hold, not when the other woman who had him first drops into the picture. No Mighty Mouse, no Popeye, no male hero popped up from anywhere to zoom to her rescue. After the private tears, after the suppressed anger, the frustration, thoughts emerged from the dust of shattered expectations: *I have to handle this. I have to handle this myself. Me. Again, I will reach into that deep well of resources within me, that hidden cavern I prefer to ignore. Difficulty unlimited. Not for the faint of heart. Things don't really slide into rational places on the surface in this world. Not this real, live world. I don't even know what I'm dealing with. Well, then, God, what about you? Are you listening? Isn't there a promise in the Bible that you won't dump more on me than I can handle? First Corinthians? Guess what? I cannot handle this. This is too butch for be!*

Before *The Elephant's Child,* along with the old Saturday morning cartoons, she remembered watching Jack Benny tell mother-in-law jokes on television when she lived in Michigan. They were never funny to her then; they seemed rather mean and cold-hearted. She nearly laughed. *Now they begin to make sense.* Unwillingly, she admitted being able to identify with those married comedians who made light of a heavy, grinding, bizarre topic. Now she knew precisely from where they came, but she could not make light of it; she could not deny the smoldering embers of molten rage building within her passive, respectful exterior.

After three months with no sign of change, Tallulah could identify and express her frustrations with silent words. She wanted to scream: *This is my family. You can't have it. You can't have my babies. They came from my body, woman. Not yours. You can't take my life away from me. You can't take my family. Get your damn hands off my kids. You have your own. How dare you try to take over my home? How dare you!* But Tallulah did not scream at anyone; she did what was most difficult for her: she held it in.

With every hope of a generational partnership down the drain, Jay came home from a problem-solving job to a house permeated with quiet, icy air. He continued his idealistic attempts to please the two major women in his life, never arguing with his sacrosanct mother, while feebly attempting to respect the boiling emotions of this creature his wife. When all three sat down together, his chosen role of intermediary seemed to come out of a box with instructions. With his Cantonese sentences longer or shorter than Tallulah presented in English, and Grandmother's sentences being stretched or shortened, it became obvious he was interpreting, rather than translating. Knowing him, Tallulah suspected sweet intentions of sugar-coating, his adoption of the fixer role neither woman desired. But neither wanted to demand more from him. The gap between the women widened. Jay's life took on a rather anxious pace Tallulah did not care to watch but knew not how to cure. Relaxation seeped out of their lives.

In order to communicate peacefully with the two people who had raised him, Jay reluctantly established a wall of separation between them and his wife. When he talked to Tallulah in their presence, she watched the smiles of his parents melt into frowns of disdain. She guessed they did not like being left out any more than she did. Tallulah soon felt she had married his parents as well as Jay. She could not appreciate the insecure qualities they brought out in this man her husband. The fumbling little boy stories Grandmother tried to share grated against Tallulah's image of Jay as a manly man she needed and wanted.

Still seeking solutions, she explored her options. *So why don't I go out and get a job if this woman wants so much to run the house? We could use the money. So what if there's an emergency and she won't even be able to call for help. So what if she cannot talk to the kids, so what if the kids cannot talk to her. So what if their questions go unanswered. Kids survive. So what if they come to depend on her more than me. So what if my chances of building an open and strong relationship with my own children burns at the stake. I have a chance to do what Jacob did, be gone and be busy. And that is exactly what I fear most, duplicating his mistakes.*

She glared into the bathroom mirror. "What are you going to do? Who are you going to be? Choose, Stupidio." *Not a rerun of my parents' lives. Not passive, not shoved into being a bystander like Idalia. Not boozing my way into oblivion like Jacob, the nervous, authoritarian monster creature.* "So find a new way, a new you. Break with the past." *But it keeps bouncing back at me. I thought I had walked away from it, but whatever stabbed me in the chest when he died remains with me, and more rot buzzes around in my head. I need help, a reminder. Something I can connect my eyes to, something to keep me on course, moving steadily forward, away from the mucky mud of habit and repetition of familiar old shit insecurities that do not help me deal with what I need to deal with, do not help me find a positive path, do not help me navigate between fighting battles and rotting as an oppressed prisoner.*

"Hair, look at you, always a mess. Yes, you can help me, my convenient, sacrificial lamb." Tallulah left no tress unlifted, making scissors separate her past from her present, shaving off all remaining stubble, happy with her smooth personal dome of a reminder, her break with the chains of the past. Afterwards, she felt freer, having demonstrated to herself an act of free will. *Remember that?* No one could take that away from her. The blade of pain remained, but she had rendered it less encumbered. And she would be kind, always kind, especially to Grandfather and Grandmother, accepting every strange food and habit they might be cemented to, and smiling if it killed her. She still wanted them to be happy.

Grandfather and Grandmother looked at the bandana wrapped around their strange daughter-in-law's suddenly bald head and took a step back, leaning toward each other in a private conversation, as they often did. Tallulah smiled, knowing at least she did not have to try and explain something they would never understand, something she barely understood herself. Jay accepted her transformation, and even found it a bit sexy.

To Grandmother, she wrote letters requiring no reader appreciation beyond the author. The writing provided a safe vent for her frustrations, as did the later shredding and trashing of the papers. *I thought we could work together, mother-in-law, equally, happily, like buddies. I help you, you help me. I thought you would be like my own mother. How the hell can two middle-class women be so different? Everything is lopsided. You tell Jay you only want to help me, but you always take over, like you don't give a damn about my intentions of partnership. Maybe my four years of childcare and home management are not much compared to your forty, but they are mine, and you have no right to try to erase them. Help without respect is interference. INTERFERENCE!! Do you hear me?*

I respect your strength and energy, actually I admire it, but I don't enjoy being pushed around by it. Polite hints are useless with you. Everything you do around me is an attempt to prove you know more and can do everything better than I can. I have no desire to compete with you. The mere idea of competition between us is outrageous, but you always seem to be pushing me into it. Why? Unless your goal is to take over, your actions make no sense. Maybe I should give control of my family to you. Just leave? I can't leave. Woman, you have turned me into a bitch peeing from tree to tree, outlining my territory, and I can't stand living like this. I must push you away or utterly drown in your faux assistance.

And I feel guilty. You and that passive hubby of yours travelled from the other side of the world and I can't even make room for you, even after I invited you to live with us. What a lousy daughter-in-law I am. Maybe I should leave, pack a few bags and drive back to Georgia. Give you my children or take them with me. Mom would be glad to have me. Jay isn't going to rescue me. I am young. I can start over. But what do you have left? Not time. You have invested everything in your family, and here I am trying to push you away. I can't do that.

Tallulah telephoned Myrna. Big sister advised little sister, "Leaving is not the answer." But leaving lingered as the most familiar and likeliest solution, a growing, appealing escape option Tallulah held in reserve. She could leave hopes of assimilation behind her, as she had so often in the past. *I know I can live on my own; I supported myself before. I know I can be a good parent; Mom can help babysit. I know I can be a good partner in marriage. I am an adult, supposedly. I don't want to run away. Why can't I be a decent daughter-in-law? Why can't I fit these two good people into our home life? What am I dealing with? What is wrong with this part of me?*

Daily, she reminded herself she remained because she chose to stay, not because she "had to" stay. She opened her reservoir of free will to move herself forward, renewing her practice of taking baby steps of personal progress, albeit the trail had become rugged terrain. She chose to face each moment as a moment to be dealt with as calmly and inoffensively as possible, shutting out naive expectations of being led by an experienced hand to glory land. Keeping an eye out for clues, she hoped to dissolve the mysteries of her jumbled, cluttered, dysfunctional concept of herself as an incompetent, ungrateful, meany daughter-in-law, but for now she waded. As for the lingering blade thing, apparently there would be no shortcuts to pain alleviation. Her slew of connections and considerations lay piled as warp and weft fibers entangled on the floor. She kicked it out of her way from time to time.

With the value of silly smiles diminished, Tallulah became firmer in her boundaries, removing Arnold from the arms of his grandmother whenever she felt he had absorbed enough attention, putting him on the floor instead, ignoring what sounded like "sheesh" coming from Grandmother, her feigned astonishment predictable and unceasing. *At least the woman is consistent.* Being immune to verbal admonition became a blessing for Tallulah; she could always pretend she didn't understand the Cantonese basics she had learned. While she couldn't prevent the rice from being rinsed, she could stop feeling guilty about not serving leftovers. She could shake her head no and not giggle, even when Grandmother tried to get her to giggle again, forever continuing to edge in at the kitchen sink while Tallulah washed dishes. Tallulah still stretched her daughter-in-law lips, but kept her feet glued to the floor. *This woman would bulldoze me right off the planet if I let her.* While weeping on the inside for a womanly partnership not meant to be, and wincing from a sense of female kinship betrayal, she made sure the boys played in the backyard every day, running around with the dog, sitting in the grass and dirt if they wanted to. When she encountered dog poop, Tallulah simply tossed it into the garden. She cherished the good health of her boys, but deplored the household atmosphere of stress, especially when it brought an unanticipated impact.

Zachary developed a lingering chest cold, and she took him to their clinic, allowing Grandmother to come along and hold Arnold. As they waited, Tallulah began to worry about Zachary's breathing, which had become rapid and shallow.

"Take a deep breath," she told him.

"I can't," he whispered.

Tallulah began to think she would be wise to go scream at the receptionist and demand attention. Instead, she restrained herself, waited quietly, on the edge of her seat, a little fucking longer, until they finally found themselves admitted to the presence of a doctor, who put a mask on her son's face and gave him oxygen, commenting on the blue color in Zach's lips, telling her she should have brought him in sooner. The white coat calmly spoke of something called "asthma," prescribing an inhaler and an expectorant, both of which Tallulah had never seen used before. She looked up "asthma" in her books at home, mortified to discover the impact stress has upon a child.

Jay drove his parents two miles to the Asian grocery stores when he could, alleviating some of their inevitable boredom. They could get on an airplane and cross the planet but refused to learn to ride city busses. After five months, no one felt much surprise when plans sprouted for their move to Dallas. Tallulah felt her hopes of approbation crumble, and she urged them to take any dishes and bedding and furniture they wanted, *but not my children*. Adverse to sacrificing her fantasy of approval from those two good people, who still bore the faces of wizened sages, nevertheless, she chopped off her dream, like the chicken bones meeting their fate on a thick board in the kitchen. She could feel the little girl inside of her whimpering in protest, but the adult Tallulah maintained a dry face. Her reality had become a matter of standing up for what she loved or losing it, and she still did not understand what more she could have done, or why the depths of her heart wrenched in agony.

Dressing her boys and herself in the odd clothing Grandfather and Grandmother had brought as gifts, making sure the old ones always had a place at the dining table, always had good chairs to sit in, a good bed to sleep in, not saying a word when muscle-woman scrubbed the temperature settings off the oven dial, had not been enough. Suspecting herself of compensating for her poor relationship with her own parents by bringing Jay's parents into their home and subsequently bending over backwards to please them, she had failed to anticipate how critical their approval was to her, how much she needed it, how deep the roots of her needs reached, and how these two innocent people were incompatible with her needs, and she theirs. Grandfather had provided an enlightening clue early in their stay, one evening when he looked at her, said something, and chuckled. "What did he say?" she asked Jay.

"He said you are more Chinese than a Chinese girl."

Subservient? Oh, shit. Not exactly the message I wished to convey. The failure is mine. What the hell happened to independent moi? Why do I so desperately need their approval? Kowtowing has done nothing to remove the stupid blade of pain in my chest.

Standing on the floor in the middle of the house purchased with three generations in mind, now emptied to two, with Jay driving his parents to Dallas, Tallulah felt her wish for a healthy, tiered family drain like blood from her heart. With tears dropping, she thought of her husband, silently modifying a Jackie Wilson tune, "Your lu-uv, keeps lifting me higher, and taking me lower, that I e-ver, have tra-velled, be-fo-or." *One thing for sure, roller coasters will never appeal to me again. Jay doesn't enjoy conflict any more than I do, but he gives in easier than I do, just to pacify the situation. It is difficult to respect him when he bows and scrapes to his mother, maybe needing her approval more than I do, surely more entitled to it. There is something crazy strong between parents and their children, sometimes unfinished business.* She realized her husband eventually would have to find a way out of his own mental jungle.

The space around an object defines the object as much as the object itself; she recalled this as a concept presented in sculpture class, from a time when things made sense. Her favorite teacher had waved his arms in the air trying to convey the general idea, demonstrating it by welding linear bars to float around the centerpoint in his own sculpture, bringing tangibility to an abstract notion thick enough in Tallulah's current predicament to be cut with a knife. *Maybe he had his own struggles with family entanglements.*

In her darker corners, the moany little girl inside continued to sob with disappointment, and a conversation rumbled within. *I tried. God knows I wrenched up my best efforts. Apparently, my best was not good enough. Am I just shit? I feel like just shit, first encouraging them into our home and then making it impossible for them to stay. Selfish. Liar liar shit pile. Hello there, Complete Failure. Your best was not good enough. You are not good enough. Face it.*

Her genetic heritage began seeping through her veins. Penetrating possibilities hissed up through the misty fumes of self-flagellation. *Here's what you need: glorious relaxation from limb to limb, anytime you want it, and you know you want it. Just drink away the pain. May as well yield. Just yield. Bring on the booze.*

Wait a minute. Is this where it came from for Jacob? My best is not good enough? What a zero feeling. Up pops alcohol as a refuge, as if waiting on the sidelines. Soothing. Tempting. Easy. Just surrender. Yuck. What a malicious beast you are. Ready and waiting to suck out my free will. No. I may be a failure, for now, stomped upon like lots of people, but maybe I can still stumble forward enough to find another path.

"Don't cwy, Mama. We can still bisit Ah Mah and Ah Yeh."

A little arm wound its way around her leg, as she dried her tears.

"When's Dada coming home?"

"Tomorrow."

"Can we go in the backward?"

"Sure."

Tallula gazed at their garden, always in need of attention. *The weeds do not abandon me, although I would not mind if they did.* The green intruders remained, patiently waiting for her thoughts to gather from vast lands untamed, expecting in vain for their steadfast, unexpiring foliage to be appreciated. *They don't die. Such tenacity. Admirable, in a way.* With Zach and Arnie occupied with toys in the sandbox, Tallulah fell to her knees at the edge of the garden, crawling into it, welcoming the healthy contact with grass, soil, and things accepting sunlight, things which grow and survive. Old Mrs. Watson came to mind, the wizard of earthy advice: "The roots, child. Get to the roots."

Tallulah began shifting the topsoil to find and grasp, those strands of eternity reaching deeper into the dirt than she could hope to fully expose. Some weeds broke off at ground level, snickering, promising a quick return. Others, like the skinny green crawly one that neighbors insisted could not be crabgrass because crabgrass grows only in Northern Yankee yards, required special attention, such as a pair of pliers attached to the whorl at the top of the root and a strong pull, defying the relentless grasp of gumbo soil unacquainted with the definition of "yield." She welcomed the textures around her, the scent of fresh soil, the sweat running into her eyes, the tangible pile of results. Leaves from surrounding bushes tickled her face. Flowers clung to her hair. The sounds of birds, neighbors, and traffic fell as treats upon her ears.

Jay. My love, my life, has a mother, has a father. Imagine that. What did I expect? I guess I thought parents to be like shoes. If one pair does not fit, go try on another. Dumbhead, it is not that simple. So many weeds in both our lives. I encouraged him to put his mother first, thinking a single flame or two would be warm, but instead a forest fire threatened to engulf our house and home. I overturned a rock, expecting a fatty worm, and a huge, hissing dragon flew up at me. The power I unearthed astounds me. Substitutes can be dangerous.

"Mama, there's a reawwy big weed over there, in the corner."

"Yeah, I know. I can't get that one out; not yet, anyway."

"Maybe you need a twuck, a supah dupah twuck, wike my orange one."

"Maybe I do."

"Here. You can bowow it, but don't bweak it, okay?" Little arms held out the treasured possession to her. Zachary's eyes didn't necessarily agree with what his arms were doing.

"Sweetie, you keep it for now."

That night, after baths and stories, she hugged Zachary until he squirmed.

"Mama, too much wuv."

"Yes, indeed." She laughed.

Sweet sons are too susceptible to mothers, who apparently can abuse their power. Mothers can perpetuate their desire to be needed, commanding, dominating others, if they are not cognizant of other possible directions for their own lives. Apparently, this role of motherhood can be stretched until it strangles. My time with my boys is now, during their formative years, even more precious than I thought, and I will do the best I can.

188

She telephoned Idalia, only to be showered with praise for the woman's son. "Oh, you should see Gregory's new baby. He's so cute. And so smart, I can tell. Eye contact. When they're little like that you can tell. He looks just like Gregory, and Monica makes the house look so pretty. Those two know what they're doing."

"I'm glad somebody does. Did you tell them how much you approve?"

"Tell them? No, of course not. I don't need to do that."

Tallulah felt in no position to guide her mother. The next day, Zachary seemed to be trying to make up for lost time, months of his mother's reluctance to leave his grandparents home alone coupled with her reluctance to take them out in public.

"Mama, can we go to the pwaygwound now?"

"Yeah, Zachie, that would be fun."

Lifting Arnold onto swings and slides, bending up and down, watching Zachary try every piece of equipment, between her positive responses to the repetitious "Hey, Mama, wook at me," she continued her private introspection. As during most of their visits to the playground, she made an effort to not be haunted by her own experience during an elementary school field trip, dragging her feet in the thick mud as she tried to stop the motion of a platform merry-go-round she had eagerly hopped onto along with her classmates. Almost immediately she had longed for a halt to the blurry world zooming past her eyes, trying to make it stop by braking with her feet, only to watch mud swallow her shoes, finally staggering into nearby bushes to puke when it ended. No adult responded to her agony then; they didn't even appear to notice the vomit of a little girl.

Watching her boys climb and crawl and swing, she realized the value of adult response to small needs no less worthy of attention because they bombard not the ears or eyes. Given enough space for good experiences, her energetic teachers glowed with enlightening activity. Focusing on their responses to her "Wow, look at Zachary slide!" and "Wow, what a great swinger you are, Arnold!" and more of the same, she perceived a quite obvious momentary relaxation in her children, like she had made a hole-in-one, home run, bingo. Give verbal approval. *Why is that so alien to me? Like pulling something new from a never-seen-before box. Yet it is so simple.* Like the clang of a church bell in her head, lightening words zinged in from the past, trampling the playground puke, coming from a design teacher who also waved his arms to get his message through the thick skulls of art students: "Simplicity is not simple!"

No, it is not. Okay, approval seems simple, but it is not. Being a bipedal primate mammal of the homo sapiens persuasion, I suppose I have a similar spot inside of me reserved for parental approbation, best doled out during the early foundational years. I should be opening an old box, not a new one, but I own no old box of warm, cuddly reassurances to fall back on when young activity invites participation. Maybe this is the spot that screamed with agony when Jacob died, making fulfillment, attainment forever impossible, moaning ever since. Was Jacob unable or unwilling to meet this basic need in a child? Jay can do it, easily, naturally. Were there no playground moments in Jacob's early years? Other than shaming his children's apprehension of snakes, he had never mentioned his young years. *Well, Mrs. Watson, I'll dig a little deeper.*

Over the following weeks, she wrote letters to Uncle Ethan, whose responses provided a few rooty details. On a summer day in rural Georgia, a five-year-old boy, the youngest member of a large family, occupied himself by throwing small sticks at the chickens gathered beside the house. After a while, and much to his delight, the birds squawked and scattered nervously every time he merely raised his arm.

When the gun went off, the boy was the first family member to dash up the porch and into the house, hoping to watch his sixteen-year-old brother practice shooting bottles again, although Dwight had already told little Jacob he was finished for the day. The other family members worked in a nearby tobacco field. The shocking scene the boy confronted did not seem real to him, but it burned like a cattle brand deep into his memory, according to Uncle Ethan.

Big brother Dwight sat on the floor in a corner of their bedroom with his shotgun still vertical between his raised knees. All around his head, red and pink flesh stuck to the walls and hung way up on the ceiling and his hair was gone and something was wrong with Dwight's face, too. It was broken and bleeding and red was coming out all over. The small boy froze, staring, backing out of the room slowly, bumping into his mother, who also had heard the shot and come running. Her scream of horror rang in Jacob's ears as he stumbled through the kitchen and ran out to the barn, shaking all over and sobbing, unable to stop for hours.

Nobody seemed to know why Dwight took his own life. Nobody could ever explain it to Ethan, but the boy saw.

Months later, Ethan and Jacob watched their eighteen-year-old brother succumb to scarlet fever, sick and hot. Their parents were still too upset over the suicide of one son to deal with the illness of another. The bright future of this star basketball player sank with his sweat into the mattress. When the fever subsided, people didn't talk about him in the same way, and he didn't seem to be able to take care of himself like he could before. How could anyone forget how to tie his shoelaces?

A few years later, in the lean times of the 1930s, young Jacob practiced his habit of tagging along behind Ethan, who was a few years older. Ethan could get Jacob to do just about anything by threatening, "If you don't, I won't play with you no more." Jacob always complied; he didn't want to be left alone.

The young brothers were playing hooky from school one day when they discovered their uncle's source of extra income tucked away in the woods. They had heard about the still and couldn't resist sneaking up and sampling its contents. When Papa found out later, he beat them with a belt until the blood ran. Jacob didn't understand why Papa got so mad; the stuff tasted the same as Papa's medicine.

Papa moved the family from the tobacco farm into town, changing jobs and business ventures again and again—Tallulah heard the echo— Criticism from the old man could be counted on for poor grades in school. "Why aren't you as smart as your brother?" and other remarks pitted one hurt child against another. Sweet, docile little Jacob turned into a wild hell-raiser during his early teen years. And, of course, Uncle Ethan wrote, nobody knew why.

Remaining home one afternoon, Tallulah watched Zachary, sitting on the floor, twisting and turning the parts of his favorite toys. Ingeniously designed robotic humans painlessly transformed into automobiles, airplanes, and other contraptions. She couldn't help wondering, *How do they do that, defying resistance as if it were nothing?* Watchful Arnold sat on the floor near his big brother, entranced at the deft hands working magic, bringing a fascinating creature into existence, striding with confidence, or an ingenious vehicle zooming across the floor and up into the air or along the edge of the couch, knocking down obstacles with no effort, continuing its heroic journey to land with a smash on a stack of graham crackers, bringing delighted laughter shared.

"Okay, guys, now sweep it up," said Mommy master, handing Zachary a whisk broom and dustpan.

"I am zupah Z-man, bwasting thoo pwanet Cwackah!"

"Blast into planet Pillow instead," she said, and she tossed down one from the couch. She flipped the cushions to the floor as well. "Here. Build a fort, too. Look, here are the walls, and you can put on a roof, like this, and hide inside." Soon finding herself more involved than the boys, she stepped away. The boys said nothing, watching briefly before returning their energy to planet blasting.

Mommy master wanted to shrink up and hide inside that fort, imagining a safe sanctuary. *Free from ripping changes that battle my bones, twisting sinewy body parts, causing unbearable agony, again and again, only to land in another impossible world where nobody knows me and I barely know myself. No shortcuts allowed, yet I strive for them, grasping at straws. Fuck it.*

Jay's parents, Ethan's letters, neither had miraculously allowed her to circumvent the difficulty of her path forward, offering no magic wand to blink away the tough stuff, providing no highly-craved substitute. Not surprisingly, Jacob-the-child carried his own problems, unconfronted, unresolved. Tallulah still felt weighed down; the blade had not vacated its premises. Her meandering had eliminated alternate routes, clarifying the residual characteristics of her own sedimentary path, requiring her to confront the everlasting beasts cementing themselves to her path, to resolve the problems.

Always a bit chicken, she had attempted avoidance maneuvers before, decorating her later student art to smother its essence when it began to speak, watering it down, because the pieces tended to reveal a true self she knew the world would trample. Why go boldly when it was going to hurt? She preferred not to invite any more uninvited personal revelations with her art; let it stay buried and private. Like guards detecting an escapee, her art professors would comment, "Getting a little artsy there."

During the months following graduation, she had painted flowerpots and tried to sell them, seeking refuge in a safe zone of cheap commercialism. A local gift shop bought her art, but no one wanted to buy a flowerpot with superficial colors bound to crumble and fall off. *I can't get away with anything, unlike other people, dang it. Other, more smiley people probably sell lots of flowerpots.*

Her chosen nitty gritty walk did not tolerate dithering vacillations, stoning signs of her hypocritical cowardice with claims of God, truth, God, truth. It persisted as annoyingly different, out of the mainstream, always real, always earthy, subliminal, taking her into muddy depths filled with reflective pools designed to reveal personal traits in need of improvement, taking her to depths she would not mind avoiding. Even bridges triggered trepidation, because she feared the pain which would follow after she crossed and they crumbled, and they always crumbled, as soon as the packed family station wagon pulled away from a plethora of problems unresolved, leaving behind a casket of forsaken opportunities and dashed hopes, reminding her.

Self-pity had its moments. Maybe she really was more of a mess than most people, at odds with herself more than anyone else. Myrna's strategy of shoving everything into the nearest closet held its appeal when monsters behind the door wanted to dance and stabbing blades lingered in jeering victory. *Maybe I am just chickenshit, seeking refuge in a fort even my little boys don't need or want. Who am I to think I can resolve everything? Find all the missing pieces? Lots of people harbor pain. Suck it up. Live with it. Life sucks. Just accept being a shit coward, another Sheridan loser. Stop looking for the damn shortcuts.*

Southern summations came trickling into her thoughts: *There's a tree stump in Louisiana with a higher IQ; Ain't got the sense God gave a goose; Been barking up the wrong tree; Goin' to hell in a handbasket; If you can't cut the mustard, lick the jar.*

She held a jar of mustard in her hand, having applied some to a hotdog. *How does one cut mustard? Guess I'll just have to lick the jar.* Or maybe not. Returning the jar to the noticeably less-populated refrigerator, she picked up a bag of spinach. "You're not so fresh, either." But she would not throw away the entire bag. For dinner that night, she would wash it all carefully, pulling off the soggy dark spots, wasting none, thinking of the canned spinach she had eaten as a child, and Popeye the Sailor Man sang for her, "I'm strong to the finich, 'cause I eats me spinach." Tallulah smiled, adding to the memory. *Ah, well. I yam what I yam.*

CHAPTER TWENTY-SIX

A week later. "Mama, why do aww these men have wong hair, wike Miss Piggy?"

"Where did you find this?"

"On the booksheff, way down at the bottom."

"Well, I guess they like having long hair, and sometimes it's just the style."

"What's a stywoe?"

"It's what's popular."

"What's a popwar?"

"It's what a lot of people like at the same time."

"Do you mean they aww want the same thing?"

"Yep."

"Uh oh, that means they have to share, wike me and Arnie. Here, you better take this. Arnie might tear the pages, wike he did with my dragon book, my faaaavorite dragon book. Oh, boy, wittle brudders are a wot of work. You need to put it up high when you're done, way up high, wike in the stars, where he can't weach it. Okay, Mama?"

"Okay, Zach. Stars it will be."

He handed her a philosophy book from her college days. Like most top students, she had read it to get good grades, never applying the concepts to her life. Now she flipped through the pages, thinking perhaps she could enlarge her present focus, which she knew to be too small, too narrow, too emotional. Over the next few weeks, while the boys napped in the afternoons, she returned to the book daily, enjoying a taste of logic and reason after having drained her emotional reservoir.

At first, the 1800s of Germany seemed long ago and far away, but not so much when she remembered the ubiquitous confederate flag decorations in South Carolina and Georgia. According to Georg Wilhelm Friedrich Hegel, both animals and man experience desires, but their consequential actions differ. While an animal obtains what it wants by naturally taking a direct approach, the self-consciousness residing in man leads him down a more complex road to success. Man's obtainment of what he wants is contingent upon his additional inherent desires, and ignites a process establishing him as anything but a solidary creature.

Tallulah somewhat balked at this concept, holding on to her respect for independence, but she continued with Hegel's views.

According to this scholar, man's desires, the things he wants, have an inescapable connection to his primal need to be recognized, accepted, and even revered by other human beings.

Tallulah caught a familiar stench.

Hegel went on to state that this dependency necessitates living in a herd, as part of a group, setting the stage for a serious social existence for him.

Tallulah found the idea of domination and subservience repulsive, setting the book aside until the next day, yet determined to keep an open mind. Being so deeply ingrained and accepted on so many levels as the norm in today's so-called civilized society, the concept of deliberate inequality gave her a bit of a gut punch, but she could not deny the bosses, the parents, the power she experienced in her own role as parent, the authority she had not wanted as a teacher, the game of Follow the Leader she so often had played as a child. Age, racial, and gender distinctions supplied further evidence of a prevailing hierarchical power structure too easily abused beyond any justifiable purpose. The worst of it stared her in the face.

And there it is, that monster on my everyday shoulders, carried by Idalia, carried by Grandmother, carried on the shoulders of every woman, that deeply ingrained subservient woman crowned with a can of elbow grease, compelling her to work hard playing second class citizen to the man she loves for no other reason than because she married him, sacrificing her own needs and interests in case they hinder his, as if his strength needed feeding. Her willful subservience contributes to the imbalance, helps him retain the master role, and he exploits it, obliterating love and devotion. "Stifle it, Dingbat!" seems too much at odds with the free will God gave me. How can anyone's happiness exist in the darkness of someone else's shadow?

Tallulah's heart hurt when she thought of the dreams of women, real and unreal, crumbling. Myrna, married for only six months before locking out the cheater. Lisa, one year and one child and bored out of her mind, ready to stand on her own two feet. Too late, they discovered holes in their romantic image of a knight in shining armor, rescuing the pretty damsel in distress, smashing the forest to clear a path for her. Nothing is free. The price of her rescue, her protection, is acceptance of her implied weakness, and behaving accordingly. Incrementally suppressing the natural urge to vomit, she must curtsy to his "superior strength," his male dominance, that bogus role of commanding king. Even in a free society, there is bondage.

However unintentionally, Idalia had provided a clear example of the social system's inevitable failure, proving the futility of waiting for heroic acts from heroic creatures who don't exist beyond beguiling fantasy. Clinging to movies and romantic fantasy, she had allowed her own strength to wither and die. *My tears fall for you. Such a waste.*

Some women awaken, responding to the imbalance of power with divorce, to prove to themselves they can support themselves quite well, dropping the shackles of dependency. Some struggle for years before going to professional therapy, if they can afford it, their brains striving to recover the logic buried beneath raging wildfires of emotions. As a lifeline, objectivity is recruited to expand the bubble of subjectivity threatening to suffocate them. Early man's choice appeared to have outlived any usefulness it may have had, becoming nothing more than a very selfish, wrong turn.

Tallulah read on. Being the one element which brings man out of the purely contemplative mode, desire transports man from an objective mode into a subjective reality, Hegel continued. His subjective reality becomes a self-consciousness containing a multiplicity of animal desires unique to the human race. Stemming from this jumble of animal desires within man is his preferred existence within the social community he chooses to live in, with each community member experiencing anthropogenic desires essential to the conscious individual. Desire for a natural object becomes a human desire only to the extent that someone else wants it. *Isn't this just plain greed?*

Social assimilation requires these individual human desires relate to perceptions belonging to other members of the community and serves to establish social position and dignity. Human value becomes contingent upon the recognition one man bestows upon another. *Good ole boys, unlimited. Sounds like neurotic neurons at play.*

Tallulah closed the book, shook her head, and sighed. Uniting these ideas with her memories of Jacob, she picked up a pen and an old spiral notebook to let him know: *Okay, okay, okay! So maybe you were not the only jackass in the world, but sometimes a herd tramples its young, in panic mode. Did our family have to live in constant panic mode? Maybe we should have stuck out our legs and tripped you, but they were not made of steel.*

Eager to please anyone outside the family, desperately seeking their approval, you yourself and you being the obvious number one priority, how could you disregard all those little people clinging to your legs and their plethora of feelings begging for your attention? Don't be surprised when I tell you your constant, unquenchable thirst for outside approval disgusted me. The hate came easily. It was already there, an everyday centerpiece on the kitchen table. All I had to do was pick it up. It was the easiest way of responding to your neglect, rejection, abuse. Were you not good enough for the civilized world, and we not good enough for you? What a stupid system.

Mom tried to reason with you, with her albeit passive interjections of fear and thread-bare reasoning bouncing off the walls of a system she adhered to as well. Instead of following any breadcrumbs of logic, you both retreated, becoming self-defensive proponents of cynicism and doubt. She became Paranoid and you reveled in the Reckless role, leaving all offspring between the building blocks of P and R. So here I am in Quandary Land. Thanks a bunch.

So much frustration and worry. I still don't understand. Perhaps you both assumed "the end justifies the means." Money would gain you social approval, buy yourself new clothes, buy your wife and kids whatever would make them look sharp as extraneous decorations tacked onto your public image, and so money became your center of focus, a panacea to cure all ills. As long as you brought in the dough, you apparently allowed yourself certain liberties: play around, seek consolation, take a drink when other pressures arose. These are all exterior, societal, and fake remedies, avoiding genuine solutions. You let demons dance upon your worries.

Not all men roller-coast through life the way you did. Uncle Ethan did not, or at least he does not now. Jay and I don't feel so inclined. We have our ups and downs, but he maintains a steady job with a steady income. It feels logical to us. Why was slow and steady never the normal for you? Were you born that way, or frightened into it?

The telephone interrupted her scribbles. A neighbor wanted to bring over her son, two years older than Zachary. "Tallulah, I've got to run to the store, and it would mean so much to me, if I could leave him with you until I get back, maybe an hour or two." Celia's call had woken Zachary, and the doorbell ended Arnold's nap. Tallulah could smell the cigarettes when she opened the front door to her well-dressed friend. Her son Roscoe ran in, as usual. Slowly closing the door to tossed words of gratitude and promises of "I'll be back soon," Tallulah held down her doubts by hoping, *maybe Zach's calm demeanor will rub off on this kid.*

As usual, Roscoe grabbed any toy he wanted to play with, giggling a lot, wearing a path between Zach's bedroom and the backyard, where he danced with the dog. With Arnie placed in his playpen so he wouldn't get run over, Tallulah opened the freezer to find meat for dinner. After enduring an hour of the boy's usual energetic zooming, she gave up trying to follow a recipe for beef stroganoff and walked over to Zach's bedroom. Zach sat on the floor, twisting two Transformer toys. Clothes and knickknacks belonging to Grandmother and Grandfather lay scattered on and around the boxes they had been packed in. "Oh, no! Zach, what happened?"

"He broke my 'bot. I'm trying to fix it."

"No, I mean with the clothes."

"Oh, Roscoe puwwed them out."

"Why?"

"I dunno. He said they were funny."

"Where is he now?"

He sighed. "Hiding behind the boxes."

"Roscoe, come out."

The boy emerged, his face twitching with shame and delight.

"What makes you think you can come into our house and pull clothes out of boxes? These things belong to Zach's grandparents."

The boy turned red in the face, but stood silent and straight, staring at the floor, as if facing a customary routine, as if waiting to be mastered.

"Do you need something to do? Come with me, outside."

They headed to the backyard. She opened the door and pointed to the nearest garden, quite overgrown.

"Just sit down there and pull the weeds. That's it, knees on the dirt, just sit there and pull up the weeds, one by one. Make a pile. That should keep you busy until your mom comes back."

She left the boy whimpering but working. Angry, she did not trust herself to stay near this male child, not after his violation of their personal territory, similar enough in impact to the wounds left by her mother-in-law, whose possessions the boy violated, ironically. Tallulah's wounds were not mingling well with her new, rather raw perceptions of dominance. Having immediately felt the warning tremors of another invasion, her conclusions bounced up. *He's like her, like Jacob, hyper, thoughtless, not considering, or not caring about the consequences of his actions upon other people. And nice-nice dummy me opened the door, again.*

Shaking her head, and shaking her arms, trying to calm down, she went back to Zach and the mess in his room, repacking the boxes and popping the toy's arm back in place. Soon afterwards, Roscoe made a run past his mom when he heard her voice spouting gratitude. "Well, Roscoe, don't we want to say thank you to Ms. Tallulah?" Having opened the door wide for him, Tallulah did not attempt to explain anything. She suspected the boy's forthcoming story of her as a meanie would cost her the trust of his mother, a trust too readily, too conveniently, bestowed in the first place. The probable loss of friendship bothered Tallulah less than the ready display of the boy's shame and delight.

She worried about the futures of her boys, and what kind of men they would become, even as she struggled to make sense of her father's past, and the clobbering, pervading impact it had on her. Hegel had presented her with a bigger picture, but not enough of the how and why.

The next day, an uninterrupted naptime allowed her to pursue his reference to another philosopher. Going back further in time to the mid 1700's, Jean-Jacques Rousseau claimed men to be corrupted by civilization. He speculated about the nomadic, hunting, gathering mode of existence which apparently worked quite well for two hundred thousand years before the concept of personal ownership infiltrated the ranks, and led to comparison and rivalry among men. When most of the world's nomadic hunting and gathering societies began to acquire land and livestock as their property, things changed. *Today's familiar gimme-that struggles were born only a few thousand years ago?* The connection between possessions and power has been ripping out the hearts of men ever since, leaving us to allow our own satisfaction and prestige to replace compassion for fellow human beings. Tallulah thought of her young boys and compared their behavior to the current actions of the human race, wanting and taking, needing to be taught about sharing and consequences. Definite similarities.

Rousseau's panorama continued. With the concept of ownership, combat became endless, as goods taken by force could be retaken by force. Eventually, men with the mostest presented seemingly logical reasons for people to unite and protect each other with laws, ultimately deceiving the poor and powerless into protecting the property of the dominating rich. Natural liberty fizzled away, and larger wars excited common men into fighting. An imposed sense of duty coupled with an induced prejudice toward perceived enemies. According to Rousseau, babies are born innocent, and all the nastiness of deceit, competition, power, fraud, and aggression are learned products of modern society, of man's social organization trumpeting position and property. Imagining her father as an innocent babe almost entered the realm of possibilities.

These ideas could explain why we are so comfortable in our own closed homes, Tallulah mused, *and so indifferent to the plights of others. We are protective of our perceived territories. We define ourselves by what we have, as I have defined myself as a mother, a role I have been known to defend with a growl or two. It is who I am, and what I do, although I know the "do" part is naturally subject to change. Not every mother is willing to adapt to the natural diminishment of her role, I suppose because she feels needed, and we place more recognition on what we do rather than how we do it, just like possessions. What we have is more important than how we acquired it.*

The natural part of us struggles to rediscover the primal affinities not only between us and our neighbors, but between different cultures and nations, between family members encapsulated in imposed roles, rarely managing to take down the mental and physical barriers thrown up to protect what we perceive as property, as personal territory. We overlook the existential compassion that binds humanity together. By doing so, maybe we overlook our own souls.

"Mama, can we go to the pool?"

Houston offered many months of pool season. Green, leafy plants surrounding an oasis of cool blue, offered hot bodies an opportunity to remove cumbersome clothing, soak up the good sun, sometimes washing away the past, at least parts already loosened. With Hegel and

Rousseau on the brain, Tallulah watched for signs of dominance and submission. They were easy to find:

Right away, Zachary made a distinction between him and his little brother, "I'm going to the big pool. You have to stay in the baby pool."

"Arnie hasn't had swimming lessons like you, yet, but I can take him in the big pool. Keep your floaties on."

Soon after, a heavyset woman surrounded by three little boys and one small girl entered the pool area, the boys eager to jump in, grabbing the girl's arm to join them. Tallulah could see the young female freeze when the woman used her loud everyone's-judging-me voice to command, "No. Don't treat her like one of the guys. She has to be a laaa-dy."

Boys engaged with boys practiced posturing, challenging each other, throwing insults at each other such as "chicken, nerd-boy, ditz, airhead," laughingly pushing down others to raise themselves above, mothers of maturity intervening if present. Young, supposed lady creatures watched the boys, with most of them being as naturally competitive, yet hesitating, the older ones not always sure of how to enjoy themselves. This setting increased everyone's awareness of physical differences. Other demonstrations of gender, size, and age dominance prevailed, too readily played at times.

"Hey, have you finished that English assignment yet?" Teenage girls lounged in chairs behind Tallualh as she supported Arnold horizontally at arm's length, helping him glide, kicking and splashing.

"Almost," came the reply from Teen Two.

"What's an allegory? I couldn't find it in the library," asked Teen One.

"It's part of *The Republic*, by Plato. A little part, called the allegory of the cave. We're supposed to compare it to television. I have my notes. Here. Take a look."

"You're so smart. I'd never make it through this class without you."

Even these two have a master/slave relationship, thought Tallulah, although who took which role could be debated. She moved away when the subject changed to: "Hey, did you watch *Dallas* last night?"

There had been several references to Plato in Tallulah's old textbook, but no allegories. Curious to know what her boys might encounter in school one day, she asked about it at the library's front desk a few days later. "Are you familiar with Plato's allegory of the cave?"

"I'll call a librarian to help you," the young man unanswered, picking up the telephone. A minute later, another young man directed her to the card catalog, flipping through a long wooden drawer of filed cards until he found, "Plato, *The Republic*, and a call number. Here you go."

Through Socrates, Plato took her further back in time. He used the enlightening powers of the sun in his imaginary scene explaining our different levels of perception. Living hundreds of years before Jesus, this philosopher seemed to have predicted the invention of television, along with all the other forms of presented images manufactured by a persuasive, modern society. A precursor to Rousseau, Plato described people who spent their lives comfortably imprisoned in a cave sometime during childhood; they were not born there. Having grown accustomed to sitting among others, sharing viewing shadows of images cast on the wall in front of them, they accepted the chains on their legs and necks. The restraints on their necks prevented them from turning their heads enough to see the constant fire producing the light behind them, nor could they see the low wall between them and the fire. The low wall served as the stage for the statues and other objects manipulated by puppeteers, sounds included. If one person happened to be released from the chains and wandered outside, into the dazzling sunlight, this person's eyes would hurt, but they could adjust to seeing the real world, and perceive the deception they had been fed. If this person went back in and tried to tell the others, "Hey, what you're looking at ain't real," the others would scoff, and the individual would appear blind and stupid to them as his eyes took time to adjust again to the limited light in the cave. "Going outside the cave just makes folks stumble," those in chains would conclude; it could not be worth the trouble. Being accustomed to a life shared would take precedence over any individual search for realities. Tallulah could hear them: "So what. I like my cave. It's good enough for me. Come on back in buddy, sitcha down, have a beer. Forget that crazy loner shit." Truth seemed not a priority for Plato's masses.

It wasn't that the shadowy presentation was bad, it was the misrepresentation. No one was telling the prisoners, "Hey, this is how I see it. It's okay if you see it another way." The chains kept them from obtaining any other perspective, depriving them of viewing the same thing from various angles. A three-dimensional world lends itself to different interpretations, all of which are to be appreciated, but only when they acknowledge themselves to be what they are: each is one view, from one pair of eyes. The beauty of her art student world had been not only its creations, but the genuine validity it gave to openly, honestly sharing various human perspectives, appreciating different interpretations of the same painting or sculpture.

Another day, another pause in her guidance of active young lives, introduced Tallulah into Plato's world of the Sophists, men who traveled about as teachers, directing young Greek men of potential leadership into the wiles of rhetoric, training them to inject verbal authority into the spoken words they wanted people to believe, usually for political or personal advantage. These men chose to regard truth as a relative entity, something to skillfully mold into any shape they desired. *Hold on a minute. This is the salesman strategy of today! Jacob's strategy. Hundreds of years before Jesus? A legitimate element of man's so-called civilization? Where is today's progress?* Now she really threw the book on the floor, lying flat on her back across her bed to stare at the flat ceiling.

Washing dishes later, she spoke to Jacob again. *So you were not the only one. You were being a Sophist, a deceived man trying to be part of the world by deceiving others. Shit.*

A worried glance from Jay playing with Arnold cautioned her to calm down. Placing both hands flat on the counter, she took a deep breath and exhaled, trying not to break anything, saving the rest of her scolding for the spiral notebook. With her philosophical clues sprinkling like baking soda on vinegary old memories, she stepped back, reluctantly broadening her perspective, reluctantly adjusting her foaming focus, once again shifting internal gears with a grinding force, unwillingly willingly applied. It would be a long night.

I may not have the power to fight the big picture, but I have the power to respond carefully to my small opportunities. I can clear much of the trail for my sons. They are not going to inherit any more of this rubbish, this trampling of decency. Greed, pride, deception, illusion do not justify the satisfying of desires at any cost. Society is barbaric to ignore the cost of young lives mangled in the process. No.

As hard as it is for me to imagine, I think I can safely assume you were a little boy once. I don't know how you started out, but the world must have become a scary place to you when you were still a kid and saw your big brother's response to this world's challenges. If he could not survive it, how could you expect to? So you shrank and followed—as I follow?—survivors, the shadow of Uncle Ethan carrying you for a few years, keeping you from being alone and outnumbered by those hideous demons of fear and doubt which plague us all, and savor snatching the vulnerable. You continued to smother your need for help by being "wild" in high school, seeking attention, acting up instead of sitting still and finding real courage.

Military life gave you camaraderie, with little chance of being alone. It encouraged you to obey blindly, living as a tool of manly action. avoiding the introspection that would raise uncomfortable questions, expose responsibilities. Alcohol helped, too, steering you clear of that damn sunlight.

You married within days of leaving the military, choosing one beautiful yet undemanding, hard-working, but conveniently no more inclined to look under rocks than you were. When you first met Mom, you enticed her with money, and money meant power to both of you. She slipped willingly into the subservient role, expecting it to be comfortable and secure, naively trusting your promise of success in an emotional relationship void of any cumbersome logic such as family planning, or troublesome occupational goals, relying upon a shower of manly words and a supply of charm to be used at will. Employment meant sucking up to the old man in charge and telling folks the golden glory stuff they wanted to hear.

This is where the unnatural dominance and subjugation concept invades modern society. Shifted responsibilities. Responsibilities out of balance. Instead of gathering essentials to build a family life upon a genuine foundation of substance and integrity, you let Mom feel needed by making construction her responsibility. You threw her a few bricks while you played and looked pretty. Responsibility is your real demon, the big guy ready to smash you to bits with unpleasant memories, the big guy you always ran from. To ever examine your past and hold your parents accountable would be to deny them their superiority, acknowledging the system of parental authority as the failure it is. It is guidance, not authority, by the way.

The many tumbles in bed kept bringing strange little creatures into your world. Mom said you would always be drunk and throw the condoms across the room. Damn wife kept getting pregnant, just kept lettin' 'em pop out, eh? So you managed to get jobs. The best ones put you on the road, away from that woman and her babies.

You were nothing like the TV dads.

You let me get hurt on my new bicycle, and you didn't help me get up.

You beat Gregory.

You were going to let me drown.

You made a joke about my very private stitches.

You and your damn cigarettes started a house fire.

You took us to Georgia and said it was a vacation, but we moved there. I lost all my friends, never saying goodbye to any of them because I thought we would be back. You lied.

You forced us to go to church. What kind of maniac shoves his kids into church with no explanation? No talk of God, the Bible, loving kindness.

And those schools, those horrid schools, where using one's brain meant being a freaky troublemaker.

Rather than risk facing unpretty truths about yourself and your background, Jacob, you allowed your psychological needs to accumulate unsatisfied, never facing them, never understanding your past or your present. You had skills, you knew how to use words to persuade people, how to get them to buy your products, how to get them to jump into bed with you when you felt the ghosts of loneliness approach. Stupid idiot.

According to your brother, you repeated your father's career pattern. The old man struggled to gain recognition, to be somebody, whatever that means, never watering the seeds of respect and admiration waiting in the hearts of his children who could make him a real somebody, never pausing to make peace with himself. Ethan said your father tried to jump off a highway bridge into the ocean. His life was out of order, too. He died in a mental institution. Why follow such a dark path?

Your need for parental attention and approval did not fade away, any more than mine did. You cried when your father died, and those were the only tears of yours your wife ever saw. Maybe you had no positive role model when you were growing up. You didn't know and didn't care to learn how to be a supportive father, as if such skill would reduce your manhood, give you less recognition. Like a commanding officer, you chose to play the dominating, critical role. You passed along what you were accustomed to, continuing to spin the ruinous cycle, zooming without thinking.

You took life at face value, as it was presented to you by those puppeteers in the cave. Your children got in the way. That drive for material success became more important than taking a toddler to the potty or drying a few tears. Racing through everything and over everyone, ignoring the collateral damage in your wake, focusing on number one, never seeing yourself as part of something bigger. Chicken-shit afraid of letting the bogeyman catch up with you.

It's okay to be afraid of responsibility, you know. It means slowing down, recognizing the needs of others as being as important as your own, even more important. Putting yourself on the same level as your children would have gifted you with a step back in time, a chance to relive your own childhood, your own stumbles, your own encounter with terror. You needed to face it to get rid of it, but you missed the opportunity. Too bad there wasn't a Damaged Child Anonymous organization similar to Alcoholics Anonymous, available for you and your need to be enveloped in the cozy folds of social acceptance. It would have been a beginning, not just a trimming of the hedge leaves for you as AA did, but finding the roots.

Many of your generation preferred to sweep fears under a rug, as if admitting their existence would have made them too vulnerable. You went through the motions with AA, admitting to being an alcoholic, easy enough when everyone around you is doing the same, but admitting there is a problem is not the same as solving it.

I am still one of those five children who got in your way. Your criticism, scoffing, chiding, jealousy, indifference, and misogyny were the antithesis of the foundation a child needs to stand on. These were your weaknesses, you sad scum of a human being. Your poor children fumbled in the pernicious dust you spewed. As a parent, you were despicable.

With every right to judge and be judged when it came to parenting, in the morning, Tallulah remembered her witnesses. "How are your folks in Dallas?"

"Doing okay. They have an Asian market they can walk to."

"That's what we couldn't give them. I thought your mom would be like my mom. I guess that's what I get for stereotyping."

"They were getting on my nerves as well. I don't think I understand them very much. So much tradition. l like that guy in *Fiddler on the Roof*."

"Tevye."

"If I were a rich man …." He laughed, kissing her.

CHAPTER TWENTY-SEVEN

"C'mon, kiddos, sunshine time." In the backyard again, she stared at the chunk of tall dallisgrass monopolizing the garden's corner. Unlike any other weed, it balked against the usual hand tug. Demonstrating no intention of yielding to any simple routine, it defied displacement with a monstrous strength and density, likely concealing a massive underground root system of tentacles daily reaching new depths. Its human challenger of the day placed the garden hose in the hands of young Arnold, who held it high, soaking the ground and himself with a gentle spray. A rainbow appeared in the misty droplets above his head.

After he finished, his determined mother stood using her foot to drive a shovel blade down into the dirt as Zachary watched her move completely around the plant, cutting through many small roots before locating the main, straight root serving as a solid anchor, the beast of defiance, the nemesis of her existence at the moment. She leaned back to slice into the deep thing with her shovel. As her feet sunk in mud, with her clothes, hair, and sweaty skin speckled with soil, she set aside the shovel to crouch over her opponent, planting her feet. Grasping the main stem at the lowest spot she could reach while still standing, she gritted her teeth and pulled, silencing expletives, wrenching the beast out with both hands, emitting, "Yaaah!" as release slammed her onto her bottom and rolled her onto her back. Her hands shoved the muddy green trophy high up into the air.

"Yay, Mama! You got it," Zachary shouted, jumping up a bit with his beloved truck in his arms. "I knew we could do it!" Exhausted Mama sat staring at the rich, clean soil inhabiting the former domain of the weed, truly dismayed at the depth. After a few minutes of recovery, she took the weed, clipped it into smaller pieces, and tossed it into the compost box.

"Where's Poochie Bear?" She asked Zach that evening as he sat on the floor in his room, building with Legos.

"Oh, I put him in the cllllloset. I can do L's now." He grinned.

"Good for you, sweetie. The closet? More like a cave. I see his leg, under everything. He's not your number one buddy anymore?"

"No. He doesn't do anything."

"He doesn't do anything. I can make him dance, see? How about if we put him way up on this shelf, where you can keep an eye on him?"

"If you want to, Mama." He shrugged.

Mama knew not if her child's need for a comfort toy had come to a complete end, just as she doubted if her process of identifying and removing the highly uncomfortable blade of something in her chest had reached completion. Loose ends prevailed. Sighing, she slid into art student mental mode once more, at the stage of final class analysis, done but not finished, where all the various perspectives merge into a point, and become subject to discussion. She visually gathered those threads of various perspectives and attempted to weave them in as weft fibers over and under the vertical warp, regarding the warp as that unchangeable, stringy, permeating, warped entity known as her father. Acceptance of her conclusive view of two worlds existing simultaneously, needed clarification of each, as well as a consequent examination of the influence each had or did not have upon the other, as far as her limited summation powers could prevail. And so she worked, envisioning the intangible.

The fibers of her youngest years boasted the brightest, cutest colors, all naturally delightful, as well as naturally tenderest in claims of physical strength, trusting, watching, learning to survive one way or another, begging to be dipped in the comforting waters of parental approval, even when that particular fluid appeared murky, emitted a suspicious odor, and failed to provide the expected sustenance. Consequently, the colors faded in her hands. Many strands lost their initial tenacity, slipping to the wayside as undeveloped potential. Signs of deprivation emerged. She worked with the faded, weary survivors slowly, gently, for they retained an inner silkiness stemming from their natural source, their original world of divine birth and glorious beginnings, a holy realm of possibility, as well as mystery.

You remain despicable to the little girl inside of me. She deserved better, something more than the illusion of a father, a mere idea dangled in front of her eyes and within her thoughts, never to be found holding her hand, never offering comfort, never confirming her personal worth, leaving it in doubt, never helping her pick up her bike and try again. That emptiness hurt, as did the sound of your voice, loud, harsh, shooting bullets at everyone in the house. Making people cry, leaving wounds unable to heal, neglecting to validate an existence.

Green preteen and early teen fibers hinted at the hormonal energy to come, as yet uncertain, clumsy, and without steady form. Void of mercy, biological cells wed to the calendar divided and increased in regularity. Pain made friends with self-conscious confusion, the result being a dogged puberty grasping at straws of survival, despite the bruises and senseless odds. Along with the stringy blends of blues and yellows, heavier purples yelped from trodden rug rags woven adjacent to the battered silk.

Again and again, you snatched the potential for stability away from me, uprooting, tossing me into a strange place, among unsmiling people who turned a cold shoulder to intruders. Because of your behavior, I floundered repeatedly among people who would never like me, becoming the guaranteed oddball with no hope of happiness, which you shot down any time it dared to rear its tender head. Nothing was certain except uncertainty. Friends, even a cousin, perched on the threshold of mitigation, you took from me. Biological changes faced ridicule. Female body parts served as your misogynist entertainment. Change is difficult; to make it worse is unforgivable. My choices were to die or defy.

Teen, ah, teen. The choice being made, the die is cast, the scene is set. Strength is gained. An identity emerges; all is defensive, but rock solid, consistent, reliable. Red hot jute moves in, trying to ignore the warp, wishing to strangle it, longing to free the world from a diabolical tyrant, and weaving becomes difficult. The physical body continues to grow, impervious to the lack of supportive conditions. It matures, resembling adulthood, appearing prepared for Jacob's world with its multitude of biased restrictions, while the brain remains undeveloped, uncertain, lingering in the natural world of the sublime. It is a dangerous time. Anger erupts from frustration. Rage erupts from anger.

I wore my anger as a suit of armor, a shiny, impenetrable fortress of young, defiant womankind. Growing up meant entering your world, the world of the phony, greedy, selfish adult. Putrid yuck. To tread upon the avenues of completion and success in your world meant self-betrayal, a loss of new and cherished identity, something not for me. I had pride. Defiance made itself essential. Those so-called life decisions, accepting eternal responsibility, or deliberately avoiding it, as you did, was a senseless no-woman's-land, to be avoided as long as possible, unless decisive steps could offer a path away from you. Then they made sense. Otherwise, and until then, it was right-on to sit back and complain, rant, and rage. I reveled in my circle of power, until God rapped on my door, "Halooo there." You had nothing to do with that.

College fibers. Steps taken. Good ones. In slides cool, royal blue, a refreshing ribbon of reason, quenching the flames of frustration. Doors could be opened without fear. Diversity, strength, and natural beauty mingled with practised concepts of harmony, balance, and kindness upon experienced trails. The world began to sparkle with drops of logic. Surprisingly, they did not evaporate upon inspection, instead bringing sustenance to dry earth. The halls of higher education never claimed to have all the answers, but they supplied intangible resources for lifelong learning. Throwing God into the picture, minus the phewy pews, this reunion with the existential, primordial world brought a little heaven down to otherwise nasty human terrain.

Food, shelter, clothing supplied. Thinking allowed. Questions answered. Oh, glory! I am free to use the brain God gave me. Life sustainable, uncontaminated by chaotic you, for once. Complete financial aid with a signature from Mom kept me out from under your damned old shaky roof. I left the cave. Remarkable. Things began to make sense; you and your ways appeared different in the bright sun. My world enlarged, encompassing so much more than any one creature's whirlpool of despair. I began to learn I had value. When the graduation cliff materialized before me, I came face-to-face with the full impact of my stunted development. Years of energy devoted to mere survival under your thumb had deprived me of arriving on time at the mental station compatible with my physical stage. Becoming aware of my own value ideally would have happened long before it was time to give thought to a self-sufficient future, to honor myself with a healthy place in society, but I had only just come to believe I was more than a piece of shit.

Teaching fibers finalized an end to the reprieve. With the potential for so much more hammering at the walls of her prison cell, Tallulah felt herself to be the one doing damage by spewing forth not so soft and silky, not so fiercely rough, plain brown, rather weak, boring threads, lacking the earthy, sunny, rich reach of a good educator. Lost again, she found herself entangled, struggling against the lack of oxygen. Familiar fibers of playful childhood jumped in, along with the ornery red jute of teen times, with neither being appropriate. Everything tumbled together until she wasn't sure who was teaching whom, who was presenting whose interpretation of youthful reality, but she knew she failed to foster peaceful moments of true creativity. Remnants of lovely college lanterns proved insufficient to shine in the cluttered darkness, or not enough of them had been collected.

Not knowing where else to turn, I let your world smack me in the face. I stupidly took steps for the sake of taking steps, for the sake of money, only to find myself back in a cave, appointed as a presenter, steadily shaken awake to the fact that I could not lead the students because I remained one myself, afraid to do damage, and thus doing damage. I remained an adolescent in mind, knowing I deprived the legitimate young ones of anything valuable; definitely stuck at the wrong mental station. As much as I adored them, they exposed me, revealing more of my weakness, my substandard development, as if I had climbed to the top of a hill and turned around only to see my beginnings remained close, too close; I had made little progress with my naive stumbles, again thanks to you. I thought I could walk away from you, and be my own person, but there you were, hiding in my head, sneaking up from behind and sucking me into the jackass master role I detested and resisted with all my might.

Marriage fibers. Strands of merciful manna gold floated down to caress the entangled pile. Halls of companionship annexed themselves to the halls of higher education. Unity business diverted her attention from employment problems she could barely fathom, much less resolve, but matrimony soon unveiled itself as not the simple love she wanted it to be. It, too, bore its contaminants. Both minds seemed too fond of old attachments, familiarity behaving like one of her eager classroom children thrusting a hand up into the air, "I know! I know!" Wiggling fingers persisted in waving claims of recognition and expectations. She wondered if battling her own brain meant undoing some deep primordial survival strategies; tenacious notions slid her too easily into the past. New roles could not be new if the brain kept jumping back to old material, slapping known objects into familiar-enough circumstances, not recognizing junk.

But she knew about junk. She knew it could be confronted and transformed. She just needed time. Swollen with their own seniority, the recognitions and associations of the past fought against giving her the clarified clock-support they knew would undo them. They knew the power of pondering, and chose to stomp the floor in protest, like a little Rumpelstiltskin, furious at having his name guessed. "Don't stop and think! Don't stop and choose!"

You infiltrated my marriage, and continue to influence my expectations, hammering my hopes with them, trying to pull me down and backwards, bombarding my defense system, turning me into a fortress struggling to maintain its flag in the air. This is too butch for be! You would even steal time from me, as you already mangled its natural flow. Change is always available. Alternatives are always available. I must remind myself I always have a choice, and need not always respond with a defensive battle cry. I will learn to choose my responses more wisely than you did. Rationally.

There will be no more naive attempts to intertwine past and present, no blending of my goals and your conventional world, no mixture of natural essence and greedy societal conflagrations. For all my years before now, I thought we lived in one world. Yesterday I thought it could still be one world; seen and unseen entities woven into harmonious balance. Mom strived and sweated for this ideal single world, but it never happened. Some things don't mix. It pains me to have to push you away, to push away so much of the world I need for survival, or believe I needed. The idea of living in two worlds simultaneously is an alien concept, in some ways other worldly.

I'm keeping Jay; my good guy. Together, we appreciate the beauty of nakedness. Physical appreciation is easy. Daring to look beneath the surface requires courage. No one wants to see the weaknesses of the person they have chosen to spend the rest of their life with. Most people think love will crumble at the sight of unprettiness. So what. If it does, chances are it was not love at all, but only one of its many imitations. We live in a society that hides nakedness.

My feelings shall not be imprisoned, whether they consist of inadequacy or anger, jealousy or fear, happiness or misery. In the same light, to automatically blast out emotions is selfish. Conflict can be dealt with in a calm, rational manner by recognizing and describing the emotions churning within, before they multiply and burst. We must be honest with ourselves before we can be honest with each other. I must learn to demonstrate my love as well as I demonstrate my anger.

With deep wounds pulled up from depths unknown and slammed onto a table in front of her, demanding attention, Tallulah knew better than to view Jay as her rescuing panacea, although he brought her joy. Letting the tantrums pass, letting the dazzle of infatuation die down, she would apply rationality and not let go of it. Marriage called for bridges, but bridges bring home the stress, and stress became a thing in itself to be recognized and described, brought into the light and unraveled. Far from having all the answers, indeed touching the garden-variety revelation of how an increase in knowledge reveals a meagerness in the amount previously claimed, the young woman vowed to try to give Jay the basic respect every person deserves, instead of either keeping him on a pedestal or jumping into blaming him for each and every frustration curdling up from her swampy quagmires.

Certain experiences helped her. Having already lived alone, she held no need to prove her womanly independence; she could support herself. Sometimes she sat down and imagined what she would be doing with her life if she had not taken those vows of marriage. Either graduate school or further employment remained her options, set aside but not abandoned. That lonely art therapy brochure tacked to a bulletin board in the art department still held intrigue; an equivalent might be within reach. She knew her personal happiness remained her responsibility, and she needed to use her brain. No one else could build her happiness and hand it to her; it came from within, from making her own choices. She promised herself she would figure out which steps were feasible and when.

Well, Jacob, so far, recovering and forgiving after conflict takes fewer tolls than your old habits and wastes less time. Jay and I can concentrate on accomplishment and set goals for ourselves instead of being bogged down all the time with self-defensive blaming. While we cannot discard our armor, we can at least hang it in the closet. I think it's okay to disagree. Conflict is an inescapable component of existence. Friction creates energy. We can channel our energy into constructive patterns. Seed harmony. Be flexible. There can be more than one good answer. We can learn to accept the weaknesses and appreciate the strengths of one another. The crappy, muddy fear you wallowed and flung at everyone is needless.

Unlike you and your society, control is not so important to me anymore, even over family activities. Preplanning everything creates boredom. Spontaneity has a place. If Jay wants to go out to eat when the meat is thawing and the menu is already planned, we can go. I can bend. Changes need the freedom to occur without planning. We can find ways to incorporate flexibility into our relationship without the roof falling in. Many preconceived images of the perfect marriage have nothing to do with reality, only with control. No one needs to dominate anyone.

She set aside her intangible weaving. It could go no further. She had hoped it would bring closure, a kind of shortcut to the end. Instead, the disgusting thought occurred to her that an attraction to shortcuts also came from you-know-who. She left the gold strands long and untrimmed. She would allow no future warping influence from Jacob, but she wasn't finished with him.

The next day she rummaged around in her head until she heard the echo of one of the few positive voices from her past: simplicity is not simple. Control would need to be redefined as guidance applied only as needed. The more she recognized it in others, the more she felt its eagerness to surge within herself, like a beast ready to jump from master to master, ready to devour anyone's good intentions. Reining it in would be ironically an act of control itself.

The spontaneity she allowed in her marriage had been learned from her children; they were the real teachers. By pausing to attend to their small needs, greater needs had become less throttling, less urgent, until it became clear that every little dribble in life is important. Children have power; they carry a celestial reality. Their entry into this world cannot be taken lightly; far from it. The independent, tremendous force within her own body as it culminated nine months of gestation told her where real power resides, and it is not in the minds of men.

Young life sat on the floor in front of her, playing games. The boys embraced every day with unrestricted curiosity, dancing to music, reminding her of human origins, especially outside, where they relished fresh air, digging in dirt, swinging in sunshine, serving as a counterbalance to the convoluted corruption cultivated by mankind. Tallulah found herself facing the kind of moral responsibility Jacob avoided. Trusting no one with her children compelled her to meet the demons and angels he had attempted to drown in whiskey. As a result, she grasped the significance of making decisions which would have an impact on other people, even while in the midst of tackling options for her own time on Earth. She often regarded her situation as the blind leading the blind. Indeed the sun hurt her eyes at times, but she refused to become stagnant water having lost its flow.

By not appreciating children, you missed something, she told him. *You missed a connection to your own soul. Children were your lifeline to heaven, and you missed it, five times. You stupid shit. Why did you have to be such a loyal cave dweller?*

That night she dreamed of Jacob. He stood in the cave and looked at her standing outside. He glided silently toward her, the shackles already loosened. She stepped back to watch him emerge, wearing a remnant of the old salesman grin, the sunlight penetrating his body as it began to shimmer, sparkling from within, weightless. A breeze began to swirl around him, its dust enveloping him, mingling, reclaiming his molecular essence. She backed away, almost tripping over what looked like a bucket of sand. Somehow, she knew what to do with it. As he neared, she tossed the first handful at him, whispering, "This is children. You used to be one, and you fathered at least five." The grains of sand mingled with his energy. She scooped up a second handful and tossed it at him. "This is art. Beautiful things can be made from junk." A third handful followed. "This is nature. Weeds can be removed." The swirling column moved him away from the cave, across the land, slowly rising to the sky, to settle and expand into a fluffy white cloud. Tinkerbell would have been proud.

Tallulah woke with a sense of loss, missing something. Physically, she felt lighter than she had in years. She sat on the edge of her bed for a minute, clutching her chest, remembering. "Tinkerbell? Really? Wait a minute. I think it's gone, really gone, after all this time. I'll be damned." Maybe blessed. Tears tangoed with smiles for most of the morning. At one point she started sorting the contents of their catch-all kitchen drawer. Zachary took notice.

"Mama, can I have this, and this?" Zach's little hands picked among the pile of rubber bands, popsicle sticks, string, and various lost parts of man-made things.

"What are you going to do with all that?"

"I think I can make something out of it."

She smiled, later ending the good day with one more entry in the spiral notebook:

I see something when I begin to erase the fears and frustrations that accumulated between you and me. Beneath the garbage, tucked away in my maze of a mind, lies that deep spot reserved for parental approval and acceptance. But this spot cannot be filled by following, by becoming a duplicate, a rerun; doing so did not work for you. In my case, this deep and permanently entrenched spot inside of me needing my father's approval did not fade away with lack of attention. Instead it sat there, a starving beast-in-waiting. Even as childbirth and parenting touched me with the sanctity of life, as long as any possibility of being filled remained, it stayed put. I guess I lost that possibility when you died. The beast screamed. I have released the beast.

Death did not awaken the beast within me. Life did. My life. That spot sat patiently inside of me while I ignored it and busied myself with other conquests. I ignored it because I lost hope of ever being able to feed it. Around it, I thought

I sculpted a superior mental wall, but someone else could have built it, and I adopted it as my own, or it may have been constructed as a community effort. Hate has a way of accepting donations and stacking them together.

Either way, the name of protection thrust me into a rut, my own cave with one line of sight. I refused the light outside, the light which would reveal the role I played in contributing to my shortcomings, highlighting the presence of choices, bringing me to a level of humility, setting me outside my shiny armor. The hate hurt only me. It did nothing to change you.

But other people helped me in the areas where I found no trace of you, the voids you left. I failed to appreciate the compensation, insisting upon you and you alone to fill a role you were incapable of filling. They did me a favor by connecting me to a bigger world. My art teachers helped me, my children lead me, and nature sustains me. I gave you a handful of each of these.

Some things transcend the demands of human emotions. The societal world we live in was never your world. You were one speck trying to stay afloat within it, controlling nothing. I will be looking for opportunity, instead of seeing only roadblocks.

I am acknowledging something bigger than the choices I made, something looming larger than the endless stream of pain and disappointment you showered upon this daughter and left behind in your wake. Those three portals connected me to a universal love. They expanded my perspective. The universal love we are all a part of includes you. It exists despite your behavior. I separated you from your behavior, and you left it behind in the big cave of deception, where your only ticket to tranquility swirled in a brown bottle.

Early the next morning, she heard the wind tossing dry leaves against the window. She looked out and saw more leaves almost ready to fall from an old oak tree in the yard.

After a few minutes, the real reason for her cognitive digging and spelunking toddled up behind her. He and his brother had so little time behind them and so many years ahead.

"Hi, portal."

"Mama, I'm not a po-tal. I'm a boy."

"You sure are." She dropped to her knees and hugged him.

"That word has the lion sound: rrrrrr. Mama, say rrrrr."

"Okay. Rrrrr."

And they growled together.

"Such a prrecious boy lion you are, Zackie."

"Mama, what's a porrrtal?"

"Hate is too heavy of a burden to bear. I have decided to love."
~Martin Luther King, Jr.

About the Author

 Beverly A. Li grew up in a large family dependent upon an unstable, alcoholic father.

Her bachelor's degree in art from Georgia Southern University included psychology and fostered a quest for self-awareness enhanced by years of journal writing.

Volunteering in her child's school led her to complete a master's degree in library science from the University of North Texas, followed by a librarian career at Lee College in Baytown, Texas.

She values life-long learning, and the sundry human perceptions of reality. Plato's allegory of the cave is a favorite. She completed graduate classes in humanities at the University of Houston-Clear Lake.

Other employment has included teaching, factory work, retail sales, and fast food.

She lived in Michigan, Georgia, South Carolina, and Texas before landing in Colorado at the base of great mountains with many hiking trails. She is blessed with good shoes, and her husband's allergy to alcohol.

Follow Beverly at:
https://www.beverlyali.com
https://www.instagram.com/beverly_a_li/
https://twitter.com/Beverly_A_Li
https://www.facebook.com/profile.php?id=100085679042016

Made in the USA
Las Vegas, NV
20 October 2022

57807057R00125